# Deadl... and I... Gossip in Little Mallow

# Patsy Collins

ISBN 978-1-914339-53-0

# Chapter 1

## Monday 24<sup>th</sup> August

"Muriel!"

Muriel Grahame recognised the voice and willed her head not to snap round in response.

"Muriel! Yoo hoo! Muriel!"

She used to advise her pupils to stand up to bullies. It wasn't easy for children all those years ago. It was just as hard for adults now, especially if they were the only one to see through the veneer of kindness and compassion. It had taken Muriel a long time to do that. Recently she'd become almost certain that not all Vanessa Meadows's gossip was innocently tactless. Some was deliberately intended to wound.

"Muriel! Over here, Muriel."

Though slightly amused at the desperation in the younger woman's voice, it was no good pretending she'd not heard Vanessa calling out as though they were friends. The other people in Little Mallow's High Street were no doubt wondering why one member of the church flower arranging team was ignoring another. What would they think?

'You worry too much about what others might think,' is how Muriel's oldest friend responded to such concerns. 'Ten to one, they hadn't even noticed whatever you thought they were going to be shocked about.' Agnes was probably right.

They'd have noticed Vanessa shouting. Still, she was the one making a mini spectacle of herself. Muriel intended to maintain her own dignity. She turned to see Vanessa waiting expectantly and raised a hand in greeting. For once she didn't obey the unspoken command to rush across the road.

Vanessa made a beckoning gesture.

Unsure what had come over her, Muriel continued to stand her ground.

Vanessa gave an exaggerated shrug and crossed over. "Are you going deaf, Muriel?"

"I am in my eighties." Muriel knew it was no answer.

"Your brother did surprisingly well in the flower show on Saturday. You must be very proud."

Muriel ignored the sarcastic tone. "Yes, I am." Was it Bert's success which had given her the confidence to stand up to Vanessa?

Bert had been placed in almost every class he'd entered. That earned him a silver cup, cash prizes, and the crystal rose bowl; a new award, for the most points from cut flower exhibits. The beautiful bowl made him especially happy. A matching bud vase was awarded as a permanent memento. Bert had given that to Muriel, saying it was thanks for filling out the entry form and exhibit cards for him.

"Muriel, are you listening to me?" Vanessa demanded.

"You were saying how well Bert did. We're delighted with the results, and his awards. They look wonderful filled with blooms, especially when the crystal catches the light. It creates rainbows on my dining room table." Oh dear, that wasn't kind. Muriel knew Vanessa had very much wanted to win that bowl, and had been confident of doing so.

"Of course it's easier for retired people, especially if they're retired from being professional gardeners!"

Odd how Vanessa referred to Bert as a professional in the context of beating her in the show, but dismissed him as an unskilled labourer at all other times. "Yes, he's skilled and experienced, but that doesn't make it easy. He gets good results through hard work, not spending money to cut corners." Muriel meant he dug the ground by hand, instead of hiring a rotovator as some did. That he made his own compost and raised plants from seed, rather than buying whatever he wanted from the garden centre.

The tightness of Vanessa's jaw and hiss which escaped her clenched teeth reminded Muriel of the rumour that, in previous years, some of Vanessa's flawless cut flowers were flown in from Holland.

Almost instantly Vanessa's lips contorted into a smile. "It's nice that people not generally gifted can be good at something. There's a girl with Down's Syndrome who goes to the Ark. The rescue shelter I fundraise for…"

Muriel nodded in lieu of the expected acknowledgement of Vanessa's generosity.

"She's good at keeping animals calm apparently, as though there's a special connection for people like her."

Muriel tried not to react. This was another 'tactless' remark of Vanessa's. In the past Muriel would have told herself it was a clumsy attempt at praise, not meant the way it sounded. Now she was certain it was an insult to both the young lady, and Bert. A suggestion he had an affinity with vegetables.

Maybe it wasn't surprising Vanessa belittled Bert's gardening talents. She'd been in second place to him in several classes. Probably that hadn't annoyed her quite as much as tying for first place in the class for a dozen hybrid tea roses. Only last week she'd bragged… yes, that was the right word… bragged that the white roses she'd been patiently nurturing, were the best she'd ever seen.

Muriel changed the subject to something safer. "You

know the flower arranging session has been brought forward to tomorrow?" Usually the public holiday put things back, so a reminder might be useful.

"Yes." Vanessa almost spat out the word. "Without even the courtesy to ask if it would be convenient! Well, I won't be able to come. I've made other arrangements."

"I'm sure we'll manage perfectly well without you." Muriel knew she'd expressed the very opposite sentiment to that which Vanessa wanted. Muriel better be careful, or she'd bring herself down to that woman's level.

Vanessa gave an unpleasant smile. "That's what I wanted to talk to you about. I've decided to donate my prize-winning hybrid teas to the church. You can call on me tomorrow morning to collect them."

"That won't be necessary. Bert, as usual, has provided flowers. I've just come from St Symeon's where we've left them conditioning in water, ready for tomorrow."

"You don't understand, Muriel. I want those white roses in the altar display. Come at twelve-thirty to collect them."

Walking to the church via Vanessa's home in Grassy Lane would take time and energy. The twenty-fifth of August was a special day. Muriel wouldn't waste it pandering to Vanessa. Muriel spoke firmly. "Bert has provided more than enough. Yours won't be needed."

"How tactless of me. You're concerned your dear brother will be upset if my roses, not his, take pride of place?"

She wasn't. Bert wasn't touchy like that. Muriel was more concerned that arriving with flowers from Vanessa would reinforce the impression she liked the woman, approved of her attempts to push herself forward, seem important, earn praise. Muriel wasn't going to keep being put in that position. Neither would she be pushed into public rudeness.

4

"Bert won't be upset if your roses are on the altar. However it won't be my decision. As they were in the show on Saturday, the others might feel they won't still be fresh enough come this Sunday." White ones showed blemishes so quickly.

"I'm sure a word or two from you will put the roses where I want them." Vanessa's tone had grown sly. "It only takes a word here or there to change people's opinions."

Muriel said nothing, hoping she'd misunderstood.

"Say something, or hold your tongue, Muriel – which of those are *you* going to do?" Vanessa taunted.

There was now no doubt in Muriel's mind. Vanessa wasn't just manipulating her, but threatening. If she didn't collect the flowers, and ensure they were given pride of place, then Vanessa would say the few words which would reveal Muriel's secret. The secret she'd held for decades, and which even now would hurt Bert, bring misery to them both.

It was now clear to Muriel the charity donations Vanessa elicited from her weren't simply Muriel's way of giving thanks for having better luck in a certain situation than had many others. They were payments for silence. Hush money. Blackmail. And it wasn't just money. Every so often, just as now, Vanessa asked for 'a little favour' which put Muriel in a difficult position or otherwise made her uncomfortable.

It had started in Bert's last few years at work. Vanessa had revealed she knew the secret which could cause him to lose respect there, and within the church where he helped out.

It got worse when Bert retired and began winning prizes and getting his name in the paper. Even that positive notoriety had unsettled him. Vanessa could have had him talked about for the wrong reasons, which would have been far more distressing. Far worse than the effect on his reputation, was what it would do to Bert himself. To discover, what he'd always known to be true, was really a lie, would confuse him. Understanding that lie was created by those closest to him might destroy his life of peace, happiness, and tranquility.

Blackmail was wrong; evil. Knowing what it was, Muriel couldn't allow it to continue... But what choice did she have? It wouldn't stop. Not ever. The situation would get worse, as it had almost imperceptibly for some time now.

Vanessa smirked. "I'll see you tomorrow morning, then?"

Muriel wanted to say no, she'd not be there. The words wouldn't come. Instead she turned her back on Vanessa and walked away.

"Muriel, I didn't hear what you said. Muriel!"

Muriel kept walking, almost straight into Aurora Evans, the newest, shortest, and most enthusiastic of the flower arranging team. How long had she been standing there?

"Are you OK?" Aurora asked.

"Fine, thank you," Muriel replied.

"You seemed," Aurora moved her hands in a vague gesture. "You know, I think that's the first time I've seen you cross."

Muriel managed a small chuckle. "You've not seen me when Bert wears his gardening boots on my clean floor! Did I look particularly cross?"

"Positively murderous!"

"How odd! I was only talking to Vanessa about flower arranging tomorrow." Muriel had no idea her emotions showed so plainly. That was something else she must watch.

"Oh yes. Tuesday instead of Wednesday. Thanks for reminding me, Muriel. I'll see you then!"

6

# Chapter 2

## Monday 24th August

"Grab your tea, lass. Skipper wants us," said Trevor Harris, Crystal Clere's mentor since she'd joined Hampshire Police.

"Righto," Crystal said. It wasn't only her shift waiting for the briefing about to be given by Sergeant Imani Freedman. Sergeant Dylan, the skipper from the team going off duty, and a few others, had stayed. That could mean something out of the usual had happened, or was about to. Good. With her boyfriend away again on a photography assignment and Crystal the tiniest bit discombobulated about her imminent job change, she could do with something interesting to keep her mind busy. Even better if overtime was involved.

The briefing started off pretty standard. Not great as the big stuff usually came first. Crystal hid her disappointment. Routine police work was important and she didn't want to give anyone the idea she thought differently.

"One last thing," the skipper said. "As you know, Crystal is leaving us very soon to join Portsmouth CID."

That was greeted by cheers, and shouts of, "Finally!" "Poor sods," and "Who's Crystal?" None of it was meant. The tone of their voices would have told Crystal that, even if two years experience of them as colleagues hadn't.

The skipper grinned. "Despite our great distress, we've arranged a surprise leaving do for you, Crystal, but as…"

"As I'm such a great detective, you knew I'd work it out anyway?" She'd guessed something was planned to celebrate her finishing her probationary period, and to wish her well as she moved from the uniformed branch into CID.

They'd done nothing to hide it. She'd done a far better job disguising the fact her family were organising a get-together for Great Aunt Agnes's ninety-third birthday.

Sergeant Freedman grinned. "As you're such a great detective, you have to work out where and when the party will be. We'll answer up to twenty questions between us, but only with yes or no."

"Oh!" That was a surprise – a good one.

"And don't think you can sweet talk Dil Dylan here into telling you. He's bet me an entire box of salted caramel doughnuts you cave and ask one of us."

Crystal attempted to look tragic. "That makes things trickier." She knew the sergeant really liked her, but he liked carbs even more. Anyway it didn't matter as there weren't so many options that a brilliant detective in training couldn't work it out.

She started at CID in fourteen days time – the seventh of September. Her shift would be working nights part of that, as would Dil Dylan's, and it seemed clear he and some of his team would be there. Trevor would have made sure it didn't clash with Aunty's party, which further reduced the number of possible dates. The fourth or fifth of September were the best bets. Although Saturday was technically her last day at the station, she wasn't working then, so the Friday was equally likely. This coming weekend was possible too, in an attempt to catch her out. Narrowing down the venue would be trickier as Gosport had a wide range of pubs, bars, and other potential venues.


A few hours later Crystal and Trevor were back in Gosport police station and due a break. "I'm just popping out for a minute," she told Trevor. "I've got detecting to do."

"Detect me a tuna mayo while you're at it, will you, lass?" he said.

"And a large, iced, skinny latte for me, please," said Sergeant Freedman.

"I wasn't actually… Oh, OK then." She wanted to make calls where she wouldn't be overheard, so may as well go to the Knitted Tea Cosy – the nearest café offering decent take-away sarnies.

As soon as she left the building, Crystal rang her mate Ellie Jenkins, who was a teacher at St Symeon's in Little Mallow. She was likely to answer as it was the school holidays.

"I'm calling about my surprise party," Crystal said, after they'd caught up on each other's love lives. Trying to get info from Ellie wasn't entirely playing fair with the challenge the skipper had set, but Crystal had been a copper long enough not to make a rookie mistake like playing fair.

"Is there something else you want me to do?" Ellie asked.

"Why, what have you done already?" If Ellie had a hand in the planning, and was willing to discuss the topic, Crystal would soon know everything.

"I did book the hall, and I've been trying to contact old friends of your aunt…"

"No, not that party! I mean, thanks for helping, but I'm talking about the one for me."

"Aren't you a Capricorn, the same as me?"

"What? Yeah, but what's that got to do with anything?"

"Then it's not your birthday, so why would anyone be organising a surprise party for you?"

"Because I'm changing jobs. You don't really think a bunch of coppers would pass up the chance for food and beer, do you?"

Ellie laughed. "Fair point."

"And I'm pretty sure Trevor would have invited you… Ah! It's on Friday, isn't it?" Crystal, and Jason, were going to the cinema with Ellie and possibly Mike. "One of you will say we're early and let's have a drink first and when I walk in you all yell surprise."

"You can check the film times online."

"Right, so you're not doing it that way…" Crystal was far from convinced on that point, but wanted to lull Ellie into dropping her guard.

"No comment – and that's all you'll get out of me without making an arrest, Officer Clere!"

"Some mate you are!"

"The very best," Ellie said.

As that was true, Crystal blew a raspberry and hung up.

Crystal did as Ellie had suggested and checked the film times. Like the update on Ellie's love life that information was inconclusive – the fact the film she'd said they were going to was showing didn't rule it out as a decoy.

Next, Crystal rang Jason in Belgium. He only came second because, if she'd got the answer from Ellie, she wouldn't have needed to use their conversation on work stuff. Not that it bothered him. The few times she'd already been involved in an actual case he'd enjoyed bouncing ideas around with her – usually mad ones. He always seemed to know when some aspect of the job caused her stress too, and was great at easing her tension. He was a keeper, as her mum often said.

"Hello, bringer of brightness and clarity to my life," he answered the call. "No, I've not forgotten to buy you a massive selection of fancy chocolate, I'm getting some decent images, and I'm well," he continued.

"Glad you've got your priorities right!"

"Are you claiming you weren't going to ask in that order?"

"I'd have asked about the job first, because that determines how soon I'll see you again and nothing is more important than that!" And that would be true, even if she wasn't expecting him to bring chocolate. Sumptuous, handmade, Belgian truffles.

"Aww. I'm pleased to say it's going so well I'll be back in time to show you how much I've missed you before we meet up with Ellie, and Mike if he's coming."

"I don't think Ellie knows. I wonder why he's being evasive? Or is he?"

"How d'you mean?"

"Well, if… No, that doesn't make sense."

"What doesn't?"

"I thought the cinema thing was a ruse to get me to my surprise party, but there's no need to pretend Mike's going."

"Maybe Mike doesn't know if he can make it? The Russians might need keeping an eye on." It was Jason's usual joke about Mike working for MI5 – which could be true for all Crystal knew. He'd never said what he did and she'd never asked, and now it felt too late to casually drop a query into the conversation.

"You didn't say, 'what surprise party?'" Crystal pointed out.

"Nooo. There's a reason for that."

"Go on."

"I don't know anything about it, but the moment you mentioned it I thought that if you believed I did know something, you'd try to get information out of me, using all kinds of feminine wiles, naughty enticements and saucy tricks. You know how I feel about that kind of punishment."

"Pervert!" She must remember to buy whipped cream before questioning him at home. "I don't believe you. Trevor will have checked when you're home and asked you to make sure I didn't arrange anything for that night."

"Ah. OK, you got me. See this is why you're the detective and I'm your emotional support virtual sidekick."

"Correct. So, you know the rules?"

"I'm to tell you nothing," Jason said.

"Not quite." Crystal explained about the twenty questions. "They won't let me actually miss it."

"I imagine not."

"So obviously you know when and where it is."

"Yes. No."

"What's that supposed to mean?" Crystal demanded.

"You just said those are the only answers you can be given."

"That's just with my colleagues and anyway, that was a general enquiry, not a specific question."

"OK, I won't tell Trevor, Imani and the others you asked, so you're not really down to eighteen."

"So, yes you do know when it is, but not where. So, it must be Friday?"

"Is that a specific question?"

"Whose side are you on? And yeah, that one is very specific. Very specifically not one of the twenty, and very specifically important to the future of our relationship."

"I'm, very specifically, on your side. Which is why I'm not going to tell you. I know you want to work it out yourself, that you'll be able to, and will enjoy proving it."

She grinned. "Yeah, fair enough." She'd enjoy trying to get him to let something slip, but she'd have felt cheated if he'd simply told her as soon as she asked. "You'll be back early on Friday, you said?"

"Just after lunch, I hope."

"And do you have to go away again before I join CID? I'm owed a few hours off and Skip said I really need to use them before I transfer. It'd be nice to spend some real time together."

"Yeah, it would. I've got tons of processing to do, and one local shoot, but I'll be home for the next couple of weeks. I was hoping we might spend next weekend together – possibly in a tent. The weather is usually good at the start of September."

"I don't know about the tent part, but yes I'd love to go away somewhere for the weekend... Would that be leaving on the Friday evening, or Saturday morning?"

"It'll have to be... Oh. Nice try! It'll be one or other of those depending on when your party is!"

"You can't blame a girl for trying. You know, this game isn't fair. If it was a real investigation I could ask whoever I liked, and as many questions as I liked."

"Yes, but the bad guys might not tell you the truth. Rumour has it they play less fair than the police."

"I'm not going to interrogate bad guys, I'm going to call an expert independent witness – or three." All she had to do was work out who those people might be.

# Chapter 3

**Tuesday 25ᵗʰ August**

Zachary Belli shook his head. The way Brambles, the house they were working at, was supplied with water was nuts. It didn't have its own stopcock. Instead it was connected to a row of four cottages a little further down Grassy Lane. To work on any of the five properties meant disrupting the supply for everyone.

"It doesn't make any sense," Zach said.

"No, it doesn't, but apparently it did to whoever owned this place back in the day. Anyway, we're about ready to sort this part of the mess out," said Zach's boss, Hugh. "You go and turn the stopcock off, kiddo."

"Where is it?" Zach asked.

"Your job to find out. Think of it as an initiative test."

Considering how crazy the whole set up was, it wasn't exactly a fair test. Telling Hugh that wouldn't get him anywhere. He was a decent boss and teacher, but didn't believe in making anything too easy for the junior member of staff.

"Do I just turn it off and come back?" Zach's girlfriend was currently staying in one of the cottages. He hoped he'd get the chance for a quick snog at least.

"What do you think?"

Zach was about to say he was paid to work, not hang about. Then stopped and did what he was constantly advised to do before speaking or acting – he thought. "No. I need to explain to the people in those houses they'll temporarily be without water."

"So, there is a brain in there! They've been informed in writing, but weren't given a time. Once you've found that stopcock, remind them all what's happening, then call me before you turn it off. That'll mean the minimum time they're without a supply."

Zach collected his phone, and the long handled stopcock key, from the van marked *'Bend Plumbing services – when you want all cisterns go, we're just around the corner'*. That corniness was devised by the man generally known as Hugh. At first Zach had assumed it was his real name, given to him by parents who'd intended him to take over the family business. Later Zach learned Hugh's real name was Kyle.

Zach rang his gorgeous Beth. "Are you in, and do you know where the stopcock is?"

"Random! But yeah, the owners said the water would be off for a while today... Oh! You're the one turning it off?"

"The very same." Zach hadn't told her he'd be working up the lane from the place she was house sitting, because he'd not known himself. He'd been dead chuffed when he learned the change of plan that morning.

When Zach reached Beth, he tried to kiss her. She dodged his lips and stepped inside. "I'm not putting on a show for that nosy witch next door," she said, before kissing him in a way which made him forget his surprise at her harsh words.

There were ornament things hanging in the hall window. As the sun shone through they made glowing patterns of light and colour on Beth's smooth, dark skin. Zach thought of stained glass windows in a church. He briefly imagined Beth in a white dress. Maybe carrying a posy of those flowers which smelled good and filled lots of vases dotted around the room. He tried to push the soppy daydream away. If it wasn't there he couldn't mind it not coming true.

"Where's Teddy?" Zach asked. Teddy was a great kid, nearly always happy, but his presence limited Zach's activities with the child's mother.

"At nursery."

Bonus. Zach explained what Hugh had asked him to do.

"Good thing I know where the stopcock is. You could spend an hour searching and not find it."

"In that case, we've got an hour to ourselves." How was that for initiative?

"An hour to do what?" Beth raised an eyebrow.

"Let me show you!" Zach pulled her into his arms.

As things started to get interesting, she pushed him away.

"What's up, babe?"

"I can't help thinking her next door has a glass pressed against the wall," Beth said, loud enough for the woman to hear if she had.

"What's she said now?"

"I'll put the radio on." Beth did that, then in a quiet voice and flat tone said, "She called Teddy a golliwog."

"You're kidding me!" He knew the woman had a habit of speaking without thinking, but come on! Surely everyone realised how offensive that would be?

"Nope. Oh, she tried to hide it. Pretended she was being nice, said a lot of stuff about his cute curls and how she loved her toy golliwog as a kid, but she knew what she was doing."

Zach didn't know how to respond. He'd briefly come across Vanessa Meadows before, and knew she said stupid things. She'd upset Kirianne, Zach's former girlfriend, with repeated unasked for advice about her appearance. Now it seemed it wasn't a case of Vanessa not knowing what to say or when to shut up, but deliberate. Beth wasn't the sort to assume every clumsy phrase was an insult. "Forget her. She's just jealous you're so young and lovely." He wanted to add 'and have me' but Beth was so independent he was scared of pushing her away.

"Maybe that's it? She doesn't seem to have anyone close." Beth turned the volume up. "Let's have some fun!"

Zach laughed as one of the bands his mum liked reverberated round the tiny kitchen. Depeche Mode, Duran Duran, Def Leppard – one of those. "She'll think we're doing something we don't want her to hear!"

"Good!" Beth kissed him again.

The DJ said, "That was Dire Straits with *Money For Nothing* – wouldn't we all like some of that?"

"I just want what I'm owed," Beth said.

"Problems with Teddy's dad?" Zach asked.

"Problems with Jo. If he wants to be thought of as Teddy's father he should try acting like it for a change."

Zach would like to be thought of in that way, and was trying to show he'd do a better job of it than the bloke who'd pretty much only contributed biologically. Beth was once bitten twice shy. "Forgot about him too. I reckon I know something that will take your mind off everything else."

"One track mind you've got," she said, taking his hand and heading for the stairs.

After they'd worked up an appetite, Beth offered to make lunch.

"Lunch?" Zach checked his watch. It was twelve-twenty,

meaning he'd spent more than an hour pretending to search for the stopcock. He was amazed Hugh hadn't called to ask what he was playing at. "Yeah, go on then." Zach was always hungry. Hollow legs, Mum said. Plus it would give him an excuse to take Beth and Teddy out, to repay the favour. "You see to that and I'll check I can turn the water off and then give your neighbours the warning."

The stopcock was right where Beth said. It was hidden by a whole load of different coloured flowering plants, some with thorns. Beth worked in a florist shop and would know all the names. He didn't have a clue. Using the stopcock key he flicked open the cover then gave the valve an experimental twist. Good, it wasn't going to be a problem. Sometimes people over tightened them. Hugh had warned of possible dire consequences of that.

Zach texted Hugh. *'Stopcock found. Just telling residents supply about to go off.'* Hopefully that'd save him an earful.

Beth had said the people in 3 weren't home. Sure enough they didn't answer, so he knocked at 4.

The lady thanked him for the reminder and said, "No problem. I'll fill the kettle now, so I'll be fine for a while."

Lastly he knocked at 1, the house occupied by Vanessa Meadows, reminding himself to be professional.

The door was thrown open. "You took your... Who are you?"

Zach explained, making sure he, at least, was polite.

"Have the Sheppards got a problem with their water?"

Zach thought of thirsty sheep, then remembered Sheppard was the name of the couple Beth was house sitting for.

"No, we're working on Brambles up the lane. The big house which is being renovated?" He put the last bit as a question. The water going off didn't seem like a surprise, so she must have seen the letter Hugh sent.

"You were in there a long time."

"Yes I was." He gave his most charming smile. The one Mum said would get him anything. "I'll be going back, once I've disconnected the water, and staying until I switch it on again." It was none of her business, but she'd probably watch and find out.

"With that darkie girl?"

"With my beautiful girlfriend Beth, yes." He gave another big smile. It probably wouldn't seem as charming.

"You'll let me know when the water goes back on?"

"It shouldn't be longer than an hour." He didn't want to give her an excuse to say they'd taken longer than specified.

"I don't want to have to keep checking."

"I'll let everyone know." No way was she getting special treatment. Nothing nice, anyway. She was lucky he wasn't in a position to make her water as sour as her personality.

Zach called Hugh. "Everyone knows the water's going off."

"Then make it so. Don't get too comfortable. It won't be long before I want you back up here."

Did Hugh know Beth was there and had deliberately sent him on the errand, to give them time together? Zach might have mentioned it. He did have a tendency to talk about her. Hugh was a good boss really, even if he did treat Zach like a stupid kid half the time.

Zach returned to house 2, for the lunch Beth had made. Salad she said. It was really good. Lots of different veg and she'd topped it with what looked like chicken. She said was fried halloumi.

He'd only just finished when Hugh called to say, "Turn it back on again, then get yourself back up here pronto."

"I have to tell them it's back on."

"No, kiddo. Their letter said it'd only be a few minutes."

"I do, boss. One of them insisted and she seems the sort to make a fuss."

"If you must, but be quick. You've wasted nearly two hours faffing about down there."

Although he'd only have to take two steps to reach Vanessa's door, Zach first walked down the shared path and turned left. He informed the nice lady in 4, tried 3 again, then went to Vanessa's. She didn't answer his knock.

Maybe she was in the back garden. He checked. There was nowhere to hide. It was much smaller than the front. Just a rectangle of incredibly green lawn, and flowers so bound up it looked like she'd taken them prisoner.

Zach knocked again. Maybe she'd been in the loo the first time? Or wasn't opening on purpose, to make his life difficult? He pushed against the door. It swung open. Zach saw through to where she was sitting in her living room.

"Hello, just came to…" he trailed off. She'd not reacted to his voice. Not even sat up. All he could see were her lower legs and feet. They seemed kind of floppy. One shoe wasn't properly on. Nasty old bat must have dozed off!

"Hello!" Zach yelled. Serve her right if she got a scare. No reaction. He banged on the door. Feeling a bit sick, he went in. Zach didn't know what he feared, until he saw Vanessa Meadows slumped in her chair with her eyes staring right at him.

She said nothing. Didn't move. Didn't even blink those terrible red eyes.

# Chapter 4

## Tuesday 25<sup>th</sup> August

Muriel Grahame found herself back at the top of Grassy Lane without consciously having moved away from Vanessa Meadows' home. She'd almost reached Main Street, when the legs which had propelled her without instruction seemed to act independently even of each other. She wasn't going anywhere, so must make herself stay still.

Fortunately her hands, gnarled but strong from decades of baking and gardening, remained obedient. She grabbed a knee with each one, pushed them together and managed to stop staggering around. Thank goodness! People would have wondered, remembered, and talked, if she'd been seen acting so strangely. Main Street was quiet, and Grassy Lane almost deserted. With luck she'd not been noticed. A plumber's van had been outside Brambles, the one detached house in the lane. The workmen must have all been busy inside for there'd been no sign of them. The same was true of the four house terrace which comprised the cottages, unimaginatively named 1, 2, 3 and 4. Muriel knew one couple were on holiday, and perhaps the others were at work. As for Vanessa... Muriel simply wouldn't think about her at all.

It was so hot. Hotter even than yesterday and the sun was right overhead. She should be careful not to get sunstroke. Muriel smiled as Agnes's advice not to worry so much about other people's opinions came back to her. Sunstroke is what people would suspect if they'd come across her out in such glorious sunshine, barely in control of her faculties. Probably it was true. She'd walked quite a distance at a brisk pace. That exertion, in such intense heat, being the final straw in an already unbearable situation.

Muriel retreated into a welcoming space in the laurel hedge. It was shaded there, a little cooler, and safe from inquisitive eyes. Gradually her heart rate and breathing slowed. Her body became still, calm and under control. Muriel headed for St Symeon's churchyard.

She eased herself down to kneel by her parents' grave. First she thanked them, as she did every year on this day, and at many other times too. Then she apologised. "I'm sorry to both of you for how I've behaved this morning. I know my decision goes against what you believed, what you tried to instil in me, but I had no choice. I did it for Bert." A moment's reflection told her she'd not been entirely honest. "My fear Bert would be upset motivated me, but I also acted for myself. I couldn't face the humiliation, the uncertainty. It seemed anything would be better than that."

As she talked, Muriel picked up a few dead leaves which had blown onto the neat rectangle of gravel. She fussed with the flowers she and Bert had placed there the day before, when they'd brought those to be arranged inside the church. Muriel continued to explain, as best she could, how desperate she'd felt regarding the situation with Vanessa. Her words probably made little sense but her parents weren't listening with earthly ears. She hoped they were hearing, understanding, and forgiving, with heavenly hearts.

Standing up to bullies hadn't been something her parents did. They kept their heads down, didn't rock the boat. That had been the right thing for them. Muriel had tried, she truly had. It hadn't been the right approach, not for her now, not against Vanessa. Muriel had done something different. A small thing. The right thing.

Muriel would have to talk to Bert. She'd put an end to one problem. Now she must face the fact it might be the start of something else. Yes, Bert must be told. She must find the right words to make him understand. If she could explain to him, have his forgiveness, then it really would all be over.

Telling Bert would have to wait. He'd be on his allotment now, or possibly already in the Kale and Snail with a pint in hand. Neither place would be suitable for her confession. She must wait for him to come to her, not confront him on his own territory, leaving him nowhere to retreat to, should he need it. It would have to be soon. Very soon.

For now, she may as well continue as if that morning had been just the same as any other. In fact that was her only option. Muriel headed into the church.

She heard voices as she approached St Symeon's flower room. Glancing at her watch she realised with dismay it was already after one and therefore she was a few minutes late for that day's flower arranging session. That would be noticed, but no matter what guess was made as to the reason, it would surely be wrong.

# Chapter 5

## Tuesday 25<sup>th</sup> August

Crystal spotted someone in the hedge where Grassy Lane joined Main Street in Little Mallow, as she drove the patrol car past. She waved. The old lady didn't see. Whatever she was hiding from, it wasn't the police.

"Was that Muriel Grahame?" asked Trevor.

"I think so. If I had a suspicious mind…"

"Which you have," Trevor interrupted.

"You're right, I do. That's probably why I think she was looking guilty."

"Of what, lass? Using shop bought pastry instead of making her own?"

Crystal laughed at the perfect example of something which would horrify the older ladies of Little Mallow. "Nothing quite as drastic as that!"

"I should hope not. If we can't rely on the likes of Muriel Grahame and your Great Aunt Agnes to do things right, then we're in a right pickle."

"I can't imagine her taking a short cut like that. She's not taking a short cut in the other meaning of the term either. There are only five houses in Grassy Lane and with the stream at the bottom she couldn't be walking up it on her way back from anywhere else."

"She was visiting someone in one of those five houses?" Trevor suggested.

"Knowing who lives there it seems unlikely." And Muriel hadn't been striding out purposefully as she usually did. She hadn't seemed her normal self at all.

"Oh?"

"Brambles, that lovely big square house at the top, is still empty. Out of the four cottages, the owners of one are on holiday, another couple will be at work, and the other two are both gossips, although of very different kinds."

"And you know all this because you've been gossiping with your Aunt Agnes?"

"Noooo – I also fact checked it all in the post office and Kale and Snail. Stick with me and I'll teach you all the best intel gathering techniques."

"Ah lass, if only I could. I'm going to miss you."

"Steady on, Trevs! I'm only transferring to CID, not emigrating."

"Talking of which, how is the house hunting going?"

"It's much more difficult than I'd expected. I've only rented before, and it only had to suit me."

"Jason hard to please is he?"

Crystal laughed. "He's dating me, remember!"

"Knows a good thing when he sees it then."

Even after years of being her mentor Trevor could still surprise her. She'd been expecting a joke at her expense and he'd said something sweet.

"Hey, lass you look proper emotional. Did I say the wrong thing?"

"I was just feeling sorry for all you lot in the station, without me to put you right!"

"We'll be fine. Without you pointing them all out, we won't have any crimes to solve. Life's going to be one long tea-break from now on."

They exchanged grins.

"So, this house hunting? Why's it hard?" Trevor asked.

"It feels such a huge decision."

"You've got plenty of time at any rate."

"True." Jason's former boss had offered them a flat at a low rent, on condition they agreed to get out quickly, when he was ready to sell it. Aunty Agnes, who Crystal had been living with for a while, said they could both stay with her if that happened, so they'd jumped at the chance.

The dinginess of the flat wasn't a problem. Slapping on a few tins of paint would soon cheer it up. The problem was Little Mallow. That was where Crystal really wanted them to have a home of their own. Living with Great Aunty Agnes was ace, especially when Jason was away on one of his photographic assignments, but it was Aunty's house not hers. It never would be.

Buying in Little Mallow wasn't an option. Not yet anyway. Way too expensive. A weird covenant kept the prices of some down a bit, but you had to have lived in Little Mallow, or had a strong connection, for fifteen years. Crystal didn't qualify. She was getting there by staying with Aunty Agnes, and she'd be doing that part time for the rest of the old lady's life.

Agnes was old. Crystal shook her head to push away the implications of that thought. Aunty was amazing. She'd probably still be going strong when Crystal made inspector and could afford to buy any one of the picturesque cottages lining Main Street, or even one of the bigger houses on Palmerston Avenue or Sparrow Lane.

"Just here on the left," Trevor said, bringing all Crystal's attention back to the job in hand.

Crystal pressed the doorbell at the property in Fareham, then stepped back so she was shoulder to shoulder with Trevor. When the door opened she introduced them both to the home owner and confirmed his identity.

"I suppose you want a statement," he said. "Look, I will if I must, but I'm not sure it's worth the effort. I only reported the theft because the insurance won't pay out without an incident number."

"In this case they won't be paying out at all," Crystal said.

"What! Why not? My bike was locked up…"

"If you could come with us, sir?" Crystal led him to the patrol car and opened the boot. "Can you confirm this is yours?" she asked.

"Oh. Wow! Yeah, it's mine. If you need proof, check the frame just there. I used one of those special pens to mark my postcode and house number."

Crystal and Trevor knew that. It's why they were able to return the stolen bike so promptly. Catching the culprit wasn't much harder. He'd abandoned the bike outside his front door, having taken it to cycle home after a night at the pub. 'You lot were too quick,' he'd moaned. 'I was going to ride it back in a bit and nobody'd have been any the wiser.' He now realised borrowing without permission was an offence he'd be wise not to repeat. He'd been celebrating getting a job after two years of unemployment and couldn't believe his stupidity in risking the new position.

After explaining the situation to the bike's owner, Crystal asked if he wanted to press charges. His lack of enthusiasm for making a formal statement suggested he wouldn't.

"Is there an alternative?"

"We can give him a caution."

"Do that then, please. And thanks for getting this back to me so quickly."

"Well done, lass," Trevor said, as she drove them away.

"For what? Oh, saving you some paperwork on this one? If I'd remembered I'd be gone to CID in time to get out of it, I might not have been so kind!"

"Born kind, you were."

"Do you think we did the right thing, letting the bloke who nicked the bike get away with it?"

"He's not getting away with it. He'll get that caution, but yes, I think we did the right thing. He was an idiot, but he's not exactly a hardened criminal."

Crystal nodded. "What do you reckon Muriel was up to earlier, hiding in those bushes?"

"Hiding? I only saw her long enough to recognise, not see what she was doing. Hiding doesn't sound like her."

"It doesn't, but she was definitely in the hedge and she looked… I dunno, flustered doesn't come close."

"Any theories?"

"If it was Aunty Agnes I'd say she was helping herself to a cutting of some rare plant, but Muriel is nowhere near as wicked as Aunty, and rare shrubs aren't generally planted in a great long line, are they?"

"Not my area of expertise, but I wouldn't have thought so. You mentioned brambles, maybe she was picking blackberries, lass?"

"Maybe." Although, as every jam and pie maker in Little Mallow knew, Sparrow Lane was the place to find the plumpest, sweetest blackberries. Muriel couldn't possibly be unaware of that. She, together with her brother Bert, still lived there in the house where they were brought up.

# Chapter 6

## Tuesday 25th August

Muriel took a moment to compose herself, then walked into the flower room of St Symeon's church.

"Made it at last!" teased Agnes, as Muriel took her usual seat by her friend's side.

Muriel responded with a smile, knowing the remark was an affectionate backhanded compliment of her usual reliability.

"Come off it," Mary Milligan said. "It's only just past the hour, and Muriel isn't the last to arrive."

"I didn't see any sign of any of you when I arrived, so I went out to tidy my parents' grave." It was true, even if the reason Muriel hadn't seen anyone was that she'd taken care to be unobserved herself.

"I know how it goes. I'm always quickly doing something in a spare ten minutes, then finding it takes twenty and I only really had five to start with," said Aurora. She hauled the tubs of blooms, which had been left conditioning in deep water overnight, to within easy reach of the older women.

Muriel smiled. From her position on the quite high chair, all that was visible of the diminutive Aurora from behind the buckets of flowers, was her peculiar hairstyle. If the red hadn't clashed with the pink roses you'd hardly have known she was there.

"I can't remember the last time I did anything quickly," Agnes said. "Except jumping to conclusions! Might as well say it before anyone else does."

Muriel wouldn't have said it, but others might, as it was often true – and the conclusions often accurate. Agnes had been right about why Daisy Bloomfield suddenly switched from being a coffee drinker to preferring tea, where Roger Milligan used to 'sneak' off to on Wednesday afternoons, and had predicted a great many engagements over the years. She'd encouraged plenty too!

Aged fifteen, Muriel and the already adult Agnes had seemed to have little in common, but these days the five year gap was nothing, and the two women were often referred to almost as a single unit. Both were in remarkably good health although at times Muriel felt every one of her eighty-eight years. She knew Agnes was the same.

"Looks as though it might just be us today," Mary said. "When young Daisy came into the Post Office yesterday she said the heat was getting to her and she might not make it."

"How long has she got to go?" Aurora asked.

"A week she said, but you know what first babies are like."

"The other two haven't said anything?" asked childless Agnes, possibly hoping to save herself and Muriel from an exchange of childbirth details.

"Not a thing, and Vanessa was in yesterday, making a big thing about buying tea even though she never drinks it."

"Say who it was for?" Aurora asked.

"She so obviously wanted me to ask that I didn't."

Agnes and Aurora both chuckled at that. Muriel too felt satisfaction that Vanessa had been thwarted in her efforts to say whatever she'd wanted to say. Such a pity that hadn't happened much more frequently, but then not everyone was as good at controlling conversations as Mary Milligan.

Perhaps running the post office, and therefore having to explain various rules and regulations, helped with that.

"Typical of that pair to leave us in the lurch without a word," Agnes said.

"That's a little unfair." Muriel knew Vanessa wouldn't arrive, but didn't wish to say so.

"Yeah, the evil Vs usually show up," Aurora said, making their reliability sound a fault, not a virtue.

"Evil Vs?" Muriel was confused by the lack of reaction from Agnes and Mary. Had they heard Vanessa Meadows and Verity Houseman described that way before?

"Sorry, Muriel," Aurora said. "I'm not going to badmouth them in church in front of you, I promise, but..." She shrugged. "Anyway, I did say they can usually be relied on to show up if they've said they would."

"I don't think any of us will mind if they make an exception today," Agnes said.

"You're right there. There will be more work and less gossip, but it will all be nicer," Mary said.

Initially that struck Muriel as a strange remark. Mary was so fond of discussing others that the post office was known in Little Mallow as gossip HQ. But then not all gossip was equal. What Mary said herself was usually positive, or at least neutral, and intended to inform or entertain. Nothing was repeated with harmful intent. That was true of Agnes. Aurora too.

"What do you think they're up to today then, the evil Vs?" Aurora asked.

"No doubt making other people's lives miserable," Mary said.

"They're not all bad. They collect a lot of money for

31

charity, especially Verity. She's always setting up raffles and things." Aurora's words sounded as though she were defending the women. Her tone didn't.

Clearly that was picked up by Mary, who made a strange noise.

"Go on, Mary," Agnes prompted.

"She's like one of those people who stop you in the street with 'just a few questions' and you end up signing over a fortune every month just to get away. Chuggers, I think they're called?"

"That's right, charity muggers," Aurora confirmed. "I know what you mean. If I see Verity approach with that look in her eye I almost throw a quid at her for a strip of tickets, just to get it over with."

"Bet you've never won," Mary said.

"I haven't... What are you suggesting?"

"Me suggest something, with Muriel sat right there? I don't actually know anything, but I'm sure people really do win those raffles even if none of us ever have or know anyone who has, and I'm sure all the money does go to the charities she says she's collecting for."

"Oooh!" Aurora's eyes became almost as large as her hair.

"And Vanessa no doubt hands over all the money she takes and has no idea how miserable she makes people when she hounds them into donating," Agnes added.

Muriel felt she must say something, but what? Defending one or both women would sound as though she was adding to the insinuations. Expressing agreement would be so out of character her friends would wonder what had come over her. She attempted to change the subject. "Perhaps, as it seems that neither lady is going to join us, we should get on with the flowers?"

"You're right," Agnes said. "Less gossip and more work you said, Mary. If we don't get on, we won't be even halfway finished before the vicar joins us for tea and cake."

They began snipping leaves and snapping away thorns from stems of flowers.

"These roses are lovely," Aurora remarked. "I can see why your Bert won all those prizes. He's very clever at growing things, isn't he?"

Muriel happily agreed. Bert wasn't often referred to as clever. Whenever it happened, the person concerned had generally done so after receiving part of the bounty he coaxed from the earth.

"He's got a knack, that lad," Agnes said as Muriel delivered trimmed stems to her.

Again Muriel smiled. Nobody but Agnes had called Bert a lad for decades. To almost everyone else he was Old Bert. Muriel sometimes wondered if she, sixteen years his senior, was known as Old Muriel, but then she'd never heard Agnes referred to as Old Agnes and she was the oldest person in Little Mallow.

"It's his birthday today," Muriel said.

"Oh yes. I guess you're not having a party for him?" Agnes asked. "You couldn't keep a thing like that secret."

A big surprise party was being arranged for Agnes's birthday, a week on Sunday. Muriel was fairly certain Agnes knew nothing about that! "Bert doesn't like a fuss. I always make him a special meal, and a cake of course, but he likes to spend most of the day on his allotment."

"Thirsty work in this heat," Mary said.

"I'm sure he'll be fine." Everyone seemed to think Muriel

was unaware Bert sometimes visited the pub, often persuading someone to buy him a pint. Or perhaps they just wanted to help her turn a blind eye. Today he'd no doubt be treated to more than one drink and would sleep it off in his shed before coming home for his tea.

For a while Muriel and the other three ladies quietly positioned flowers and foliage in the containers they had before them.

The peace was broken by Mary asking, "Did you hear about the patient who went to his doctor…"

"No, and neither should you have done. These things are confidential." Muriel spoke far more sharply than she'd intended.

"It's a joke, Muriel, not real. My grandson told me it."

"Oh, I see. I'm sorry. Have I spoiled it?"

"No, don't fret. The patient goes to the doctor with a cucumber sticking out of his ear, a tomato up his nose and a beetroot… somewhere else. The doctor takes one look and says, 'I know what's wrong with you, you're not eating properly!'"

The others chuckled and Muriel said, "I must tell Bert that the next time he comes back from the allotment with a marrow tucked under his arm and his pockets full of potatoes." In many ways Bert was still the lad Agnes called him, and that applied to his childish sense of fun.

"That reminds me, please thank your brother for the runner beans," Mary said.

"Thank you for taking them off our hands. It's feast or famine, with runners. I hate to waste good food, but there are only so many beans you can eat and they're not the same frozen or salted." Muriel knew Bert received cans of beer from the post office in exchange for surplus vegetables, and he had a similar arrangement with the Kale and Snail. Although he produced impressive quantities of beans and marrows, she didn't think they'd buy enough beer to do him much harm.

"It was Ellie Jenkins who told Adam that joke," Mary said. "She read the class a few, saying she wrote them down so she didn't forget and asked her pupils to get people to tell them different types of jokes and write those down."

"Clever way to show the value of writing," Aurora said. "Better than the boring stuff we did in our day."

"I thought the clever bit was asking for different types so she doesn't have the same one twenty times. Adam has doctor ones. Do you know any I can pass on?"

"I know one," Agnes said. "The receptionist says there's a patient on the line who says he's invisible and the doctor says to tell him the he can't see him right now."

"I saw one on Facebook." Aurora tapped away on her phone. "Here it is. I told my doctor that I broke my arm in two places. She told me to stop going to those places."

"Good advice," Muriel said.

"I think we're all done, ladies. Shall I put the kettle on?"

"Good idea, Mary. And bring out the cake!" Aurora said.

# Chapter 7

## Tuesday 25<sup>th</sup> August

Zach gulped at the air. His lungs felt both empty and as though they'd burst. His vision swam. He couldn't look away. He didn't know if he wanted to rush forward to check if Vanessa Meadows was really dead or run away and try to pretend he hadn't seen anything wrong. It didn't matter as he was unable to do either. His feet wouldn't move.

When he'd been a kid, and things got too much, he'd been told to focus on one thing at a time. Concentrate on details. What could he touch, hear, see, taste, smell?

He was holding the door. Keeping it half open. Or half closed? Details. Painted wood under his hand. He moved his thumb a little. Yes, real wood. Hugh had taught him to tell the difference. You needed to know what you were up against, before cutting or drilling. There was music coming from next door. Beth listening to the radio. The world hadn't stopped, not for her. Not for him.

Zach could smell the flowers in the garden. Beth loved flowers. He never bought them for her. It seemed silly when she worked in a florist shop. Mum said working in a supermarket didn't stop her wanting the fridge and kitchen cupboards full of food. She'd then admitted she'd prefer something different from what she handled every day. If Zach was thinking of a gift for her, Mum could recommend a particular brand of chocolate. He'd bought her some. He'd noticed others made into flower shapes and bought those for Beth. Now he often gave her little gifts of things shaped like flowers or decorated with them. Sometimes she got him something too. It was their thing.

Beth, Mum, Hugh. It would be OK. He could look now.

Zach had never seen a body before. Even so, he was certain Vanessa Meadows was dead. There was the strange way she was slumped in the chair, lack of movement in her chest, and her eyes. They weren't right.

It didn't look like she'd died peacefully in her sleep. At least not how that appeared on TV. It seemed more as though she'd been trying to get up. She had weird red dots on her face. Her eyes were the worst. It looked like blood had leaked into them. They couldn't have been like that when he'd spoken to her earlier. He'd definitely have noticed. They were so red, and almost glowed. No wonder people closed the eyes of dead people. He couldn't do it. Zach forced away thoughts of vampires and zombies. That stuff wasn't real.

Zach guessed he should try CPR. He didn't really know how. Couldn't touch the body. It would be too late. He'd knocked on the door and waited, gone out to the garden...

Zach returned to Beth.

"What on earth is wrong?" she asked.

"Heart attack, I think."

"What? Zach, what's happened?" Beth looked so scared.

"Not me. I must be in shock." He gestured towards the neighbouring house. "She'd sort of collapsed. I think she's had a heart attack."

Beth guided him onto the sofa. "We should call an ambulance."

"No point. She's dead."

"You're sure? Maybe they can do something?"

He shook his head. "She's dead. Her eyes..." He felt

himself shivering and was glad of the warmth of Beth's body as she held him tight.

"We still have to tell someone. Would it still be the ambulance, or maybe it's the police?"

Zach's phone rang before he'd made a decision.

It was Hugh. "What are you playing at?"

Zach replied without knowing what he was saying.

"What's up, kiddo? Everything OK?"

"She's dead."

"Who is?"

"I went to tell her the water was back on. She's…"

"Dead? You're absolutely sure?"

"Yes."

"Where are you now?"

"House 2. Beth is here."

"Have you called an ambulance or anyone?"

"I didn't know who." Zach could hear the worry in his own voice.

"Stay there. I'll come down."

"Thanks." Hugh would know what was best and tell him what to do. He always did.

They walked out to meet Hugh who squeezed Zach's shoulder and asked Beth if she was OK.

"I'm fine. I was inside the whole time, so I've not seen anything. Zach says she looks weird."

"I see you're upset, kiddo but you could be mistaken and the lady's just fallen asleep. I remember my gran would do that sometimes, just drop off while you were talking to her and I'd be sure she was dead. Proper scared me it did. You go in, I'll just check."

Zach wanted to believe he'd made a mistake. That she was asleep. A trick of the light had made her eyes seem red.

Hugh soon rejoined them. From the doorway he said, "She's dead alright. Looks like she might have had some kind of seizure. Come outside, lad, and get some fresh air while I call 999."

Zach went out to him.

Hugh made the call, giving only the bare details. "Look, kiddo, we're going to have to make this official."

Zach nodded. The situation couldn't just be ignored.

"Unless there was something seriously wrong with her that the doctor knew about there'll be an investigation. The police will be involved. You need to get your story straight before that happens…"

"You mean because of my brother? It's OK, Beth knows about that."

"Good. That's good."

"I've made tea," Beth called and they went back inside.

Zach felt slightly better. Mum always said honesty was the best policy. She'd been right when Dom got into trouble and she suggested Zach tell both Beth and his boss. It might come to light now and it would look worse if he'd hidden it. There was something else he needed to come clean about.

"Boss, I talked to Beth as soon as you sent me down here. She knew where the stopcock was. I wasn't searching for it the whole time. I, we were… indoors. I didn't even go and look until just before I called you."

"Ah. That explains it." Hugh looked relieved. "I did think that with the residents all warned what would happen, you'd be able to get one of them to tell you where it was."

"That's what you meant about getting my story straight? You can't think I did something to her!"

"No, of course not. But on the face of it, it does look odd that a plumber took over an hour to locate a stopcock."

"Zach hasn't done anything wrong, I know it," Beth said.

"I know. I just meant we don't want to be contradicting each other, or to leave out something important."

"That makes sense." Zach glanced at Beth and saw her nod.

"Right you two, talk me through what happened."

Zach told Hugh everything. Except the details of what he and Beth did to make him lose track of time. That'd be embarrassing for her and wasn't anyone else's business.

Hugh didn't say much other than stuff like, 'OK, go on' until Zach got to pushing open the door of the dead neighbour's house.

"Why did you go in?"

If Hugh thought it sounded a strange thing to do, what would the police think? Because his brother almost killed someone, a fishy sounding story from Zach involving initiative tests and bunking off work to go to bed with his girlfriend, who he knew had been upset by the dead woman, was less likely to be believed.

"What do I tell the police?" Zach asked after explaining those concerns to Hugh.

"Tell the truth," Beth said, before Hugh got the chance to speak. "You haven't done anything wrong. There's no need to hide anything."

"Of course not," Hugh said. "But I do think…"

The sound of sirens ended the conversation.

# Chapter 8

## Tuesday 25th August

As Mary filled the kettle for the flower arrangers' tea, Aurora lifted the finished arrangements into their positions atop pedestals, in the entrance porch, and on the altar. Muriel didn't offer her assistance with the physical work. Whenever she'd done so before, Aurora had asked her to stand back a bit and check each display was positioned at just the right angle, so that's what she did.

"Talking of cake, is the vicar's supply sorted for next week?" Agnes asked. "I'm doing a Victoria Sandwich for tomorrow. I'm not sure about anyone else."

"He'll have the remains of the cherry sponge we've got today and I'll drop off a lemon drizzle on Friday," Mary called from the kitchen. "I think you're the other person on the rota, Muriel, so he'll get coffee and walnut on Monday."

"I will, of course, take him a cake, but perhaps ginger for a change." It had been Vanessa who'd frequently referred to Muriel's speciality and had her pigeon holed as making only that. It hadn't really mattered, but had irritated her.

"Jerry likes your coffee and walnut," Aurora said.

"I'm sure he does, but, other than being especially partial to the lemon drizzle which Mary makes so well, he likes all cake to the same enthusiastic degree."

"He is very easy to please," Agnes conceded. "I've always

41

thought he'd make a good husband. The right sort of vicar's wife would be a real asset to Little Mallow, and to our dear reverend. It's a shame he never married."

"I wonder why he hasn't?" Aurora said. "Jerry Grande's a nice looking man and..."

"There's too much of it about!" Agnes snapped.

"Too much of what?" Aurora asked, not sounding happy.

"Confirmed bachelors."

"What have you got against them?" Aurora asked.

"No wife means no weddings! I like a wedding. Blushing brides, beautiful dresses, flowers, champagne, dancing. I want to see my niece Crystal, and little Ellie married here, but there's no sign of it happening."

"Ah, I see," Aurora said. "I thought you meant a certain sort of man without a wife."

"Don't know what you mean."

Aurora glanced from Mary to Muriel as though asking for help.

"I think Aurora means someone like the verger," Muriel attempted to explain.

"Nice man that, as long as you don't get him on the phone," Agnes said, still seeming confused.

"Yes. Quite. But, well, if he married there wouldn't be a bride," Muriel pointed out.

"Oh!" Clearly Agnes now understood the point.

"I never knew Arnold was gay," Mary said.

Mary not knowing made Muriel doubtful. Mary knew everything. She didn't always talk about her knowledge, but if she ever said 'I don't know anything about that' it usually transpired there was nothing to know.

"Is that not right? Oh dear… I just assumed, which of course we never should. I could be wrong." Muriel was almost certain she was right, but horrified she'd revealed something which wasn't common knowledge, and which the people concerned might prefer stayed that way. What had got into her today? She must get herself under control.

Muriel missed part of the conversation, but tuned back in to hear Agnes say, "Yes, that's very true," in a tone she recognised.

"Are you plotting something?" she asked her old friend.

"Matchmaking again, I think," Mary said. "She's got that gleam in her eye."

"Maybe I have. So, the verger… Is it that Scottish friend of his you mean?"

"Cameron," Aurora supplied.

"Charming man," Agnes said, "And the verger's been different lately, as though a sadness has been lifted."

"Yes, I'd noticed that," Muriel said. "Perhaps he was lonely before. He's never been really close to anyone… not that I'm sure he is now, not in that way…"

"Don't sweat it, Muriel," Aurora said. "It's no secret. They went to France together, remember."

"Oh!" Mary said. "How did I not know that?"

"He'll probably still have the flowers and cake and I'm sure those two boys will look very smart in suits, and they might have pretty relations who'll be bridesmaids," Agnes murmured.

"Well, that's Arnold sorted, and your Crystal is getting on well with her photographer chap, isn't she?" Mary asked.

"She is. They'd be living together if it wasn't for me, but I'm too selfish to kick her out."

Muriel knew it wasn't selfishness on Agnes's part. She appreciated the help her great niece provided, and probably wouldn't be able to stay in her own home without it, but would never do anything to impede either Crystal's romantic relationship, or career in the police.

"That leaves us with Ellie Jenkins," Agnes continued. "I'd like to see her married to the vicar's nephew."

"The whole of Little Mallow would like to see those two married, with the exception of Mike and Ellie themselves," Mary said.

"You're right, except maybe for one, or perhaps two, of your exceptions," Agnes said.

The vicar joined them then, telling Mary her grandson Adam would be helping the verger until she was ready to go. The conversation then turned to the long run of good weather, the beauty of the flowers, and the ladies' artistry with them. Everything was just as normal, even Aurora saying 'I shouldn't really' when offered cake, before eating at least as much as anyone else. Only Muriel was different. In one way she felt lighter, but another weight would surely descend soon.

"I'll clear up today," Muriel said, indicating the empty tea cups and cake plates.

Once the crockery was returned to the cupboard, she stepped into the nave to look at the coloured light spilling through the stained glass windows onto the stone floor and oak pews.

She thought of her near gaffe when talking of the verger. Muriel knew she'd meant no harm, had just been taking an interest in the man and sharing her observation with friends. The vicar once told her that's what most gossip really was. That and a way to spread information. She was so glad Jerry Grande was their vicar. He had a way of expressing things which helped you understand, not just God, but the world.

"It's truly beautiful, isn't it?" said the man himself.

"The light? Yes, it is. Divine light, perhaps?" Muriel suggested.

"That's how I think of it. As though God is looking down, and revealing the best of us."

"You couldn't blame him for wanting to see us through a rose tinted filter. We might be made in his image but we're flawed. Most of us anyway, I didn't mean to imply…"

"I like to think I'm as human as everyone else," Jerry said.

Muriel considered him to be human in the very best sense of the word, but judged it safest to simply nod.

"Muriel, what you were saying about God seeing us…" Whatever the vicar had been about to say was drowned out by first one, and then another, siren.

"Police and ambulance, I think," the vicar said. "I wonder what can have happened?"

# Chapter 9

## Tuesday 25th August

Crystal pulled up outside Gosport police station. As she turned off the engine a thought struck her.

"Something wrong?" Trevor asked, leaning back in from outside the car.

"What? Oh, no, no." She got out and locked up, wondering how long she'd been sitting there, looking at the concrete wall. "It's weird. I've known since I started here how long it would be for and what would happen next. Moving to CID is what I've always wanted and what I want now, but somehow I hadn't quite taken in that after next week I won't be coming back here. Not officially anyway."

"You'll miss the place?"

His tone invited her to make a joke and she almost did. "I'll miss the people. You, obviously, and the skipper, and everyone. Good grief, maybe even Dil Dylan."

Trevor grinned and said, "Steady on, lass. You're only transferring to CID, not emigrating!"

Once inside the station they caught up on paperwork. Routine stuff, which allowed Crystal to puzzle over the date and location of her leaving do. She'd already ruled out this coming Friday. It was the least likely anyway, and after talking to both Jason and Ellie she'd been even more sure. The clincher had been overhearing a couple of colleagues standing outside an open window discussing the subject. The sentences, 'I'm so looking forward to Crystal's party on the twenty-eighth,' followed by, 'yes, the party this Friday should be fun,' were so obviously staged for her benefit.

Crystal couldn't resist playing along. She'd stuck her head out. "Did you want me, Ruth? I thought I heard my name?" She'd attempted to look smug, as though she thought they'd accidentally given her information.

There were a limited number of suitable venues. It needed to be somewhere which served alcohol, and food, and where space for a dozen or so people could be booked. It would almost certainly be somewhere they'd used before. There were three options close enough to the station for people to leave their cars there and walk, or get a taxi, home. Another two were further away. The times they'd had birthday bashes in either of those the skipper, who didn't drink, borrowed a minibus and acted as their taxi. That gave Crystal a useful question to ask.

"Your turn to fetch lunch, lass," Trevor said.

"I got it yesterday!" But the skipper and the same colleagues who'd had the badly staged conversation were approaching. Crystal guessed she was being got rid of for a reason. "There's something I want to do anyway, so OK."

She left noisily and snuck back quietly, but was spotted before she got close enough to hear more than 'Queens'. That could be a clue, deliberately misleading or otherwise.

Crystal walked rapidly up and down Gosport High Street, sticking her head into almost every establishment serving food or drink. That confirmed her feeling that only one of those was a likely candidate for her leaving do. Reasons for discounting others were – no booze, size, recent arrests on the premises which would make things awkward, food which was a crime all by itself, and food which was fab but way too fancy and pricey.

Crystal bought herself a burger, ate it too fast, then returned to the station. As well as what her colleagues had asked for, she'd bought a salted caramel doughnut for Dil Dylan, which she left in an airtight box, topped with a note saying, *'Sorry you'll lose out on a whole tray of these!'*

"Confident, are you, lass?" asked Trevor when he saw it.

"I can't believe you, of all people, doubt me!"

"I don't think anyone does. I tried to bet on you doing it but nobody would take me on. Not even Sergeant Dylan."

That confidence made it even more important she succeed. Before Crystal could ask the first of her twenty questions, Sergeant Freedman collected her coffee.

"Thanks, and I've got something in return for you." Her tone was far more serious than her words.

"What's that, Skip?"

"Despatch just called through with a sudden death. Grassy Lane, in Little Mallow. You know where that is?"

"I do."

Crystal drove so Trevor could eat his sandwich. On the way she said, "I know where and when my party will be."

"Yeah, right. And I'm supposed to say something like, 'who told you it's Saturday at the Kale and Snail', and you reply 'you just did.' You won't catch me out that way, lass."

"Ah well, it was a good try, and you've just ruled out one location and date for me."

"Unless it was a double bluff."

"Which would be sneaky."

"So, you're no further forward, are you?" Trevor asked.

"OK then, I have a question for you – will the skipper be driving the bus?"

"Ah. Yes, that's a very good question."

"Yes or no, Trevs."

"If I tell you the truth, it will be misleading and…"

"Ruth and Kev have done enough of that already?" She didn't mind him knowing it hadn't worked. Trevor was playing the game within the rules, but he was on her side.

"You're too good!"

"But not so good I don't need any answers," Crystal pointed out.

"I see why you asked that question. Can you get the same information with a different one?"

Could she? What she wanted to know was whether it was one of the three pubs near Gosport police station. "Will you be walking home afterwards?"

"Yes, most likely."

That was very helpful. Two were within easy walking distance of Trevor's home, The Queen's Hotel and Five Alls. He'd have answered 'yes' if it was one of those. Nelson's was close enough for him to walk, but if the weather wasn't good he got a taxi. The fact the event would happen early September in the south of England meant he'd expect good weather but wasn't relying on it.

"I'll have to report that you asked a question," Trevor said.

"That's fair… Actually, I asked two. It might be fun if you reported the one you didn't answer, not the one you did."

He laughed. "Oh lass, that's wicked."

"I knew I could count on you!"

As they turned into Grassy Lane, Crystal recalled seeing Muriel Grahame there earlier that day. She really hoped the body they'd been called out to was of the homeowner, Vanessa Meadows, and not her great aunt's oldest friend. Aunty Agnes took a weird delight in having outlived people younger than her, but she'd be terribly upset at the death of Muriel.

When Crystal and Trevor arrived, Pete the paramedic was on scene. He confirmed the person concerned was dead and it didn't look as though it was due to natural causes. It sounded like the very first murder case she'd ever had any involvement in. So much so that Crystal wondered if it was some kind of prank staged for her benefit.

One look at Vanessa Meadow's body showed that wasn't the case.

# Chapter 10

## Tuesday 25th August

Muriel tried to clear her mind so she could concentrate on getting Bert's birthday tea ready. It was his special day. She should be thinking of what would make him happy, not worrying what her fellow flower arrangers had thought of her arriving late, commenting on Arnold's private life, or not taking the slightest action to stop them talking negatively about the awful Vanessa Meadows. She hadn't even walked away to avoid being party to the gossip and speculation.

Muriel took her snippers into the garden to gather herbs. That familiar task didn't occupy her thoughts. What had Mary and Agnes meant about Vanessa making people miserable before extracting money from them? Did they really know anything? It was so difficult to be sure when people insinuated, instead of just saying what they knew in a straightforward manner.

That wasn't a problem with Bert. Muriel had heard him referred to as simple. It was true, in the best sense of that word; uncomplicated. He'd always struggled with reading and writing. No matter how she'd tried to help him, he just couldn't transfer the marks he saw on paper to thoughts in his head. It had troubled her greatly. She was sad for him that he'd not gain the pleasure she did from losing herself in a novel. She'd worried for herself at her inability to teach him, until she learned about dyslexia. It made life harder for Bert, but he'd overcome that disadvantage and worked at jobs he enjoyed. For him, as her, gardening brought contentment and satisfaction. When he retired she'd suggested he get an allotment. A piece of ground not owned by his employers, or shared with her, but entirely his to do in as he pleased. It had delighted him, and he'd shown he had real skill. He entered competitions and won prizes, and more than kept them in seasonal produce.

Vanessa had been right about one thing, Muriel was proud of Bert. She was so pleased that what he most enjoyed was producing things for others; fruit, vegetables, and flowers. He looked so happy when presenting her with an armful of blooms. She knew that although he didn't turn down beer, or money to buy beer, from his other beneficiaries, that wasn't his sole motivation.

Muriel rubbed oil, salt and pepper onto the chicken to ensure it would have a crisp, tasty skin. It would be served with lots of fresh vegetables, all grown by Bert. Roast chicken was something they frequently had on a Sunday, but Bert considered it special to have a roast in the evening on a week night, even if it was similar to the meal he'd have a few days before or after. The duplication wouldn't happen that week, as it was Agnes's birthday party on Sunday. There would be a plentiful and varied buffet, quite a lot of it cooked by Muriel herself. Bert would enjoy that.

Should she have made more effort for him? When he was little they had parties in the garden for him and his friends. Muriel and Mum made a huge cake, heaps of sandwiches and a big fruit jelly. There was ice cream too, usually a block cut into slices and put between wafer biscuits. Something similar was done for Muriel. As her birthday was later in the year they had chestnuts and crumpets toasted on the fire. Being held indoors they were more sedate affairs, with best dresses, board games, and charades.

For Bert they had all kinds of races and games, with small prizes for the winners, when they could work out who that was. Generally the sack or three-legged races resulted in a slightly grazed heap, and Chinese whispers and musical chairs in giggling disarray.

That was a long time ago now. Bert was still happy to attend parties and other social gatherings where food and drink was involved, but didn't like being the centre of attention. Even at the flower show he'd vanished before the prize giving ceremony. Yes, she'd been right to carry on as usual and make a nice meal just for the two of them.

Muriel stuffed the chicken cavity with sprigs of thyme, sage and a few bay leaves. They made such an appetising smell as the bird cooked and added flavour to the gravy. She scrubbed baby potatoes and tender young carrots, ready to be par boiled and put, along with whole shallots and wedges of sweet peppers, to roast beside the meat. All would be basted frequently with meat juices and a little butter, in between stages of making his cake.

Birthday cake would be their dessert, unless Bert got home for tea time and they had it then. That wasn't likely, but she'd prepared a 'fancy' apple pie just in case; an open tart with the apple slices, skin on, arranged in a rose pattern. She'd once called it *tarte tatin* in her youth. Neither Bert nor Dad liked it under that name, but both enjoyed it when reintroduced a year later as untopped apple pie.

Muriel had already made the sponges for Bert's cake and left them to cool. It was to be a variation of a classic Victoria sponge, four layers high, instead of the usual two. In Bert's opinion, the way to make any cake better was to make it bigger. He did have a point.

Muriel built up the cake tiers, using generous layers of soft vanilla buttercream and tangy damson jam between each light, buttery sponge. Bert didn't go in for piped icing, but had been impressed when she first produced a cake topped, not with the traditional even dusting of icing sugar all over, but with his name left uncovered in the middle. That had been relatively easy to do the first time she tried it, by using a piece of waxed paper carefully cut into the four letters of his name. She'd saved that, so now the process was extremely simple. It still pleased him just as much.

The rest of the vegetables; tiny broad beans, shredded runners, and beautiful florets of cauliflower, were ready in steamer baskets. She heard Bert let himself in, earlier than expected. Rather than removing his boots as he usually remembered to do, he rushed straight into the kitchen.

It was his birthday, so she didn't reprimand him. She started to ask if he'd like tea and birthday cake now, and have dinner a little later than their usual time of six-thirty, when she saw how excited he was.

He spoke so quickly, Muriel couldn't understand what he was trying to tell her.

"Slow down, Bert. Take a breath…"

He took several.

"That's better. Now tell me what's happened."

# Chapter 11

## Tuesday 25$^{th}$ August

Crystal didn't know Vanessa Meadows well, but was certain that's who lay slumped in front of her. The cause of death also seemed clear. The red bruises on the neck, blood in the woman's eyes, and red speckles known as petechiae across her face, all told the story.

"It looks as though she's been strangled. From what despatch said, the marks on her neck weren't showing when she was found. She can't have been dead long."

Pete the paramedic, and Trevor, both agreed.

Crystal called Sergeant Freedman. "I'm sure it's murder." It wasn't just Vanessa's appearance which suggested foul play. Her home was aggressively tidy, yet the small table next to her chair seemed out of place. Too far away for her to have easily reached anything on it. In the way of anyone sitting on the sofa. A small vase of flowers was knocked over. A book lay splayed open on the floor.

"I'll inform CID and be there as soon as I can," Sergeant Freedman said. "You know the drill in the meantime."

"Yes, Skipper. We'll secure the scene without contaminating it, ask the person who discovered the body and anyone else who might have heard or seen something, to stick around for preliminary statements."

When Crystal ended the call, Pete said, "Most of the people you'll want to talk to are waiting in house 2."

Odd, that was the home of the Sheppards and they were on holiday. "Who are they?"

"The lad who found her, bloke who called it in, and a girl. The lady at 4 is in. She asked what had happened. I told her everything was under control, but she probably guessed nothing could be done."

"OK, thanks." The arrival of a paramedic who waited outside for the police, would have been a big clue.

"I'll go and get something to eat if that's OK?" Pete asked.

"Sure."

"You two want anything?"

They both declined. Crystal stood by the front door as Trevor checked there was nobody else in the house. It wasn't likely the killer was still there, but it would be stupid not to look. Trevor soon reported a negative and the fact it appeared she lived alone – which was no surprise.

"Back door is bolted," Trevor added.

Good. That increased the chances the killer was seen entering or leaving. As the pathway was shared with the house next door, which was currently occupied by several people, that wasn't an unreasonable hope. "There was some disturbance in the living room. She probably put up a fight."

"Not much of one."

"True." Crystal was sure that if someone had tried strangling her, or even Great Aunt Agnes, they'd have done more than drop the book they were reading and knock a table askew. "Let's see if anything else is disturbed."

"Nothing obvious upstairs, but you take a look, lass."

Both bedrooms looked like a B&B ready for the guests. The same was true of the bathroom, except for one detail. "You're such a bloke, Trevs!" Crystal called as she came back down. "The toilet seat is up."

"Ah… I think there's something else too." He indicated

the draining board, on which stood a teapot, small jug, and two cups and saucers.

"She had a visitor, male, and he was here for a little while," Crystal said.

"Someone she knew and trusted – hence not much of a struggle."

"We'll make a detective out of you, yet, Trevs."

He grinned.

"I've missed something, haven't I?" Crystal deduced. "Yes, the cups are the right way up. Washed and dried, but not put away. I don't see a tea towel." The washing machine was in the kitchen, clearly empty. "I can't see her putting a used one back in the cupboard…"

Trevor carefully pressed the pedal on the waste bin. "No teabags – or anything else."

"There wouldn't be teabags, but I'd have expected a bin liner, wouldn't you?"

"Yeah, it's spotless. But no teabags? She used leaves?"

"No. Well, it wouldn't surprise me. I meant they'd be in there." Crystal indicated a ceramic pot marked 'compost' on the counter. "Aunty has one. Egg shells, vegetable peelings and teabags go in. Oh, that's really odd…" There was what looked like an extra large teabag in there.

"Coffee bag," Trevor said after a quick sniff.

"That's a thing?"

"They were quite popular for a time. Probably before you were born."

"The things I've missed out on in life, coffee bags, mods and rockers, crinoline skirts."

Trevor narrowed his eyes. "Don't you have witnesses to

annoy so I get a break?"

"I do, and as there's a garden seat out front that looks like it should just about take your weight, you can secure the scene and rest your weary bones while I do that."

"It's not too late to fail you on your SOLAP, you know!"

Crystal was laughing as she left the house. He'd been referring to the student officer learning and assessment plan which she'd already completed.

As Crystal stepped next door, Trevor positioned the chair so it blocked access to the dead woman's home. "I can inform the resident at 4 and keep an eye on it at the same time," he said.

In 2, Crystal found Beth Philips, the strikingly beautiful young woman who worked for Paula's Posies in Little Mallow, with two men she didn't know.

Beth explained she was house sitting. "The Sheppard's are due back the day after tomorrow. Teddy and I will have been here a fortnight then. He's at nursery now." She introduced her boyfriend.

"Pleased to meet you," Crystal said. Zach seemed vaguely familiar, but gave no indication they'd met before.

"And I'm Hugh," said the older man, in a deep, calm voice. "It's me who made the call. We're plumbers, working on Brambles up the lane. I sent Zach to turn off the stopcock. He had lunch here with Beth. When he went back next door, to say the job was done, he found the homeowner dead."

Hugh seemed to need to talk, which wasn't uncommon when someone had suffered shock. He was explaining why working on one house required disconnecting the supply to the others when Sergeant Freeman arrived.

"Your DI will be here as soon as he can," the sergeant said as they went outside.

Skip meant the decidedly attractive Detective Inspector Shortfellow. Crystal would be working for him when she transferred to CID. To some extent she'd been doing that already, as she'd handled a few routine enquiries for him. The uniform branch assisting CID wasn't unusual, but Crystal had done more of that than she would have, if she'd not been on track to become a detective.

Crystal hoped the DI's arrival wouldn't mean their departure. That wish was instantly granted by Sergeant Freeman saying, "We're to take preliminary statements. Just the bare facts – no leading questions, and keep witnesses apart, although I see it's too late for that."

"Yeah, was before we got here. There's another one at 4. I don't think she's spoken to these three. Trevor's just notifying her. House 3 seems to be empty."

"The deceased's ID is confirmed?" Skip asked.

"Trevor and I both knew Mrs Meadows, the homeowner, slightly and are sure that's who it is."

"OK, I'll check the other house is unoccupied, then take one of those three." She tilted her head to indicate the people inside house 2.

Before she could do that, Trevor returned. "A Mrs Helen King lives in 4. She's shocked, but not particularly distressed I'd say. She's happy to wait in for someone to question her. She says Mr and Mrs Stone, who live at 3, both work. They left at about eight, this morning, which is their usual time. She'd not seen the deceased this morning, or noticed anyone coming or going except the plumbers."

Hugh came out to ask what was happening. He addressed the question to Trevor, who took him to the patrol car to 'run through the details'.

The skipper suggested Zach, who'd found the body and still seemed shaken, come into the kitchen for a chat.

Crystal was left with Beth.

"How are you doing?" Crystal asked.

"Me? I don't think I've really taken it in. I didn't really know her and I haven't seen her, since… you know."

"Could you tell me the last time you did see Vanessa Meadows?"

"Yesterday. She was working in her garden."

"Could you go through what happened this morning?"

When DI Shortfellow arrived, he had DC Neil Ingerson and Sergeant 'Captain' Kirk with him. SOCO were right behind. Crystal, Trevor and the skipper went out to meet them.

"Is it worth us taking a look, or have you solved it already?" Neil asked Crystal.

"There are a couple of details I'm not absolutely clear on," she admitted with a grin.

"Who, where, how, when and why?" Captain suggested.

"That about sums it up!"

"And we were thinking you'd be an asset. Come on Neil, looks like we're going to have to do some work after all."

The DI, who'd spoken briefly to Sergeant Freedman, followed his team into Vanessa's house. He didn't stay long. By the time he re-joined them, Crystal, Trevor and Skip had shared what they'd learned from the initial statements.

Outside the terrace of houses, Skip summarised it all for the DI. "Deceased is Vanessa Meadows of this address. Zachary Belli came to cottage 2, where his girlfriend Beth

Phillips is house sitting for the owners who are on holiday. At about 12.25 Zach informed those residents who were home, that's Mrs King and the deceased, the water was about to be switched off. He turned the stopcock, then returned to Beth until his boss called to say the water could go back on. That was 12.35. Zach then told Mrs King the supply had been restored and attempted to inform the deceased. On obtaining no answer, he checked the back garden then knocked again. He opened the door and saw something wasn't right. After ascertaining she was dead, he called his boss at one pm. Mr Hugh Bend came to check for himself and called us about quarter past. All witnesses have been co-operative. None of them were aware of anyone else coming or going."

"Thanks, Imani. Anything jump out?"

"No, sir. Zach seems agitated, but he's not seen anyone dead before and she's not a pretty sight."

"Trevor? Officer Clere?"

Crystal told him what they'd seen in the house. "To me it suggests Vanessa entertained a male visitor who might well have done some clearing up."

"Yet didn't straighten the living room?"

"Either he wasn't the killer, or maybe he thought it would look like she'd had a heart attack. That was Zach's impression and the killer might not have realised the bruising would come up later."

Hugh came out, introduced himself and said, "If you've not got any more questions for me, can I get back to work? I was part way through something and it needs to be finished before it'll be safe to lock the place up."

"Can you tell me why, when the water was only off for a few minutes, people were informed both before and after the event?" the DI asked.

"Mostly in case it takes much longer than expected. We'd get no end of complaints otherwise. The lady who came home when it was off might still be thinking she had no water hours later, if we didn't go back and say."

Crystal cleared her throat.

"Officer Clere, you have a question for Mr Bend?"

"Yes, sir. Was that a hypothetical example, or were you referring to an actual person who returned to one of these cottages today, Mr Bend?"

"An actual person." He looked thoughtful. "I was up at Brambles when I saw her walking by and assumed she lived down there, but she could have just been visiting."

"When was this?" Crystal asked.

"Just after the water went off."

"Which was when exactly?"

"I'll check." Hugh consulted his phone. "Zach called me at 12.27, so 12.30? Oh, hang on, I think it must have been after it went back on, or I'd not have been where I could see her. 12.45 maybe? Sorry."

"It might be helpful if we had a copy of your call log, to confirm timings," the DI said.

"Sure. How will you get that? I need my phone for work, so I don't want to be without it for longer than necessary."

"That won't be a problem, sir." Trevor took a photograph of Hugh's screen and made a note of what Hugh remembered being said during each call.

"Can you describe the lady you saw?" Crystal asked.

"Old, thinnish. Grey hair, boring clothes."

That was an accurate description of Muriel Grahame.

# Chapter 12

## Tuesday 25ᵗʰ August

Bert spoke slowly and carefully. "It was that woman you don't like, Mure. Her at Grassy Lane."

"I told you never to talk to her." Fear made Muriel's tone sharper than she'd intended. For years she'd been paying a high price to ensure Bert never heard what Vanessa could say to him. Had it all been for nothing?

"You don't have to worry about that now. Nobody's going to talk to her ever again. Mure, she's dead."

"Vanessa Meadows is dead?" She had to be sure he'd really said those words and they'd not come from her own head.

"They took her away in an ambulance, with her head covered over."

There seemed no room for doubt. Muriel saw no reason to pretend to be sorry.

"It must have happened when you were at flower arranging this morning."

"How do you know all this, Bert?"

"Everyone was talking about it in the Kale and Snail… I was there because the vicar and verger happened to remember it was my birthday and wanted to buy me a drink."

The alcohol must be what was affecting Bert's speech. She'd not seen him under the influence for so long, she'd forgotten the signs. In his teens, he'd gone through a phase of drinking far more that was good for him. Muriel had, probably rather forcefully, warned him of the dangers. She'd meant only to protect him from excess, not make him feel guilty over moderate consumption. "That was nice of them, and I can quite see you couldn't refuse."

"Helen King came in and told us all about it. That's how I know. All she said to start was that she needed a brandy. When she'd drunk it, she told us what happened. She said the same things over and over. Shock, the verger said, and got a blanket for her."

Muriel noted Bert was more concerned that Vanessa's near neighbour had been distressed than about the woman's death.

"What happened to Vanessa? A heart attack?" Muriel tried to suppress the uncharitable opinion the woman hadn't had a heart to give out on her.

"People reckon she was killed! The police were there a long time and they've been asking people where they were. You were in church flower arranging, weren't you, Mure? I know it's not your day for it, but you said this morning you were going."

"Yes, I was there. The day was changed because of having the floor re-varnished."

Bert gave a small nod and looked relieved. Not, Muriel thought, because he considered she might have been involved. It was more like satisfaction he'd understood and remembered correctly. "I told Trevor that's where you'd have been when…"

That conversation with the police officer had also occurred in the pub, Muriel suspected. It was far more likely Trevor Harris had joined his friend Jerry Grande for a drink there than Bert having been sought out for questioning.

As Muriel made a pot of tea, she recalled the day's events. How would they appear to others? She'd been inside the church for all but the first minute or two of the flower arranging session, and stayed on a while afterwards. That was alright. She'd been in the churchyard for a time beforehand too. Possibly someone had seen her. Even if they hadn't, she imagined her true explanation would be believed. She'd told her friends what she'd been doing and they'd not doubted her. It was before that which wouldn't be so easy to account for, should anyone ask.

She'd not gone straight from home to St Symeon's church, but had first visited the school of the same name. The school where she'd spent her entire working life. She hadn't gone in, wouldn't have done even if it hadn't been closed for the holidays. Muriel stood outside remembering and thinking gratefully about the life she'd had. The education, the career, the freedom to choose.

Ellie Jenkins, one of the school's current teachers, happened to pass. She stopped to say a few words. It was during that conversation Muriel saw a way to be free of Vanessa's hold over her.

Muriel had walked briskly to Grassy Lane until she reached Vanessa's home. Perhaps too briskly for such a hot day, as afterwards she felt quite overcome for a short while. She'd sought shade in the laurel hedge and soon recovered, physically at least.

When Muriel reached the churchyard, she'd gone the long way around to the graveyard, avoiding the doorway leading to the flower room. She went to where her parents lay in rest. She'd whispered her thanks to them, as she often did, for giving her life and opportunities. She'd try to explain why continuing to keep the secret had become a burden she could no longer carry. Why it no longer mattered as it once had.

She hoped she wouldn't have to explain herself to the police. If Trevor Harris knew she was flower arranging, and that was confirmed by the others, perhaps she wouldn't need to?

"Is dinner ready?" Bert asked. "It smells good."

"Not yet. Would you like birthday cake now, and I'll delay dinner, or… "

"Yes, please, Mure!"

"Go and take your boots off and wash your hands then."

He decided to change into clean clothes too and was upstairs doing that when there was a knock at the door.

# Chapter 13

### Tuesday 25ᵗʰ August

After Hugh, the plumber, had supplied his phone record to Trevor, and answered Crystal's question, he again asked if he could go back to work.

"You can, but I'll need you to make a formal statement at some point," DI Shortfellow told him.

"Anytime you like. I can come back right after I've checked everything is OK at Brambles. It will be. Ryan knows what he's doing, but I'm the boss, you know?"

"Of course, sir. We'll just walk up with you and have a word with Ryan in case he can give us a description of the lady you saw, or noticed anyone else coming or going."

"Oh, OK." Hugh seemed a little surprised, but not concerned.

"You go on with Mr Bend, Officer Clere. I'll catch you up."

"Any good is he, your boss?" Hugh asked Crystal as they walked up Grassy Lane.

Rather than explain her current employment situation, Crystal said, "Yes, he's good. Very fair and very thorough."

Hugh nodded. "Soon have this sorted out then."

The DI quickly caught up with them.

"Do you want me to tell Ryan what's happened, or do that yourselves?" Hugh asked.

"He doesn't know?" the DI asked.

"I just told him the kid found someone ill and we called 999. I was hoping he'd overreacted and she was asleep or something."

"Does Ryan know the deceased?"

"Not as far as I know."

"In that case we'll tell him."

"What's going on, boss?" a man called as they entered the building.

"Come down a sec will you?" Hugh shouted.

Someone thundered downstairs.

"You lead," the DI murmured in Crystal's ear. The thrill that gave her was entirely due to being actively engaged in a murder enquiry and nothing to do with the tall, handsome man being close enough for her to feel his breath on her neck.

The other plumber stopped short when he saw Hugh had company, one of them in uniform. "Is Zach OK?"

"Yeah, he's fine. These two will explain, and might have some questions. When that's done you can knock off for the day. I'll finish up here for now and see you at Bury Road in the morning."

"Sure, Boss."

Hugh turned to Crystal and the DI. "Tell Zach the same will you? When you've done with him he can go home."

"Not a problem," Crystal said. "Is he to go to Bury Road tomorrow too?"

"Yeah. This house is empty and a long term project. We only work on it when we've nothing else on. Tell Zach he can call me if he wants."

"Will do." Crystal then faced the other man and introduced herself and the DI.

"I'm Ryan Fells," he supplied. "I don't know what's going

on. The boss just said Zach had found a problem and they'd called an ambulance for someone."

"It's a lovely day, shall we step outside?" The hallway of the house was dark and cramped due to building materials leaning against the walls. Crystal thought they'd all be more comfortable outdoors, especially if there was somewhere to sit.

Ryan led the way to a cast iron patio set, with four chairs.

Once the three of them were seated, Crystal asked the plumber to confirm his full name and address, learning that he lived in Little Mallow.

"Mr Fells," Crystal said. "Unfortunately your colleague Zach discovered the dead body of one of the residents of the cottages."

"Jeez, poor kid. Who was it?"

"Vanessa Meadows. Did you know her?"

"I know who you mean. She ran the fancy chiropody place in High Street. Didn't realise she lived in Grassy Lane though. She wasn't very old…"

"No and her death was unexpected, which is why we're making enquiries. Did you see anyone go up or down the lane today?"

"You think she was killed?"

Unsure how to reply, Crystal glanced at the DI.

"We have to keep an open mind and investigate all possibilities," the DI intervened.

"Oh. Right… A couple drove out just as we arrived, that'd be about eight. Todd… Stone I think it is and his wife. They've gone out just as we've turned up other mornings so I guess they were off to work. Then I was mostly inside, except for getting stuff from the van. I didn't notice anyone else until I popped out to get lunch. I saw Old Bert's sister – Maria, is it?"

"Muriel Grahame?" Crystal prompted.

"Yes, her. I think the postie went by on his bike about then too. You know about Zach and Hugh. I didn't notice anyone else, but I was in the back of the house a lot of the time."

"What about a young mother and her son?"

"Beth from the florist shop?"

Crystal nodded.

"I saw them walk out when we were here last week. Wednesday morning that would have been. She said she's house sitting down there. I didn't see her today."

Crystal glanced at the DI in case he had further questions.

"An ambulance came by earlier. You didn't hear that?" DI Shortfellow asked.

Ryan pulled ear buds out of his top pocket. "Hugh isn't an Abba fan!"

Crystal thanked Ryan for his help and asked him to call if he remembered anything else.

"What do you think?" the DI asked as they walked away after taking the men's formal statements.

"Ryan Fells seemed to be telling us the truth, although I suspect he didn't like Vanessa, so maybe knew her better than he implied. And if he was so absorbed in his music that he didn't hear the sirens, then he might not have noticed Hugh going out and down the lane. If he realised Hugh was't there he'd just think he was getting something from the van."

"I agree. Hugh Bend possibly had the opportunity to commit the crime. We'd better check Ryan really went to the post office and not in the opposite direction."

"I can do that, sir." Hopefully without adding another suspect to the list.

"This Muriel Grahame, you know her?"

"Yes, quite well. Actually Trevor and I saw her at the top of the lane this morning. She's in her eighties and a friend of my great aunt. They're both in the church flower arranging group – so was Vanessa. I have a hard time imagining Muriel doing anyone any harm, she won't even repeat juicy gossip. As for strangling someone considerably younger…"

"No, it does seem unlikely. Still, we'd better talk to her. I think it might be best in her case, and probably many others, if you approach this as informally as possible. Talk to anyone who might have seen someone coming or going and get all the gossip from those who are willing to repeat it. Find out who might have had a reason to kill Mrs Meadows."

"Will do, sir. Sir, it's probably nothing, but when I saw Muriel this morning something seemed out of place. I'd like to go up to the top of the lane and take a look."

"OK. Return to the scene after that. I've spoken to Sergeant Freedman and she's okayed you staying on to help out."

"Thank you, sir!"

He smiled. "You'll be officially involved in the case as much as possible, even if by some miracle it's wrapped up before you're formally a member of CID. I won't have anyone left out of the loop. Anything at all, however minor, let me know and that includes your gut instincts and hunches, as I trust your instincts. I don't want any mix ups because any of us aren't fully informed."

"No, sir… Zach Belli, there's something familiar about him."

"There's nothing on him, but his brother Dominic has a record for endangering the life of a friend."

"Oh!" Dom Belli was someone she had met.

"You were the arresting officer." It wasn't a question.

"Yes. I never met Zach, but Dom was involved in a very stupid prank. He's also the one who stopped it becoming a tragedy by telling his mum what happened and taking me to the location so I could…"

"Save the boy's life?"

"Do my job, sir." She hoped the DI didn't think she'd brought it up to make her look good. "I did what any police officer, or almost anyone else come to that, would have done. But that's not the point. Zach isn't a clone of his brother. I don't believe he's the killer. If he was, he could have pretended she was still alive when he went back to tell her the water was on, and apparently set the T.O.D later and have his boss and colleague witness he hadn't done it."

She'd not phrased that very elegantly, but he seemed to take her point as he nodded and walked back towards the crime scene.

# Chapter 14

## Tuesday 25th August

Muriel opened the door to Ellie.

"Good evening, Muriel. I've got a little gift for Bert."

"That's very kind." As far as she knew, Ellie had never before bought him a birthday present.

"It's sort of a joke really. At the show we were talking about giant vegetables. He said he'd once seen a runner bean over three feet long and wished he could have had seeds. I thought he might be teasing me and looked it up. The record is thirty-nine inches!"

"Goodness!" Why was the girl so agitated?

"Then adverts for seeds of all kinds of extra large vegetable came up. You know how when you search for one thing… Oh, maybe you don't?"

"On a computer, I suppose you mean?" Muriel was old, but not completely out of touch with the modern world.

Ellie looked even more uncomfortable. "Yes. Well, anyway I ordered some. I didn't expect them to arrive before his birthday, but they just came, so I thought I'd bring them."

"Won't you come in?" Muriel belatedly asked. Maybe Ellie seemed nervous because she felt she was intruding?

Bert appeared, presumably to see what the hold up was, and repeated Muriel's invitation. "You can have some birthday cake."

"Thank you." Ellie waited until Bert departed for the kitchen to say, "Muriel, I'm very sorry about what I said this morning."

Muriel was at a loss. They'd spoken, Muriel remembered that. She recalled how she'd felt afterwards, but not the exact words used.

"I was rude and there was no call for it," Ellie said.

"Tea's ready!" Bert called and they both went through to join him.

Bert had taken control of the cake knife. He handed a very generous portion to Ellie.

Catching her expression, when he cut a second slice, Muriel said, "You have that slice, Bert. Ellie and I will share this."

While Ellie was explaining to a delighted Bert about his gift, Muriel thought back to what Ellie had said that morning. She'd made some lighthearted comment about them both being outside the school in the holidays. They'd gone on to discuss differences in their experiences as teachers and changes at St Symeon's school. They'd talked about that several times. Muriel enjoyed hearing about modern approaches, so it was unlikely Ellie would feel the need to apologise for raising the subject.

Ellie had said many things were changing. How, what were once considered taboo subjects, were now facts readily accepted by children. "I have pupils whose parents are mixed race or same sex for example and none of them think anything of it. I'm sure it would have caused a sensation in your day!"

Muriel had agreed it would. She'd wondered how she herself would have reacted. Most likely not well when judged by today's attitudes. "I do hope I never made anyone uncomfortable or put them at a disadvantage because of something which shouldn't have been a problem."

"I'm sure you'd never have blamed the child, Muriel. Those who blame anyone, especially children, for things beyond their control are the ones with the problem."

Ellie had continued talking, but Muriel hadn't been listening. Until that moment she'd dreaded telling Vanessa that she'd no longer be bullied by her. Had been intimidated about facing the woman's anger and hearing the horrible things she'd say. Her threats to speak out, to reveal the truth to those who mattered most to Muriel. And then, as she thought about those people, how they were likely to react if they learned her carefully guarded secret, she'd suddenly realised she didn't have to fear Vanessa.

Had Ellie thought she'd offended Muriel because she'd been lost in her own thoughts, and eager to act on them?

Once the cake was gone, Muriel told Bert to put his seeds somewhere safe. He was so very pleased with them it was extremely unlikely he'd lose them, she just wanted to speak to Ellie alone.

"My dear, nothing you said this morning warrants an apology," she said.

"I snapped at you, when I knew you intended to help. I'm touchy about it, but should never have taken it out on you."

"I don't recall… With what happened afterwards…"

Ellie nodded. "Vanessa's death was such a shock. It's because of that I wanted to apologise. We think we'll always have another chance to put things right. Vanessa didn't get that chance."

"No." That woman could never have lived long enough to apologise to all those she'd upset and offended.

"When I said I'd like to get a reputation, I didn't really mean it as a reaction to what you'd said."

"Oh?" What had she said?

"It's just that everyone seems to think of me as Miss Jenkins the school teacher."

"I suppose that's true." If anyone ever referred to Ellie and then clarified who they meant, they almost always did so by mentioning her profession.

"It bugs me. I'm good old dependable Miss Jenkins. Always there, always doing what's expected of her."

"Is that a bad thing?"

"It depends who's thinking it. If it's my pupils or boss that's great. But there are others I'd rather saw me as a single young woman. Someone they could ask on dates. Whom they might want to make an effort for, and not take me for granted."

Muriel was certain Ellie was thinking of the vicar's nephew, Mike. She had a point. For years people had assumed the two of them would marry, but their relationship didn't appear to have altered at all.

"If I'm always thought of as Miss Jenkins, then that's how I'm likely to stay," Ellie said, echoing Muriel's thoughts.

"I didn't think you wanted to get married?"

Ellie looked startled. "Why do you say that?"

"I'm not sure. Just an impression I had. I'm sorry, I shouldn't have said anything." Muriel hoped she hadn't inadvertently been rude.

"I'm glad you did. Perhaps you're not the only person who thinks that way?"

"Perhaps not." Muriel's own experience with potential suitors had been deliberately, rather than unintentionally, discouraging, but still meant she had no advice to give.

"Am I forgiven for snapping?" Ellie asked.

"I still don't feel my forgiveness is required, but yes, of course you are."

"Mure, is dinner ready now? It smells really good."

"It won't be long."

"Would you like to stay and have some?" Bert asked Ellie.

"You'd be most welcome, but it's a roast and I've basted most of the vegetables with the meat juices."

"I won't, but thank you both very much," Ellie said.

"Thank you for my seeds," Bert said.

"You're very welcome. Do let me know how you get on with them."

"I will, Miss Jenkins," he said, making both women smile.

They waved her off, then Muriel turned on the heat under the vegetables. She lifted out the chicken to rest, drained the juice for the gravy, sprinkled the roasted vegetables with chopped herbs and returned them to the oven.

"Roast chicken! You're good to me, Mure."

"Well, it is your birthday… Maybe you'd like to pour us a glass of sherry while I do the gravy?" Sherry was reserved for special occasions. Today qualified as a special occasion.

Bert filled the glasses so well it was a delicate manoeuvre to clink them together before they each took their first sip.

"Happy birthday, Bert." His seventy-second. Hard to believe it, but the tiny bawling bundle he'd once been was now a man who fitted the nickname of 'Old Bert' which the residents of Little Mallow had been calling him for years.

# Chapter 15

## Tuesday 25th August

Crystal walked up Grassy Lane to where she'd seen Muriel that morning. There was no sign of blackberry plants, just a long row of tall bushes with large shiny leaves. Some stems were damaged. More than they would be if a slight, elderly woman had stepped into them for a moment. Maybe Muriel saw the damage and investigated? With any luck, that's not all she'd have seen. Crystal returned to the cottages and reported to the DI.

"How well do you know Beth Phillips?" he asked.

"Not very, but she seems nice."

"Have another chat with her. She's given us the facts. Now I'd like to know what she really thought of the victim."

Crystal again asked Beth how she was doing.

"I've been better, but I'm fine really."

"It's an upsetting thing to happen right next door."

She nodded. "Yeah. Poor woman. I'm so glad Teddy wasn't here."

"If it helps, it doesn't look like a random attack. More as though she was targetted personally."

"I'm not surprised!"

"Oh?"

"I shouldn't have said anything."

"Anything you can tell us might help catch who did this. That's what's important now."

"You're right. OK. Vanessa had a knack of saying the

wrong thing and upsetting people. You know, congratulating them for being pregnant when they've just put on weight, or saying they'd made a brave choice after a drastic hairstyle. I'd heard she was seriously tactless before she ever said anything to me, and tried to believe that's all it was, but... She didn't let things go."

"How do you mean?"

"In the shop once she asked how she should refer to me. When I reminded her of my name she claimed she wanted to make sure she didn't cause offence. She proved she knew not to use offensive terms by listing a bunch of them."

"That sounds more than tactless."

"Yeah. I wasn't absolutely sure, but did think she was amusing herself by trying to wind me up when I wasn't in a position to do anything about it."

"She was racist then?"

"Maybe, but it's not just that. It was like she probed for weaknesses. She didn't mention it again, but started making a big thing of checking the change I gave her. "

"Did you think it was personal?" Crystal hoped to verify the woman was generally unpleasant, rather than learn Beth had felt victimised enough to want revenge.

"Gawd, no. She did it to everyone. If she was in the shop when a man bought flowers she'd ask who they were for and why he was buying them, even when it was clear he'd rather not say. Actually, especially then."

"She was like that all the time?"

"Pretty much. I've remembered one time when I bested her. She'd said it must be hard for someone like me in a village where I'd stand out. I didn't know if she meant black, or a single parent, but got the feeling I wasn't really her target and she was having a dig at one of the other customers. I said I've always found being tall an advantage, which got a snigger from everyone but her."

"Good for you!"

"It helped that Zach warned me about her. Apparently an ex of his was sensitive about her weight. Vanessa kept saying things like she looked fine, puppy fat was usual at her age, or women are supposed to have curves."

"Poor kid." Crystal hadn't realised Zach knew Vanessa, but she'd not been the one to interview him. "Did Vanessa continue being unpleasant when you came to house sit?"

"Oh yeah. It's been easier though. In the shop I'm trapped. Here I can say I'm busy and keep walking."

"You enjoy housesitting?"

"Yeah. I've been doing quite a bit – anywhere I can take Teddy, get him to nursery and still do my normal job. Ken and Carol, who I lodge with in Palmerston Road, are great, almost like grandparents to Teddy, but I think it's good for them to have a break from us now and then."

"Makes sense. Do you get paid?"

"Yeah, it's all done through an agency. There's different rates for if I look after pets or anything like that."

Crystal nodded. An agency meant references and a background check and she already knew Beth didn't have a record.

"I could do with a cuppa before I go into work. Want one?" Beth offered.

"Yes please – and I'm going to need to take a formal statement about this morning."

After that was done, Beth asked what she should say at work. "I suppose it's OK for me to go in now?"

"It is, yes. It's fine to say Vanessa is dead, but we'd rather people didn't speculate too much. It's usual for the police to make an initial enquiry into any unexpected death. If people think there's more to it, we might not get all the information, and gossip can cause needless upset."

"No problem. I don't want to talk about it anyway."

Crystal went to look for the DI and found DC Hetherington. Thinking it might not be tactful to ignore Anne in favour of her boss, Crystal reported to her.

Afterwards, Crystal asked if Vanessa had any family.

"The neighbour didn't know of any, so there can't be anyone close. We're not sure if he's her next of kin, but we found her passport and that gives Arthur Rendall as the emergency contact. The local force is going to notify him and have him get in touch."

"What's next?" Crystal asked.

"I'm going to talk to Mrs King. Want to join me?"

"Sure."

"I'll ask the questions to start with, but you can add some, especially if your local knowledge will help us."

Mrs King talked a lot but, due to having been in her back garden most of the time, couldn't tell them much, except she'd had the impression Vanessa was expecting a visitor. "I can't remember exactly what she said, but it was in her manner when we discussed the fact the water was going off today. She seemed a little excited."

As Mrs King told them all she knew about the events of the morning, she referred to Zach as a nice young man, Beth as a kind young lady, and Teddy as adorable. Vanessa was described as community spirited and industrious. "She set up a Neighbourhood Watch scheme with her friend Verity

Houseman, and is always getting involved in things. She cares about local issues and her flower arrangements are very pretty. She does them for the church... Oh, did... and if anyone was ill or anything she'd often take them an arrangement of flowers from her garden."

Crystal thought the woman was trying hard to think of positive things to say and prompted Mrs King with, "I understand Vanessa could be quite... annoying." Aunty Agnes had said a lot worse!

"I confess we weren't close friends," Mrs King said.

"Any particular conflicts?"

"No, nothing like that..." She looked puzzled. "Oh! You suspect this isn't a natural death?"

"We have to consider all possibilities until we know the facts," Anne said.

"Yes, I see. She's a good few years younger than me and as far as I know her health was good. Of course you'll need to ask difficult questions. You're right that she could be annoying... Not on purpose perhaps, and not to the extent that anyone might... It was more that she didn't know when to let things be. Most people sense when someone doesn't want to discuss a particular topic, or get involved in something, without it being spelled out, but not Vanessa. She kept on until you had go along with what she wanted, or to outright refuse to discuss the matter. Not everyone was able to stand up to her enough to do that."

"Anyone, or any incident, in particular?"

"Nothing springs to mind. Nothing major I mean. She'd do things such as complaining to the council that our lane wasn't gritted, sending the letter on behalf of us all and not telling us until after, and she wanted to hold all our door keys for emergencies. Somehow none of us wanted to. My daughter who lives in the flats in Castle Street has my spare, so it was easy for me to say no. Mrs and Mr Sheppard gave in I believe. I gather Mrs Stone had to refuse quite forcefully. This is petty stuff, not enough…"

"We're just building up a picture," Anne reassured her.

After they updated the DI on what Beth and Mrs King had to say, he asked Crystal when her shift was due to end.

"Not for… Oh, twenty minutes," she said after checking her watch.

"You'd best get back to the station then, Officer Clere."

"Yes, sir."

Sergeant Freedman was still in Gosport Police Station. "DI Shortfellow asked that you be allowed to work on the case as much as possible. He pointed out that with you being a Little Mallow resident you'll be able to find out stuff unofficially, and you're almost in CID anyway. I assume I did the right thing in being convinced?"

"Yes, Skip."

"Thought so. I said if you're on duty and Trevor can handle the taskings alone, or someone can cover, you can go whenever he wants you. If you're not on duty it's up to you."

"Thanks, Skip."

"He's briefing his whole team tomorrow. He'd like you there. It's fine with me but you're not on duty. He can't authorise overtime as you're not working for him yet, and I can't as I don't have a requirement for it."

"I understand. I'll go. Jason's away, so it's no biggie." Besides, after what the DI said about keeping everyone informed, what choice did she have but to go unpaid? Who was she trying to kid? She'd have wanted to go to that briefing even if she'd had to pay for a ticket.

# Chapter 16

## Wednesday 26<sup>th</sup> August

"Muriel, have you heard about Vanessa?" Mary Milligan asked as soon as Muriel stepped into the post office.

"She's dead," Cherry Baines said.

Muriel knew she'd be expected to express shock and say it was awful, but simply couldn't. She never had been able to lie convincingly. "Bert told me yesterday." That at least explained her lack of shock.

"Did he say she was murdered?"

Muriel was surprised at the relish with which Cherry spoke. As a rule she wasn't much of a gossip.

"He said some people thought so. He didn't know if it was true." Usually Muriel expressed her doubts about the truth of a rumour in such a way as to stop people expanding it. This time she felt her tone encouraged further speculation.

"Strangled they say," Mary supplied. "While we were in church arranging flowers and wondering where she was. That lets the four of us out, not that you or Agnes could have done it. Vanessa was a strong woman."

"Yes."

"We'll make sure she has beautiful flowers, for her funeral," Mary said.

"Yes, of course." They could do no less for a member of the flower arranging group.

"Although I don't know when that will be, or who will arrange it. As far as I know she didn't have any family. Did she ever mention any to you?"

"Not that I can recall, Mary, no."

"And none visited her I don't think?"

"I wouldn't know." Now Muriel did want to end the conversation – before she was asked anything which forced her to be less than honest in an attempt to hide the fact she'd occasionally and briefly been inside the woman's house.

Muriel didn't go straight home. Instead she went to St Symeon's church. She attempted to pray, but found it impossible. She understood why forgive and forget were so often put together. At times it was only possible to do one when you could also do the other. She sat, letting the peace and coolness soothe her, until she heard a quiet cough.

"Sorry, I didn't mean to startle you," said Jerry Grande.

"I came in…" She'd been going to say for peace and quiet, but didn't want to imply his presence was resented. It wasn't, as she felt calmer now. "It's soothing to sit here."

He nodded. "It seems a common feeling. When we first asked for volunteers to church sit, so we may safely remain open throughout the day, I was delighted by the response but feared the novelty would wear off. To a small extent that's happened, but it has been more than compensated for by others being willing to stay longer than they originally thought they could manage."

"I hadn't noticed nobody was here." Although the church hadn't been empty. The vicar had been there all along.

"That makes me feel better about taking so little heed of your arrival. I'm afraid I was so engrossed in what I was doing my effectiveness was that of a sleeping guard dog."

"No doubt you'd have woken up and barked had the need arisen."

"Perhaps so. I've been looking at old parish records. The

other trinity of hatches, matches and despatches." Jerry chuckled at the slight pun.

Why was he telling her this? What had he found? "I didn't realise they were kept within the church."

"They're not. I came here to work, partly as I take a turn church sitting when I can, and because it's much cooler than my office. Although calling it work is a little disingenuous. I have no official reason, although I suppose it could be argued that an interest in my parishioners is part of my job."

"I'm sure it is." She'd rather he restricted his interest to the present or, better yet, the future.

"And the past impacts on the present," Jerry said.

"I suppose so." He had! He'd discovered something he'd not expected to see and was trying to tell her.

"It really is fascinating looking back. Probably it would be anywhere but it's especially so with Little Mallow. So many people who were born here also ended their days here. It's sad though, because it makes me realise how many children born as recently as a hundred years ago didn't make it into adulthood."

If the vicar was thinking of a hundred years ago as recent, he was looking at very old documents, not those relating to anyone currently living in Little Mallow. Or perhaps, as he was a kind man, trying to give Muriel that impression.

"I remember my grandmother saying she was one of twelve," Muriel said. "Some had died as babies. She didn't know what of and said babies just died in those days."

"Their deaths may have been less well understood, but I'm sure they were loved and mourned just the same. The loss of a child is a terrible pain. The loss of any..." His train of thought seemed to be lost as he didn't finish the sentence.

After a pause he said, "Oh dear, our conversation has turned dark for such a lovely day!"

"Perhaps we should follow Agnes's example and concentrate on the weddings?"

"Matchmaking again, is she?"

"Quite possibly." Muriel wasn't going to repeat her mistake of mentioning Arnold in connection with weddings. With Mike being the vicar's nephew the relationship, or lack thereof, between him and Ellie was also best avoided.

The vicar gathered together his paperwork. "Time for me to return to the vicarage. You're very welcome to come in for a cup of tea if there's anything you'd like to talk about."

"Thank you but it's not me who is coming to church sit."

"No, it's Verity Houseman. I'll be happy to leave everything in her capable hands as soon as she arrives."

"If she does," Muriel said. Then, realising that sounded as though the woman was unreliable, said, "She wasn't at flower arranging yesterday."

"Oh. She's not called to say…"

Muriel didn't say Verity hadn't bothered letting the flower arrangers know. She didn't want the dear vicar to think her uncharitable. For that reason, when Verity arrived, Muriel greeted her pleasantly. "I hope you are feeling better after whatever problem kept you away from flower arranging yesterday?"

"Much thank you. It must have been the heat. I wasn't myself at all or I'd have phoned to let someone know I wasn't coming." Verity smiled, inviting sympathy.

The vicar provided it. "I'm so sorry you were indisposed. Are you sure you're well enough to stay now?"

"Oh yes. The coolness will do me good. When I heard

about Vanessa, I thought I must be suffering a fever!"

Jerry gave his condolences and offered to pray with her.

"Thank you. I'm not ready for that, but when I am…"

"Of course, of course."

Verity and the vicar spoke for a few minutes about what a loss Vanessa was to the community, a conversation Muriel didn't contribute to.

"Thank you for your kindness, vicar. I won't keep you any longer, after all I'm here to help not hinder!"

He smiled uncertainly, then obeyed the dismissal.

Muriel would have followed, but Verity put a hand on her arm. "Do you think things will be different now?"

"Vanessa will be missed of course. I'm sure you'll feel it most keenly. You were such close friends." She hoped that sounded like a compliment.

"It's true I was the person closest to her. She wasn't always understood."

"Perhaps not." Why else would she have commanded so much respect in Little Mallow?

"Maybe she seemed a little forceful, bossy even, but it got results. She did so much good work for charities."

Muriel felt she was being prompted to say something in particular.

"You helped her," Verity said.

That seemed like another prompt. "I made some donations, that's all."

"Come now, there was one particular…"

To Muriel's relief, the conversation was interrupted by Verity's phone. As the younger woman immediately answered it, Muriel didn't feel she was the one being rude by turning away and walking home.

"Muriel, wait a minute!" Verity called.

Muriel didn't wait. She recalled walking away from Vanessa, pretending not to hear her shouts. Vanessa had prompted Muriel into saying certain things, and referred to charity donations. That had progressed to blackmail. Was Verity now treading the same path?

The evil Vs the two women were called, because they were friends, and possibly because they were as bad as each other. Muriel had endured years of torment from Vanessa. She wasn't going to put up with someone else taking over practically the moment that had stopped. She couldn't.

Maybe she was mistaken about Verity. It had taken her a long time to realise the truth about Vanessa. Perhaps now she was trying to compensate by jumping to conclusions. She hoped so and must find out before saying, or doing, anything about a situation which might be all in her head.

When Muriel reached home, she discovered a uniformed police officer waiting on the doorstep.

# Chapter 17

### Wednesday 26<sup>th</sup> August

"Zach, got a minute?" Mum asked just as he was going out.

"Yeah, sure. I'm off to Beth's, but I didn't say what time."

"Give her my love. What happened must have been awful for the poor girl."

He'd told Mum about finding a murdered woman yesterday and she'd been full of sympathy for the shock he'd had. They'd not gone into much detail before he'd left again. Beth had asked him to stay the night and he was hardly going to say no. She'd never done that before, or asked him for anything really, so he hadn't wanted to keep her waiting and thinking he'd changed his mind. "She's OK, Mum. She didn't see anything and it's not as though she liked the woman. I don't think anyone did. Did I tell you she's the woman who upset Kirianne?"

"Oh! No, that's... But it's not about that. There was a murder in the village where Beth lives and whoever did it is still out there. That's scary."

"Yeah. It doesn't seem real somehow."

"And you're OK, love? Really OK?"

"Yeah." He was over the shock, but it didn't feel like the whole thing was over.

"What is it?"

"Nothing. Well, I mean I am OK, but it's Ryan. He keeps saying how us three are OK because we couldn't have done it."

"Zach?"

"I mean of course we couldn't. Because we're not like that... But it might look like we could. I was in the house. If she wasn't already dead I could have... And Ryan went off to get lunch, so he said. I didn't see any sandwiches or anything. That meant Hugh was alone. Any of us could have done it."

Mum looked worried.

"It's OK, Mum. Of course we didn't. It's just odd he keeps saying we didn't have the... Opportunity? That's the word I want?"

"Yes."

"I get he's trying to reassure himself or whatever, but why say that? It'd make more sense to say we've no reason to do it. None of us have."

"This woman who died – she was awful to Kirianne?"

"Yeah and a lot worse to Beth!"

"She was unkind to two of your girlfriends, one of which is Hugh's daughter?"

"Well, yeah but you don't kill people for saying horrible things."

"Oh, Zach love. People do all sorts of nasty things for almost no reason at all. Beth will be able to tell you that."

"I was thinking of offering to stay with her again. Well, until she goes back home."

"She's still in the house next to where it happened?" Mum looked shocked.

Zach nodded. He'd thought that was obvious. He'd stayed with her the previous night – not something he could have done at her lodgings. Carol and Ken, whose house she rented a room in, were nice people, but you could just tell they wouldn't like it. "I'll offer to stay then, shall I? I didn't

91

want it to seem like I was taking advantage of the situation."

Mum tried not to laugh. "Oh, Zach! I'm amazed you ever got the nerve up to ask her out at all!"

"Yeah, well I did!" Tried at any rate. After the way things ended with Kirianne he'd not had much confidence. Luckily Beth guessed what he was trying to say and helped him out. He'd since hinted he'd like her to be more than be his girlfriend. Although he hadn't spelled it out, she must know what he wanted, but she'd not said a word about it.

"I'm getting married."

Zach thought maybe he'd imagined Mum saying that, because it's what he wanted to do. Then he looked up and saw she was anxious.

"That's great, Mum! Congratulations!" He hugged her.

"Really? You're OK about it?"

He didn't know how he did feel. "Geoff's a nice bloke, and he'll be good to you." Geoff had been a friend of Dad's. Sometimes the two got mixed up in Zach's memory. He'd say 'Dad took us here' or 'I remember Dad doing that' and then realise he must have been dead by then. When Zach and Dom had been kids they'd thought of Geoff as a kind of uncle and not realised he was anything more than a friend until very recently. Maybe it had only started in the last year or so?

"Yes, he's a good man," Mum agreed.

"When's it happening?"

"We haven't set the date. We wanted to be sure you were both OK with it."

"I am, Mum. Dom will be too." He'd better be. He'd caused Mum more than enough grief – as Zach would point out next time they spoke.

"I'll live with Geoff of course, but not here. Maybe in his house, I'm not sure. He suggested we get somewhere else, that's not his or mine, but ours."

"Oh, right." It hadn't occurred to Zach how his mother's marriage might affect him. "You'll sell this place?" It was the only home he'd ever known. The tiles on the front step were laid by Dad. He knew that was right as he'd seen a photo of him doing it.

"I'll split the money three ways. Your brother won't get his yet. Don't go telling him either. If he thinks easy money is coming his way he won't try to earn any and like as not get himself into even more trouble."

Zach nodded. Dom was no more sensible with money than with anything else.

"You can have your share as soon as you're ready to get a place of your own. It won't pay for a whole house, there's still a mortgage on this one, but it'll be a good deposit. Even for somewhere big enough for three."

"Fat chance of me ever needing that!"

"Have you proposed?"

He shook his head. "I'm sure she'd say no."

"I'm sure she's not going to say yes unless you ask."

# Chapter 18

**Wednesday 26<sup>th</sup> August**

When Crystal arrived at CID, she was treated as though she were already part of the team. That meant she got a cup of tea the way she liked it, and a bit of cheeky banter from Neil and Captain – also the way she liked things.

The DI said they'd go over what they knew so far, explaining to Crystal he did that daily on every case. "It's a reminder for those who already know and an update for those who aren't yet fully informed. Better to risk going over old ground than miss something potentially important."

"Yes, sir." It made sense. In Crystal's experience, repeating the facts could help her see things differently. She took the empty seat beside Anne, who smiled in greeting.

"Vanessa Meadows was fifty-three, fit and healthy. Self employed with a comfortable income. No criminal record, bar speeding. She gave a lot of time to community projects, and donated to a range of charities. She was respected in Little Mallow although not particularly liked. She was divorced, no children. No recent contact with her ex?" The DI looked in Neil's direction.

"He says not and his details aren't in her address book. He has a slight motive in that he was paying her maintenance despite her having a profitable business doing people's feet."

"She's a chiropodist?" Anne suggested.

"Yeah. That's the word. They've been divorced over five years, he isn't local, and his alibi checks out."

"Thank you, Neil. Vanessa Meadows owned her home,

and had savings, so inheritance is a possible motive. We don't yet know who the beneficiary is. An Arthur Rendall is the emergency contact on her passport. Anne?"

"Arthur wasn't home when local officers called round. A neighbour said he was on holiday, so I phoned the contact number on the victim's passport and got his voice mail. I left a message asking him to call us back."

"Thank you." The DI went through the main points from witness statements and evidence found at the scene.

Only one aspect was news to Crystal – the discovery of an apparently clean tea towel in the wheelie bin outside Vanessa's back door.

"The autopsy will confirm, but I don't doubt she was strangled. All the common indicators are present."

"Do we have the T.O.D., sir?" Neil asked.

"Based on the paramedic's evidence, after 11.30 and before 13.00. If the two plumbers, Zach and Hugh, told the truth, we can narrow it down to between 12.25 and 12.39. Before you ask, the phone records which they made no objection to providing, back them up. Again it's something the autopsy might help with, but I think we should work on the assumption that time of death is accurate."

"It seems the younger one had plenty of opportunity," Captain said.

"It does and he phoned his girlfriend quite a bit earlier than the time he estimated. Both men were surprisingly vague about when Zach went down to those cottages. There's no apparent motive though. They live in Gosport and didn't know the woman."

"Sir?" Crystal raised her hand as she spoke.

"Officer Clere?"

"Zach did know her, at least by reputation. She'd been very unkind to a former girlfriend, something he told Beth, his current girlfriend, about."

"Indeed? That's the young woman who told us the deceased made racist and other unpleasant comments to her and generally got people's backs up?"

"Yes, sir."

"So those two both have motives of a sort?"

"I suppose so, sir." Crystal didn't like that thought. "Beth needn't have told us, and she didn't have an opportunity... Unless she and Zach were working together." Crystal didn't believe it, but it was at least theoretically possible.

"Other people with opportunity but no apparent motives are Muriel Grahame, a friend of the deceased who was seen in Grassy Lane that morning, and Helen King who is one of the residents."

"Mrs King didn't like Vanessa either. And the postman was on scene at about the right time." Crystal could also have pointed out Muriel and Vanessa weren't actually friends, but didn't want to seem to be undermining her boss even before he officially was.

"That's true, sir," Anne said. "About Mrs King not liking the deceased. It didn't seem a strong feeling, but she could have been playing it down. She also claimed the deceased had given the impression she'd been expecting a visitor."

Rats, how could Crystal have forgotten that?

"Could that have been Muriel Grahame, Officer Clere?"

"Unlikely, sir. They didn't socialise and were both due to meet for flower arranging in the church at one."

"Then we need to find out if Vanessa really was expecting someone and, if so, who, and if they did indeed visit, and when. If they're not our killer maybe they saw something useful."

"Sir, could it have been the plumber she was expecting? They knew the water was going off," Neil suggested.

"I don't think so. Not the way Mrs King said it." Anne glanced at Crystal.

"I agree, sir. According to Mrs King, Vanessa was annoyed the water might be off when her visitor arrived."

The DI nodded. "Officer Clere, SOCO agreed with your assessment Vanessa had a visitor who drank tea with her, and washed up afterwards. They, or someone else, wiped over quite a lot of the surfaces, presumably with the tea towel which was later discarded. It's possible the person who washed the cups is a different individual from the person she was expecting. Either of them, or someone else entirely, could be our murderer. Any thoughts?" This last comment was addressed to everyone.

"I think it's most likely that her expected visitor is the killer, sir," Anne said. "There were already a lot of people about. Two more who didn't get spotted seems a stretch."

Crystal agreed, but Neil spoke before she could say so. "We don't know when the expected visitor was due to arrive. The plumbers hadn't given a time, so that person could have come and gone long before Zach arrived. Then the killer slipped in after she was told the water was going off and before it went back on."

"Why would the victim leave out the washed cups, wipe off their fingerprints and hide the tea towel?" Anne asked.

"The killer could have done that. Maybe he interrupted her clearing up after her guest?" Neil said.

"Any more thoughts?" the DI asked.

"It looked as though the victim put up some resistance, but not much. The killer is likely to have been someone reasonably strong. Not necessarily a man, but probably not an elderly lady. It's possible they sustained injuries. She had long nails," Captain said.

"Zach had fresh scratches on his arm," Anne surprised Crystal by saying. "He said he got them turning off the stopcock. Sergeant Freedman who noticed them said they looked more like thorn scratches than defensive wounds."

The skipper would know. She'd broken up plenty of fights, and dealt with too many domestic abuse cases. That's probably why she hadn't mentioned the scratches to Crystal.

"Muriel Grahame's in her eighties. At her age she'd bruise easily and she doesn't have any marks," Crystal said. "She's strong for her age, but no match for Vanessa. Neither is Mrs King. Beth or any of the men could have overpowered Vanessa, especially if she was taken by surprise."

"Anything else?" When nobody spoke the DI invited Crystal to sum up.

"So… The killer is either someone we already know was on scene, or someone who got past those people without being spotted. They either washed the cups or interrupted Vanessa doing that after an unknown visitor left. Which means it's either someone she knew well enough to invite in for tea, or it's someone she didn't know well enough to invite in for tea?" Crystal asked.

The DI smiled. "Exactly. Given your local knowledge, can you provide a list of possibilities for the first category?"

Crystal felt she must warn him it wouldn't be very helpful. "In Little Mallow that doesn't narrow it down much. Visitors, unless particularly unwelcome, are always offered tea. Oh… It was coffee not tea, wasn't it?"

"Do you think that's significant, Officer Clere?"

"It might be, sir." Crystal wished she'd asked Trevor more about coffee bags. "I'll make a list, taking it into account."

"And how are you getting on talking to locals?"

Crystal didn't reveal the local, who'd so far provided almost all her information, was Aunty Agnes. "The flower arranging ladies met at one in the church. Mary Milligan, who runs the post office with her husband, was serving until just before she left. It's always busy at lunchtimes as they make filled rolls, so there are witnesses. I've not obtained statements, but I'll be happy to if required."

"Not at this stage. What about Muriel Grahame?"

"I'm due to spend a few hours at her home this morning, so thought she'd speak more easily then. However I've discovered she was slightly late at flower arranging which is surprising as she had time to get there after leaving Grassy Lane – I tried and did it in much less than the time she had available." That wasn't incriminating evidence, but was puzzling and just possibly relevant.

Crystal continued, "Aurora Evans gave Agnes Patterson a lift, after they'd had lunch together. The vicar came into the flower room at the end of the session, which I understand is usual. He, together with the verger and two other people had been up the tower doing something with the bell, so they're all in the clear." One of the other people was nine-year-old Adam, who'd left a message with his gran at the post office to say he had 'really useful and important information'. Normally Crystal would take a claim like that from him seriously. He had a knack of noticing useful details. In this case she didn't see how he could help. Grassy Lane couldn't possibly be visible from the church tower, and if he'd known any hard facts Mary Milligan would have passed them on, not said, 'Do us a favour and have a chat with him, would you?'.

Crystal's phone rang. She apologised, noticing it was Aurora calling as she switched off. "The nearest I have to a suspect is Verity Houseman. She was expected at flower arranging but didn't show up. She's a friend of the deceased." Crystal couldn't help being a tiny bit pleased Verity didn't have a watertight alibi.

"She's not lying dead on her living room floor, I take it?" the DI asked.

Nooo! If she was and Crystal, who'd spent most of the previous day and evening in Little Mallow, mainly investigating the crime, had failed to realise it was a double murder, she'd have destroyed her CID career before it started. "I'll just check, sir."

She stepped away to make the call. Luckily Verity's number was listed and she answered straight away. After a short conversation Crystal was able to report, "Verity says she was ill yesterday. As far as she knows Vanessa had intended to go to the flower arranging session."

"Thank you. While you were speaking to her, Arthur Rendall returned our call. Captain is speaking with him now. Does Verity Houseman have any possible motive for killing her friend?" the DI asked.

"None I'm aware of, sir."

Crystal's phone sounded to announce a text. She should have switched it back off after calling Verity. She pulled it out to do that and read Aurora's brief message. "Oh!"

"An important update on the case, Officer Clere?"

"Maybe, sir." She handed over her phone so he could read it. *I know who did it – call me.*

# Chapter 19

## Wednesday 26<sup>th</sup> August

Zach carried in an armful of plastic piping. He was about to ask what the boss wanted him to do next when he heard, "… doing much better now."

He didn't ask who Hugh and Ryan were talking about. If it was a bloke he'd hope it was him, but they'd take the Mick or say something sarky whether it was or not. Most likely it was Hugh's daughter Kirianne. Hugh was often telling them how much she was improving. Ryan hoped that was true, but from what he'd seen it wasn't. He didn't want to have to reply with false enthusiasm, so started gathering up the bits of plaster and old piping they'd removed. He'd have to do it anyway, so there wasn't a lot of point in waiting until he was told.

The work didn't distract Zach from thoughts of Kirianne Bend. He'd first met her at college. She'd been a bit on the skinny side even then, but a total stunner all the same. Way out of his league looks wise. She'd also been nice. Really nice. Always smiling and if she saw someone on their own she'd bring them into a conversation or invite them to sit with her at lunchtime. Her kindness gave him the confidence to ask her out. He didn't think she'd laugh in his face as she said no. She'd smiled shyly and said she'd love to see a film with him.

Zach and Kirianne went out a few times. Nothing serious. Then she dumped him. That she did it wasn't a surprise, but her bitterness had been. She said he'd been using her, had only been interested as he hoped for a job with her dad.

101

He'd felt horrible. It was true about him wanting the job, but he hadn't asked Kirianne out because of it. He'd not even realised Hugh was her dad when he applied. Zach found out after his interview. Hugh suggested he come to a barbecue that weekend and 'meet everyone' before making the final decision about taking him on.

Everyone turned out to be some regular clients, his workmate Ryan, a very short lady with massive red hair who did the accounts, the families of all those people, and Hugh's wife and daughter. He and Kirianne had laughed when they were introduced, admitting they already knew each other pretty well.

Vanessa Meadows had been there too. Zach hadn't been sure how she fitted in. He'd asked Kirianne, adding, "I don't want to say the wrong thing."

"She's that Vanessa I told you about. She shouldn't be here really, but she overheard Mum mention it and made sure she got included."

Zach steered well clear of her.

The barbecue food had been great. Not just burgers and buns, but kebabs, corn on the cob, chicken, giant roasted chillies stuffed with tasty rice, fancy coleslaw and baked potatoes. It had started off fun, but at one point Kirianne went to help her mum with something. After that she didn't eat another bite and was clearly unhappy. She'd dumped him the next day.

Zach worried that with them splitting up he'd lose his chance of the job. He'd seen how much Hugh loved his daughter, and guessed one word from her would ensure he didn't get accepted. That was further backed up by the way Ryan was treated as one of the family. Clearly Hugh didn't keep his business and family life completely apart.

When Zach went to the office a few days later he was asked if he still wanted the job. He'd said he did and tried to convince Hugh he'd not regret taking him on.

"You and Kirianne, it's not going to be a problem is it?"

"There is no me and Kirianne. I'd have liked there to be, but no, there won't be a problem."

There hadn't been. Whenever he'd met Kirianne from then on the brief, out of character, display of bitterness had entirely gone. She'd been really nice again, and behaved as though their few dates and break up had never happened. He'd done the same. He met Beth soon after.

Kirianne had got even thinner and clearly wasn't well. When Hugh finally revealed his daughter had an eating disorder, Zach had already guessed what was wrong. It was selfish, but he felt he'd had a lucky escape.

"What's up with you?" Ryan asked, making Zach jump.

"Oh, nothing… Actually I was thinking about Kirianne."

"Boss says's she's getting better."

"He keeps saying it. That doesn't make it true."

"Have you seen her since she started the counselling?"

"Yeah… once." Actually she had looked less haunted then, and chatted to him sounding really positive. She seemed genuinely pleased he was still with Beth, and talked about going back to college to finish the course her illness had disrupted. She'd still been horribly thin.

"I've seen her a few times. It's slow going but she's looked a little better each time. I really think she's turned a corner," Ryan said.

"I hope you're right."

After work, Hugh said he'd give Zach a lift home. "You and Ryan can stop for a bite to eat, if you like."

That offer was made quite frequently. Zach, feeling awkward eating in front of Kirianne, usually made an excuse. This time he'd have accepted, if he'd been going home.

"Ah… Thing is, I won't be going back to Mum's tonight. I'm not happy leaving Beth and Teddy sleeping next to a house where there's been a murder." Plus he didn't know when he'd next get to spend the night with Beth and wanted to show he'd take care of her way better than Teddy's dad ever did.

"No, it's not a nice thought. Is the kiddie OK?"

"Yeah. We've not tried to explain it to him. He's too young and he didn't know the woman."

"We?" Hugh asked.

"Huh?"

"You said 'we've not tried to explain.' I didn't know it was quite like that with you two."

Zach shrugged. Until yesterday he'd have said Hugh was right. Beth kept him at a distance in some ways, and refused most of his offers of cash or help. When he'd been to see her after work the previous day he'd suggested staying the night, so she'd be safe.

She'd agreed, and she'd asked his opinion on trying to explain the murder to Teddy. And she'd agreed to him taking her and Teddy out for the day that Saturday. He was borrowing Mum's car, and they were going to walk in the New Forest, have a picnic and paddle in the sea. Cheap things, but fun. The sort of things families did.

# Chapter 20

## Wednesday 26ᵗʰ August

Aurora's cheery, "Hiya, Crystal, how are you? I saw you this morning and was thinking how hot you must be in that uniform at the moment," when she answered the call didn't sound like someone with hard facts about a murder.

"I got your text during a meeting about the murder."

"Oh, sorry to interrupt." Aurora did sound sorry, but not very.

"You're not interrupting if you know who did it. Do you?" Crystal tried not to snap in her impatience.

"Well… Arnold suggested I speak to you. He said I could do so in confidence and that you'd listen."

"Of course I'll listen, but if it's something directly related to a crime I may not be able to keep it to myself."

"I don't really want you to. I want you to prove me right."

So, Aurora didn't know who did it. That wasn't surprising, but was disappointing. "Right about what?"

"I'm convinced Verity is the murderer."

"Based on?"

"She's an evil woman and we all know she was up to her neck in all that business about Castle View."

"OK, so, you don't have any actual proof – you're basing this on what you know of her personality and past?" And Aurora's very strong personal dislike going back to childhood, Crystal thought, but didn't say.

"Exactly. I know the woman."

That was true. She'd known Vanessa too. It was possible Aurora had a reason to jump to the conclusion she had. Maybe she'd noticed something without fully understanding its significance. And she might be able to shed some light on Vanessa's mystery visitor. "Fair enough. I'll be in Little Mallow later. Can we meet for a coffee or something?"

"If it's coffee you want, you'd better come to mine."

"I'll do that, thanks." Aurora made excellent coffee, and always had cake or biscuits on offer.

Crystal returned to the briefing. "Sorry. False alarm. She just 'knows' because she knows. There's no evidence."

"And who does she 'know' did it?" the DI asked.

"Verity Houseman."

"Ah." The DI knew Verity had been implicated in a previous crime, although lack of evidence meant she'd not been arrested. "You've not missed anything, we're still waiting for Captain to finish speaking to Arthur Rendall."

They had a long wait. The time wasn't wasted, as they dealt with paperwork. Perhaps more importantly, in career terms, Crystal made more hot drinks, so she knew how everyone liked theirs.

"That was interesting," Captain said when he returned. "Arthur Rendall is the victim's godson. He said he didn't know her particularly well and hadn't seen her recently. He has no reason to suspect anyone of wanting to harm her."

"You informed him how she died?" the DI asked.

"He asked what had happened to her, sir. Said he'd guessed, as soon as he realised Hampshire Police wanted to speak to him, that it was about her as he has no other connection with the county. He was thinking maybe she'd had an accident, but when I notified him about her death at home, he guessed it wasn't natural causes."

"I see. Was he able to tell you who benefits financially?"

"He said it's possibly him, as he's the nearest she had to family, but more likely she'd have left everything to charity. He thinks he's the executor to her estate. She asked him a year or so ago if he would do so and he'd agreed. He's not positive as she didn't mention that again. He is sure she made a will as she told him the name of the solicitor. I've got them checking, which is partly why I was so long."

"Good work, Captain."

"There's more, sir. Arthur supplied an alibi before I got a chance to ask. He's on a cycling holiday in the Peak District. He spent yesterday morning looking round Peveril Castle. He was due to return home tomorrow, but said he'll come directly here as soon as possible. He supposes there are arrangements to be made, and legalities to be completed."

"There will, of course. When can we expect him?"

"Unclear, sir. He doesn't drive, so will come by train. As he has his bike with him that might not be quick or easy to arrange. To be honest, he seemed more concerned about the difficulty with travel arrangements than upset about the death of his godmother."

"Her fan club isn't large, is it? Anything known about Mr Rendall?"

Captain shook his head. "No record. No driving licence. He lives on the outskirts of Manchester and works in a chemist. Single, no children. He's the talkative type."

"Thank you, Captain. We'll consider him further when we know the contents of the will, and have spoken to him in person." The DI took a sip of coffee. "Actions for now are to ask Zach if he'd thought Vanessa was expecting him or any other visitor. Neil, you do that. Give him the chance to tell us he knew Vanessa. Ask, if he doesn't volunteer the information. And take a look at those scratches."

"No problem, sir."

"Anne, find out who the postman was and ask if they saw anything useful." The DI glanced in Crystal's direction and grinned, "or committed the murder themselves."

"Yes, sir."

"Officer Clere, try to find out if Vanessa really was expecting a visitor and, if so, who it was, and continue your other enquiries in Little Mallow."

"Yes, sir."

"Captain, press release, please. Say..." He stopped when Sergeant Kirk waved his phone.

"The solicitor calling back, sir." At a nod from the DI, Captain answered. After the preliminaries the only things he said were, "When was that?" and "Thanks very much." He ended the call. "The will they hold was made a little under three years ago after the death of the previous beneficiary, Iris Rendall. The new will has two beneficiaries. Arthur Rendall is the executor as he thought, and..." He stopped when his phone buzzed. "That's him now, sir. Shall I?"

"Please."

The only inputs from Captain were, "I'll check and let you know," then "Yes, sir, I understand," and, "That's right, sir." Finally he ended the call. "Mr Rendall is very anxious to assist us and tackle any legal responsibilities, despite the difficulties over travel arrangements. He's arranged to take time off work and discovered he can catch a train, with his bike, which will get him here about two tomorrow afternoon, after a journey of over six hours."

"Heroic of him!" Anne said.

"He was laying it on thick," Captain agreed. "He's heard from the solicitors that he inherits the house and has declared his intention to stay there while everything is sorted out. He wasn't happy when I said I'd let him know, but worked out that, as it was a crime scene, we may need access. He's very willing to co-operate in any way he can."

"Thanks, Captain. You were telling us about the will. Two beneficiaries?"

"Rendall gets the house and all 'monetary assets'. Verity Houseman inherits all the deceased's personal effects. From what I saw in the house, that might be worth quite a bit."

Clearly it wasn't only Crystal who realised that added weight to Aurora's theory Verity was the murderer, as the DI asked Crystal, "Heard any rumours about that?"

"No, sir. I'll add it to my list of things to find out."

"Discreetly, please. Anne, you have a chat with the woman and see if she was aware."

"Will do, sir."

"I'll double check with SOCO that they've finished with the scene, but I don't think we have any reason to prevent Rendall taking up residence. We'd better give it another look over while we have the chance. Any volunteers?"

"I'd like to do that, sir," Crystal said. "I knew her a bit and know some things about her – that's not likely to be the case with most victims. I'd like to try to see how what her home tells me ties up with what I've seen from outside." She didn't want to give the impression she expected to stumble across a vital clue which a whole team of more experienced officers had missed.

"I'll come with you," Anne said. "I didn't know her at all

so we can compare notes."

"OK, I'll leave you two to sort that out," the DI said.

After the briefing Anne asked when Crystal was on duty until, so they could visit Vanessa's house.

"I'm not actually on duty now. I just wore my uniform as I wanted to look professional." And it gave her confidence.

"OK, but a word to the wise – don't do too much volunteering for unpaid overtime."

Crystal nodded. She'd thought she was doing the right thing, but her new colleagues might not see it that way, and maybe it would set a precedent she'd later regret. "I didn't think. I'm just keen to learn all I can."

"Enthusiasm is good, but you can't let cases take over your life or you'll end up with nothing but the job… Don't look like that. I have a life! My uncle was a detective and he gave me that advice when I talked to him about joining up. Neil, my mentor in CID, said the same. Cases can consume you if you let them, you need to learn to take a step back."

The advice seemed well meant, not a lecture. "Thanks. I'll keep that in mind."

"So, when shall we do this?" Anne asked. "It would suit me best if it were this evening, but if you've got plans?"

"I haven't, not for tonight. My boyfriend is working away. I have things to do today though, so this evening would be perfect."


After making Crystal a coffee and buttering thick slices of malt loaf, Aurora repeated her belief that Verity had got away with criminal behaviour in the past and was completely evil.

Evil was pushing it, but Crystal disliked Verity and had

been sure she wasn't totally innocent in that previous case. However the Crown Prosecution Service decided there wasn't enough evidence to secure a conviction, so no action was taken. They'd put the main perpetrators behind bars and Crystal had attempted to follow DI Shortfellow's advice to be satisfied with that result.

Crystal repeated to Aurora more of the DI's comments. "She may have lied over that, but perhaps she was pressured into it or had some reason we don't know about. There's absolutely no evidence she was involved in any direct action, or benefited in any way from the crimes committed."

"Yeah, OK. I see you had to let her get away with it then, but that doesn't mean you have to now."

"We won't, not if she's guilty. If you have any evidence…?"

"Pretending to be friends with Vanessa was dodgy. They were thick as thieves alright. People talked to them because they knew all the gossip and could be maliciously entertaining. Plus they did 'good works' and people like your Aunty Agnes wouldn't want to seem unchristian, but I don't believe anyone really liked either of them and I don't believe they liked each other."

Crystal had barely known Vanessa, and mostly only spoken to Verity in a professional capacity, but hadn't liked either woman – possibly because Ellie, the sweetest and most forgiving person ever, had referred to them as unkind.

"You have a point, but there's a big difference between being a gossip and a cold blooded murderer, Aurora."

"She's worse than a gossip, I know she is…"

Crystal would very much like to prove Verity guilty, but mustn't let that cloud her judgement. It was possible no real evidence was found against her before because there hadn't been any, due to her being guilty of nothing but a few lies. Crystal shifted the focus of the conversation. "Do you have any reason to think Vanessa was expecting a visitor the morning she died?"

Aurora frowned. "I feel I might have thought that. We'd been expecting her at flower arranging, so maybe that's why she didn't come. We'd been expecting Verity too…"

"Don't worry about it." Crystal didn't want Aurora filling in blanks from her imagination and wish to see Verity behind bars. "This malt loaf is great. Did you make it?"

"Not worth the faff. They've got a two for one offer in Morrisons at the moment."

"Thanks, I'll pop in."

"Have another slice. If you don't I'll eat it all and I really shouldn't."

As they both chewed Crystal wondered if there was anything more she could get Aurora to help with. Saying Vanessa and Verity weren't really friends made it pretty clear she hadn't heard one had left the other a legacy. There was something else Crystal wanted to know more about and Aurora was the ideal person to ask. "You like coffee…"

"Just before oxygen on my list of priorities."

"What about coffee bags?"

Aurora shuddered. "The real thing or nothing for me. Don't tell me Vanessa used them?"

"OK, if you don't want to know that's the case, I won't mention it." Crystal drank more of Aurora's delicious brew.

Aurora grinned. "At church she had instant, but made a big thing of it as though she was doing us a favour and said she drank the real thing at home. Oh! On Tuesday Mary Milligan said she'd been in the post office buying tea… That was at flower arranging so she must have been dead by then. It's real, isn't it? Someone really strangled her?"

The cause and exact time of death hadn't officially been announced. Probably Mrs King who lived in the cottages opened her kitchen window at some point when the matter was being discussed by CID and then remembered she needed to buy a stamp and now everyone in Little Mallow knew every detail.

"Afraid so… Aurora, do you really think Verity…?"

"She IS evil." Aurora sighed. "But maybe not that evil. I can't see her actually…" Aurora lifted her hands as though imagining strangling someone. She went pale.

It seemed a good idea to get the discussion back on track. "So, these coffee bags – do you put them in a pot, like teabags?"

"No, you put them in the bin – all they're good for. They take so long it's cold before you drink it. Even then it's like gnat's pee."

"So you'd need more than one for a pot?"

"I would – and so would Vanessa have done. For someone who didn't like instant she didn't half put in a lot."

Crystal finished her coffee. She called the DI the moment she was out of the house and reminded him what was found in Vanessa's kitchen. "Sir, a single coffee bag wouldn't make two drinks. Used teabags should have been on the scene. As they weren't, somebody removed them – and presumably had a reason for doing that."

"You could well be right," DI Shortfellow said. "Leave it with me."

# Chapter 21

## Wednesday 26th August

The police officer waiting for Muriel, after her unpleasant encounter with Verity in St Symeon's church, was Crystal. She lived with Agnes and had offered to help with food preparation for the surprise birthday party.

"Sorry about the uniform, I had a meeting in Portsmouth this morning, and I'm working later," Crystal said.

"And you've had to wait for me, I'm so sorry."

"I've literally just got here." She held up one of the two bags she had with her. "I've got my normal clothes in here, if there's somewhere I can change?"

"Of course. Up the stairs and first on the right." That was the bathroom and if the girl had just finished work she might want to use the facilities.

"Great." Crystal came in and handed Muriel the other bag. "This is stuff for the party – or will be once you've shown me what to do with it."

When Crystal returned, wearing what she considered normal clothes, Muriel relaxed. The skintight stretchy shorts, almost concealed by a large T-shirt, made it easier to think of her as Agnes's great niece and not a policewoman.

"Right, what shall we do first?" Crystal asked.

"I thought the scones, sausage rolls and cheese straws could all be made today and frozen. If they're served warm it will be as though they were freshly made."

"Great idea!"

"The pastry will need to chill, so perhaps we should begin

114

there?"

"That's for the sausage rolls, right? I hope the sausages I bought are the right size. The fat ones looked too fat, but the others were definitely too skinny."

Was the girl teasing her? "They won't go in as they are."

"Oh?"

Clearly Crystal had meant it when she'd claimed to be relying on Muriel's expertise to turn her ingredients into something edible. Muriel had thought that empty flattery, but now looked forward to sharing her knowledge. "We'll skin them and add sage and onion. It gives the finished rolls more flavour and a lovely texture. Juicy, Bert calls them."

"Perfect. Dry sausage rolls are hard going. Shall I chop some onion? I'm good at chopping." She grinned. "And stirring. You can count on me for that!"

Although she didn't get the joke, Muriel returned Crystal's smile.

"Should I have bought a pack of sausage meat, not actual sausages?" Crystal asked. "I saw some."

"I've never found any that's good quality. It usually has a very low meat content, with a lot of rusk and fat. You can't make good sausage rolls without good sausage meat."

Muriel made pastry as Crystal chopped and stirred. While they worked they discussed the party. "Did you have any luck tracing people from Agnes's past?"

Crystal laughed. "Yes! Aunty Agnes asked me to help her transfer the details from her old address book into a new one. She told me who everyone was, how she knew them, and when she last saw them."

"Oh." It was very convenient that Agnes was fond of reminiscing.

"Most of them were people you'd already mentioned, but there were a couple of others. I attempted to contact everyone. Unfortunately, most of her old friends really are old. I didn't find many I didn't already know about, who'll be able to make the journey."

"That's a shame," Muriel said.

"One old neighbour who'd been thinking of revisiting the area said she'd come. So did a lady who remembered me from when I was little although I don't recall her. I think she'll get a lot of cards too. She'll like that."

"Will that alert her to the fact something special is being done for her birthday this year?" Muriel asked.

"Do you think she already knows? She's been mentioning parties a lot lately. I'd think it was a hint, but in that case she'd have started sooner and not been so subtle."

"I'm sure she hasn't guessed. Yesterday she suggested she and I go for a meal together after church."

"What did you say?"

"That I would book us a table at the Kale and Snail."

"Excellent!"

Muriel smiled at the approval in the young woman's voice. "It struck me that would be a good way to get her out of her house and heading towards the hall on the day."

"Good thinking. I couldn't see how you'd manage that without her realising something was going on."

What a nice young woman Crystal was. "Are you looking forward to your move to CID?"

"Yes, very much."

"Next month, I think Agnes said. Will it be a big change for you?"

116

"Yes and no. I'll have loads to learn – lots of courses and exams and things and I'll be assigned a new mentor to show me the ropes. I've already worked with the team before so the people and offices are familiar. Actually I've unofficially joined them from this week, to help with the investigation."

"I didn't realise..." Muriel didn't need, or want, to ask which investigation. She'd prefer not to discuss it at all.

"I hope what happened won't cast a shadow on the party," Crystal said.

"I don't think it will. If anything it will make people more determined to enjoy themselves and for Agnes personally, well, as you get older there's a satisfaction in outliving others. I don't mean Agnes was pleased at the news."

"It's OK, I understand. Actually, Muriel, I do need to talk to you about the death."

Oh dear. "Officially, you mean? I'd have to go to the police station?"

"No, no, I just have a few questions – a few things to clear up really."

"Oh, I see." She wiped down the table. "Well, if you think I can help?"

"I understand Vanessa carried out fundraising for a number of charities?"

"Yes."

"There's been speculation not all the money was handed over."

"As far as I know it was." That was true. There was more she could have said on the subject, such as how would she or anyone else know if it was otherwise. She resisted the temptation to say something unkind and unproven.

"You knew Vanessa quite well?"

"Not well, no. She was one of the flower arrangers of course, but we didn't socialise. Which would you like to do, cheese straws or scones?"

"Scones if you'll tell me how. I've never got the hang of them. Aunty's are better than mine. Yours are better still!"

Muriel was pleased at the praise, feeling it was justified. "We'll do a batch each and you can copy me. Start by weighing everything and sifting the flour."

As they did that, Crystal said, "On the morning of the day Vanessa died, I thought I saw you in Grassy Lane. Were you going to visit her?"

"No, no. You didn't see me visiting Vanessa that day." Muriel spoke forcefully, as though putting conviction into her voice could make it true. Probably it *was* true. Muriel hadn't noticed anyone in the lane, so how could they have seen her?

"But you did at other times." It wasn't quite a question.

She demonstrated cutting the butter into the flour and rubbing it in. "No, not visit exactly, but I occasionally went to her home to give her money for a charity."

"You didn't do that in church?"

"Vanessa thought it better not. Now add the sugar, sultanas and about half the milk mixture."

Crystal did as instructed. "You did go to Grassy Lane yesterday though?"

She seemed to know, and Muriel hated to lie. "Just a little more liquid in yours. That's it. Keep stirring. It doesn't seem like it will come together at first and the temptation is to add too much and make it wet." She mixed hers and showed Crystal the correct consistency. "I was a little early for flower arranging, so took a longer route, then ended up late." She tipped the scone dough onto the floured board and patted it down as she spoke.

Crystal smiled. "I know what that's like! You don't use a rolling pin for that?" Crystal gestured to the dough.

"No, it's liable to get too thin." She demonstrated gently pushing the dough level, using the first joint of her thumb as a gauge for the thickness.

"Ah! That's where I've been going wrong. Mine tend to come out like biscuits. This cutter?"

"Yes, that's the one. Stamp it in firmly, getting it as close to the last cut as possible. Mark them all out and then you should be able to pull the rest away."

Crystal did as instructed, leaving behind a tight cluster of perfect circles. "Oooh, that's really satisfying." She picked up one of the raw scones, brushed it with milk and placed it on the baking tray. "Muriel... I saw you that morning, right at the top of Grassy Lane, sort of in the bushes. Maybe you were blackberrying?"

"No. It's a laurel hedge there. Just as well, I..." She'd replied without thinking, and found she didn't have a complete answer. "It was the heat. I felt quite overcome and needed to get out of the sun." She gathered up the remaining dough and patted it down again to hide her discomfort at having revealed more than she'd intended.

"It was hot, wasn't it? We could have left these outside to cook!" Crystal put the trays in the oven. "Do you use a timer or your nose?"

"Pardon?"

"Aunty says she can smell when things are cooked. I think I can too a lot of the time, but I'm really impatient and keep wanting to open the door and look, unless I can see they've definitely not had long enough. Talking of enough, do you think we need more food than we're making today?"

"There will be more. There's the birthday cake your cousin Yvonne has arranged, sandwiches to be prepared on the morning, a selection of cheese, crackers and fresh fruit. Don't worry, in my experience parties like these are generally over, rather than under, catered for."

Muriel relaxed now that Crystal's attention was firmly back on food preparation. She'd been foolish to be alarmed.

"Are we making the cup cakes today too, or is it just the sausage rolls to go?" Crystal asked.

"The cakes will dry out if we freeze them." Even so, Muriel was tempted to take the risk, rather than bake before church on Sunday morning.

"Not if they're iced and put in plastic boxes," Crystal said.

"The icing will get wet and spoil as they defrost."

Crystal seemed delighted with that response. "That's what Aunty said! It probably would if you had that hard stuff like on Christmas cakes…"

"Royal icing?"

"Yep, that. But I was thinking of doing soft toppings. Carrot cakes with cream cheese frosting, lemon ones with a mousse topping and chocolate sponges with chocolate ganache. I've done all those before and it works really well."

"Then you will be teaching me something."

"Trust me – I'm a police officer."

Muriel trusted that Crystal took both her aunt's birthday food, and cake in general, seriously enough not to risk wasting great quantities of it. "I'm familiar with most of the things you mentioned, but not the mousse topping."

"That's super easy, I promise."

It was. First Muriel impressed Crystal by adding finely chopped lemon verbena as well as fresh juice to the sponge mix. Then they shared a light meal and pot of tea. When the cakes had cooled the young woman stirred lemon curd into clotted cream and swirled it on top of the lemon cakes.

They were just about to ice the other flavours when Bert came in and offered to help wash up. Crystal handed him a mixing bowl and spoon to lick, and congratulated him on doing so well in the flower show.

Muriel didn't realise until too late that Crystal had brought the conversation round to Vanessa. "What happened to her must have been an unpleasant surprise?"

"She was a horrible woman who upset Mure and I'm glad she's dead. The day before my birthday she said she couldn't put up with it any more and now she doesn't have to."

Muriel was shocked at Bert's anger, and the fact he'd realised quite how distressed she'd been with regard to Vanessa's demands. She didn't want it to seem to Crystal that either of them were irrationally emotional or vindictive. "I *was* cross," she admitted. "It was so hot and Vanessa wanted me to go to her house and collect some flowers she thought would be better than Bert's on the altar."

"This was recently?" Crystal asked.

"Yes, Monday."

"And your birthday was the day after, Mr Grahame? Oh gosh, that was the day she was killed! I bet you can remember where you were when it happened?"

Muriel wasn't fooled by the apparent innocence of that question. Not that it mattered. "Bert was at his allotment, weren't you?"

"No, I wasn't. I went there before but... We went

somewhere else for a while. The beach. Maybe. I don't remember."

That sounded extremely unconvincing to Muriel. What must the young police officer be thinking?

"You went to the beach with someone?" Crystal asked.

"I was just there, I weren't doing anything wrong." Bert went out.

Thankfully the subject wasn't raised again as they finished baking the sausage rolls, icing the remaining cakes and clearing away.

When Crystal had changed back into her uniform she said, "I know you don't gossip, Muriel. That's not what I'm asking you to do. Your impressions and anything you hear could be very helpful in catching Vanessa's killer. If anyone you mention is innocent then anything we learn will be confidential. And if they're guilty – it's important to catch them. For all we know, they may do it again."

Muriel thought it must seem unusual to Crystal that she didn't just say everything she knew, suspected and guessed, as most Little Mallow residents would most likely do unasked. Muriel couldn't, but she must try to help. "What we were talking about earlier. The charity donations, I do think the money would have been handed over. Vanessa didn't seem particularly interested in material things… She probably gave the impression the donations were from her, took credit for them."

"That's interesting. Thank you. Aunty said something about her pushing people into donating, sometimes almost aggressively. Do you think that was true?"

You weren't supposed to speak ill of the dead, but some people made that the only option short of never mentioning them at all. "Yes, yes I do."

# Chapter 22

## Wednesday 26th August

Crystal had just got back to Aunty's, after baking with Muriel, when she got a call from Anne.

"I know it's earlier than I said, but I was wondering if you were free to check out Vanessa's cottage now?"

"Yes, and I'm in Little Mallow already."

"I'll meet you there. Thirty minutes ish?"

That gave Crystal just enough time to visit the post office. She had a plan to bring up the topic she was interested in, but didn't need it.

"We were just talking about Vanessa," Mary Milligan said. "Are you investigating that?"

"I'm not officially with CID yet, but can pass on any information." Crystal hoped that would stop those present from pumping her for information.

"We're wondering who gets the house," Mary said. "She didn't have any family, did she?"

"Not that we know of," Crystal agreed.

"Probably all goes to charity," one customer said.

"Yeah, for something with her name on!"

That remark confirmed Muriel's suggestion Vanessa liked to be recognised for any money she gave. It wasn't a big stretch to imagine she collected it in an annoying manner, but that seemed an unlikely motive for murder.

"Were any of you near Grassy Lane Tuesday morning?"

There was a regretful shaking of heads.

"CID are very keen to hear from anyone who was. They might have seen something without realising the significance." Crystal's unofficial request for information would likely reach as many people as Captain's press release. She waited until the post office was temporarily free of customers. "Mary, I've heard it suggested Vanessa was expecting a visitor yesterday morning?"

"She said so, and bought teabags when she doesn't usually. She wanted me to ask." Mary sighed. "I wouldn't give her the satisfaction. I'm not sure she'd have told me. She was like that sometimes, dropping hints, trying to get a bite, then leaving you wondering. Still, I'd have asked if I knew it was important."

"It might not be, but we have to investigate all possible lines of enquiry." Now she sounded like a press release! "I know that's what the police always say, but it's true. Any idea when the tea drinker might have been due to arrive?"

"No… Well, she didn't say she wasn't coming to flower arranging, so it must have been before or after that."

"OK, thanks." Aunty had told her the flower arranging was done on a different day from usual, due to something being done to the floor of the room they used. Vanessa could have forgotten about that.

"You didn't ask when anyone else was in here," Mary observed.

"It's not a secret, I just don't want to put ideas in people's heads. If it gets around she invited her killer for tea when she had a perfectly innocent visitor, that person might not want to come forward. The same would apply to anyone who was in the lane, or passing it."

"I see what you mean. I'll say if I hear of anything, but won't ask. Now, Agnes's party – I'm going to the cash and carry tomorrow for the drinks. Anything else you need?"

"As long as there's a selection of cold drinks and an ocean of tea, we'll be fine!" With Dad and Uncle Leonard in charge of wine it wasn't likely there'd be a shortage of that. Muriel had said there would be enough food... but she didn't eat much and her tastes weren't very adventurous.

Crystal took a couple of notes from her wallet. "Can you get some of those spicy kebabs on little skewers? Chicken satay and that sort of thing?"

When Crystal met DC Anne Hetherington she told her what she'd discovered since leaving CID.

"You've spent the whole day investigating?"

"No, mostly baking with Muriel Grahame."

"Who is one of our many suspects, I believe?"

Crystal couldn't tell if Anne was teasing her. "Muriel explained her presence in Grassy Lane, and slight lateness at flower arranging, by saying she'd left home early, so walked the long way and then suffered with the heat."

"Yeah that's plausible."

"Actually, Muriel's brother Bert could probably also be considered a person of interest," Crystal admitted.

"Oh?"

"He's made no secret of his dislike of Vanessa. He's not alone there. And I doubt he'll be the only person to be vague about where he was at the time she was killed."

"How vague was he?"

"His story is that he was walking somewhere, maybe on the beach and he might have been with someone else."

"That's not at all convincing."

125

"No. Even his sister looked doubtful. He's a gentle sort and has a reputation for being a bit simple. I really can't decide if he's not clever enough to hide his feelings towards Vanessa and create an alibi, or if he's clever enough not to pretend, and not to say he was somewhere, such as the allotment site, when it was likely they'd be people there who'd know he wasn't."

"If his sister was present when he spoke to you, maybe he was doing something, or with someone, he didn't want her to know about?"

"Good point." Crystal made a mental note to check whether Old Bert had been in the Kale and Snail at the relevant time.

"Are we looking for anything in particular?" Crystal asked as she followed Anne up the path to Vanessa's home. "I'm interested in how you work, what your thinking is. I know we're not going to find a dropped cigarette which solves the case…"

"Mostly I'm just getting a feel for the victim. If this wasn't a random attack, it might help. Things like whether she was living within her means, or way above or below."

"That makes sense." The cottage was about what they'd expect from a financial point of view – Vanessa's work was well paid and her furnishings were good quality without being ultra expensive. Same with make up and toiletries. There was a single, half full bottle of wine in the fridge, some salmon, plenty of fresh salad, punnets of fruit and a small bar of chocolate with one square gone.

"A healthy, well-balanced diet," Crystal said.

"Yep. Looked after herself, but wasn't obsessive."

Crystal thought eating only one square of chocolate was obsessive, but Anne's slender figure persuaded her to keep that to herself.

Vanessa's clothes were good quality classics. Not flashy but not cheap, with a very limited colour palette.

"Practical. Safe," was Anne's verdict.

"Controlled," Crystal added.

"Her shoes are the only hint of extravagance."

"Really?" Crystal didn't recognise the brands. They looked boringly sensible to her.

Anne made a Google search and showed Crystal the result. "Expensive, but you'd expect a chiropodist to take care of her feet."

If Anne thought those prices only hinted at extravagance rather than being crazily, eye wateringly, nosebleed inducingly, bonkers then Crystal needed to rethink her clothing options for when she started in CID. Or maybe she could stay in uniform forever? Whatever, a chat with her conservatively but well dressed friend Ellie was in order.

The interior of Vanessa's house was completely colour themed, with everything matching. There were no photos or holiday souvenirs. Nothing to show her likes or interests except the flower arranging equipment. There were masses of vases and bowls, pins, wire and foam. Even a selection of test tubes. Both women conducted internet searches and discovered all that stuff really was used for getting flowers to stay where a person wanted them.

"Way too formal for me," Anne said. "I like flowers, but in simple posies."

Thank goodness for that! Crystal had started to think Anne approved of all Vanessa's choices and would consider her a slap-dash mess. "Same here. Anne… You mentioned she wasn't obsessive. I'm not so sure. She seems very controlled," Crystal said. "It's one thing to be really tidy, or watch what you eat, or have all your underwear matching, but she's like that with everything."

"It's not normal, is it?" Anne said. "And did you see her back garden? Scary."

"Scary how?" It was ridiculously controlled and neat, which seemed perfectly in keeping with the house.

"Look at the front."

Although Crystal had walked through it several times since the murder, she did as Anne instructed. "That's much nicer." She still didn't understand.

"It's much more like the other three. She's made a show of fitting in. That much is normal, but with most people it hides something. Well, not hides, but they're more relaxed behind the good front. More themselves."

"You mean this…" Crystal indicated the spotless room, "Is the real Vanessa?" Yeah, that was kind of scary.

"Do you understand that covenant thing, which means houses here aren't worth much?" Anne asked. "The DI mentioned it."

"A lot of the houses belonged to one person, like two hundred years ago. She left them to the people who lived in them, but they couldn't sell to outsiders and current owners still can't. That brings the price down a bit. It doesn't apply to every house here – not sure about this one, but I know someone who does."

Crystal called the post office. While Mary Milligan went to check, Crystal said, "She and her grandson Adam between them provide half the answers to… "Yes I'm still here. It is? Thanks!" She put her phone away. "It's outside."

"Meaning?" Anne asked.

"The covenant doesn't apply. This place will be worth the full market price."

"An absolute fortune! And a good motive for murder, wouldn't you say?"

"I would. Arthur Rendall made a real point of how difficult it would be for him to get here. Was he definitely on that holiday?"

"It seems so. Captain had another chat with him after you left. Rendall says he can prove where he stayed the nights before and after the day Vanessa was killed. He'd booked in advance meaning the B&B owners will have records and would remember if he didn't show up. He had lunch in a pub, but paid cash and it was busy, so no proof there. He might be remembered by a family he saw several times. They had three kids and a dog with three legs. Because of his jacket and sharing a picnic table with him, when he was eating cake, one of the kids called him the Battenburg man. They drove past on the day in question, and the boy waved."

"That's a lot of information and should be easy enough to check," Crystal said.

"Something on your mind?"

"I just wondered why all that was got out of him by phone, rather than waiting until he comes here. Or don't you think he will?"

"We're confident he'll turn up. Local uniformed officers are making enquiries and I reckon they'll confirm his claim, partly because none of this was 'got out of him.' He volunteered the lot saying he realised his inheritance meant he'd be investigated, even though he'd not known he was mentioned in the will. Personally, as he's the executor, I reckon there's a good chance he did know."

"I'd have thought so too... And it would explain why he

gave so much detail to show he wasn't here. I suppose he couldn't have got down here and back again between the times he can prove he was in the Peak District?"

"The DI will be pleased to know that interests you, as although it's a long shot and checking will be boring, he'll want someone to look into it."

"And I've just volunteered?" Crystal guessed.

Anne grinned.

"Fine with me." Crystal knew CID wouldn't be all excitement – there would be lots of dull routine and plenty of it would come the new girl's way. She might as well accept that and learn to do it well so it wasn't time wasted.

"That's enthusiasm I do approve of!" Anne said.

Presumably those tasks had previously fallen to Anne. "Some pointers to get me started and a check I've not missed anything would be appreciated."

"You have a deal."

"What about Verity? The house contents must be worth a fair bit. Maybe she knew what she was getting or, because Vanessa didn't have family, thought she'd get the lot?"

"That was my thought when I spoke to her," Anne said. "Verity pretended to be surprised she was mentioned at all. I think the real surprise was that she didn't get everything."

"And we do know she's not always entirely honest."

"She tried covering up for her cousin, didn't she? She was lucky she shut up before she was jailed for perjury. People can behave out of character to protect their family; do you think it was just that?"

"I don't know her all that well. Before that I'd have said she was honest, but someone who's known her since they were kids is convinced she killed Vanessa."

"Anything to go on?" Anne asked.

"She's pure evil! It was Aurora Evans who said it. You remember the short lady with massive red hair?"

"I do, yes."

"She's never liked Verity. Maybe with good reason, but she doesn't know anything. Did Verity say any more about why she wasn't at flower arranging?"

"Too ill, like she told you. It came on suddenly and she slept most of the day. What she described sounded like sunstroke and it was really hot."

"True." It still was very warm.

"We may as well look at the stopcock," Anne said.

Despite having been told where it was, that was easier said than done. It was located in a flower bed and to turn it you had to push your arm through roses bushes. They didn't try as nobody disputed it had been used.

"Zach was probably telling the truth then, when he said that's how he got the scratches on his arm."

"Ah, yes. Looks like it," Crystal said. That sounded better than, 'I never noticed the scratches, or wondered why he was wearing a long sleeved top on such a hot day.'

"Is there anything else you want to check out?" Anne asked.

"If you've got time, can we walk through what we think might have happened?"

"OK. Are you strangling or being strangled?"

"I'm pretty sure you're tidier than me, you be Vanessa."

"OK, but remember this is a walk through, not an action replay!" Anne said.

Almost as soon as Anne opened the door to Crystal, they

131

agreed Vanessa most probably let her killer in willingly. A strong person could have overpowered her on the doorstep and dragged her to where she was found, but the tiled hallway and living room carpet would have shown signs of that. Crystal had noted both were unmarked when she first arrived on the scene.

"So, he sits down, or maybe goes up to the loo, while she makes the tea?" Crystal said. "If he'd got the cups and everything out he'd have known where to put them back."

Anne laughed. "You don't have brothers, do you?"

"No." Crystal followed Anne into the tiny kitchen.

"Knowing where something lives is no guarantee it'll be put away, that's all I'm saying. But she could have had the things out ready."

"Yeah. There was the toilet seat. The killer didn't bother putting that back down, so maybe he considered he'd tidied up properly. That's even more likely if she'd put the cups out beforehand. So, one of them makes the tea." Crystal opened cupboards and found what Anne said was a coffee pot, plus a sugar bowl. "She knew him well. If he took sugar, that would have been out, and she bought the tea just for him."

They easily found the almost full packet of teabags.

"So, he wasn't trying to hide the fact they drank tea, but did hide the used bags."

"Not very well," Anne said. "They were in a bin liner in the wheelie bin, along with the wrapper from the box and the foil seal from a carton of milk. Forensics have them."

"OK. Good." Crystal did her best not to jump to conclusions. If there was anything but tea in the bags then forensics, and the autopsy, would find it.

# Chapter 23

## Thursday 27<sup>th</sup> August

"You be careful out in the sun today, Bert," Muriel said. "Take some water with you and try to stay in the shade."

"Don't worry, Mure. I'm used to working outside. I won't come over faint, just because it's a bit warm, like these kids who spend all day in cars and offices with air conditioning."

"I know, but it's hotter than a bit warm." Muriel didn't say more. Nagging seldom worked with Bert. Instead she made him a bottle of lemon squash. He'd be much more likely to drink that than water. She was probably fussing for nothing. As Bert had said, he was used to being out in all weathers, and he had his shed to shelter in.

The heat affected people differently. Muriel suffered if she did anything strenuous and, as she got older, she needed to take more care not to burn. That didn't bother some and they'd come back from foreign holidays pleased with their already peeling suntans. Like Verity Houseman…

"Verity said the heat made her too ill for flower arranging. I'm not sure that's true." Muriel wasn't gossiping, just thinking out loud.

"I didn't see her that day, Mure…"

"Ignore me, Bert. She probably was ill." Muriel didn't have any proof the woman hadn't told the truth, on that one occasion. Or any occasion. She'd heard it said Verity once lied to the police, but she wasn't going to start taking heed of rumours simply because she disliked the person being slandered… probably slandered.

133

Muriel was washing up the lunch things when Verity's car pulled up outside. She hastily dried her hands, picked up her handbag, and stepped out of the front door. Was acting out a charade a lie?

"I can see you're busy, so I won't come in," Verity said.

As the only words which came to mind were, 'I had no intention of inviting you,' Muriel said nothing.

"I'll come straight to the point... Now Vanessa is gone, I'm taking over from her."

"Taking over? I don't understand."

"Oh, I think you do," Verity said.

The only community roles the two women held were things they'd done together. Flower arranging, the New Hall Committee and Neighbourhood Watch, so Verity taking Vanessa's place would achieve nothing. She could hardly mean Vanessa's chiropody practice, as that must require specialist training and Muriel knew Verity hadn't continued her education after secondary school. The only difference had been... Oh. "You mean collecting for charity?"

Verity gave a most unpleasant smile. "If you want to call it that."

Muriel felt sick. Verity really did intend to blackmail her, just as Vanessa had. Just as when it had been Vanessa making the demands, Muriel would not, could not, be party to it. She couldn't stop it right then and there, so must stall for time. "I'm in a hurry just now, I don't have time to go in and write a cheque."

"I prefer cash."

"I only have a little change on me."

"At least you, for one, understand that won't do. Let's make this nice and simple. £100 on the first of each month, starting in September. That will be easy to remember, won't it?" Verity grinned nastily and walked back to her car.

That feeling of being out of control returned to Muriel. She had to lean on the doorframe to avoid stumbling like she had in Grassy Lane after... After what? She'd thought that was the end of the danger, the humiliation, and fear of worse to come. All that should have died with Vanessa. Now it was happening again.

Muriel had tried so hard to convince herself she'd been wrong about Vanessa. That she was just so passionate about getting money for those less fortunate that she was a little unscrupulous about how she did it. Muriel told Crystal she believed that money really had reached the charities. She still thought so. Perhaps that's what would happen to any money Verity might extract. Somehow that seemed less likely. Verity had made no effort to convince either of them it wasn't blackmail pure and simple.

Muriel hadn't gone back inside. Unconsciously she'd closed her front door and walked in the direction Verity had driven. Now she saw the awful woman's car stopped ahead. At first Muriel thought Verity was waiting for her. Then saw she was speaking to someone standing on the pavement. When that person reached into her handbag, Muriel saw it was Cherry Baines. She looked most unhappy.

When Verity raced off, Muriel sped up herself.

"Good morning, Cherry."

"Good morning, Miss Grahame."

"Is everything OK?"

"Yes." She sighed. "No, not really. Money worries, that's all. You know how it is."

Muriel, who'd been fortunate enough to always have

sufficient funds to meet her needs, nodded as though she was familiar with the problem.

"The kids need new school shirts and I've just… Oh well, I suppose it will wait a week."

Muriel felt certain Cherry was also a victim of blackmail, although what that young woman could have to hide she had no idea, and no business wondering about. Muriel didn't want to push Cherry into revealing she had a secret. What she did want was stop that one mistake, omission, perhaps even sin, from haunting her for life. "Cherry, did Verity suggest you donate to one of the charities Vanessa Meadows collected for?"

Cherry nodded unhappily.

"She told me she'd taken over doing that. It seems she's just as persuasive and perhaps even more ambitious… Try not to let her take money you don't have to spare."

"It's not that easy to say no," Cherry looked miserable.

It *was* blackmail then. That wasn't Christian. It wasn't right. It wasn't fair. "How much did you give her?"

"Fifty pounds."

Muriel extracted that amount from her own purse and gave it to Cherry.

"I can't take that!"

"Please do." It was only half of what Verity was expecting from her. A sum she could afford, but must not pay. If she paid, it would never stop. Each time would just be a temporary reprieve. That's what she'd given Cherry. That was all she could do – for now.

Muriel felt desperate. Had Vanessa told Verity her secret, and that of Cherry? Or perhaps the facts had come to light only after Vanessa's death. Blackmail was evil. The police might see escaping from it as a motive for murder. She should tell them about Vanessa and how she'd extorted money from her, and from others too. If they found out another way it would look very bad.

Verity had implied multiple victims. As Muriel knew she wasn't the only person who'd felt manipulated into donating to the charities Vanessa had collected for, that made sense. What she could, should, do was share with the police the fact that others were in the same position. Looking into all the victims would be better than them concentrating on just one – Muriel herself.

Muriel would go into Gosport immediately, before losing her nerve. It wasn't just the police station she would visit. She had shopping to do and now that she'd given Cherry fifty pounds, what she'd told Verity about having to go to the bank was true.

When Muriel reached the bus stop a small group of people were gathered there, saying what a terrible thing Vanessa's murder was. When invited to contribute to the conversation Muriel found she had nothing to say.

"I'm so sorry," one person said. "I was forgetting she was a friend of yours."

That, Muriel could answer, by explaining it wasn't true. No, she mustn't say that. How would it look? "There's the bus," Muriel said when those who'd been waiting longer than she, failed to react to the sight of it.

"We're not waiting for that," one woman said. "We've a coach trip booked."

"I hope you have a nice time."

They thanked Muriel and wished her a good day as she boarded the bus. It was such a relief to be driven away from Little Mallow and everyone who was talking about

Vanessa's sudden death. Muriel didn't want to listen to rumours and speculation, much less contribute to them. Is that what she'd be doing if she went to the police?

It wasn't Muriel's place to help expose the problems of Cherry, and the others Muriel guessed were blackmail victims. In any case she might not be right. And how could she explain she was being blackmailed without revealing the secret she'd kept so long? A secret which wasn't hers alone.

She'd still not decided whether to proceed by the time she reached Gosport. The police station was located very close to the library, so Muriel went there first and exchanged her books. Then, as that was also close by, she visited the supermarket.

It was tempting to get back on the bus with her purchases, especially as she'd come out without her little shopping trolley, but she made herself return to the police station. She could see no obvious way inside. The building was joined to the council offices. Muriel had been in there several times, completing the paperwork for Bert's allotment and attending to various other matters. She couldn't recall any indication of that being a way to reach the police. She decided to have tea at the Knitted Tea Cosy while deciding what to do.

As Muriel approached the tearoom she noticed Arnold the verger, with Cameron. Should she join them, or go without fortification? She couldn't very well have tea there at a different table. The matter was decided when Cameron looked up. He smiled, exchanged a few words with Arnold, and gestured for Muriel to join them.

The two men rose and greeted her pleasantly. Cameron pulled out a chair for her. Arnold took Muriel's bags and placed them in the corner behind his seat, where they'd be in nobody's way. They were very gentlemanly, quite formal. They didn't touch one another, or express words of endearment. Even so, there was something in the way they worked as a team to make her feel comfortable which convinced Muriel she'd been correct in her belief they were more than simply friends.

"Am I right in thinking you're attempting to get away from talk of the shocking news, dear lady?" Cameron asked. "Arnold appraised me of the fact you never gossip, and that most of your fellow Little Mallow residents do little else."

Muriel nodded.

"Then you are safe here, as the subject is not one we're involved in, or of our concern."

"Everything in Little Mallow is something to do with me," Arnold said, although not in a reproving manner. "I'll be very happy not to talk about it. It's much better to wait until the facts are known."

"I quite agree," Muriel said.

Muriel's relief was short lived, as she looked up straight into the face of Verity Houseman. Had she followed Muriel, seen her hesitate outside the police station and come to issue threats against going in? Or maybe assumed she had gone in and now wanted revenge?

"Hello, verger. Do forgive me interrupting you when you're with friends, but I didn't get a chance to..." As Verity's glance switched from Cameron to Muriel she stopped abruptly. Some of the horror Muriel had felt was mirrored on Verity's face. Clearly Muriel wasn't the reason for the woman's presence in the coffee shop.

Verity acted as though she'd not already spoken to Muriel that day, greeting them all with fake warmth and continued what she'd started to say. "I didn't get a chance to offer you raffle tickets the other day. It's in aid of The Ark and there are some excellent prizes. I didn't want you to miss out."

Cameron declined, with great emphasis, on the grounds he never gambled. His confidence gave Muriel the strength to say, "No thank you." When Cameron reached for Arnold's hand the verger shook his head. Verity took herself off. It seemed to Muriel she'd taken offence too.

"I think you upset her," Arnold remarked.

"Good. She's an atrocious woman and I like blackmail even less than gambling."

"Blackmail!" Muriel exclaimed.

"I don't think…" Arnold began.

"I do. Not in a legal sense, but she approaches people in groups so they feel uncomfortable being the one to say no, and drops little hints like 'I sold tickets to two people I never expected to see together, of course I'd never gossip about such generous contributors to the rescue centre'."

"I see," Muriel said.

"I don't…" Arnold began.

"Of course you don't." Cameron turned to Muriel. "Arnold doesn't speak ill of anyone, however much they deserve it. But it's true I'm afraid. She tried it with me last week. Something along the lines of knowing that some people like to keep their relationships private and how I could rely on her."

This seemed to be news to Arnold.

"Oh?" Muriel asked, willing Cameron to continue.

He obliged. "I told her there's no such thing as bad publicity and that all my sins were already public."

Muriel glanced down to where he was still holding Arnold's hand. "Love is not a sin."

# Chapter 24

## Thursday 27th August

Crystal was making notes about Vanessa's murder, trying to decide who she should speak to next, when someone knocked on the door.

"Stay there, lovey, I'll go," Aunty Agnes said.

Crystal heard the sound of the door opening and Aunty saying, "Hello, Beth. What a nice surprise. Do come in."

"Hello, Mrs Patterson, Is Crystal in? I just wanted a quick word."

"Yes, she's here. Come in, come in."

Crystal smiled as she heard Aunty returning. Clearly Beth wasn't going to be the one person who escaped with no more than 'a quick word'. Even the postman rarely managed that! Something tickled in Crystal's subconscious.

As Beth manoeuvred Teddy and his pushchair into the house, Muriel arrived. "As you have a visitor I'll come back another time," she said.

"Don't be silly," Agnes chided Muriel. "It's lovely to have so many visitors. It's just like a party and I do like a party!"

"Party!" Teddy exclaimed.

"Exactly." Then Aunty, bless her, suggested Beth help Crystal make tea and take it into the garden, where she and Muriel would be sitting in the shade. "And this young man too, if he's happy to come with us?" She must have guessed whatever Beth had to say could be for Crystal's ears only.

"Teddy, would you like to go with these nice ladies into the garden? I'll be there in just a minute."

He nodded slightly doubtfully and Beth unstrapped him from his pushchair

"I'm sure we have some squash for him and there's some C. A. K. E. too, if he's allowed that?"

Teddy let Aunty take his hand and lead him away.

"Just tea for me, please," Muriel said before following. "I not long ago had refreshments with Arnold and his friend Cameron in Gosport."

Aunty Agnes glanced back. "Oh, did you now? Tell me, were you…"

Crystal turned her attention to Beth. "Would Teddy like cake? We have plenty."

"I'm sure he would – he eats a lot! The Sheppards said to make ourselves at home, and it's been like a holiday with all the nice food and the garden… As we're both here, I could ask Mrs Grahame about that. Do you think she'd mind?"

"Muriel, like Aunty, is Miss, not Mrs," Crystal corrected. "No, I don't think she'd mind talking about gardens."

"I'm only looking after the house, you see. Vanessa Meadows was doing the garden… She did it when I wasn't there. Although I know a lot about flowers I know nothing about gardening. There might be something urgent I need to attend to. It'll be bad enough for them to come home and find a plague of Teddy shaped locusts have emptied their kitchen cupboards and fridge, I don't want it to look like the same thing has happened to their garden."

"I'm sure Muriel will know. Is that what you wanted to speak to me about?"

Beth shook her head. "The thing is, last night I saw Verity Houseman poking about outside Vanessa's house." She paused as the sound of laughter reached the kitchen. "She was lifting flower pots and I thought she might be looking for a key. Lots of people leave one in places like that."

"Yes, they do." Vanessa had – it was found in the same search which revealed the discarded tea towel, and used by Anne when they'd gone in the previous day.

"It might be perfectly innocent. They were friends, and she didn't take anything, but it was very late. Just after midnight."

"She didn't get in?"

"No. I watched for a while and she didn't go round the back, just walked away after a bit of a search. I'm fairly sure she didn't see me."

More laughter erupted from the garden.

"OK, thanks. I'll pass that on to CID. Someone might come to take a statement." It would be difficult for Beth to get into Portsmouth, and as she was currently right next door to the crime scene, it was likely an officer would be there sometime that day.

"No problem. Anything I can do to help catch who really did this will speed up the time anyone innocent is under suspicion."

She must mean Zach. Her concern didn't tell Crystal anything. Pretty much anyone would realise the police needed to consider the possibility he was involved.

"Yes, it will. And so will anything you remember about events yesterday. If you saw anyone else for instance, or you realise anything you told us wasn't accurate."

"Right."

Crystal could deduce nothing from Beth's tone. "There are cold drinks in the fridge. Help yourself to whatever Teddy would like, and something for yourself if you'd

143

prefer that to tea."

Yet more shrieks of laughter sounded. What was going on out there?

"Do you think that's enough cake?" Crystal asked.

"I expect so. Miss Grahame said she didn't want any."

Crystal added six jam tarts and a few chunks of chocolate brownie. "Better?"

Beth returned her grin. "Perfect."

When Crystal and Beth carried apple juice, tea, and cake outside, the reason for the laughter became clear. Aunty, Muriel, and Teddy, all had loads of flowers stuck in their hair. Aunty acting like a kid was nothing new, but it was quite a revelation to see Muriel decorated with colourful blooms. She'd removed her shoes and looked like a hippy as, giggling, she added more flowers to the abundance already woven into the little boy's dark curls.

"Mummy, Mummy!" Teddy said, indicating it was Beth's turn for a floral makeover.

"Tea first," Agnes said.

Teddy was very polite with his please and thank yous and very enthusiastic with his cake eating, which delighted the older women. When the cake was gone, Beth was encouraged to choose flowers to go in her hair. Crystal got out of it by saying she would wash up and had to make a work call.

She called DI Shortfellow and told him what Beth had said about Verity's late night visit.

"And what do you make of that, Officer Clere?"

"There's something in the house she wants but can't wait until she officially inherits it. I'm tempted to say it's something which implicates her in the murder, but we or

SOCO would have found that already. There was absolutely nothing which seemed out of place or was unexplained." Some of her flower arranging and kitchen equipment would have made decent murder weapons, but couldn't have been used to strangle anyone.

"Perhaps she wanted to leave something?"

"Ooooh! Can we let her get in? The place is so neat, it'd be easy to spot whatever she left."

The DI gave a bark of his own distinctive laughter before ending the call.

Glad that everyone was having so much fun, Crystal took her phone into the garden. She took a photo of the other four all covered in flowers and prompted Beth into asking for Muriel's help with the garden.

"I'll be happy to come and take a look," Muriel said.

The three visitors left together soon after, with Agnes inviting Beth and Teddy to call in any time they were passing, especially if they wanted cake.

"I like her," Aunty said.

"I do too." Crystal really hoped Zach wasn't the murderer. It was easy to imagine him losing his temper about insults to his girlfriend and her son. He was young and strong, it wouldn't have taken him long to overpower Vanessa. Zach could have carried her through the hallway, rather than needing to drag her. Crystal reminded herself she didn't know what kind of person he was. Just because his brother Dom was a reckless idiot didn't mean Zach was.

"… a good mother too. Dear little Teddy is polite but not too polite."

"Oh?" Crystal asked.

"Polite means she doesn't take the easiest route of giving

him what he wants all the time. He knows not to snatch, but to wait until something is offered him, and he knows to show gratitude when it is. That kind of thing takes effort and patience."

"Yes, it must do. And the not too polite?"

"He wasn't scared to say or do the wrong thing, as he might if bullied or she was too quick tempered with him."

"I see what you mean. I'm also starting to see where my deductive genius comes from!"

"Talking of which… Sunday should be a good chance for you to talk to people about Vanessa," Aunty said.

"You want me to come to church?"

"You could do if you'd like, but I was thinking of here. I'm sure a lot of people will be calling in to wish me a happy birthday."

"I imagine so." Crystal smiled. If Muriel was wrong and Aunty had guessed something was being done for her birthday, it was clearly a small party at home she'd be expecting. The big do in the hall would still be a surprise.

"Something on your mind, lovey?" Aunty asked.

"I've not got any further working out the details of my work leaving do."

"You'll do it and you'll solve the murder too. Anything I can do to help with either, you let me know."

"Thanks."

"Someone in Little Mallow is bound to know something. You just need to ask the right people the right questions."

"We're working on it."

"Tell Trevor Harris he's very welcome to come round. He likes cake – and your cousin Yvonne."

"Not matchmaking, are you Aunty?" From the gleam in the old lady's eye, she obviously was.

"Of course not! I just thought he could help with the questioning."

That was a good point. Crystal didn't intend to use the party for a murder investigation, but people would be talking about the subject. With both of them there, the chances of overhearing something useful was doubled – and Trevor did like cake – and cousin Yvonne.

"And if you get a chance, make sure Beth knows she's welcome here anytime. She seems like fun, and with a little kiddie I don't suppose she goes out much."

"Probably not. She does have a boyfriend though. It was him who found the body."

"They're the nearest you've got to witnesses, aren't they?"

That was true. There were so many people coming to the party it couldn't hurt to add a few more, as long as they got in a bit more food.

Crystal's phone buzzed.

"Answer it, lovey. It could be the breakthrough you need."

Crystal glanced at the display. "Maybe it could!" She clicked to accept the call from Adam's mum, Lorna Milligan. "Hello, Lorna. I'm sorry I didn't get back to Adam. It's been hectic." She hadn't entirely dismissed the boy's claim to know something useful, but it hadn't felt like a priority. He was a great kid, super keen to prove his detective skills, and had been useful in the past. Because of that she'd wanted to spend time with him, when she could talk to him properly, not just two minutes on the phone.

"Yes, I can imagine. I don't want to be a nuisance, but I

promised Adam I'd relay some very important – according to him – information about the case. He insists it could be a vital clue and wouldn't leave until I crossed my heart and swore on my hair straighteners!"

Crystal laughed. "Gotta love him! Did you say he's gone somewhere?"

"I've sent him and Josh to stay with my mum as I'm worried he'll accidentally get mixed up in something."

Crystal was relieved at that. Adam did treat detecting as a kind of game and perhaps wouldn't realise the danger. "What's the vital clue?"

"I can give it you word for word as he made me write it down. 'Verity Houseman was telling another big fat lie. She wasn't sick when the murdering was done. I went up the tower with Reverend Grande and Mr Stewart and Linzie, the campanological metallurgist'." Lorna said that last bit slowly and slightly doubtfully.

"Sorry, the what?" Adam loved learning big new words and sharing them with others.

"I may not have got that quite right, or he might not have, or maybe they were teasing him. She's some kind of expert on church bells. Apparently St Symeon's has a particularly interesting example of whatever type it is."

"Oh, OK. Go on."

"Adam said, 'I saw her in her garden as soon as we got to the top. She was digging potatoes and had done a big long row and that's really hard work.' He even noticed that the soil was still dark on the row she'd just dug, but paler where the sun had dried out her earlier efforts."

Crystal had no doubt Adam's evidence was accurate. He understood the importance of that and was very observant.

The church tower would have provided an excellent view of Verity's garden, and Adam was up there only just after the time Vanessa died. If Verity had taken a break from her spud harvest to kill her friend, Adam would have seen her arrive home. Obviously he hadn't. But if Verity was well enough to dig potatoes, why hadn't she gone to flower arranging? The session had been on a different day from usual. Had she simply forgotten and then lied rather than admit her mistake? "That is interesting. Will you tell him thank you for me?"

"I will. I assume I can't add that you rushed off to arrest her?"

"Sorry, no! He's given her an alibi. Please tell him that proving people innocent is as important as discovering they're guilty, and that I'll be passing on his information to CID."

Crystal was about to call the DI to report this latest suspicious behaviour from Verity when she thought better of it. She never called the inspector at Gosport station directly, so shouldn't keep doing that with DI Shortfellow. Instead she called Captain, taking care to address him properly as Sergeant Kirk. Skipper felt presumptuous when she wasn't yet directly under his command.

"Thanks, Crystal. The DI just told me she was seen snooping around the victim's home last night. She's up to something alright. If it's not murder what is it? There's the question."

"And a very good question it is too, Sergeant."

"Promise you'll phone me the minute you get the answer."

"Deffo!"

# Chapter 25

## Thursday 27<sup>th</sup> August

"Did you say your son is just two?" Muriel asked Beth as they walked towards Grassy Lane. It was Agnes who'd told her that on a previous occasion, but Muriel didn't want the young woman to feel people were gossiping about her.

"Actually he'll be three on Wednesday."

"Oh, another birthday! And you'll be having a party for him?" Muriel spoke quietly, so as not to excite the interest of little Teddy, who was dozing after some energetic play and impressive consumption of cake and other sweet treats.

"No."

"Tea with your family?"

"No."

Oh dear, Muriel should have picked up Beth's discouraging tone the first time she answered in the negative. "I'm very sorry. I didn't mean to pry, or... I've been making a lot of birthday cake and other party food lately and it's made me remember parties from when I was young. Such happy memories."

"And I'm a bad mother for depriving Teddy of that?"

"No! No, not at all. I'm so sorry, I..."

"Don't be. I'm the one who should apologise. I'm a bit touchy on the subject." Beth took a deep breath, then nodded as though she'd reached a decision. "My own childhood wasn't great. I thought I'd do so much better, but I've just made different mistakes. I can't afford a party and I'm pretty much all the family he has."

Muriel was touched the young woman had opened up to her, and she wanted to help. Even these days being a single mother couldn't be easy. "A party at home needn't cost much. When I was young, and when Bert was too, parties were just games. Lots of running round mostly. Races sometimes, with sweets for prizes and musical chairs and we'd have sandwiches and a birthday cake and jelly and ice cream for tea. That was a real treat then. I expect children still like it now everyone has a freezer?"

"Yes they do. Maybe I'm just being stubborn. I can be. Zach offered to pay to take Teddy and a few other kids to MacDonald's. I wouldn't let him, just because I'm annoyed Teddy's bio dad never helps at all. Carol and Ken are great, but a house full of noisy kids would be too much for them."

Muriel hadn't been thinking of Beth using the small patch of ground outside the house in which she and her son lodged. She'd been imagining Teddy, young Adam Milligan, and a crowd of other laughing children in a much larger, flower filled space. "You could use my garden," Muriel said. "I'd be happy to provide sandwiches…"

"No. Thank you though, that's really kind. You've shown me I could do something. A picnic on the beach maybe? I'll have a think."

Muriel said no more on the subject. Beth had admitted to being stubborn, so pushing her into immediate acceptance wasn't going to work. She'd do some thinking of her own.

When they reached the cottages, Teddy woke up. As Beth removed him from his pushchair, Muriel looked around the Sheppard's front garden. "The most urgent thing is watering the containers," she said when they joined her.

"I did give them some yesterday."

"In this weather they need a good soaking every day."

With Teddy's laughing help, the pots and hanging baskets got that, as did he and his mum. Muriel escaped with just a few splashes, which in that heat weren't a problem. The process was repeated in the smaller back garden.

"Anything else I should do?" Beth asked.

"Ideally mowing the grass and dead heading."

"I understood the first half of that, and they do have a mower."

That proved to be a cordless electric one. It was the same kind of thing as the lightweight strimmer Muriel used at home sometimes. With Muriel holding onto Teddy, so he was in no danger, she instructed Beth on how to start it.

Muriel cut off the dead blooms, handing them to Teddy. "Help me count," she told him, in the hope of keeping him occupied, before remembering he was two years younger than the pupils she used to teach. To her surprise he got all the way to ten without much prompting.

"What's next?" she tried.

"Again!"

"OK. Let's put these on the compost heap first then."

As Muriel cut faded roses, she noticed that although there were buds on a large bush of white hybrid tea roses, and it was clear previous flowers had been removed, there were none now in need of removal. A suspicion began to form.

Once Beth had finished mowing, Muriel asked her if she'd picked any flowers.

"Sweet peas. Mrs Sheppard asked me to do that. She said it encourages them to produce more."

"She's quite right, but I was thinking of roses. White roses."

"It's funny you should say that. I noticed lots when we

152

first arrived and they all seemed to go over at once."

"I don't think they went over. There's something I'd like to check in Vanessa's garden."

There were no white roses in the pretty patch in front of the house, so they went around to the end of the terrace and into the back. The space there was barely a garden at all. Why would anyone who professed to love flowers do this? Everything was so sterile, so rigid, so joyless.

"No white ones here," Beth said. "Do you think someone is going round stealing bunches of them?"

"That isn't what I suspect, no." It only took Muriel a few minutes to walk around the awful fake turf, looking at each trussed up plant, to be sure she was correct. Just as well, because they'd only just reached the front of the house again when a thin young man in garish clothes cycled up.

"Hello, ladies! I'm Arthur Rendall. Vanessa's godson and the new owner of her cottage. It's a pleasure to meet my new neighbours."

They introduced themselves, explaining they weren't his neighbours, but did live in the village and that Beth was housesitting next door.

Afterwards Muriel said, "I was taken by surprise and didn't think to offer him my condolences."

"I thought of it, but I'd have been lying if I said I was sorry Vanessa Meadows was dead! Sorry, didn't mean to shock you, but I didn't like her."

"Neither did I."

"Oh… So what were we doing in her garden?"

"Looking for proof she cheated in the flower show."

"And did you find it?"

"I did."

# Chapter 26

## Thursday 27th August

After work Zach went home. Mum had left a note. 'Grapes in fridge. Use the car if you want. Love you. X'.

The grapes were for Teddy. Zach took them straight over to where Beth was staying. Zach had been teaching Teddy to count with chocolate buttons. Letting him eat the appropriate amount for the highest number he got to without a mistake was a great incentive, but Beth wanted Teddy to develop good eating habits. Zach saw the sense in that, but also wanted the boy to be interested in school stuff. Zach hadn't been, and clowned around rather than pay attention. Luckily he didn't get into much trouble but leaving school with few qualifications had limited his options.

"Counting, Zach?" Teddy suggested.

"After tea," Beth said. "We've got lovely runner beans and yummy courgettes!"

The enthusiasm was to persuade Teddy to eat them. Apparently if people knew you had access to a kitchen, it was impossible to walk around Little Mallow in summer without at least one person giving you one vegetable or the other, or both.

"What have you two been up to today? Anything fun?" Zach asked over a meal light on fish fingers and heavy on seasonal veg.

"Teddy and I went to a garden party!" Beth showed him photos of them and two old ladies all wearing lots of flowers in their hair. They all looked so happy it was impossible not to smile.

"That's a serious amount of cake and stuff. Did Teddy eat it all?"

"About half of it! Agnes, who'd cooked it all, invited us to call in any time."

"Nice."

"And then Muriel, the other old lady, walked back with me to check the garden here is OK. I asked her, she wasn't checking up on me. We had quite a chat. They're both really nice. I thought they were scary. Well, Muriel is a bit, but she's nice too. She used to be a teacher and was really impressed with Teddy's counting."

Zach was well chuffed to hear that. He wanted to show he was a good influence on Teddy. With that in mind, Zach put a piece of very un-yummy courgette into his mouth. On the plus side, compared with that slimy stuff, the beans really did seem lovely.

"How did this garden party come about?"

"Agnes is the great aunt of Crystal, the police officer who came on Tuesday?"

"I remember."

"I told Crystal about seeing Verity snooping round. I didn't mention you were here. Maybe I should have. I don't want it to seem like we have anything to hide."

"We don't. Tell her if you like, but I didn't see anything you didn't. What did she make of it?"

"Same as us, I reckon. That it was weird and suspicious. She didn't say that, but she didn't dismiss it as nothing."

"I don't suppose we'll ever know."

After tea, Zach produced the grapes for Teddy to count, which met with Beth's approval. Teddy went straight from one to ten without the slightest hesitation!

155

"Have you been practising, little man?"

Teddy's response was to count to ten again. Time to move on. Giving the boy a lot more than twenty grapes at once probably wouldn't end well, even if they were small. "What comes next?"

"Compost!"

Zach laughed. Where had that come from? "Um, no. Eleven. Can you say that? Eee lev en."

Teddy tried. He'd done well enough to earn one more grape before Beth declared it was nearly bed time.

"I'll go and run his bath," Beth said.

That meant Zach would be bringing Teddy upstairs, and helping get him washed, in bed and to sleep. It felt great she was letting him be involved.

Teddy was lively and giggly until they got him into bed. He would have stayed that way during his bedtime story, except Beth read calmly and stopped whenever he moved. Soon he was fast asleep, looking even cuter and butter wouldn't melt than when awake and laughing.

Downstairs, Beth said, "Muriel suggested holding a birthday party for Teddy in her garden, wasn't that a nice thought?"

Zach tried to hide his jealousy that she'd let an old dear she hardly knew do that, when she'd refused his offer to take Teddy and his little mates somewhere. "Yes, really kind. Will it be on his birthday?"

"I said no."

That made Zach feel better in one way, but it was a shame Teddy would miss out. Beth too. "Why? If she's nice and likes you both…"

"Because I'm proud and stubborn."

"No. You're strong, independent and completely able to look after yourself and Teddy on your own."

"That's really how you see me?"

"Yeah, I do. I know it… But Beth, babe, just because you can doesn't mean you have to. I'd like to help make things a bit easier for you. Both of you."

"I know. But I really am proud and stubborn, Zach. I'm not going to take money from you, or let you pay for things all the time. Look, I had one boyfriend I thought I could depend on, thought I could have a proper family with. He couldn't commit to that, so…" She shrugged.

"I'm not the same." Even as he said it he knew that wasn't enough. He'd have to find a way to prove it. He supposed sticking around was a good start. That's what Mum said when he'd asked her. He'd have another chat with her. As she'd just agreed to marry someone, she must know what persuaded a woman to do that.

"I was talking to Ryan today," Zach said.

"The guy you work with?"

"Yeah." She knew that. They'd met several times.

"OK, what did he say?"

"That Kirianne is getting better. Hugh's been saying it a lot. I thought he was kidding himself, but Ryan says she really is."

"That's good." She didn't sound that pleased, but then she didn't know Kirianne. What she was like before, and how she became.

"I was thinking – what Vanessa said to her, could that be what caused Kirianne's problems?"

Beth seemed more interested now. Probably she'd remembered him saying how ill Kirianne had got. "Can't have helped, can it? I'm not sure about causing it as such. Maybe it was the trigger, but I think she must already have been at risk. Women are always getting comments about their weight and most don't get eating disorders, they just get annoyed."

"I suppose."

"I'm not blaming Kirianne, Zach. Just saying not everyone is the same. If Vanessa had said something about my weight I'd have made a point of eating cream cakes in front of her... Then she'd still have pushed me into something I didn't want to do and made me unhappy."

"You're stronger than Kirianne. You wouldn't let someone like Vanessa ruin your life."

"Not ruin, no. She did spoil it a bit though. I hardly ever stayed for coffee after church, because I couldn't face having to be nice to her. That must have made me seem standoffish. It's taken me a long time to make friends and feel comfortable here. Vanessa's not totally to blame, but her nastiness didn't help. I'm sure that whatever caused Kirianne's problems, Vanessa added to her misery."

"I think she did it on purpose. That she hated to see people happy."

"That would explain why she didn't like Teddy!"

"And Kirianne. She was always happy and always loved, because she was a really nice person – she cared about people and they responded. Vanessa was the opposite and it made her jealous."

Beth jabbed him with her finger just under his arm pit.

"Owww! What was that for?"

"Just demonstrating that people can hurt others when they're jealous."

Wasn't that the exact point he'd just made? "You know, I've been thinking about Kirianne dumping me. She wasn't upset when Hugh introduced me as his new employee. She was upset about something later, but I had no idea it was me until she dumped me. Maybe Vanessa said something?"

"Wouldn't put it past her."

Zach became certain it was true. "Kirianne said I'd used her to get the job, but if she'd thought about it she'd have seen it wasn't true. Hugh hadn't known I was dating her, or he wouldn't have introduced us like that. Vanessa put it in her head."

"And then she dumped you and broke your heart?"

"For about a week, but then I met another girl, far more gorgeous and lovely."

"If that's not me, there's going to be another murder in these cottages!"

Zach knew she was joking, but also that she wanted reassurance it was her who mattered most. Not because she was insecure, but because she cared what he thought about her. He set about doing his best to prove how much he fancied her.

"Something on your mind?" Beth asked a while later.

"That I was lucky. If Kirianne hadn't dumped me we probably wouldn't have lasted anyway. But I wouldn't have been single when I met you. Great result for me! For Kirianne it was the opposite. Vanessa didn't just make her cross or sad for a while. She was so miserable she got really sick. She could have died."

Hugh must have known. Not long after Zach started working for him he'd said he was sorry it hadn't worked out with him and Kirianne and he knew it wasn't Zach's fault. If he knew who was responsible then he'd also have known what else Vanessa pushed Kirianne into.

"Beth, when Hugh came here... You know, on Tuesday morning, did he tell the police he knew Vanessa?"

"I didn't hear him say it, but then it would be obvious, wouldn't it?"

Would it? "Did you hear me tell him which house the dead person was in?"

"Yes. You said you were here at 2 and it was next door. Does it matter?"

"Probably not." Hugh hadn't asked which side though.

"If something is bothering you, you could ask him about it."

"Yeah, I could."

# Chapter 27

**Thursday 27th August**

Dil Dylan had stayed on after his shift to talk to Crystal.

"Thanks for the doughnut, Crystal. I know I'm going to lose that bet. I only agreed because everyone said I'd give you extra clues to help you find out otherwise."

"Would you have done?"

He blushed. "You could probably still persuade me, but I don't think you'll need to."

"Nope! I've worked it out already." Well, she'd worked out a way to hopefully get the information. "You never doubted my brilliant deductive skills, did you?"

"You'd better get yourself over to CID where they'll be appreciated," Sergeant Freedman said from behind her.

"Oooh, what's happening, Skip?"

She grinned. "Don't ask me. You're the detective!"

When Crystal reached CID HQ in Portsmouth, she learned Arthur Rendall had recently arrived in Little Mallow, direct from his holiday. He'd volunteered to come in and answer questions.

"Anne, will be with me. Officer Clere, you're observing."

"Thank you, sir."

"Before we talk to him… Local uniformed officers contacted the owners of the B&Bs he claimed to have spent the nights before and after the murder. It appears he was where he said he was. Is it possible he could have got here, committed the murder and got back to the next place?"

"It's not absolutely impossible, sir, but very unlikely," said Crystal who, with help from Anne, had investigated that. "Getting back by six is no problem. If he didn't leave until eight-thirty he couldn't have got here by train or bus before the T.O.D. He'd have needed at least another hour. With a car it's just about doable, if there's no traffic and he didn't worry about speeding. He doesn't own a car or hold a licence, so renting legitimately wouldn't be an option. Admittedly a murderer may not worry about getting points on the license he doesn't have, but no traffic in over 200 miles isn't likely. Plus an unknown car in Grassy Lane, or anywhere in Little Mallow, would likely have been seen."

"Ah yes. Young Adam was about," the DI said.

Crystal smiled. If he'd not been up the church tower no doubt Adam would have seen something useful. She wondered where he'd been before and which route he'd taken to get there. It was worth asking.

"Sir, do I have time to make a quick call? There's something I'd like to check with an informant."

"If it is quick."

Crystal rang Lorna Milligan and asked if Adam had seen any unusual traffic in the hour or so before he went up the church tower.

"Like orange sports cars?" Lorna asked, referring to previous evidence of criminal activity spotted by Adam.

"I don't want to be more precise right now. It's very unlikely he did see anything relevant."

"I'll ask him. He's cross I'm keeping him away from the action, but I expect he'll talk to me if it's to help you."

"Thanks. I'll ring back later!" Crystal ended the call.

"Let's see what Rendall has to say for himself then," the

DI said.

Crystal's first sight of Arthur was a slight shock. His name had made her imagine him as older than twenty-seven, which she knew from their checks he was. He looked younger and was startlingly good looking, if you liked the half starved look. He must have liked it himself as his skin tight head to toe lycra emphasised his extreme thinness, and the bright colours made it extra hard to miss.

If cycling was that effective for weight loss, maybe Crystal should take it up? She wondered how far Arthur cycled at a time, and how fast he went – which gave her an idea unconnected with calorie neutral pizza eating.

The DI introduced himself, and the two women. "Thank you for coming in. We'll be recording the interview, Mr Rendall, in line with our standard practice, but you're not under caution and are free to leave at any time."

"Right. OK, sure. Where would you like me to start?" His voice was low and slow, as though he was considering every word.

"With your movements on Tuesday, that is the twenty-fifth of August."

"Right. As I said on the phone I was on a cycling holiday in the Peak District and couldn't have got here that day in time to… in time to see her before she died. I'd booked all my accommodation well in advance. Monday night I stayed at Mam Tor View. I have the receipt here." He produced it.

"This is dated the twenty-fourth," Anne pointed out.

Arthur Rendall gave her a beaming smile. "That's right. I pay a deposit when I book, and the balance on arrival, so I can get away quickly the next morning. I like to be on the road before there's much traffic about."

"I see," the DI said. "And how early did you get away that morning?"

"I told your officer on the phone eight-thirty, but thinking about it, maybe it was slightly earlier. Eight-thirty is when the cooked breakfast is served. I was first in the dining room and only had cereal and toast."

"How much earlier? An hour?"

"Oh no! Ten minutes perhaps? I understand you like to be exact about these things. I'm afraid I didn't look at my watch." Arthur pulled a strange grimace which was probably supposed to look apologetic.

"I see. And then?"

Arthur was very eager to talk. The DI and Anne let him. He repeated his statement he'd stayed in his booked accommodation, and produced more receipts. He'd spoken with people who might remember him. He had no receipt for visiting the castle. He probably was given one, but couldn't find it. As proof he'd been there he showed the information leaflet.

"That's very helpful, thank you. May we keep these for now?" the DI indicated the paperwork Arthur had brought.

"Yes of course. I don't know why I kept them really, but I'm glad I did."

"You'll appreciate that, as the main beneficiary under your godmother's will, it's important we're very thorough in obtaining information which eliminates you."

"Yes… I didn't know she'd left me the house, but I see it seems to give me a motive."

"Indeed, but did you have the opportunity?"

"No, like I said, I was in the Peak District and don't drive." The pitch and speed of his words went up a notch.

"That's unusual."

"I suppose so, but I've never felt the need."

"You've visited your godmother in the past?"

"Yes. Mother and I used to come quite often."

"How did you get here?"

"On the train."

"I see. Would it have been possible for you to have made the journey on the day in question?"

"I wasn't there." Arthur seemed cross. Crystal thought that was understandable – he'd said that more than once, using a lot of words.

"I see." The DI picked up the castle leaflet. "You were at Peveril Castle?"

"Exactly."

"We need to know if it was theoretically possible. If it wasn't, we can eliminate you from our enquiries."

Arthur explained at length that he doubted the trains would get him there and back in a day, and there was no train to Little Mallow anyway. He'd probably have had to go to Portsmouth and get a ferry across the harbour and that still left him several miles away.

"Indeed, as you initially stated, it would not have been possible for you to have left..." DI Shortfellow selected a receipt, "The Mam Tour View at eight-thirty, or even eight-twenty, and got a train or bus and reached your godmother's home whilst she was still alive. By the way, how do you know what time that would have been?"

"I don't... I'm not sure. The policeman I spoke to must have told me. Officer Curt, was it?"

DI Shortfellow shook his head. "He can't have done. We

165

didn't know ourselves at that point."

Crystal knew that was a lie. Arthur Rendall had lied too. Captain hadn't told him.

"I don't mean he told me the precise time. He said it was that morning, and as I've said, I couldn't have got there in the morning." Arthur spoke as if explaining himself to a wilfully disobedient child.

In turn the DI looked as though he saw he'd asked a silly question, although his, "I see," told Crystal he still felt fully in command of the interview. He sat back and placed his right hand on the table – the signal for Anne to take over.

"Mr Rendall, we have reason to believe your godmother was expecting a visitor on the day she died. Do you have any idea who that might have been?"

Arthur put his hand to his face and screwed up his eyes. "No. She was very active in different community groups. Neighbourhood Watch she said, and other things. She had lots of friends, so I expect she often had people coming round. I can't think of anyone in particular."

"Will you be staying at your godmother's house, that is 1 Grassy Lane Cottages, Little Mallow?"

"It's my house now. Yes, that is where I'll be staying. I have funeral arrangements to make and the transfer of Vanessa's personal effects to the other beneficiary of the will. I was informed it wouldn't be a problem."

"No, not at all. We've completely finished examining the scene and have taken away *all* the evidence." She put a great deal of stress on the all.

"Evidence?"

"Those things which may assist us with our enquiries. It would be helpful if we could have your phone, Mr Rendall."

Crystal knew it would be extremely helpful. If Arthur consented they'd have it examined to reveal his movements on the day in question. That would either eliminate or incriminate him, with almost no room for doubt.

"I'll need that!" he snapped. He continued in a wheedling tone, "to arrange the funeral and let people know about it, and I'm sorry, but I don't see how it will help find my godmother's murderer."

"It most likely won't," the DI said. "It may however be helpful in eliminating you."

"I still don't understand, but don't want to be difficult. Would it be possible to check my call history now and return it to me before I leave?"

"That would be an admirable compromise. Thank you."

It was actually far from ideal. As all he'd offered was his call history, that was all they could currently take. Still, it might tell them something.

Anne stepped outside the interview room. The DI barely had time to say so, for the benefit of the recording, before she returned. "Mr Rendall, what can you tell us about your godmother?" she asked when she'd resumed her seat.

"How do you mean?"

"The kind of person she was. If anyone may have had a reason to harm her."

He seemed to think hard, then said he'd not known her well. She'd been a great friend of his mother. That was when they lived near each other. After both moved away in different directions it was just very occasional visits and then Mum died and he'd hardly seen Vanessa after that.

"When was that?"

"Mum died three years ago, almost exactly. That's why I

was away. I was the one who found her and I don't like being in the house on that day."

"The date?"

"Twenty-fifth of August."

"I'm sorry to ask," Anne said gently, "how did she die?"

"Suicide. She was depressed. I tried to help, but she thought I'd be better off without her."

"And you still live in the same house?"

"Yes. She left me well provided for in that way, but I miss her so much."


"What do we think?" the DI asked after Arthur's phone was returned, and he'd left.

Anne indicated Crystal should go first.

"He put on an act of being extremely helpful, but didn't really care about catching the guilty party. His inheritance is plenty of motive. And it's a huge coincidence Vanessa was killed on the anniversary of his mother's death. Maybe it unbalanced him?"

"Anne?"

"I agree, sir. Plenty of motive and his helpfulness only extends to clearing his name. Although he seems timid, I think he has a temper. He didn't like it when things didn't go precisely his way. His mother's death isn't an obvious motive, and could be coincidence, but there could be something there."

"Maybe the holiday wasn't a distraction from that memory, but planned to give him an alibi?" Crystal suggested. "And he's a cyclist – that might help him get about quickly in a way which would be hard to check."

"So, Officer Clere, you now doubt your own findings that he couldn't have got there and back in the time?"

"No... I said it wasn't absolutely impossible."

"And that extra ten minutes helps," Anne pointed out.

"If it was a bit more than ten, and the autopsy gives us a slightly later T.O.D. it could have been done in a car, and trains and taxis might just about work."

"You're both liking him for this?" the DI asked.

"Yes, if he could have got there. Pity he wouldn't relinquish his phone," Anne said.

Crystal nodded. Maybe the reason Arthur was so reluctant to give up his phone was that he knew it would incriminate him. On the other hand, she'd be lost without hers.

"OK. I agree. Officer Clere, check those train timetables again, and accept the blame when your colleagues in Gosport complain they're tasked with making enquiries with taxi and bus drivers, and on the Gosport ferry."

"Gladly, sir."

"And we'll ask for more enquiries in Manchester about the possibility of him having access to... Yes, what is it?"

"Excuse me, sir, but there's been a report from a lady living in Little Mallow. Thought you'd like to know, in case there's a connection to the murder," an officer said.

"You were correct. Tell me."

"A Verity Houseman says she's been followed, sir. There's no evidence and she can't give a description, except she senses a man and sees them out the corner of her eye."

"OK, thank you."

"Yes, sir."

"You can speak to her, Officer Clere."

# Chapter 28

**Thursday 27ᵗʰ August**

"Bert, it was really you who won the hybrid tea class in the show," Muriel said as they had a cup of tea and the last slices of his birthday cake.

Bert shook his head. "Tied. Hers were as good as mine."

"Maybe, but they weren't hers."

"I knew something weren't right."

"You didn't say anything at the time." It didn't matter now, the woman was dead after all. Muriel just wanted Bert to have the satisfaction of knowing he was a better gardener than Vanessa had been. She hoped he also realised he was a better human being in every way. If he didn't understand already, she doubted she'd be able to explain.

"I didn't know then. That other one, she's been saying things."

"Verity Houseman?"

"Yeah. She keeps saying how I was lucky to win so many classes and how I must have been disappointed not to win that one. I didn't know what she was getting at, but she was up to something."

"She's as bad as Vanessa was, Bert."

He nodded. "I've seen her talking to people, same as she does to me. They don't like it, but she does. She keeps on at 'em. I've seen her."

If Verity's blackmail activities were blatant enough to draw Bert's attention, she wasn't being at all subtle. Behaviour like that was likely to get her into trouble – with the police, or someone else.

"How did you know it weren't right about the roses, Mure?"

Muriel explained about Beth's request for help, and how that led to the discovery Vanessa had taken the roses from the Sheppard's garden.

Bert took another bite of cake, chewed, swallowed and said, "Good."

"How is it good?"

"The Sheppards don't put anything in the show. Say they're not good enough. I've tried to get 'em to, and they said they might, but it was their holiday so they didn't. If we tell 'em they'd've won, we can get 'em to to do it." Clearly he thought that was an excellent idea.

"You want them to enter so they beat you?" Muriel asked.

"No, so that I can beat them – fair and square, not by cheating."

Muriel was so proud of him.

"It's little Teddy's birthday next week. Beth can't have a party for him, because she doesn't have space," she said.

"There's room here, Mure. It could be in our garden."

"What a good idea! Hopefully the weather will still be nice, but if it rains we could use the car port. I could make cakes and sandwiches."

"Will you want me to go out?"

"Of course not, unless you'd rather not be there." Muriel was worried Bert might feel hard done by. There was to be a proper party for Agnes, and one for Teddy, whereas he'd had nothing more elaborate than a meal at home with her. She began to apologise.

"It's clever of you, Mure. I'll get three birthdays. Teddy would like jelly and ice cream."

Muriel chuckled. "Yes, I'm sure he would. I'll make sure we have that. What else would he like?"

"Beer!"

"Bert!" She was laughing. He hadn't really expected that to work.

"Crisps," he suggested. "And balloons."

"We can do that." The balloons would make the garden more appealing to small children – and they could be played with and thrown about with little risk of injury to themselves, or damage to her borders.

"We can have races! I'll get sacks from to allotment and we can do potatoes in spoons instead of eggs."

Now Muriel had even more reason to persuade Beth to let it happen.

# Chapter 29

## Thursday 27<sup>th</sup> August

Crystal went directly from CID headquarters in Portsmouth to Verity's home. She explained that when she arrived.

"I'm glad someone is taking this seriously."

"Of course we are."

"The policeman I spoke to didn't believe me."

"I'm sorry he gave that impression and promise this will be properly investigated." Crystal took Verity's statement, which was very vague. She was careful to give no indication she might not be one hundred per cent convinced. Even Verity must tell the truth sometimes.

"Can you think of any reason this is happening?' Crystal asked.

"There's obviously a maniac about. He killed my friend. He could be after me."

"Did Vanessa ever mention being watched or followed?"

Verity shook her head. "She wasn't as sensitive as me."

Crystal gave Verity advice on personal safety and a direct number to call any time if she felt in danger. It wasn't unreasonable the thought of an unidentified killer in the area worried her, but it wasn't particularly likely he'd switch from quick, efficient murder to stalking.

After sending through Verity's statement Crystal made a Google search. Cycling from Manchester to Little Mallow would take an average cyclist almost twenty-four hours. However speedy Arthur was, he couldn't have done it in five. Oh well. She had another look at the train timetables.

In order to reach Vanessa's home before she was killed, Arthur would have had to catch a train at or before seven-twenty-five – almost an hour prior to the time he stated he left Mam Tor View. He'd also have needed to travel the twenty odd miles to a suitable train station, plus make the shorter journey from the destination station, either Fareham or Portsmouth, to Little Mallow, which would take up yet more time.

Crystal supposed she should call the DI and tell him the enquiries with local taxi firms and bus drivers he'd just requested would be pointless, but couldn't face it. Instead she went into Gosport station herself.

"Sergeant, Dylan, you're still here," she said.

"Not still, again. Why are you here when your shift has ended?"

Crystal, who hadn't realised how much time had passed since she'd arrived for work that day, explained about the taxi and bus enquiries being a real long shot.

"OK, I'll keep that in mind. Any questions you want to ask me about your leaving party?"

"Nooo. Didn't I tell you I'd sussed it already?"

"Ah, yes. I was forgetting that. I'll see you there then, that is if I don't see you before."

"Looking forward to it!"

As Crystal drove back to Aunty's, where she was staying another night, she reviewed her progress with that particular investigation. She was satisfied she'd correctly narrowed it down to two possible venues and either next Friday, or Saturday, with Friday being most likely. Since working that out, she'd got no further forward.

Crystal rang Jason. "Will you have much work on next

week?" she asked after the kind of soppy chat which made her laugh, and miss him even more.

"I should have some free time."

"In that case, can we take Aunty Agnes out for a meal next Friday?"

"If you think she'd like that."

"She mentioned she's never eaten Turkish food in her life and I want to show her she's not too old for new things."

"Ah, yes – I think that would appeal to her."

"I'll tell her then, so she can look forward to it?"

"Yes. Sure. You sound kind of… Oh, if we can take Aunty Aggie out on Friday, that's not when your party is."

"Correct! Am I a brilliant detective or what?"

"The best! I'll reward you with the most popular Turkish dish of all – grilled camel testicles!"

She hoped that wasn't a real speciality, because Aunty would find it just as amusing as Jason to see Crystal faced with a plate of it.

"We'd better not make it too early, in case I'm held up as I do have a shoot that day. Say eight, unless that would be too late for her?" Jason said.

"Earlier would be better."

"Give me a minute and I'll double check the timings."

Crystal's phone rang and she thought it was Jason calling back. It was Lorna Milligan. "Not sure this will be of any use, as it's after the time in question, but my hair straighteners are again in mortal peril if I don't pass it on. Adam did see a bicycle – not suspicious, but unusual."

"Really! That's brill!" If Arthur somehow got his bike on a train in time, it would have made the last bit of his journey quicker, and very hard to prove. This might be a breakthrough!

"Oh. That'll teach me to dismiss stuff as irrelevant. He saw her at about quarter to three."

"Her?"

"The postie. He said it wasn't the usual man and thought she must have had to do her own round first, which is why she was late."

Not the evidence Crystal had been hoping for then. It would be accurate – with his grandparents running the post office and his own eye for detail, Adam could be relied on to tell the difference between an unknown man on his own bike, and a female using one supplied by Royal Mail.

Crystal answered another call, again expecting it to be Jason.

It was Anne. "There's been a couple of interesting developments I thought you'd like to know about."

"Go on."

"First, Arthur's phone log revealed he called Vanessa the day she died. She's his godmother and they spoke on the phone every few weeks, but it's odd he didn't mention it."

"Yes, that's interesting. Most people's reaction would be something along the lines of 'I was only just talking to her'." It was hardly a major breakthrough, but did suggest Arthur wasn't being completely open with them.

"I agree, and I checked with Captain. He didn't mention it then."

"Two things, you said?"

"The tech people have been doing their thing with computers and found internet searches of train times between Manchester and Fareham. Not just that, but departure, change and arrival times all typed up in a neat list."

"Oh." That wasn't good – Crystal had been the one checking up on that and found no trace Arthur could have made that journey within the time frame. "I must have missed something."

"Maybe not. What where you checking?"

"If he could have made the journey to Little Mallow in time to kill Vanessa if he'd left anywhere close to the time he and the B&B owner say he did."

"These timings are for well before that. Leaving at 5.05 in the morning."

"That's strange. Why would he go so early? And what about… but this is good. It should be much easier to check with such precise details. We might even get lucky with CCTV if the station was fairly empty."

"I'm emailing it to you now."

"Thanks. Has Arthur been confronted about these details being on his computer?"

"Nope. Ask me why not."

"Why not?"

"Because they weren't found on his, but on Vanessa's!"

"What!"

"Told you it was interesting." Anne said, "Talking of which, the DI has approached me about being your mentor when you join us."

"Oh!" Crystal had expected it to be Neil Ingerson, based almost solely on the facts he was older and more experienced than Anne. "That would be great," she said, despite being far from sure. As far as Crystal could tell Anne was a good officer, and when they'd interacted before they'd communicated easily and pleasantly. They were on the same wavelength workwise. On the downside, Anne didn't seem much fun. The rest of the team teased Crystal and joked about. Anne was always very straight, a proper grown up. Although only two years older than Crystal she was already married. The couple had a mortgage and were applying to be foster parents. Maybe that's why the DI thought it was a good idea? Anne could be a steadying influence to Crystal's obvious enthusiasm.

"I've never mentored anyone before. The other option is Neil Ingerson, who was my mentor. I've found him encouraging and helpful."

"I'm sure he is – and that you'd be too." Crystal didn't want to get off on the wrong foot with whoever it was, and didn't want an unwilling person to be assigned the task. "Whatever the DI, you, and Neil, decide is fine with me."

"My wife Chrissie said it might be good for my confidence to mentor someone. She's a football coach and said it did wonders for hers. Of course it's you the situation is really supposed to help."

"I don't see why it shouldn't work both ways – especially if you're hoping for promotion."

"I am, yes, when I'm ready."

"And me. If we do end up together I promise to make it clear that any of my terrible mistakes weren't your fault."

"And, if it happens, I'll try to stop you before you make any but the most innocuous of errors."

"Deal," Crystal said, hoping innocuous meant what she thought it did.

Anne had emailed as promised. '*The attached is the whole document. It doesn't look as though Vanessa emailed it to anyone. She printed one copy. She made several internet searches for train times, all leaving Manchester Piccadilly which is the nearest station to Arthur's home. Plenty of other searches, but none seem relevant. All this is dated early July. Naturally we'll be speaking to him on the matter.'*

Crystal opened the attachment and studied it.

*Travel details Tuesday 25th August*

*Leave Manchester Piccadilly 5.05 1 change 4hrs 44 min*

*Arrive Fareham 9.49*

*Arrive my house 10.30*

*Leave my house 15.00*

*Leave Fareham 15.35 1 change 4 hrs 54 mins*

*Arrive Manchester Piccadilly 20.29*

Very odd. Arthur wasn't named and neither was Vanessa.

Crystal called Anne back. "Two questions. Could this have been planted on her computer?"

"Unlikely. It's password protected and the searches weren't all done on the same day."

"Right. Does Vanessa's address book show anyone else living in Manchester?"

"No. There's no suggestion she knew anyone else there. We've got her phone log and Arthur's is the only Manchester number. She did call him shortly before these searches were made, and again soon after."

"Interesting, thanks."

Jason called back while Crystal was trying to make sense out of it. "How about we take Aunt Aggie out the following week? It won't interfere with our camping trip, I'll definitely be here then and we could go as early as they open, and it would mean spreading out the excitement and it can be my birthday present to her."

That seemed like a lot of reasons for delay, so maybe he'd agreed to the earlier date as a bluff and now had to get her to change it without giving the game away? Yes – very likely. Which meant her leaving do was almost certainly next Friday.

Crystal rang Trevor and asked if he liked Turkish food.

"No idea, lass. Why?"

"Jason is taking me for a Turkish meal next week and mentioned camel testicles, so I was thinking I'd bring you back a doggy bag."

"Um no, that's OK."

"Are camel testicles a real thing?"

"Baby camels are a real thing. Please don't make me explain more than that!"

"I'll let you off if you promise me Jason won't be making me eat them next Friday evening."

"Of course he won't."

"Because we'll be at my leaving do, not in a Turkish restaurant then, right?"

"Damn!"

"Don't feel too bad – I already tricked him into giving the date away. Just thought it would be fun to do it to you too. I'm really ringing about a different party. The one for Aunty Agnes's birthday. You're invited."

"Yes."

"I thought you could make some casual enquiries. We've got so many people coming and you know a lot of them so I don't think it will seem odd. Besides, Aunty likes you."

"Everyone likes me, lass, I'm just that nice. You're a bit

late with the invitation though as that's already been made and accepted."

"Aunty invited you? She's not supposed to know!"

"Don't fret, lass. It was your cousin Yvonne who asked."

"Oh." That was good news, and interesting too. Yvonne must have asked before the murder, long before. She'd said she'd be bringing someone when the party was first suggested. Crystal knew the pair had got on well when they met earlier that summer, but hadn't realised they'd kept in touch. "You're a sly old dog!"

"Less of the old, you cheeky pup!"

Crystal grinned, then returned to pondering the train timetable produced by Vanessa. If Arthur had caught the 5.05 train, he'd easily have reached Vanessa's home in time to kill her. But the B&B owner had confirmed he didn't leave there until some time after eight. Arthur hadn't made Vanessa's specified return journey either as he checked into a different B&B at six, and had the receipt issued when he checked in to prove it. That wasn't such a problem, as he'd have had time to catch a different train after killing Vanessa.

Crystal soon decided she needed something chocolatey to help her think. Remembering Teddy had finished off the brownies, Crystal went to the post office. Seeing Beth there meant she was able to invite her to Aunty's party. Neither that sense of accomplishment or the chocolate provided any startling revelations into Arthur Rendall's movements.

Crystal couldn't think of any reason, short of planning her own murder, for Vanessa to send anyone those times. They suggested Vanessa really had been expecting a visitor. That person was most likely to have been Arthur Rendall, who apparently didn't arrive. How likely was it that someone else picked that same day to kill her?

# Chapter 30

## Friday 28th August

"I'm really going to miss coming here," Zach said, when Beth let him into 2 Grassy Lane Cottages. "And not just because of…" He pointed upstairs. They'd spent more time together while she'd been house sitting, and these last few days it had felt almost like they were a family.

"It's been good in some ways, but I'll be glad when the Sheppards get back tomorrow and we're not staying next door to where a murder happened," Beth said.

"Sorry, babe, I hadn't realised how horrible it must feel."

"I'm not that bothered really… not about her, but I don't like knowing the murderer is still about."

"Whoever did it is probably long gone."

"I'd like to believe that, but I can't. This isn't finished. Her friend Verity has been back."

"Yeah, I saw her. She was just…"

"Since then, in the day. Vanessa's godson is living in the cottage now. They had a right set to. Verity wanted to take some things from the house, said Vanessa left them to her. Arthur Rendall, that's the godson, wouldn't let her. He said everything had to be valued for probate."

"Maybe you should tell the police?"

"I meant to when I saw Crystal earlier. What she said made me forget."

"What's happened now?"

"Nothing bad. We've had an invite to Agnes's party."

"Are you going?"

"I could. It's Sunday afternoon and wouldn't be too late for Teddy. Crystal said not to bring anything unless I wanted to get a card. Apparently none of the family are getting gifts, so it'd be weird if I did. Do you want to go? She said you're welcome."

"Yeah, why not?" Zach wasn't interested in going to an old people's party, but maybe Beth had asked because she wanted his support? He'd ask Mum to get him some food to take with them, so they didn't go empty handed.

Beth called Crystal, accepting the invitation for all three of them and telling her about Verity's visit to Arthur.

"He hasn't given you any trouble, has he? This Arthur bloke?" Zach asked afterwards.

"No, he's been really friendly."

Zach was suddenly a little less disappointed Beth wouldn't be staying in the house much longer.

After tea, which was macaroni cheese, served with more than enough fresh vegetables, Zach helped Teddy decorate a huge birthday card for Agnes. It was made by Beth from a couple of boxes fished out the recycling bin. She glued them together, so the sides showing what had been in them were hidden. She even made the glue from flour and water!

"How do you know how to do all this stuff?"

"Having a kid and no money makes you really creative. Well, it does if you want the kid to be happy."

Zach hugged her. She'd not said much about her childhood, but he'd heard enough to know Teddy was better of with just her than he would be with her family around.

"Want to show Zach how you do potato prints, Teddy?"

"Tato prints!"

Beth cut a potato in half and made two different flower

183

shapes from them, and put paint into yoghurt pots. She took everything outside. Once she'd covered half the lawn with newspaper, Teddy was allowed to get to work. He stamped yellow flowers liberally on the front, back, and inside the card. Then red ones, orange and finally purple. After that Zach had the brilliant idea of using a piece of carrot to make leaves. It was a messy process, and surprisingly noisy. It was a lot of fun too. The finished result looked pretty good, Zach thought. Like the fancy wallpaper he'd seen in a big posh house on a school trip once.

They left the card to dry before attempting to write in it.

"Thanks for that," Beth said when they'd finished. "As a reward, you can get the paint off Teddy!"

Kids are really slippery when wet, Zach discovered. Announcing that to Beth made her laugh so much she was no help. It took ages, but eventually Beth agreed her darling boy was clean enough to sleep between sheets belonging to the people who'd entrusted her to care for their home.

Zach read Teddy a story, doing funny voices. That made him laugh a lot, but didn't send him to sleep. By the time Teddy had said, "Nother one!" three times, Zach was imitating the calm, slow tone Beth used the night before.

When Beth came in to kiss Teddy goodnight, the boy was drowsy, and she'd changed into a slinky silk thingy. "Might as well make the most of having the place to ourselves before I'm back living with Carol and Ken," she said.

"Good thinking."

He reached for her, but she ducked away laughing. "Oh no you don't! Not until there's not a trace of paint left in that bathroom!"

This parenting stuff was harder than he'd realised. A lot harder – but Zach reckoned it would be worth it.

# Chapter 31

### Friday 28<sup>th</sup> August

When CID interviewed Arthur Rendall again, his clothing was still all over lycra. The tightness made his elbows, knees, and other body parts, far too noticeable in Crystal's opinion. His top was cherry red with lime green sleeves – hadn't it been the other way round last time? Or had it been yellow and pink like his leggings? How could the combination be both forgettable and unforgettable at the same time? One thing Crystal did know was that she was going to go easy on witnesses who messed up that kind of detail.

When Arthur was confronted with Vanessa's research into train times he was unusually quiet for a while.

"You've seen this before, Mr Rendall?" the DI asked.

Arthur nodded. "Vanessa sent it."

"Why didn't you tell us this before? We did ask if you knew who she was expecting to visit her."

"I was upset. I'd just lost someone close to me on the anniversary of my mother's death. As I gained financially in both cases I was worried I'd be suspected. Anyway, I'd told her I wasn't coming, so she wasn't expecting me!"

"When you visited previously, did she send a timetable?"

He shook his head. "She said what time to arrive, but left the arrangements to me."

"If you'd followed these instructions, the journey would have been a long one for a relatively short visit?"

"Probably the point of it. She didn't like me, didn't ask me

185

for the pleasure of my company." He sounded bitter.

"Why then?" the DI asked.

"She was Mother's friend. I visited for her sake. Vanessa didn't appreciate it! She was always trying to manipulate me, upset me." Apparently her influence was still working – Arthur's usually calm, measured tone had morphed into a rapid squeak.

"Why didn't you say you knew it was possible to get here by train, and back again, on the day in question?

"I didn't come and I didn't know. I didn't check if she was right. Maybe she just wanted to waste my time. I knew it would look bad as it was likely I'd inherit at least something." He had his anger and voice back under control.

"You were her executor, surely you knew the contents of the will?"

"She was always changing it. Putting me in and taking me out again. OK, I'll be honest, the last time she said anything on the subject I was to get everything, except a few personal things – as the will is now, I suppose. Knowing her, she'd make me come down just to tell me I was disinherited."

"When she did that before, did she say who'd get the money?

"Charities – different ones."

"I see. When is the last time she made a change?"

"I'm not sure. I sent flowers for her birthday. That was in May and she mentioned it then."

Arthur seemed to relax. Crystal would have thought he was telling the truth, except the will the solicitor held was almost three years old. That was the only change since Vanessa made her first will with them ten years before.

"What was the last contact you had with your

godmother?" the DI asked.

"The morning she died, I called to say I wasn't coming."

"You hadn't told her before, when she first suggested it?"

"I told her I had a holiday planned. I really did, it was all booked up and everything,"

"How did she react?"

"Annoyed. She said I must change it. It wouldn't have been easy. I tried to tell her, but she called me selfish. Said she missed her friend and implied I was the one who drove Mother to take her life." Arthur was whining again.

"That must have annoyed you?"

"I hung up on her."

Crystal was sure that last statement was a lie.

"Mr Rendall, do you use a computer?"

"Of course."

"It would be helpful if we could have access to it."

Arthur looked smug. "Well, you can't. I use one all day at work, but that belongs to the chemist shop and most of the contents will be 'medical in confidence'. You might have more luck with the library, but of course I'm not the only person who will have used that."

"You don't own one yourself?"

"Not unless you count my phone. You've already looked at that, but feel free to do so again." He slid it across the table, towards DI Shortfellow.

The DI picked it up, asked Arthur for the passcode and presumably attempted to look at his search history.

"Do you use email, Mr Rendall?" Anne asked.

"At work, not personally. As with driving I don't see the need. I can phone or text people or speak to them in person." Then, after a pause, "If you tell me what you're looking for, I might be able to help."

The DI returned the phone. "Please stay local, Mr Rendall. It's likely we'll have further questions for you."

"Of course. Anything I can do to help, officer."

After the interview, the DI informed Anne and Crystal there was no email app on Arthur's phone, nothing for any messenger service or social network and his internet searches were sparse. "He'd recently looked up Peveril Castle. I went back as far as firework displays local to him last November, with no train enquiries. Nothing about accommodation in the Peak District either, so it's likely he used the library computer for most searches."

That meant finding anything and tying it to Arthur would be far from easy – perhaps impossible.

"Any thoughts?" the DI asked.

"I was right about him having a temper," Anne said.

"Yes. He got it under control quickly, but he's emotional and impulsive – and I'd say either secretive or a loner."

"I'm sure he wasn't the one to hang up, when he called Vanessa that last time," Crystal said.

"Does that tell us anything?"

"I thought so at the time… maybe it just shows the rest was true. But it wasn't, not about the will, was it? Maybe he thought it was? I mean, if he didn't kill her. Perhaps she taunted or manipulated him by saying she changed it – pretending she'd put him back in could have been a reward for the flowers." And maybe Crystal should stop burbling her stream of random thoughts in front of the DI.

"Could be. She sounds awful," Anne said, making Crystal feel a bit less silly. "Arthur was instructed to make an unnecessarily inconvenient journey on the anniversary of his mother's death. It doesn't seem likely she wanted to comfort him, does it?"

"I'd like to know if he really had booked his holiday as far in advance as he claims," Crystal said.

"Then you'd better check, hadn't you?" the DI said.

Anne helped Crystal with that task. They discovered Arthur had made very few calls. Some were to Vanessa. She'd called him slightly more often. There was one, local to him, number Arthur called occasionally, one he called every week usually once, sometimes twice. All those calls were short. There was one Premium rate line showing long calls about once a fortnight.

"There's a big batch of calls in April," Crystal noted.

A check showed them all to be to hotels and B&Bs in the Peak District. Some he'd only called once, some twice.

"He phoned round making enquiries and found some were already fully booked?" Anne suggested.

That's what Crystal had thought. "Yeah, or too expensive. And he called back the best options to make bookings?"

"Gut reaction – could he be our man?" Anne asked.

"Yes. He has at least two strong motives. It's theoretically possible he could have done it in the timeframe with a car. I know we were told Mam Tor View said he left after eight, but we haven't got that from them directly. It wouldn't hurt to ask, would it?"

"Wouldn't have thought so."

Crystal tried and got an engaged tone. "Should we check his regular calls?" Crystal asked. She wanted to.

"Try the local ones."

The infrequent ones were to the chemist's where he

worked – all early in the morning.

"Phoning in sick?" Anne suggested.

"That was my thought. Has quite a few sick days, doesn't he?" Although tempted to make a joke about it being a pity he didn't know where to get medication, Crystal resisted.

The other local number was a take away.

"Didn't he have any friends?" Crystal asked.

"Doesn't look like it," Anne said. "What do you make of him as a person?"

"I quite liked him to start with. I'm not so sure now. He seems one of those people you're really pleased to have as a neighbour when you first move in, then end up avoiding."

Anne laughed. "That sounds like the voice of experience!"

"It is, but as far as I know, those people didn't kill anyone, unless it was by boring them to death with… Anyway, shall I try the premium rate line?

"You don't want to do that," Anne said

"Because of CID's budget?"

"Because it's a sex line. A fairly cheap one, which explains why I've seen it enough times to remember. It's quite tame and perfectly legal, but… All this," Anne gestured to the phone records, "tells us a lot about Arthur."

"Yeah, he's a sad lonely, wan…"

Anne grinned. "User of sex lines? Precisely."

"I'd really like to know if I was right and Arthur was lying when he said he hung up on Vanessa."

"Of course you would."

Crystal tried the Mam Tor View and got the engaged tone again.

They informed the DI that Arthur really had booked his holiday before Vanessa summoned him for a visit.

"Where does that get us?" he asked.

"He didn't cycle up and down hills just to give himself an alibi – but it does strengthen his motive," Crystal said.

"How so?" DI Shortfellow asked.

"He doesn't seem to have much in his life, so the holiday would have been important to him."

"Anne?"

"I concur, sir. I bet if a search of his house is made, we'd find it just as Mother left it."

That thought gave Crystal the shivers – not least because she was convinced it was true.


When she left the CID building, Crystal went back to the flat she and Jason were renting. She wanted to be there when he got back from Belgium. They'd stayed there together a few nights, but this would be her first opportunity to welcome him home.

Crystal remembered Aunty saying you just had to ask the right people the right questions to find out what you wanted to know. Crystal really wanted to know for certain when and where her leaving do would be.

She'd narrowed it down to two pubs and was almost certain it would be in exactly a week's time. She had nearly all of her twenty questions left, so could just ask any of her colleagues. That felt like cheating. Come to think of it, she could probably have done the whole thing by asking, 'Is it this Friday?, next Friday?, in The Nelson etc, but where would have been the fun in that?

Crystal rang the first possible location, saying she was

from Gosport Police calling about the party they had booked for next weekend – just in case she was mistaken about the date.

"Sorry, we don't have anything booked for the police."

"I know it's supposed to be a surprise and you may have been asked not to give out any information. I'm not asking you to tell me anything, other than that you'll be careful not to serve peanuts. One of the guests is severely allergic."

"We really don't have anything booked for the police."

"Maybe it was booked in the name of Trevor Harris, or Imani Freedman?"

"I'll check. Hold on."

Crystal held.

"Sorry, no parties booked at all. We might be able to do something. How many people is it for?"

So, it wasn't there. Crystal tried the other pub and only got as far as saying they may have been asked not to give out any information.

"That's correct. We can only give info to the person booking it."

"I'm glad you're on the ball about this. You know it's a test for officer Clere? That's who the leaving party is for?"

"I didn't know that."

"She's going to CID so we want her to practise her detection skills." Crystal explained the rules which she was currently breaking.

"Sounds fun. Will she do it?"

"Yeah, I think so. Might need all the questions though! There are so many pubs in and around Gosport and she doesn't even know what day it's going to be!"

"What happens if she doesn't work it out?"

"She'll still be there. We've got some of her friends pretending to take her to the cinema, so they'll just bring her instead – and then we'll tease her so much she'll be really glad she's going!"

"I bet! Well, I look forward to finding out if she's solved it on Friday. See you then!"

"You certainly will." Crystal wondered how long it would be before the person she'd spoken to realised she hadn't said why she'd called.

When Jason came home he hugged her awkwardly – on account of the humungous box of chocolates he carried. "I've missed you and I know you've been pining away without me, but I've got something to make up for it."

Crystal took the box. "Better have a couple of these first then, to give us the energy."

Jason grinned. "You're terrible!"

"One of the many reasons you love me."

"True."

Later Crystal noticed the time. "We'd better get moving or we'll be late meeting Ellie."

"It doesn't take you an hour to get dressed."

"She suggested we grab something to eat first. We're meeting her at the Kale and Snail."

"And Mike?"

"She didn't say, so I guess not."

"Shame. I was going to try to find out what it is he does for a living… Maybe it'd be easier if he's not there. Ellie must know."

"Yeah, but if he really is in MI5 she might not tell you."

"I'll settle for knowing his cover story."

Ellie was on her own in the pub.

"Is Mike coming to see the film?" Jason asked after they'd greeted each other, got drinks and ordered food.

"I told him not to bother," Ellie said. "No, not like that… He couldn't be sure he'd get here in time and I didn't want him driving down in a rush."

Ellie didn't mention Mike again. Crystal would have brought him into the conversation if she could and not just to help satisfy Jason's curiosity. Crystal was wondering about Ellie and Mike's relationship. She'd never really understood it. They'd known each other forever and obviously cared a great deal, but were they just friends, a bit more than that, or maybe about to become a proper couple? That conversation was probably best saved until it was just Crystal, Ellie, and a bottle of prosecco.

Jason's attempts to turn the conversation to Mike's job resulted in Ellie talking about getting ready for the new school term, asking about Jason's trip to Belgium, and enquiring about Crystal's visits to CID.

Crystal couldn't blame Ellie for not answering the questions they didn't quite ask – especially when she couldn't answer Ellie's queries about the murder case. She either didn't know, or the information wasn't something she was currently able to share. Despite all that, they managed a lively chat until their food arrived.

"Do you two have any plans for the weekend, other than Agnes's party?" Ellie asked a short time later.

Crystal was rostered to be working, but as she had leave to take, Jason was home, and it was Aunty's birthday, she had the weekend off. Sunday would be spent with family, who were gathering for Aunty's birthday. That evening was occupied by Ellie, which only left Saturday.

"Decorating our flat," Jason said.

"Do you want a hand?" Ellie said.

Was it mean of her that Crystal didn't? She wanted it to just be her and Jason.

"I'm a dab hand at the prep. Masking off the woodwork and sugar soaping and clearing up afterwards," Ellie said.

That was Crystal's cue to nip to the loo. After Googling sugar soap she decided they needed Ellie's help. Getting the paint to stay on the walls was more important than it being just the two of them doing the job.

When she rejoined Jason and Ellie she said they'd love some help on Saturday if she was up for it.

"Great. Have you got everything you need?" Ellie asked.

"We'll be hitting the DIY store as soon as it opens for paint and brushes and things." Although precisely which 'things' were needed was a mystery.

"Are you just painting?"

"Yes."

"Arnold has all the brushes, rollers and stuff. I'm sure we could borrow them."

Crystal and Jason liked that plan, so Ellie texted Arnold.

"At the risk of sounding like a schoolteacher... If you don't buy everything until tomorrow, you'll have used half the day before you get started. Once you've got your furniture all covered up it's easier to keep going."

"Good point," said Crystal who hadn't considered how they were going to avoid getting paint where they didn't want it.

"Let's do it now, and see the later showing of the film,"

Ellie suggested.

By the time they got to the store, Arnold had texted back to say he'd meet Ellie at the church in the morning, so she could take whatever decorating equipment they wanted.

"How much prep are you doing?" Ellie asked.

"As little as possible," Crystal told her.

"Hopefully it won't need much," Jason said. "Everything seems fine. No crumbling plaster or peeling paper or anything like that."

"Yeah, it's clean and tidy, but super dull. Most of it's a dusty looking version of magnolia. The bathroom is tiny and painted navy so that needs brightening up."

"Have you picked your colours?" Ellie asked.

"Not yet."

"You do that then, and I'll get the rest."

"Do you think she realises we don't have a clue?" Jason asked, when Ellie left them to it.

"Probably – but let's 'fess up anyway."

They choose a lovely romantic peach for their bedroom, a soft terracotta for the kitchen, delicate green for the lounge, and primrose for the bathroom. Those would all look OK with the dark green carpet. They'd hoped to replace it with something looking less like wet moss, but with everything Ellie picked up, and the paint, they were already over their entire decorating budget.

The results better be worth going without pick and mix in the cinema!

# Chapter 32

## Saturday 29<sup>th</sup> August

Muriel looked round at Little Mallow's village hall after helping set up for Agnes's birthday party the next day. There were masses of flowers, on tables and windowsills and in containers hanging from the walls.

A long row of tables was covered in pristine white cloths and disposable platters ready for the food. Crystal's fears there wouldn't be enough were most definitely unfounded. Already several people, despite having been told it wasn't necessary, had delivered non perishable contributions – packs of crisps and other savoury snacks, jars of pickles, boxes of biscuits, and tubs of chocolates.

As Muriel stepped into Main Street she saw Verity. The woman smiled nastily and began walking determinedly towards her. Salvation came in the unlikely form of Mrs King. Muriel generally tried to avoid conversations with her because, although it was considerably less malicious, she gossiped just as much as Verity did and Vanessa had. That day it seemed like a good thing. Either Verity would join the conversation or she wouldn't. If she joined, Muriel would find a way to leave her trapped talking to Mrs King. That shouldn't be difficult, Mrs King would be very reluctant to lose her entire audience at once. If Verity decided not to join them, then Muriel just had to keep Mrs King talking until Verity had gone. That would be only too easy!

"Mrs King!" Muriel called. As anticipated, Mrs King was willing to be detained. Mention of the weather provoked details of the Sheppards' holiday, the fact they were back

197

and very shocked about Vanessa. How terrible to have that happen actually next door – terrible for Beth too.

Muriel let her ramble on. No doubt she'd been used to gossiping with Vanessa, who'd devoured every word hoping for something she could use.

Verity had stopped walking. She'd first studied her phone and then the greengrocer's window. Muriel was certain she wished to say something without the benefit of a witness. She'd have joined the conversation otherwise, rightly confident they'd both be too polite to say she wasn't welcome.

"A man named Arthur Rendall has moved in," Mrs King said. "Vanessa's godson, he is."

Muriel explained she'd met him.

"I don't know what to make of him," Mrs King said. "He's very friendly, always ready to chat, yet he seems sort of secretive. He keeps his bicycle in the house so you never know if he's in or not."

By then Verity had walked by, exchanging a nod but no words with the other two. Muriel hoped she'd keep walking all the way home.

"I'll tell you something for nothing, he and Verity don't like each other, not one bit. Had a proper row this morning they did. I was on his side there."

Muriel was warming to Mr Rendall.

"She said it wasn't right him not letting her have some things of Vanessa's. From what I've heard he inherits the house, and she gets everything else – but not yet because of some legal thing. Would that be because of how she died, do you think?"

"Possibly."

"Well, he tried to say he wasn't supposed to release anything yet and she was saying it was only a little thing, not worth any money and it would only take her a minute to fetch it. It was obvious he wanted shot of her but she said Vanessa had some information about the organisations they both did fundraising for and Verity needed it to check their vital work continued. He said that if it really was urgent she could have it. Don't suppose he had much choice really?"

"Possibly not." Muriel had the horrible suspicion the information Verity wanted was details of whatever hold Vanessa had on her blackmail victims. She must have previously shared the information with Verity, but not the proof.

"Well, so he said to tell him what it was and where and he'd get it for her. It turns out she didn't even know what she wanted! I reckon she wanted to look at where Vanessa died, or maybe she was checking what was there in case she didn't get it all?"

"Possibly."

"She said she'd know it when she saw it and it'd be where Vanessa kept her personal documents. He said she was out of luck and you could tell he was pleased! He said no books, computers, papers, or anything like that were left in the house as the police had it all."

"Oh!"

"Well, I suppose they'd need to check in case there was anything to show why she was killed. Threatening letters do you think it could have been?"

Muriel didn't. If such things had been received the whole of Little Mallow would have heard. It seemed cruel to be so negative when Mrs King was enjoying herself so thoroughly, and had helped Muriel avoid an unpleasant confrontation with Verity, so she didn't say so. Instead she said, "I wonder how Verity would have recognised those documents?"

"That's a very good question!"

While Mrs King was pondering that, Muriel made her escape. She had thinking of her own to do. Did this mean Verity didn't know Vanessa's secrets? And that the police did?

Once home, Muriel called Crystal. She stressed she didn't have first hand knowledge, was just repeating what she'd heard, "As you wanted to know about Vanessa's charity activities I thought it might be important."

"Yes, it might. And this happened today, not yesterday evening?"

"That's what Mrs King said. She only mentioned the one instance, but it did sound like a continuance of Verity's grievance, so perhaps something similar occurred the day before. Does that help?"

"It's certainly interesting. I don't suppose you have any idea what kind of information Vanessa might have which could be so important to Verity?"

"Mrs King didn't say." That wasn't what Crystal had asked. Muriel must find the courage to admit she'd been blackmailed. There was now a real danger the police would learn Muriel's secret. It would be better, much better, if they didn't also consider it a motive for murder.

On the whole, Muriel was glad she'd repeated Mrs King's gossip. It did mean she'd been gossiping herself, but that wasn't such a bad thing if it went some way to helping with police enquiries.

# Chapter 33

## Saturday 29th August

Early on Saturday, Ellie brought the equipment she'd borrowed from Arnold, which included several large dust sheets. "While I was collecting this, Mike turned up," she said.

"You don't have to stay and help us. We'll be fine." Crystal was glad she'd not yet confessed they had no experience and little idea about decorating.

Ellie laughed. "Have you Googled sugar soap yet?"

"Was it that obvious I'd never heard of it?"

"Yes. Your faces, honestly! What was your plan? Buy one brush each, prise the lids off the pots and start painting?"

"Pretty much."

"Sorry, it's not quite that easy and it'll take longer than you think, but it's worth doing it properly."

"I agree. That doesn't mean you have to give up a day with Mike to help us."

"Actually, when he heard what I was doing he offered to help. I said I'd ask you and let him know."

"It's a yes from me," Jason said.

"And me," Crystal said. "I'm getting the feeling we need all the help we can get!"

Mike came, confessing he was no expert. Luckily, Ellie directed operations and made sure everything was done correctly. Once the prep was finished and she'd showed them how to use the roller trays, she offered to see to lunch.

Crystal was amazed it was already past twelve. Ellie had

been right it was going to take longer than they'd thought.

"How's the investigation going?" Mike asked.

"Early days yet." It was hard to believe Vanessa had still been alive five days previously.

"Maybe we can speed things up. Who are the suspects?" Mike asked, grinning.

It was very tempting to give a complete answer, but it wouldn't be professional to be so indiscrete. She had a mental count up – Arthur Rendall, Hugh Bend the plumber, his employee Zach. Possibly Beth, if she was covering for Zach, Verity Houseman, Mrs King, Muriel Grahame and her brother Bert. "We've whittled it down to nine, if you include the imaginary postman, and why wouldn't you?"

"You're investigating all nine?" Ellie asked.

Crystal shook her head. "CID are. Some to a greater extent than others obvs. It's frustrating I'm only half with them. If I'm there at the right time for the DI's daily briefing I find out everything that's been going on. Otherwise, I get updated on actual results, but there's a lot happening which I'm not involved in."

"You'll be with CID full time very soon," Jason said.

Crystal knew he was comforting her. She wondered how Jason felt about it. Her becoming a detective was something he'd known from the start – but she remembered Anne's warning about it taking over her life. There was a danger of that and she needed to talk to him about ways they could limit the impact on their relationship. Not now though.

"Yes, I will. Ignore my moaning. It's a murder. It happened in Little Mallow, and I was virtually on scene at the time. It feels like it should be my case, so everything which happens that I'm not involved in feels like I'm being shut out. That's ridiculous. Police work isn't a one man show. It's teamwork."

"Sounds like the team have a lot on their plate."

"We do! We have people with possible motives and people who may have had an opportunity, but there are problems with all of them."

"The godson who inherits must be top of the list," Mike said.

If even Mike, who lived in Durham, had heard the rumours about Arthur there was little point denying he was a suspect. It would be better to make clear that his guilt was far from certain. "Arthur probably couldn't have got here on time."

"Probably?" Mike queried.

"He said he didn't leave his B&B until gone eight. If that's right, he couldn't have got here by train. We've made enquiries with taxi ranks, bus companies and all sorts, but found nothing to suggest he did, or even could have, made the journey. That reminds me…" Crystal left the room and tried calling Mam Tor View again. There was no reply, and no voice mail option. She rejoined the others.

"Could he have got here by car in time?" Ellie asked.

"He doesn't have one and doesn't drive. Never even had a provisional licence, and he doesn't have any friends to drive him. And it's really unlikely a strange car wouldn't have been noticed in Grassy Lane."

"That's true," Ellie agreed.

"What about the imaginary postman?" Jason asked.

"A plumber, who isn't a suspect, thought he saw him go by. He wasn't very sure and my expert civilian witness says that wasn't possible, as a woman did his round that day, later than usual."

"Mary Milligan?" Mike guessed.

"Close. Adam."

"OK, then there was no postie. If the guy who thought he saw him is local, perhaps he just expected to?" Mike said.

"Yeah, that could be it."

Mid afternoon, Crystal went into the hall to answer her phone. She could hardly believe her ears – Muriel repeating gossip? And what could be so important in Vanessa's paperwork that Verity tried to take it at night, and went back twice in daylight?

Crystal called CID. Neil answered the duty phone.

"Should I come in to look through Vanessa's paperwork? Being local might mean something jumps out for me," Crystal offered after passing on Muriel's information.

"Is there something you're trying to get out of at home?"

"No, the opposite."

"Then don't volunteer like that. You'll have plenty of weekends cut short when there's no choice."

"Was that work on the phone?" Jason asked, when Crystal returned.

"Yes. Don't worry, I'm not going to slope off and leave you to do everything here." Even if she had volunteered to do just that!

Decorating took all day, and despite the special undercoat Ellie had bought, the bathroom was going to need another coat, but it looked really good – even with the green carpet.

Ellie and Mike said they'd see them both at Agnes's birthday party the next day.

"I've made a couple of broccoli and stilton quiches, which

I'll drop off at the hall before church," Ellie said.

Crystal phoned Aunty about Mike and Ellie, asking if she knew what was going on with the pair of them.

"Nothing much as far as I can see. That girl is wasting her life," Aunty said.

"Don't let her hear you say that!"

Agnes cackled. "Don't worry, I've not lost my marbles yet! And I'm wrong of course. Not having a man doesn't mean a wasted life. Muriel and I have been happy, but I'm not sure little Ellie has the life she wants."

Neither was Crystal. Ellie was proudly independent and most definitely didn't need a man around all the time, but that didn't mean she didn't want one. When she got off the phone Crystal discovered Jason had made a call of his own – to order a takeaway.

"Am I good to you or what?" he said.

"Depends. Are you going to put all the furniture and stuff back, while I soak in the bath?"

"No. We're going to do it together, while obeying Ellie's instruction not to get the room steamy until that paint, and the next coat, are completely dry."

That was fair and sensible. Sometimes being a grown up was no fun.

"I think we're allowed to get steamy ourselves."

And sometimes it was!

Anne phoned Crystal quite late that evening. "You said you've got things on this weekend?"

"There's been a development, hasn't there?" Crystal demanded.

"Answer the question first."

"It's my great Aunty Agnes's birthday party tomorrow. Lots of my family I haven't seen for ages, including my parents, are coming for the day. I really have to be there."

"Crystal, I'm not asking you to come in, I'm telling you not to. What I want to know is, as you can't be involved, would you still like to know if there had been an interesting development?"

"Oh yes!"

"I got through to Mam Tor View and asked for the exact time Arthur left. The owner was sorry, she couldn't say precisely, but as she'd told the other police officer, he definitely could have been there when he said."

"Could have, not was?"

"Yeah. Arthur had asked for something simple before she started the fry ups, as he liked to get an early start. She told him to help himself and he was gone when she came down just after eight."

"That still doesn't give him time I don't think... Oh, she didn't see him at all that morning?"

"Nope. Arthur could have caught any train after the 5.05 which we know he wasn't on."

"Which means he could have done it!" In Crystal's mind, and she guessed in Anne's too, it was almost certain he had.

# Chapter 34

## Sunday 30th August

"I'll pick some salad stuff and take it to the hall while you're in church, Mure," Bert said.

He'd already delivered as much as would be needed to go in the sandwiches and for use as garnishes. Maybe a small plateful or two would be a good idea though and he obviously wanted to increase his contribution. "Alright, but then come straight back to get ready. Remember, everyone needs to be in the hall ready when Agnes and I arrive."

Bert showed her his watch as proof he'd be keeping an eye on the time.

Muriel walked to Agnes's home before church. Some of the family were already there; Agnes's niece Marguerite Clere with her husband Dave, and Agnes's nephew Lionel. After greeting them all, Muriel wished her friend a happy birthday and gave her a bunch of garden flowers and a birthday card.

"Thank you. Oh, what a pretty one." Agnes put the card on the crowded mantlepiece. "And you're looking very nice yourself."

Muriel, who was wearing the very best of her Sunday best in anticipation of the party, smiled to acknowledge the compliment. "As do you. Elegant in fact."

"I'm trying to convince people I'm growing old gracefully. Do you think it will work?"

"Of course," said Dave Clere. "If they've never met you and don't get close enough to hear a word you say!"

"Oi, cheeky!"

"Not wrong though, am I?"

It didn't surprise Muriel that Agnes took his teasing comment as a compliment.

Agnes's niece Yvonne appeared from the kitchen to offer Muriel tea. "And a bacon sandwich if you fancy it?"

Muriel, who'd had breakfast, was persuaded to go halves with Crystal, who'd just arrived with her boyfriend Jason.

"If we're going to church, we'd better make a move," Yvonne said, once they'd all finished eating.

"We'll stay with Crystal," Marguerite Clere said. "We've hardly had time to talk to her lately."

Muriel knew Crystal, her parents, and uncle would be making the sandwiches and laying out the rest of the food as they chatted. As other family members arrived in Little Mallow, they would go to the hall in time to help, and then surprise Agnes.


Vanessa's untimely death was announced in the church service, although not the manner of it. Her flower arranging skills were mentioned, as was the fact she was so well known in the village that her death would impact on everyone to some degree. The vicar talked about it not being their place to judge and God forgiving people their sins. Muriel supposed he meant the murderer, not Vanessa.

Jerry also mentioned Agnes's birthday, personally wishing her many happy returns. He prayed, giving thanks for her life, and for that of all those we love, whether with us for a short or long time.

After the service almost everyone wished Agnes a happy birthday. Some gave her cards. A few said, 'see you later.'

That had become such a common expression even Muriel wasn't sure if they were referring to the party.

"Would you like me to take you straight to the Kale and Snail for your lunch?" Yvonne asked. Then, as arranged, she added, "You'd be rather early though. How about I take you down to have a quick look at how the work on the castle is progressing?"

Agnes had unknowingly been primed for this, by several people telling her the scaffolding was being removed. As had been hoped, she readily accepted the idea.

They couldn't see very much from the road. "It's a lovely day for a walk, shall we go along the beach for a better view?" Yvonne suggested. They didn't go far on account of the shingle being so difficult to walk on, especially in their good shoes. It was however far enough to observe that the tower had been extensively rebuilt.

As they returned to the car, Muriel said, "We're still early and haven't had much of a walk yet. Maybe you could drop us off at the top of Main Street, Yvonne?" That was also part of the plan, as she wanted Agnes to approach the village hall, believing she would continue past to the pub.

When they drew close to the new village hall, Muriel said, "Earlier, I smelled something lovely coming from the hall garden. It reminded me of daphne, but it can't be that at this time of year, can it?"

"No… I wonder what that could be."

"Shall we go and see?" Muriel suggested.

"Alright. Muriel dear, don't you think we should have a very light lunch today?"

"Because of the heat?"

"No, silly. I have guessed you know! We'll get back home

and all my family and some friends will be there, ready to shout 'surprise' sing *Happy Birthday* and serve up huge quantities of sandwiches and cake."

"Oh! I thought we'd been so clever keeping it quiet."

"You overdid it. There's been so little fuss made this year, I just knew you were all doing something special."

"There's no fooling you, is there?" As they walked up the path towards the hall, in search of the mysterious plant, Muriel moved so Agnes was ahead of her and would see the door standing open.

Agnes was quick to notice. "We'd better let the verger know, so he can come and lock it," Agnes said.

"Let's just put our heads in and check everything is OK." Muriel pushed the door and gestured for Agnes to precede her.

There was no shout of 'surprise'. Instead, what seemed like hundreds of people sang *Happy Birthday* to an amazed Agnes. All of her family and her local friends were there, plus most of the other villagers and a few people who'd moved away. Everyone had dressed up and looked splendid.

As the assembled crowd launched into For *She's A Jolly Good Fellow*, Muriel noticed the buffet table had been moved from where she'd helped set it up, into the first room. It was an odd thing to have been done, but scarcely mattered.

"I can hardly believe this," Agnes said with a wobble in her voice when the singing ended. She dabbed happy tears away from her face. "So many of you and all those flowers, it's lovely. Thank you. Thank you."

# Chapter 35

## Sunday 30th August

"Go on, call," Jason said over breakfast on Sunday morning.

"Call who?" Crystal asked. She wanted to phone CID, but was trying not to seem, or actually be, work obsessed.

"Your handsome inspector. See if they've brought your suspect in."

He wasn't her inspector yet but, as there was no denying the handsome part, Crystal didn't challenge Jason's remark. "I think I'll ring Anne instead. She's very pretty, I'll be sure to introduce you sometime."

"Good idea," Jason said. It was unclear whether he was referring to her first or second sentence.

"No," was Anne's response to Crystal's query as to whether Arthur had been brought in for interview. "The DI said the landlady not actually having seen him that morning is a long way from proof he left earlier than he said. The CPS will need a lot more than that, so he's waiting for the results of the enquiries about taxis and buses."

"Oh flip! I told Sergeant Dylan they were low priority."

"I know. Luckily for you it was me who called to chase it up and, low priority or not, they were working on it."

"Thanks, Anne."


As more and more of Crystal's family arrived at the hall to help get ready for Aunty's birthday party, it became noisy and chaotic. She hoped it wouldn't be too much for Jason, whose own family were fewer in number and quieter than her rabble. She was glad there were so many of them though, as there was a lot of food to deal with – and doing it together made it fun.

Crystal was pleased to see Muriel had been right, and if anything there was more food than was likely to get eaten. She was relieved the iced cakes had defrosted just as well as she'd promised Muriel they would, and it wasn't obvious which scones she'd made and which were Muriel's.

Jason was suitably impressed by her domestic skills. "Can you do it again without Muriel's help?"

"Now I know where I went wrong, yes."

He shook his head."You're going to have to prove that."

"And then that I've not forgotten – maybe on a weekly basis?"

"Sounds about right."

"Where do you want the other tables, love?" Dad asked.

"I don't think there are any more small ones."

"I meant long ones for the rest of the food."

"There's more?"

"We've barely started!"

Arnold located another couple of long tables, which he set up in the other part of the hall. "Perhaps everything still sealed in packaging should be left that way?"

Even following that suggestion, there was far more than could be accommodated on both buffet tables. It took a while to juggle things so the excess which needed to be refrigerated was put safely away. They were only just ready in time to gather ready to sing *Happy Birthday* to Great Aunty Agnes. Her surprise and joy made all the planning and preparation worthwhile.

Crystal heard hysterical laughter coming from the corner of the hall's garden where she'd sent Jason for a bit of peace after coping with her family. She found him surrounded by some of her laughing relatives, seeming even more amused than they did.

"What's going on?" she asked.

"We're telling Jason about Ralf."

"Why would you do that?" There were plenty of stories from her childhood which showed her as clever or cute. Why did they pick the single most embarrassing incident in her life ever? It didn't take much of her detective skill to work out they were telling it precisely because it was so embarrassing – and because, to anyone but her, it was far funnier than it was mortifying. She left them to it.

As Crystal mingled, she encouraged talk of the murder, and asked about the friendship between Verity and Vanessa. That just resulted in mentions of flower arranging, charity fundraising, and community projects. Asking about Vanessa personally was slightly more interesting. Some people, mainly those who didn't know her well, praised Vanessa's 'good works'. Others called her a snoop and gossip. Crystal didn't come across anyone who seemed to like the woman.

The most interesting comment was one Crystal overheard in the loo. A voice she didn't recognise said, "Verity hasn't learned anything from her friend's murder – she's been hinting she knows who did it."

"With any luck they'll prove her right!"

Ooooh! Frustratingly both women had gone by the time Crystal was able to leave the cubicle. She dashed into the corridor.

"What's up, lass?" Trevor asked, when she almost collided with him.

"Did you see two women come out?"

"No, but the far door was just closing."

Crystal looked, but there were so many people she couldn't work out who she'd heard. "Someone knows something and I don't know what or who they are!"

"About the murder?"

"Yes." She explained.

"If they're talking about it, they'll tell others and it'll get to you eventually."

"Yeah, I suppose." And maybe it would be no help at all.

"I'm sure you know lots of things I don't. Care to share?"

Crystal washed her hands, then found a quiet-ish spot to tell Trevor that Arthur Rendall might have left the Peak District earlier than he'd said. "The family Arthur claimed would alibi him have been traced. They remember meeting the Battenburg man, as the boy called him. None of them were absolutely sure if they'd seen him on the day in question."

"Frustrating, but maybe not surprising."

"Yeah. I don't remember much about people I've met on holiday." Even so, she'd hoped the kid would be another Adam and provide crucial evidence.

"You were thinking he might have got a really early train and there'd be CCTV?" Trevor said.

Was it so long ago she'd talked to him? "At least we got something definite there. CCTV footage shows nobody remotely matching his description caught the 5.05 train from the station Vanessa suggested, or any alternatives he might have used due to starting from his holiday B&B

214

instead of home. As it gets busier it's harder to be sure."

"There are other forms of transport."

"Buses are out, they don't connect up well enough. Such a long taxi journey would be remembered. He couldn't hire a car without a licence – not legally, and there's no indication he called anyone about it or knew how to drive. Or had any friends who could have helped."

"Sounds as though, despite the lack of evidence, you haven't ruled him out."

"He has such strong motives."


Crystal didn't ignore Aunty Agnes, but mostly kept her distance, so she could talk to those she didn't often see. Aunty did a lot of that. She also joined in dancing to the *Hokey Cokey, Birdie Song* and every other similarly cheesy, but hard to resist, number Uncle Leonard could route from his iPod through the hall's speakers.

At one point Aunty beckoned in Crystal's direction and pointed to the garden.

"Everything OK? Music not too loud?" Crystal asked when they were together.

"It might be if you hadn't, very sensibly, invited everyone who lives nearby."

"Luckily they're all people we thought you'd be happy to have here."

"You're quite right. Now, where has that boy got to?" She waved and beckoned to Jason.

He soon appeared, with a, "What's up, Aunty Aggie?"

Aunty better not be about to recall another excruciating incident from Crystal's adolescence.

"Dancing, that's what," Agnes said.

"Have I been doing it wrong?" Jason asked. He very much had. As that was to amuse the children who were present, and occupy them in instructing him on the correct moves, he was in no danger of being told off.

"I don't get to do enough of it. I can't do the proper ballroom stuff, no matter how carefully I watch Strictly, but I'm not so bad at the silly stuff."

"You were ace, Aunty Aggie. Throwing great shapes!"

"Hmmm." Aunty gave Jason 'that' look, although he'd long since lost his terror of it. "Thing is, you only get to do that kind of thing at parties like this… and weddings."

"I suppose," Jason said.

"I want to dance at Crystal's wedding. I'm not normally an impatient person, but once you get to ninety-three you can't wait long." With that, she returned to the hall.

Crystal wished Aunty had recalled the time she'd jumped onto the stage at school assembly and announced the 'truth' about Santa, only to discover the man she'd seen wasn't the real Santa, and the elf wasn't an actual elf either.

Jason took her hand. "Crystal, I love you, and you love me."

"Yes," Crystal managed to squeak. But there was her career. And his. And they'd not really been together all that long. How would he cope with her erratic hours, and likely near obsession with any big cases? How would she cope with his absences on foreign assignments?

"We'll talk about this, but not here, not quite yet," he said.

"I think that's a very good idea." She already felt a warm glow – what would an actual proposal be like?

"Will you be in the station or CID tomorrow, lass?" Trevor asked, when they met at a buffet table.

"A bit of both, I think."

"Someone wants to come in and talk about the murder."

"This happened yesterday and you're only now…"

He shook his head. "I wasn't in yesterday either. Muriel just told me she has something to confess."

"Muriel! What? No, that can't be…" Muriel wasn't going to confess to murder. Please don't let it be that. "See if we can do it as soon as we come on shift. That way if she does say anything useful I can pass it straight to CID."

"I'll set that up then."

As Trevor walked away, Crystal wondered why he'd taken the Saturday off. She hoped he hadn't told her, and the murder and her imminent transfer meant she wasn't paying attention. Could it be connected with the fact cousin Yvonne had only arrived at Aunty's on Saturday evening, not spent all day with her as she usually would?

# Chapter 36

## Monday 31st August

"We've put out as much of the food as possible," Arnold told Muriel. "However there's a lot more in the kitchen."

"Why didn't you use the tables we set up yesterday?" she asked, trying not to sound critical.

"We have, however they proved insufficient and we deployed reinforcements. I'd always thought the expression groaning under the weight an exaggeration," Cameron said.

"Whatever are we going to do with it all?" Muriel asked.

"Perhaps you can recruit more small boys?" Cameron suggested. "There's a young lad out there doing a fine job."

Muriel looked in the direction Cameron indicated and saw Teddy. "Excuse me," she said and made her way over.

"Lo!" Teddy said, then continued eating.

"Sorry," the young man with him said. "I know we should have waited. Someone saw Teddy eyeing the cakes and gave him a plateful. It'd have been cruel to take them away."

Muriel smiled, reassuringly she hoped. "Please give him more as soon as he can manage them."

"Oh, OK. Thanks."

"I'm Muriel Grahame. You, I take it, are Zach?"

"Oh! Hello. Yeah. That's me. You're the lady who offered to let Beth use your garden for," he nodded at Teddy.

"Yes. And you're the man who'll persuade her to accept."

"I don't know. She's hard to help sometimes. Won't take anything she considers charity."

"It's not charity. And it wouldn't be for her, it would be for her little boy. And for me. I'd like to do it."

"Yeah? If we talk her round I'll give you some bread."

"For the sandwiches?"

He laughed. "Sort of. I meant money to buy the food."

"Looking at how much food we have here, I'm sure there will be enough left over." Teddy's birthday was only three days away. Many of the items would keep perfectly well in airtight containers. Others could be refrigerated or frozen.

"Yeah, there's masses and it looks good stuff too."

"That's settled then. Now, how do we persuade your young lady to agree?"

"If she thinks it's best for Teddy she'll say yes. He was a bit young last year, but I reckon he'd love it this year. Let's swap numbers in case we think of anything."


"Muriel, can I give you a lift back to Aunty's once we've cleared up a bit?" Yvonne said as what had been a delightful party finally drew to a close. "The Cleres are taking her in a few minutes and they'll have Crystal and the birthday cake too, so that car will be full, but I won't be far behind."

How tactful of Yvonne to show Muriel was welcome to join them. However, Agnes would no doubt prefer to expend any remaining energy in conversation with people she didn't see very often.

"Thank you, but no. I'm rather tired. I'll wait for the verger to lock up, then have an early night." She'd not been sleeping as well as usual. There was too much on her mind.

"Aunty must be tired too, although she's not showing any sign. It'll hit her soon, I expect. I'd best go get her."

Muriel began selecting items which would keep until

Teddy's birthday. Bert, who'd not been much in evidence during the party, made a considerable contribution to the clearing up. True, some food went into his mouth, but he packed up far more to be taken home for their own use, as well as Teddy's party. Once that priority was taken care of he began wiping down those tables which were empty.

"My dear lady, what a triumph!" Cameron said.

"I do think it went very well, but can't take all the credit." She was willing to accept some. False modesty could be so irritating, and she'd worked hard.

"Then teamwork is clearly one of your many talents."

Muriel told Cameron she was following his suggestion of feeding a portion of the leftovers to small children. "That won't make much of a dent I fear."

"We know of a place which offers support to homeless people. I took the liberty of calling to ask if they would be able to distribute food such as this. They'll happily do so if you feel that's appropriate."

"What an excellent idea! Are you able to deliver it?"

"It would be my pleasure."

They worked together, collecting everything which remained unopened. Muriel felt much happier knowing the food would be eaten rather than going into the bin. It seemed possible the leftovers would be appreciated and enjoyed just as much as the original offering.

Arnold, followed by Bert, joined them when the last of the furniture had been put away.

"Please allow us to drive you both home," Cameron said.

Muriel was grateful on account of the bags and boxes they had. By the time she got out of the car she wondered if she'd have managed the walk even with nothing to carry.

Bert evidently noticed her weariness. "Sit on the sofa, Mure. I'll bring you a cup of tea."

When she awoke, two hours later, he was replacing that stone cold drink with a fresh one.

"Would you like any sandwiches or cakes?" Bert asked.

"Perhaps a lemon one, if any are left. You get yours too and join me here." They didn't generally eat from their laps in the lounge but she felt like making an exception.

When he was settled, Muriel asked Bert what he'd been doing on the morning of his birthday.

"Nothing."

"No, Bert, not nothing. You went to the allotment?"

"You know that... Then I went to get seaweed."

Ah! A walk on the beach wasn't a convincing explanation, collecting seaweed to feed his plants was. "Why didn't you say when you were asked?"

"Because of her."

"Crystal? You could have told her."

"I didn't know if you're supposed to take it but it weren't just that. There were kiddies there. The one who got herself killed, she said I was a nasty old man. People would think it weren't right. I know what she meant. It's not true, Mure."

"Oh, Bert. Of course it isn't." Poor Bert. If he felt he must defend himself even to her, he would have been in torment about what others might suspect. If Vanessa wasn't already dead Muriel would gladly have brought that about.

"That's why I told you not to talk to Vanessa. She said horrible things."

"It's not just her. The other one, she's been saying it too."

"Verity Houseman?"

221

"Yes."

"She has to be stopped! This simply can't go on." She'd spoken to Trevor Harris and intended to reveal Vanessa had been blackmailing her. Now it seemed she must do more.

"The other one has stopped."

How to make Bert understand the problem and that it wouldn't go away? "Yes and Verity has taken over."

"She's the same?" Bert asked.

"Worse. It's not just you and me she says things about. I think she does it to lots of people. Some of it's true and she threatens to tell others if they don't give her money."

He balled his hands into fists. "Is she doing that to you, Mure?"

Her dear, placid Bert looked so angry. As angry as Muriel herself had felt each time she'd realised one of the evil Vs was deliberately blackmailing her. "I won't pay her, Bert. We can't give in to that kind of thing."

"It's not just us who wants her to shut up?"

"No." Others were being threatened, made miserable. Were perhaps feeling as desperate as she once had. "Bert, I need to go to the police and explain. Is that OK? If I tell them she's said nasty things?" Although what had been said to Bert seemed to give him a slight motive, Muriel thought the police more than bright enough to realise others were very likely to be in the same position. Possibly many others.

"If you think that's best, Mure. Will they make her stop?"

Muriel couldn't reassure him. Once deprived of a way to profit from keeping her secrets, Verity might seek revenge by revealing them in the most damaging way possible. Muriel did the most comforting thing she could. "Let's have some more tea and cake."

# Chapter 37

## Monday 31st August

Crystal rang Sergeant Kirk to say Muriel had some kind of confession to make. "She asked to speak to me and Trevor. Although he gathered it was connected with the murder it doesn't seem likely she's going to claim responsibility."

"You want to interview her yourselves?" Captain asked.

"If that's OK? I thought we'd pay her a visit. If things take an unexpected turn we could always bring her in."

"Alrighty then."

Muriel, who was clearly uncomfortable, made tea and offered a plate of leftover party food. "There's still a lot left, far more than we can eat."

"If it's really going spare, Trevor and I could take some into work." Crystal made the suggestion as it would make them both popular and wasting good food, especially some she'd given up a day off to help make, seemed a serious crime. It had the bonus of helping relax Muriel a little.

"Please do that. We shouldn't have brought it all home, but compared with what was there at the start it didn't seem to be so very much."

"What was it you wanted to tell us, Muriel?" Crystal asked once they'd all sampled the refreshments.

"It's about Vanessa."

"OK." She'd guessed as much.

"I'm afraid it might be rather a long story and perhaps of very little help to you."

"No rush. We get cake, so it's not wasted time!"

223

"I lied to you."

That was a shock.

"I'm so sorry. I did have a reason, but I see now that misleading you… It was a mistake."

Poor Muriel. Obviously it was frustrating when witnesses didn't tell the truth, whole truth and nothing else, and it could lead to delays in establishing the facts, but it was hardly unusual. "You're putting that right now."

Muriel nodded.

"Did you go to Vanessa's house, on the morning she died?" Trevor asked.

"Yes. I didn't go inside, but I did walk down Grassy Lane and stand outside."

"Why?"

As Trevor was asking the right questions, Crystal kept quiet.

"I wanted her to see me. See that I was there, but that I wouldn't go in."

"Because…?"

"I had to show I'd no longer allow her to blackmail me."

That was another shock for Crystal. It must have been for Trevor too. He hid it well.

"I think I said she'd told me I was to go to her house that morning and collect roses to go on the altar?"

"You mentioned being cross about it." And had given the impression she'd not gone.

"Bert had donated lots of flowers, as he does throughout the summer. She wanted hers displayed instead. I was to collect them and persuade the others to have them included in the altar arrangement, as payment for her silence. Not the only payment."

"What was she blackmailing you about?" Crystal asked.

"I'd rather not say. I was naive and hadn't realised until the day before that her manipulation was blackmail. She used to ask me to do little favours, or call at her home to make charity donations. It made it seem as though we were friends, that I approved of her behaviour…"

Crystal could see how humiliated Muriel was, but had to continue. "You paid her money?"

"Charity donations. I think she did pass them on."

"So, you went to collect the flowers?" Crystal asked.

"No. I wasn't ever going to do that. I'd been going to tell her so. I changed my mind, didn't walk down the path."

"Did Vanessa see you?"

"Yes. That is… I waited a little while. I'm certain she'd have been looking out for me. I didn't speak to, or see, her."

"Did you see anyone at all?"

"No. I heard a radio playing. I'm not sure from which house the sound came."

"You just walked away?"

"I don't remember much from when I stood outside her house to when I reached the top of the lane. I'd resolved to stand up to her. I demonstrated I could have done her bidding and chose not to. The reality of doing that was almost overwhelming. I've kept the secret such a long time."

"Was anything else you told us… not quite right?"

"No."

"Did you see anyone else in Grassy Lane?"

"I didn't see the men, but there was a plumber's van."

"Did you notice anything else unusual?"

225

Muriel frowned. "I… No, I don't recall."

"If anything does come back to you, please let us know." Muriel hadn't mentioned seeing the patrol car, so Crystal didn't have high hopes she'd spotted the murderer and would be able to describe him.

"Is there something else?" Trevor asked.

"It's not the end of it! When I heard Vanessa was dead I thought the blackmail would die with her, that my secret was safe. Verity Houseman has taken over. She's demanded money from me, and I know she's taken it from others."

That probably solved one mystery. The documents Verity was so keen to get hold of could well be proof of whatever her victims wanted kept quiet. Verity's blackmail would be dealt with, but the murder was still the priority.

"You think Vanessa blackmailed others?"

"There were others. I saw a person give Verity money and I spoke with them. Verity having taken over from Vanessa was mentioned. The person knew what I was referring to. And Vanessa made comments to people on subjects I think she'd have liked to blackmail them about. Verity said the same things. Nasty things."

Crystal recalled the snatch of conversation she'd heard, about Verity not having learned from her friend's death. It did seem as though she might well be attempting to blackmail the wrong person.

"Do you think any of the other blackmail victims might be willing to talk to us?" Crystal asked.

"I can't give you names, I just can't."

Crystal didn't feel able to push her further right then. It seemed Trevor didn't either as, after a pause, he asked her to go over the events of the morning Vanessa died. She repeated her previous statement of walking to Vanessa's house, leaving without speaking to her, and then becoming overwhelmed.

"When I came to as it were, I was inside the hedge, which seems strange to me."

"You said it was hot and you wanted shade," Crystal said.

"I was the wrong side of the road… unless I got right inside the hedge. I don't quite see how I could have."

There was something Crystal didn't quite understand. "What made you sure Vanessa wouldn't tell people your secret once you stopped doing what she asked?"

"I wasn't. I had thought of telling her that if she did, I'd denounce her as a blackmailer. I would have done so, and therefore lost her the respect and reputation she'd so ruthlessly obtained. However I decided against threatening her. That would itself be a form of blackmail. I hoped she'd realise the danger herself and hold her tongue."

"It was a risk," Crystal said.

"Yes."

While Crystal was trying to think what to ask next, her phone rang. It was Anne, so she excused herself and stepped outside to answer.

"When are you interviewing your suspect?" Anne asked.

"Right now."

"I assume she didn't do it?"

"It seems not – although she's revealed she has a motive." Presumably that's what stopped Muriel telling the truth from the start. That and not wanting her secret exposed.

"A lot of people are giving us information. Zach and Hugh are coming in to do the same. You're cordially invited to join in the fun, as soon as you can."

"As long as my skipper agrees, I'll be on my way when I've finished here."

Crystal went back in to hear Trevor trying to persuade Muriel to tell them what she was being blackmailed about.

"It might help us and perhaps we can help you too."

Knowing Muriel's hatred of gossip and old fashioned outlook it might not be anything bad, just embarrassing.

"I really can't tell you. Not yet. It's not my secret. There is something else I can tell you. Crystal, you asked Bert what he was doing on the day Vanessa was killed, and he said he was walking on the beach. I don't think you believed him."

"I…"

"It didn't sound like him, did it? But he didn't tell you why. He was collecting seaweed for his allotment. He didn't say as he wasn't sure it was allowed."

Crystal thought Muriel might still be holding something back. "Is there anything else you can tell us?"

"I don't feel that I can. I'm sorry."

Crystal reached across and put her hand on the old lady's. "Thank you for what you've told us. It must have been difficult. If you remember anything else, or feel you can tell us more, you know how to get in touch. You can speak to either one of us on our own, or even to a different officer if you'd feel more comfortable with someone you don't know."

"Thank you."

"Don't forget you promised us some cakes," Trevor said.

Crystal was concerned she didn't have time for that. However Trevor's reminder seemed to cheer Muriel a little, so she waited. By the time she'd given them each a platter of food, Muriel appeared calm.

"Well, what do you make of that, lass?" Trevor asked, as

she drove him back to Gosport police station.

"I think it was true, but she's holding something back."

"Just whatever that secret of hers is, or something more?"

"More. But whoever she was protecting by not saying what the blackmail is about must also be a suspect."

"Suspect! I can't see it, but you do have to consider her and whoever else shares the secret."

"Old Bert," Crystal said. "He's the only person, other than Aunty, she's close enough to, and she is protective of him."

Trevor nodded. "From what I know of Bert he's a good person, but he could have done something which seemed shocking to Muriel."

"I've had a horrible thought... He'd be protective of her wouldn't he? Spending his birthday gathering seaweed is more plausible than taking a random walk, but it's a long way short of a cast iron alibi."


While waiting for the plumbers to arrive in CID, Crystal reported on what Muriel had said. She also shared out the cakes, proudly saying she'd made them when they received praise – omitting the fact she'd not done so for their benefit.

"How widespread do you think the blackmailing is?" Neil asked. "I mean, did Vanessa put her life in danger and is Verity doing the same, or were they just being nasty to Muriel because they had something on her?"

"Good question. I don't know... Muriel said it took her a long time to realise exactly what was happening and although she thinks there are other victims she could be mistaken. I'll ask around. I know some people who, if it was widespread, would probably have heard something."

"You missed this morning's briefing, but I believe you're

up to speed on everything, Officer Clere," DI Shortfellow said. "Do you have any questions?"

"Which charities did Vanessa leave money to?" Crystal had almost asked Muriel which Vanessa had coerced her into donating to, thinking it might shed light on her blackmail activities. She'd judged it better to ask at a different time when the implication wouldn't be so clear and Muriel would therefore be more likely to tell her.

"None. Not a penny," Anne said.

"That's odd when she worked to support several and it doesn't seem as though she particularly cared about Arthur getting all her money."

"It's odd under any circumstances," Anne said. "Doesn't everyone leave money to charity?"

Crystal shrugged. "I don't know. I have, but only because I was persuaded to make a will when I joined the force and I didn't have a partner at the time." She should update that.

"Talking of needing a will, what's that?" the DI asked, indicating a cup cake.

"Carrot cake with cream cheese topping, sir," Crystal informed him.

"Does carrot cake have raisins in?"

"That one doesn't. Nuts, but no dried fruit."

He ate it. "Officer Clere, you're with me. Do not say a word unless I give the signal."

"Yes, sir. No, sir. Thank you, sir!"

He emitted his trademark burst of laughter and strode away to an interview room, with Crystal scurrying after.

The plumbers, Hugh and Zach, declined to be interviewed separately. It wasn't ideal, but as they'd come in voluntarily, the DI said he wouldn't push it, at least until he'd heard what they had to say. That turned out to be that Zach spent much longer in the house with Beth, prior to discovering the body, than they'd originally said.

"I knew Zach's girlfriend was there," Hugh said. "As Beth lodges with an old couple and has a kid, they don't get much time alone. We weren't particularly busy, so I gave him a chance to spend a bit of time with her."

Crystal's mind was racing. By doing that, and sending Ryan to the post office for rolls, he'd given himself time alone. That meant he'd had the opportunity to kill Vanessa. Hugh went in to check Vanessa really was dead – which would explain away any fingerprints or hairs of his on the scene. Did he have any motive? She longed to ask questions, but managed not to interrupt the DI.

"How long were you alone in Brambles, Mr Bend?" The DI asked.

"Me? I wasn't… Oh, yes Ryan went for lunch." There was a pause before he answered the question – while staring at the desk. "Must have been getting on for an hour."

Easily enough time to strangle someone.

"How well did you know Vanessa Meadows?"

"Not very."

Interesting that both he and Zach had initially given the impression they'd not known her at all.

"You liked her?" the DI continued.

"No." Hugh sounded sure about that. It was a very common sentiment.

"I see. Why is that?"

"Because every nasty thing anyone has told you about her, or hinted at, is true."

"I've been told she was very unpleasant."

"That will be people not wanting to speak ill of the dead. She was a lot worse than that. I can't say I was expecting her to be murdered, but it wasn't that big a shock."

"Any theories about who would want her dead?"

"Everyone she'd ever spoken to I'd imagine. But wishing someone was dead and making it happen aren't the same thing."

"No. Are you one of those who wished she was dead?"

"I'm not sorry about it."

"When you were informed one of the residents of Grassy Lane was dead, were you told who that was?"

Crystal was really pleased the DI was asking all the questions which were going through her mind. Not just because that gave her the answers. It also showed she was thinking along similar lines.

"I don't know if he told me her name. He probably didn't know it then." Hugh glanced at Zach.

"I don't think I did say, just that she was next door."

"I see."

If they'd rehearsed what they were going to say, they'd not been very thorough. Either that, or Zach hadn't told his boss about Beth's treatment by Vanessa.

"That'd be next to the house Beth was looking after?"

"That's right," Hugh said.

Zach nodded.

"I see. How did you know it was 1, not 3?"

"Zach pointed that way, and as I'd gone down the path to see him, I saw the door was wide open."

"Zach, you knew Vanessa?"

"Of her – I've not really spoken to her myself, but she

was horrible to... to an ex girlfriend and to Beth."

Crystal thought that was news to Hugh – he'd stiffened as Zach spoke.

"Why weren't you honest with us before?"

"Because of Dom. I thought it would make you suspicious of me," Zach said.

"That wouldn't, but the lying has. Think carefully, is there anything else you've not told us?"

"No... Well, not about us. I think maybe Vanessa's door was open when I went back to tell her the water was on. Not at first I don't mean, after I'd gone into the garden."

"How sure are you it wasn't like that before?"

"It definitely wasn't open when I went to say the water was going off. Not locked, or a chain or anything, but shut. She opened up really quickly and started to talk, then stopped and seemed surprised. I thought she was expecting someone she knew, or who definitely couldn't be me."

The DI placed his hand on the desk.

"How do you mean?" Crystal asked.

"Well, if she was expecting a woman, or a delivery. Obviously I wasn't one of those."

Crystal bit back the words, 'I see'. She was going to have to come up with her own alternative. "Go on."

"When I'd spoken to her she closed the door hard, almost in my face. When I went back, I don't think it was open. When I saw it was later I thought she'd heard me and opened it then. I thought that meant it was OK to stick my head in and tell her the water was back on."

"You've thought about this a lot," Crystal said.

"Yeah, I have – going over and over it, but I'm nor

making things up."

"And there's nothing you've left out?"

"I don't think so." He seemed uncomfortable.

Crystal wondered if he could have been blackmailed. What would a man in his twenties want kept quiet? "This other girlfriend Vanessa wasn't nice about?" Maybe she wasn't as ex as Beth had been led to believe?

To Crystal's surprise it was Hugh who answered. "My daughter, Kirianne. It was just nasty little jibes, schoolyard stuff, nothing serious, but Vanessa Meadows was no kid. She knew what she was doing. It doesn't bother Kirianne now, but she was proper upset about it for a while. Really knocked her confidence. She got over it. She's going back to college and has a part time job. That's where she was on Tuesday, in case you're interested."

Crystal glanced at the DI, then told the men they'd need to give updated statements. Those didn't reveal any additional information.

"What are your thoughts, Officer Clere?" the DI asked.

"They both had time to kill her, sir, and a motive. Sort of the same one. They could have done it working together, or on their own, or with Beth, who also had reason not to like Vanessa. It's interesting Mr Bend provided his daughter's alibi. Oh, and this backs up Muriel's idea there might be a lot more people who had reason to wish Vanessa dead."

"Is there, do you think, anyone in Little Mallow who can be eliminated at this point?"

"My great aunty Agnes, sir."

Before the DI could react with more than a laugh, Neil rushed up. "Sir, another woman's been strangled in Little Mallow!"

# Chapter 38

## Monday 31st August

"Have you heard that Verity was attacked?" Agnes asked, even before Muriel was through the front door.

"No! Is she...?"

"She's OK, but someone tried strangling her. I admit that when she said she was being followed I thought she was making it up, trying to get attention. Crystal gave me a proper ticking off, saying that attitude sometimes stopped female victims of crime from coming forward. I saw her point, and I don't usually think women who are scared are making a silly fuss over nothing, but with Verity..."

"This attack really happened?"

"Oh yes. She has red marks on her neck. She's been showing everyone."

Muriel could see why Agnes initially suspected Verity of having made something up to get attention. She was quite sure most of Verity's, 'I have it on good authority,' stories involving scandalous allegations were entirely fictitious.

"Has the person responsible been arrested?"

"No. She didn't see him well enough to identify him. Just said he had rough hands and a deep voice. The police are trying to find out where everyone was when Verity was attacked. Where were you, Muriel? Oh, don't look like that – I'm not accusing you for goodness sake! I'm trying to help eliminate people. If you were with someone, or saw them, then they're in the clear."

Muriel hadn't thought Agnes was accusing her. She'd

been more concerned about Bert – who had a deep voice and hands roughened with garden work. She'd told him something had to be done to silence Verity. Surely he couldn't have…? "When did this happen?"

"Verity was quite vague, probably about half nine this morning."

Muriel almost laughed. "Yes, I was with someone! Your Crystal, and Trevor Harris came to talk to me." Bert went to the allotment. She hoped there had been others there, who'd be able to back up his alibi should that be needed.

"Talking about what?" Agnes asked.

"I was telling them the evil Vs were blackmailers."

Agnes gasped. "You know that… You wouldn't have said it unless you knew for certain. I can only think of one way you would. Muriel my dear, they were blackmailing you?"

Muriel couldn't deny it. Neither of them said anything for quite a time.

"About Bert?" Agnes eventually asked.

Muriel felt as though the air had been sucked out of her. She fought for breath before asking, "You knew?"

Agnes shrugged. "I'm not sure whether I did at the time, or just guessed. Nobody talked about it and I'd almost forgotten. But there's the one thing you don't ever say."

It was such a relief both to share her secret, and that her oldest, dearest, friend realised Muriel had never outright lied to her. She always called Bert by his name, never referring to him as her brother.

"You mustn't pay her, you know that, Muriel."

"I know, but how do I not?"

"We'll think of something. First, I'll put the kettle on."

When the tea was made, Agnes said, "Crystal is amongst those talking to possible suspects for the attack on Verity."

"Are there many?"

"It seems so. The police think both attacks may be linked."

"They must be, don't you think?" Muriel asked.

"I do. Crystal says they're not jumping to conclusions – meaning I am! Still, they're concentrating on those who were in the area when Vanessa was killed, or had a reason to do her in, and trying to eliminate people."

"I see the sense in that."

"She says it's not easy. The godson gets the house, so he's an obvious suspect. He was on a bike ride when Verity was attacked. As he doesn't know the area he couldn't say where he went, which could be true. And they don't think he could have got here in time to murder Vanessa."

"Did I say I met him?"

"No. What did you think of him?"

"He seemed very friendly." Agnes's words had triggered a memory. "I've seen a bicycle somewhere."

"The vicar's, I expect. He leaves it in strange places sometimes. I once saw it dangling from a low tree branch and thought someone was playing a trick on him, but he'd hooked it up there himself because there was nowhere suitable for him to lean it."

"It wasn't his. I'd have recognised that."

"You'd know if it was the godson's. Mary said he told her he'd added colourful dayglo tape whatever that is, and luminous paint to the frame and has several sets of lights and reflectors, to try to make cycling in traffic safer."

"I remember now. He arrived on it when Beth and I met

him." It wasn't that distinctive machine which had flitted across her thoughts, but something ordinary.

"Let's talk about something more pleasant. My party for instance."

"Yes, that was very nice."

"You did a wonderful job, Muriel. It must have been a lot of work."

"You know I enjoy baking and I didn't do it all myself. Crystal spent a day cooking with me."

"She kept that quiet. And you were very sneaky, pretending we'd have lunch in the Kale and Snail, when you've never set foot in a pub. I can't believe I fell for that!"

"We could really do it one day, if you'd like to?"

"I would, yes. Tell me, at the party, did you notice Yvonne with Trevor Harris?"

"I did. He seems like a nice man and clearly he's respectable and honest. I don't think there's anything to be concerned about."

Agnes laughed. "Oh, Muriel! I'm concerned there isn't anything going on. I think they'd make a lovely couple. She's been widowed a couple of years, which is about the right interval. Do you know if he's ever been married?"

"I don't. Crystal could probably tell you, if you think it's important."

"Oh yes, of course I could ask her. Although I don't suppose it matters. Unless… He's not like the verger, is he?"

Muriel knew what Agnes wanted to hear. "Not judging by the way he was looking at Yvonne. I take it you only noticed them together actually at the party?"

Agnes gave Muriel a questioning look.

"You should have been paying attention when they arrived and left – together, both times!"

Agnes chuckled delightedly. "Muriel, there's hope for you yet!"

"Is there any hope you're going to pour that tea?"


Muriel answered the telephone. At first she thought it was a crossed line as she seemed to have joined a conversation part way through. Eventually she realised it was Beth's boyfriend Zach and he'd launched into what he wanted to say without any of the usual preliminaries. A moment later she gathered Beth had almost agreed to Muriel holding Teddy's birthday party.

"Sorry, but I went on about you being a lonely spinster who loved kids but didn't have grandchildren and how she'd be doing you a favour. Don't let on we were talking about you though. She doesn't like talking about people behind their backs, not people she likes anyway."

"That's an attitude I approve of. Where is Beth now?"

"At work. You know, the flower place?"

"Yes, I know it."

Muriel set off the moment the call had ended. She was in luck as Beth was the only person in Paula's Posies when she arrived.

"Beth, my dear, I've come to ask you again if you'd agree to my garden being the venue for Teddy's party. Talking about parties from when I was younger brought back so many happy memories which I'd very much like to relive. There wouldn't be the expense of food, as I've frozen some of the surplus from Agnes's birthday." Hopefully that would convince her there was no whiff of charity about the offer.

"Are you really sure?" Beth asked.

"Certain."

"Then thank you. It will be great for Teddy. For both of us really. Other parents at nursery invite us to things but I don't like to go too often as I can never return the favour, so Teddy misses out as well as me."

"As do the other parents. Beth, I'm sure you're invited because you're both wanted."

"You're a nicer person than me, Miss Grahame. So maybe people do really want you, not just what you can do for them."

"Less of that, young lady! Self pity is unattractive and your attitude is very rude. Yes, it will give me pleasure to host Teddy's birthday party, but I've not attempted to befriend you simply for access to your delightful son."

"I didn't mean…"

"No, I know you didn't, child. Forgive me. Now, will you let your young man help? As I said, there's no cost for the food, but a small contribution from him would pay for a few small prizes. He is very keen to be involved."

"I don't like to ask him for anything."

Muriel used the expression she'd put to good use in her teaching days when a child was being uncooperative.

Beth shook her head. "I know what you're going to say. I'm not asking, he's offering."

"I'm no expert on young men, but I understand it's possible to hurt their pride."

Beth smiled. "OK, OK, I give in. Zach can pay. Not too much though."

"Just a few pounds, I promise. Now, to the details. I assume that actually on Teddy's birthday is the best date?"

"Yes, it would be. Miss Grahame, there are eleven kids at the playgroup Teddy attends. He gets on well with them all, so how do I choose who to invite?"

"Invite them all. Eleven is quite a lot, but it's short notice so it's unlikely they'll all be able to attend. If they all do that's OK. The weather should be dry, but we have a big car port. We don't use it so a neighbour keeps their campervan in it. They're away at the moment."

"What time shall I say?"

"When do you finish work?"

"Usually three – then I collect Teddy. If we made if 3.30, that would allow everyone to come straight from nursery."

"Perfect, and perhaps we had better say a finish time. 5.30? Two hours will be long enough."

"Thanks, Mur…Miss Grahame."

"You're welcome, and please call me Muriel. I'd like us to be friends."

Muriel didn't intend to go straight in when she got home. Instead she planned to go next door to the aptly named End House and asked the men who were renovating it if it would be possible for them not to use any very noisy or dusty equipment during the two hours of the party. At the last minute she did go home – to collect the few remaining items of food from Agnes's party, not reserved for Teddy's.

"Is this a bribe?" a very young looking man asked her.

"Yes it is."

"Then I accept. And if there's anything left over from the kid's party you can count on us to dispose of that too!"

"I shall keep that in mind."

When Muriel returned home, she rang Zach and confirmed the party was to go ahead.

"Great! I'll try to get some time off work. Anything I can do to help?"

"I suggested to Beth that we have a few small treats for prizes and we thought you might like to pay for those."

"Beth agreed?"

"She did."

"Chilled! Get whatever you think and let me know what I owe you."

"It would be helpful if you could let me know how many guests to expect. Beth is inviting the children from Teddy's nursery, but if there are any family members…"

"She's not close to her family. In the year and a bit I've known her she's not seen any of them."

Beth had said her childhood hadn't been a happy one. Muriel hoped the future would be better. "You've been Beth's boyfriend all that time?" He'd implied that previously, but it had seemed to Muriel quite a casual relationship.

"Sort of. She's reluctant to commit. Because of Teddy's dad, you know?"

"No, I don't know him."

"He's not around. That's the problem."

"You know what I think would be the best thing for young Teddy? A reliable father figure who cares about him and his mother. I shall tell Beth so." Muriel was amazed at herself. She seemed to have caught a dose of Agnes's matchmaking.

# Chapter 39

## Tuesday 1ˢᵗ September

Sergeant Kirk called Crystal. "I've got an update for you. The doc confirmed there's no bruising or other indications of strangulation on Verity Houseman."

"She made it up?"

"I'm not saying that, but maybe she exaggerated? There was a lot about him looming over her and not being able to breathe and everything going black."

"She is a drama queen. There were real injuries though?"

"A slight red rash. She mentioned rough hands. Most likely she was grabbed round the throat by someone wearing hard gloves and the injury was caused by those and her struggling to get away."

"That would be scary. After what happened to Vanessa she'd think she was going to be strangled to death."

"Yeah, that's what we thought. Anything else strike you?"

Crystal tried to picture Verity scared with a man leaning over her. "She got away. He was bigger than her, had his hands around her neck holding firmly enough to leave marks, had her terrified, and she walked away from that."

"Her story is she must have passed out and he thought he'd killed her but didn't have time to check because someone came along."

"Possible I suppose."

"She thought she'd heard a dog barking and a little while earlier she'd seen Aurora Evans with a dog."

"Aurora doesn't own a dog. Shall I talk to her?"

"No, we're on it. You're to confirm whether the plumbers were all where they said they were."

Crystal did as instructed and learned from Mr and Mrs Smith that Bend's plumbers arrived at eight and spent the entire day installing a new bathroom.

"They didn't go out to lunch?" Crystal asked.

"The boss brought something with him when he came back," Mr Jones said.

"That's right. Hugh went to get a part. Everything delivered here the Friday before but something was broken," Mrs Smith said.

"He couldn't wait for a replacement to be sent as we wouldn't have had a loo!"

"Can you tell me exactly when he left and returned?"

Mr Smith looked at his wife. "No, sorry."

"The boys were in and out of the house a lot."

"They did a smashing job. Come and see."

As she dutifully admired the gleaming bathroom, Crystal wondered how easy it would be to convince the couple something was damaged when it wasn't, or even break it to give Hugh a reason to leave.

Once she'd made her escape, Crystal rang Hugh to ask if she could have a word.

"No problem if you don't mind coming here." He gave the address where he was working.

When Crystal arrived, Zach was in front of the house, getting something from the van. He confirmed the plumbers worked the whole of the previous day at the property she'd just visited. Zach and Ryan didn't leave at all. Hugh went out mid morning to replace a broken part for the flush.

"Is that usual?" Crystal asked.

"It's not usual for things to be broken, but it happens. Or pieces are missing from deliveries or we're sent the wrong thing, or need something we didn't expect to need."

"And it's always Hugh who goes for it?"

"Usually."

She'd typed his statement and had him sign it electronically when Hugh and Ryan came out.

"What's the problem here?" Hugh asked in his deep voice, as he pulled off his hard looking work gloves to reveal large, rough hands.

Crystal mustn't jump to conclusions. Lots of men had quite deep voices, and hands which showed they worked for a living. She should also avoid antagonising someone who was either innocent, or who prowled around Little Mallow strangling women. "My boss is the problem! I, er, I mean he wants statements, saying where you were yesterday."

"You can check with the people we did the job for," Hugh said. "These two were there all day. I was, except for fetching a replacement flush lever."

"I know. Zach has already confirmed you were where you said you were, but my boss likes his paperwork."

"Ryan, you stay and help the lady out. I'll carry on with Zach until it's my turn, if that's OK?"

"Perfect."

Ryan said the same as Zach.

"Was it usual for Hugh to get your lunch?"

"He buys us something once or twice a week."

"And it's always him who collects it? Sorry, as I said my boss is a stickler!" She attempted to look hard done by.

"And he's never bought me so much as a bag of crisps!"

"Often he'll get something because we pass a burger van or whatever. Or if he has to go out, like yesterday, he might bring something back. Other times he'll send one of us. That's what happened the day Vanessa Meadows was strangled. I went up to the post office and got filled rolls."

If that had been planned in advance, he hadn't told his staff, as Zach had eaten with Beth and therefore presumably wasn't expecting Hugh to provide food for him.

"When was that?"

Ryan shrugged. "I don't know the exact time. The post office was busy, so around lunchtime."

"You said Hugh didn't leave until Zach told him someone had died. If you weren't there, how can you be so sure Hugh was?" She hoped she sounded puzzled, rather than accusing.

"He'd plumbed in the downstairs toilet. We'd started that the day before. Zach and me that is, but could see it would be a pig of a job. The soil pipe was at slightly the wrong angle for standard fittings to, well to fit, and it was concreted in so we couldn't easily have moved it."

"And how did Hugh resolve this difficulty?"

"Custom shaped a coupling at the right angle. He showed me right after Zach called to say the water was back on. It was perfect – as you'd expect from him."

"And it wasn't there before Zach went on his errand?"

"Couldn't have been, could it? He hadn't made it then."

"It couldn't have been made in advance?"

"We only found the problem the night before."

Hugh could have come back in the night, but as DI Shortfellow hadn't drawn the plumbers' attention to Hugh's lack of alibi, Crystal thought she'd better not do it. "You mentioned seeing the postie that morning. Was it the usual man?" If it was, he'd go straight to the top of the suspect list as both Royal Mail and Adam had said he shouldn't have been there.

"I suppose... I'm not sure I saw his face and I don't know his name. Sorry."

"Not to worry. It's just nice to tie up any loose ends."

"Your boss really likes his Ts crossed, doesn't he?"

"Like you wouldn't believe!" Rightly, on account of Crystal having made it up. DI Shortfellow wasn't one to cut corners, but she considered him thorough rather than fussy.

To further distract Ryan from Hugh's weak alibi she said, "The people where you worked yesterday are delighted. I could see why. I'd love new tiles in our the bathroom if we could afford it. The ones we've got are hideous!"

"You could paint them."

"Really?" She'd only said it as a diversion, but it actually sounded a good idea. "Is it the same as painting walls?"

"Pretty much. You need to make sure they're absolutely clean and the grouting is neat and tidy, and buy the right kind of paint. It needs to be waterproof and hardwearing."

"That's brilliant. Thanks for your help. Can you tell Hugh I'm ready to speak to him?"

Hugh said he'd been gone almost two hours that morning, which was longer than she'd thought after speaking to the others. He explained he'd needed to go to a couple of different places before he found what he needed, and then bought lunch. When asked, he produced receipts for both.

Crystal called the DI and said Hugh's opportunity to kill Vanessa had been confirmed, and he'd had an opportunity for the attack on Verity.

"And motive?"

"I didn't mention Vanessa. He seems unaware we know how weak his alibi is. I was tempted to ask him if he knew Verity was a blackmailer, but thought it might be better to let someone more experienced do that."

"You thought correctly, Officer Clere."

"Will there be anything else, sir?"

"See if you can find out any more about the blackmailing activities of both women."

"Yes, sir."

"And well done, Crystal. Not asking the wrong question, or not asking the right one at the wrong time, isn't an easy skill to master."

Crystal believed Muriel had been blackmailed by both women. Muriel was very unlikely to make anything up and in this case it gave her a motive for a murder she'd potentially had the opportunity to commit. Crystal still needed proof.

By definition, blackmail victims wanted to keep their secrets quiet, so they weren't going to tell Crystal. They might confide in someone they trusted, such as the vicar.

Crystal went to St Symeon's church and found Arnold. It was worth asking him – he might have received confidences and although his relationship with Cameron was nothing to be ashamed of, Vanessa seemed nasty minded enough to think it was. Crystal doubted Arnold would have given in to blackmail, but he could have been approached.

When asked if that was the case, Arnold said, "No, quite the opposite. Vanessa offered to make things easier for me by telling others."

"Are you sure?" This was pretty much the only positive thing anyone had said about Vanessa, beyond her skill at manipulating plant material.

"She said something about it being difficult for a man in my position to have people wondering about such things and she was in a position to stop the rumours."

"By making your relationship public?"

"What else could she have meant? Oh... to give the opposite impression?" he looked troubled. "Perhaps... I thanked her and said it wouldn't be necessary. You see, she had an unfortunate way of saying things. I felt that, however well meaning, her input might make things worse."

"She did that kind of thing a lot?"

"I'm afraid she was something of a gossip, so if she said anything straightforward, people assumed there was more behind her words. For example, when telling a woman she was pleased to see she'd recovered from a stomach bug, she mentioned that a man, a married man, but not that woman's husband, had also suffered with it. That was true, and many others in Little Mallow, myself included, were afflicted, but something about her tone hinted at cause and effect."

Arnold's tact in not mentioning names made the story difficult to follow, but Crystal thought she'd got it. "Vanessa was hinting to the woman that she knew about an affair?"

Arnold sighed. "I thought she was attempting to make others think that, but if you're right and she was a blackmailer then yes, I think so. And yes, what she said to me about Cameron could have been an attempt to see if I wanted our relationship to remain secret."

"How did she react when you refused her help?"

"She wasn't especially happy."

"You don't look happy yourself, Arnold."

"You've made me see something else in a different light. Vanessa warned me to be careful spending time with young Adam, saying people might get the wrong idea. At the time I thought she was trying to be helpful and it made me see how very trusting Adam was. I spoke to him about it. Reminded him he should always let people, his parents or grandparents, know where he was going and who with and not to keep any secrets from them."

"That's good advice. Do you know where Jerry is?"

"The vicarage I think."

With just that little bit of help Crystal managed to locate the vicar. And his teapot and cake tin.

She began by repeating Arnold's words about Adam.

"Ah! He did approach me a while ago on the subject. I'll speak with him again. I'm as certain as I can possibly be that there's no problem."

"Me too. I'm sure nobody else thinks there's anything wrong with him spending time with the boy, but I thought that if I said so he might think I'd been looking into it."

"Yes, I see that. How did the topic arise? Assuming it's something you can share…"

"We have reason to believe Vanessa Meadows was a blackmailer. If that's true, it's a possible motive for murder. I wondered if either of you know of any potential victims."

Jerry shook his head.

"I'm not asking you to name them or reveal their secrets."

"Because you know I can't." He smiled. "In this case not just because of my job. I don't know of anyone being blackmailed, by anybody."

"Arnold said he didn't. When he considered some of the

things Vanessa said in that light, he thought she could have been trying to find out if people were sensitive on particular subjects or dropping hints about her knowledge."

Jerry sighed. "She did drop hints, and you and Arnold are right, it's possible she was trying to convey that she could talk or not as she choose. Drink your tea, help yourself to cake, and let me think."

"OK, but... Sorry about this, but we think Verity Houseman may have taken over where Vanessa left off."

Without a word, but looking troubled, Jerry left the vicarage kitchen and headed for the church.

Crystal did as instructed. She'd eaten a small slice and almost emptied the pot, by the time he returned.

"I find I cannot assure you that Vanessa Meadows was incapable of blackmail. Blackmail is very wrong. Murder is worse. If I knew of anyone who, for any reason at all, had good reason to kill her, I'd find a way to give you a hint. I know of no person I feel could be guilty."

"Thank you. And Verity... She was attacked. If she was targetted, rather than it being random, the person might try again and be more effective."

"I don't know if she's a blackmailer. I sincerely hope not, but she and Vanessa shared information and outlooks... Recently she mentioned a certain person wasn't the saint she pretended to be. Verity gave the impression she thought she was speaking in confidence to one person, but I and others were able to hear, including the subject of her remark."

"Muriel Grahame."

Jerry didn't have to answer for Crystal to see she was right. "Had Verity ever said anything like that before?"

"No, never... At least, not about Muriel."

# Chapter 40

## Tuesday 1<sup>st</sup> September

"Bert, sit down a minute. I want to talk to you." Muriel gestured to the kitchen table which held a full pot of tea and the usual accompaniments.

"What have I done wrong now?"

For a moment it hurt that he'd jumped to that conclusion just because she wanted a word. Then she saw his grin.

"I know I've been a sore trial to you, Mure, but you've got nothing on me this time."

"Nothing? You mean there's nothing I'm going to get to hear about?"

"You hear everything. People think that because you don't gossip you don't know, but they forget that while they're using their lips, you're using your ears."

She did, but not consciously. Bert knew that, he wasn't accusing her of eavesdropping or looking out for things people would rather she was unaware of.

She placed a small plate in front of Bert. Over the years a piece of cake had said so many things. I forgive you. I'm sorry. I love you. Now she wanted it to say so much more. No, not quite that. It was all the same really. Muriel lifted the cake from the tin.

"It's a bit pale," Bert began to say. His words died away as she cut into a simple Victoria sandwich, rather than the coffee and walnut which had recently been what she most often made. "Are you alright? Mure, you're not going to tell me you're ill?"

"No, nothing like that. It's your favourite, isn't it?" She indicated the cake.

He paused and then gave a small nod. "I like 'em all. Don't go thinking you can fob me off with a smaller slice of anything else because you've got it into your head the one you've just baked isn't my favourite."

She put a large piece on his plate. Should she speak now, or let him eat first? As he'd lifted the cake she kept quiet.

He put it down untasted. "What is it, Mure? You've something to say. The longer you leave it the harder it will be."

She smiled at his repeating her advice to him on so many subjects. It was very appropriate as, after more than seventy years, doing what she'd decided she must, was getting harder by the minute. He loved her, she was sure of that. Things might be difficult for a while, but she owed him the truth.

She'd thought and thought about how to say it. No approach seemed quite right, so she decided on a simple statement of fact. "Bert, I'm not your sister."

"Yes you are."

She'd tried to prepare herself for him to be shocked, hurt, angry that he'd been lied to throughout his life. It hadn't occurred to her he might not believe the truth.

"I pretended, and Mum and Dad did. It was a secret. Nobody was supposed to know."

He looked puzzled. "You've been here my whole life."

"I have, yes. I am the same person you've known since you were little, but I've never been your sister."

"But you are, Mure. Mum and Dad were your mum and dad. That makes us brother and sister."

"They were my parents, yes. They were your grandparents." She could see from his face he still didn't understand. "I'm your mother, Bert. You're my son."

He didn't say anything for quite a while.

Muriel longed to ask him what he was thinking. To answer that, he first needed to work it out for himself.

Eventually he said, "I didn't think it was true. Mum told me. She said you were my mum. It were near the end. I thought she'd got mixed up, like she did sometimes."

"Mum told you?" Muriel had wanted to tell Bert the truth as soon as he was old enough to understand. Mum said it wouldn't be fair. She'd hidden Muriel's shame for years, raised the boy as her own, now Muriel wanted to make her out to be a liar and deprive her of a son. Keeping quiet had deprived Muriel of the same thing. Muriel never had a serious relationship – she couldn't face telling new boyfriends she'd had a son, and she couldn't marry and keep the truth from her husband. If she couldn't be honest she thought it best not to get involved.

"She got a bit 'motional," Bert said.

"Not with me," Muriel said.

"I said she'd always been harder on you than me. 'Too hard,' she said. That's when she said you were my mum. I didn't think it were right. She talked like I was still at school sometimes."

In Mum's last year she'd occasionally spoken to Muriel as though the shock of her pregnancy was a fresh wound. Perhaps it was just that she'd gone back in her mind, not carried that bitterness through the years? "She spoke of Dad as though he were alive sometimes. I didn't tell her. I couldn't."

"Nor could I. And when she said you were my mum I didn't ask what she meant. I thought it was that she knew the end was near and was glad I had you."

It was probably part of that. Muriel felt certain there was more to it. Mum had finally released her from secrecy, given her back the son she'd taken at birth.

"What happened, Mure? How did you have a baby?"

"You don't know how these things happen?" He'd always been shy around girls, but...

"I meant the man. Did he make you?"

"No, no. Nothing like that. He was a navy lad, here doing specialist training. Good looking, charming and already going up the ranks. Mum and Dad liked him, until Mum found out we were... She said he wasn't to come near me again and he didn't. I don't know what he'd have done if he'd known he started a baby. His ship had sailed before I knew myself. His name was Albert. Albert Flax."

"Do you have a picture?"

Muriel shook her head. "I'm sorry."

Muriel wondered about telling Bert more. That Albert had written to her after he sailed wanting to stay in touch. She could have told him about the baby, and thought he might have married her if he'd known. Muriel hadn't wanted to be a wife and mother, not then. She didn't want to follow a sailor on his various postings, and wait dutifully at home changing nappies when he was at sea. She wanted a career and a life of her own. Her parents had wanted that for her too. She decided not to tell Bert that for a time, before his birth, she'd wanted it more than she'd wanted him.

"Why did you do it, Mure?"

"Pretend I was your sister?"

He nodded.

"I thought it best for both our futures. Things were different then. A mother without a husband, or a baby without a father, would be talked about, judged. If I'd tried to bring you up myself, I couldn't have gone to college or got a job. We'd have had no money for food or somewhere to live. No garden for you to play in." That last, she guessed, would carry the most weight.

"Mum and Dad would have helped."

"They did, by taking you on as their own. They wanted more children, so it seemed the obvious answer." Mum had suffered numerous miscarriages after Muriel's birth, something Muriel was glad Bert had known nothing of. It had been so hard for them all. Her parents probably would have helped her, even if Muriel hadn't gone along with their wishes, but at the time she'd felt she had no choice.

They drank their tea and Bert ate his cake without speaking for a while.

"I'm going to dig over the spud beds again. Every year I leave a few in and they sprout where I don't want 'em. This year I'll get out every one."

"Get enough for tea and we'll have egg and chips." The allotment was where he always went when he wanted to think, or to work through emotions. She knew him so well. Her Bert, her son.

# Chapter 41

## Tuesday 1st September

While at work, Zach thought he heard Kirianne's voice.

That was confirmed by Hugh saying, "Hello, sweetheart!"

"You left your salad behind again. Mum asked me to drop it off."

"Cheers. That's soooo incredibly kind of you."

"I know I'm a fine one to talk, but you should eat it. All that green veg and avocado will help with your cholesterol."

Zach didn't catch Hugh's response, but it made Kirianne laugh. Ryan had said Kirianne was improving. The fact she and Hugh were talking about food in a way which amused them did make it seem she must be. Zach wanted to see for himself that was true, so he quietly moved nearer.

Ryan had been right. Kirianne looked so much healthier than the last time he'd seen her, and even that had been a big improvement from when she was at her worst. He didn't still fancy her, but could see why he once had.

Zach had missed part of their conversation, but it was obvious they weren't still talking about salad.

"… feel I can be me again. I know it's awful to be pleased another person's dead, especially as the old vulture was killed."

"No, in her case it's not awful to feel like that. The world's a better place without her. Just don't say it. People might get the wrong idea."

"What and think I killed her? I'd have liked to…"

"Shh. Forget about Vanessa."

Zach crept away, wondering why Hugh sounded so worried. As Zach was thinking that Hugh didn't usually care what other people thought, Kirianne walked towards him.

"Oh! Zach I... um, hello. How are you?"

"Hello. Yeah, good." It was so awkward. She must have guessed he'd overheard some of the conversation and Zach didn't want to ask after the health of someone who'd dropped out of college due to her illness, and was still too thin.

They talked about the hot weather and then Kirianne said she'd better go, or she'd be late for work. Zach knew it was a part time job, but it was further proof Kirianne really was getting better.

Zach remembered how angry he'd been when Beth said Vanessa was horrible about Teddy. Vanessa's comments to Kirianne had been of a different nature, but no kinder – and the effect had been much more serious. How did Hugh feel about that? Was it him, not his daughter, he was worried people would get the wrong idea about? Or would it be the wrong idea? Yes, of course it would. Hugh was a good bloke, not a killer.


"I hate all the horrible rumours going round since Vanessa was killed," Beth said that evening. "It's making people suspicious and nasty."

"Yeah, I know what you mean."

"I even heard somebody say Old Bert had strangled Verity. He's such a nice man, so gentle and funny."

"Funny?"

"Yeah, he loves to moan! He can work his 'poor old back' or dodgy knees into any conversation and you can see the gleam in his eye when he spots an opening."

"Okaaay."

"Maybe you needed to be there? The other day I saw him as I walked Teddy back from nursery. We talked about the weather and Teddy told him it made him thirsty. Bert thought that was hilarious. We were near the Kale and Snail and he insisted we go there. He got juices for us, a pint for himself and crisps all round because we needed the salt."

"What was funny about that?"

"He met someone else who was just going in, got them talking about the weather, said about us being thirsty and needing the salt and all that and somehow got them to pay for all of it!"

"No!" That was quite funny, unless... "Was this a man?"

"Yes, Zach. A good looking man with a lovely Scots accent." Then she laughed. "Don't look like that. It was the verger's friend."

That didn't make Zach feel any better.

"The Verger's *boyfriend*. Nice man, well they both are, but he's really charming."

That was OK then. "Why would anyone think Bert attacked anyone?"

"Apparently Verity said the man wore gloves. Bert often does. I think to give him a chance to moan about his arthritis. I admit it's unusual to wear gloves in this heat. But anyone could put on a pair, couldn't they?"

"Yeah, 'course they could. I'm sure that Old Bert bloke is harmless, but next time you want a drink in the pub, let me buy it, OK?"

"If I get crisps as well, it's a deal."

# Chapter 42

## Wednesday 2nd September

It was going to be a tiring day for Muriel, and emotional in different ways. She must summon her courage and ask Trevor and Crystal to come and see her again. Telling them her secret would be difficult. Not as hard as she'd feared telling Bert might be, but not as easy as the reality had been.

The flower arranging session in church, which should have been relaxing and enjoyable would be marred by the presence of Verity. Would she taunt Muriel? Or reveal the truth about Bert and therefore expose Muriel as a liar, a fraud, a... No, she wouldn't speculate on what the others would think of her. Agnes had once given her a fridge magnet which said, 'what others think of us is none of our business.' She'd do well to remember that.

After flower arranging would be Teddy's birthday party. That would be the most physically tiring, but had the potential to be the most uplifting. The reactions of the adults she was far from sure about, but she was confident that with a garden to play in, and plenty of nice food to eat, the children would enjoy themselves.

Wasting useful daylight seemed justified if it conserved her energy for when she'd most need it. Muriel didn't get out of bed until all she had time to do before breakfast was water the pots and hanging baskets. After clearing up from that meal, and preparing jelly for later, she planned to do nothing but sit and read until the two police officers arrived.

Bert joined Muriel on the sofa, without saying a word. He'd not done that in a long time. When he was younger he'd sit beside her when he had a decision to make, or problem to solve, or was just unsettled. Often he'd ask her advice, but not always. He'd once said just being close to her helped him think. Presumably he was attempting to come to terms with the fact she was his mother. It would be a lot for anyone to take in, even if they usually found adapting to change relatively easy.

Muriel knew that if Bert wanted to speak, he'd do it when he was ready, so continued leafing through *The Garden*.

"Mum used to read a gardening magazine."

"Yes, she did. Actually it's the same one. The Royal Horticultural Society sends it out to members." Would that continuity reassure him?

"I do what you said, Mure. When I'm sad about Mum and Dad, I talk to them."

"I do too. I put flowers on their grave and tell them what I'm thinking."

"I don't do it there."

"No?" Muriel prompted.

"I tried, but it made me think of them being dead. Vicar saw me. Knew I was upset."

"Reverend Grande is a good man."

Bert nodded. "He said the real them isn't in the ground, but in heaven and everywhere. Like God. And if we want to talk to 'em we don't need to be in church or at a grave, we can do it anywhere."

"That makes sense." Muriel was impressed Jerry had explained it in such a way that Bert would understand, and be comforted.

"I like to talk to 'em. But it's not like when they were here."

"I know." Muriel squeezed his hand.

When Bert said no more she read the magazine, choosing an article she wasn't particularly interested in, so as not to get completely engrossed and risk missing an important cue from Bert.

"Mure?" he said after a few minutes.

"Yes, Bert?"

"I like them being our mum and dad."

"I did too."

"An' I like you being my sister."

"You've been a good brother, Bert. Really good."

"Can't you keep being my sister?"

That suggestion was something she'd never considered. That Bert might be angry with her for lying, or bitterly hurt she'd rejected him as a son, had been risks she'd faced when telling him the truth. Although she didn't like seeing him confused it had been a huge relief to face nothing worse.

"Can't we do that, Mure? Me still be your brother and you be my sister?"

Really, what Bert was proposing was little different than what her parents suggested when she'd discovered she was pregnant with him. She asked herself the same question she had then. Could it work?

She'd agreed before, for both their sakes. To allow him to grow up free from the stigma of illegitimacy, and with two loving parents instead of just one. To allow her to continue her education and follow her dream of being a teacher. It had worked then and they'd both been content, happy. If she agreed now it would be for Bert alone – so that he could continue the life her original deception had allowed him.

Yes, it would be better for Bert this way. He needn't

adapt to a change in their relationship. He needn't try to love her as a mother – and later mourn her as one. Perhaps her instinct to keep the truth hidden had been right? Had she told him, confused him, upset him, just to free herself of the fear of her secret being discovered?

No. Because of that, but not just that. She couldn't give in to blackmail. That was wrong. And it wouldn't have removed the fear. Payment only brought temporary relief to her, and rewarded and encouraged the blackmailer. There had always been the risk her secret would come out. That risk wasn't ended with Vanessa's death. She couldn't have allowed Bert to learn the truth from someone like her. Like Verity.

Now it wasn't just those women who knew. The police soon would. The idea didn't frighten her as once it would. It would be such a relief to no longer fear discovery. It would help them too. They'd said the information might help them catch the killer. No matter who their victims, murderers could not be allowed to continue. With Verity's attack it seemed the person responsible might be trying to do that. Perhaps they were both being silenced because of what they knew and had taken payment to keep quiet. A very high price indeed!

Agnes knew Muriel's secret, but Agnes had always known and it hadn't mattered. If her other friends knew, would it matter to them? Probably not. As Ellie Jenkins had said, things were very different now. What had seemed shocking when Muriel was a teacher was the norm for many of Ellie's pupils.

Muriel wasn't really still ashamed of having a child out of wedlock, and certainly wasn't ashamed of her son. She doubted that these days anyone would hold his illegitimacy against either of them. That didn't matter either way. Her own pride in her son wasn't important. Bert mattered. If he wanted her to continue as his sister, that's how it would be between them, no matter what anyone else knew or thought. "Yes, Bert. If that's what you want, I'll keep being your sister."

"Thanks, Mure."

"The other's not to be a secret now though. I must tell the police, and I'd like to tell the vicar."

"That's OK, Mure."

Shortly before the police were due to arrive, Muriel sent Bert out, to get the garden ready for the birthday party that afternoon.

"I have things to collect from the allotment."

"Well, come straight back!"

"Yes, Mure."

# Chapter 43

## Wednesday 2<sup>nd</sup> September

Crystal and Jason had intended to sleep in. A call from Anne woke them. "The DI asked me to brief you. There have been more interesting developments."

"Go on," Crystal said, as she slid out of bed.

"I hardly know where to start…"

"Anywhere," Crystal said, heading for the kitchen. "So far all your interesting developments had lived up to that description. As long as you don't miss anything out, I don't think it'll matter in what order I hear them."

"It might, but here goes. We've had the autopsy report. Captain was right – Vanessa scratched her attacker."

"Zach had fresh scratches on his arms." Which reminded her why she'd not noticed them herself. "And Arthur's arms have been fully covered each time he's been in."

"It might be more productive to let me finish each point before you start analysing it."

"Sorry." Crystal switched on the kettle.

"There was very little material under her nails. The pathologist thinks we're looking for a single set of three marks. He also said the lack of bruising suggests there wasn't much of a struggle. Rather than trying to fight him, she was reacting to not being able to breathe."

"So the killer must have been stronger than her, which means it's unlikely to have been Muriel or Vanessa's neighbour Mrs King… Sorry, had you finished the point?"

"Nope." There was a pause. "She'd ingested a sedative. It

wouldn't have completely incapacitated her, just made her drowsy." Another pause followed. "That's it for interesting development number one. You may react now."

Crystal thought Anne might actually be teasing her and wished she knew her well enough to be sure. So as not to disappoint her if she was, she put plenty of enthusiasm into her response. "Arthur works in a chemist's! I can just imagine him offering to make the tea, then Vanessa saying she didn't feel well, and him apparently concerned and coming close. Maybe putting his hand on her forehead to check for a fever. Any attempts to defend herself could well be delayed until it was too late."

Anne laughed. She turned it into a cough, but she definitely laughed. "Don't get too excited. Remember, there's almost always a beneficiary when someone dies and sometimes that person isn't a murderer."

"You're right, sorry."

"Don't sweat it. I like him for it too. But it's a prescription medication which means it'd be almost impossible for him to have got hold of some without anyone noticing – they're very careful about that kind of thing."

"They'd keep records if any went missing?"

"Neil's asking about that now."

"Any chance it's very rare and therefore easy to trace?"

"It could hardly be more common. It's regularly prescribed it short term for anxiety and insomnia."

"So, the killer brought it with them and made the tea?"

"Possibly. OK, probably," Anne said.

Crystal pondered. "It would have made killing her easier, so that puts Muriel and Mrs King back in the frame."

"We know Muriel had a motive. It's possible Mrs King

was being blackmailed too. One thing which might help, is that waiting for the sedative to work would add at least half an hour. We might... Hang on a sec."

Crystal hung on.

"Neil says none of the drug used on Vanessa has gone missing from the chemist shop where Arthur works."

"I didn't really think it would be that easy," Crystal said. "But..."

"Ooops, sorry!"

"His boss was asked the same question at the time of Arthur's mother's death."

"He was suspected over that?" Crystal asked.

"Not suspected particularly, but it was investigated. She committed suicide using those same sedatives. His was the only real evidence of her state of mind, as she'd cut herself off from most people. That was consistent with her depression, which had been diagnosed, although the doctor hadn't considered her a suicide risk."

"Ooooh!"

"Which brings us to interesting development two."

There was more? "Go on."

"Arthur is coming in this afternoon. He wants us to look at his phone again. Apparently we were too stupid to realise it proves beyond doubt that he was where he said he was at the time we're trying to make out he killed his godmother."

"Oh!"

"Quite! We're really hoping he's badly faked something that'll do the exact opposite of what he intends. You'll be joining us?"

"Of course! Thanks, Anne. Great briefing!" Crystal made

two mugs of tea and carried them back to the bedroom.

"You have to go into work early?" Jason guessed.

She could easily have said she had no choice. He'd have been fine about that. How would he feel about the truth – that although she didn't absolutely have to, she was going to get into her uniform rather than back in bed with him?

"Not exactly. Anne said one of our two chief suspects is coming for an interview, which will most likely bring us a lot nearer to solving this thing."

"You've gone from nine suspects to two already?"

"Not exactly, but two seem more likely than the rest."

Hugh had plenty of opportunity to attack Vanessa and could have been planning his revenge for months. He ran his own business and employed staff, so was used to being in control, and his reputation was important. He wouldn't have quietly paid up if Vanessa and Verity found something to blackmail him with.

There was no need to speculate over Arthur's motives – money and revenge. Maybe he was right and could prove he wasn't in Little Mallow when Vanessa was killed. If not…

"It's OK, Crystal. I get it. You can't give me the details yet, and you need to be there for that interview."

"I do, yes. It's this afternoon."

"Excellent!" Jason gave her the full benefit of his wicked grin and comical eyebrow waggle as he gestured for her to get back into bed. "I want to talk to you."

She grinned. "That's what we're calling it now, is it?"

"No. I'm counting on plenty of the steamy, naughty, saucy stuff, but we really do need to talk… About Aunt Aggie's hopes of dancing."

"You said we'd discuss it later!" She didn't want him to

propose. Well, she very much did, but not until she knew saying yes would be fair to them both.

"You don't want to?" He looked confused.

Did he mean talk, or get married? "I do." She took his hand. "I really do love you. I think we have a future..." They didn't if she couldn't be totally honest. "But we've only been together three months. We shouldn't rush into anything and there's work. It'll get in the way. For example, as I'm heading over to CID later I'm going into Gosport station early to catch up on paperwork. I don't have to, but..."

"You know that camping weekend I promised you?"

"Threatened more like!" Hotels existed for a reason.

"You know you'd love it! But... There's this amazing old ruin I've wanted to photograph for ages. I've just had a text saying I can have access for a couple of hours on the Saturday. It's not a job, so I don't have to. It'd mean delaying our trip, and yet..."

"Oh!" Was Jason explaining exactly the same situation as had been worrying her? Yes, she thought so, which meant... "You just wanted to talk about the talk, not have *the* talk?"

"Yeah. I thought we should maybe wait until you've finished your CID training. See how we both feel about everything then?"

"Good plan. And as we've saved time by not doing much talking, maybe I don't have to put my uniform on just yet."

"Oh go on. You won't need it much longer – it won't matter if it gets a bit creased!"

"CID chucked you out already?" Dil Dylan asked.

"I'm just catching up on paperwork." Leaving stuff unfinished wasn't fair and she was sure the return of the stolen bike and a few other things hadn't been written up yet. She was wrong. Trevor had caught up with everything. "And I thought he'd miss me!" she joked.

"He will. We all will."

If Crystal couldn't work on her old job, she'd use the time to try to make progress on the new one. "Sarge, do us a favour and try to strangle me."

"Do what?" Sergeant Dylan asked.

"Imagine you came across me and I was unaware of your presence. What would you do?"

"Not strangle you! I wouldn't do anything, obviously, but if I did think it was a good idea to put my hands on you, it wouldn't be round your neck."

She grinned. Not so long ago a remark like that would have made her uncomfortable. She knew him better now. He might half mean it, but he'd never do anything about it – not while she had a boyfriend and he was a senior officer at any rate. "Indulge me. I'm an evil blackmailer who you think can incriminate you as the murderer of Vanessa Meadows. Try and bump me off."

"Ah, right. I still wouldn't strangle you. I'd whack you over the head."

"I don't like that note of certainty, Sergeant Dylan! Come on, get with the programme. It's strangulation or nothing."

"OK… I suppose I'd…" he moved closer. "You've not just had a defence training refresher and want to practise your moves, have you?"

"I'm a woman in my fifties and don't know you're there."

Dil Dylan moved behind her, put his arm around Crystal's neck, grabbed her shoulder, and pulled. She'd known it was coming. He was being gentle. And, as he'd said, she was trained. Even so she wasn't at all confident she could have got away if this had been for real.

"Why would the killer have attacked Verity from in front, and how did she get away? And why, if she thought a maniac was following her, was she out walking alone?"

"You think she's making it up?" Dil asked.

"I didn't at first. Now I'm wondering. Imagine you wanted to pretend you'd been strangled, what would you do?"

"If I tell that boyfriend of yours we've been doing role play, will he dump you and you'll come to me for comfort?"

She laughed. "Behave! Now go on, fake a strangling."

He put his hands on his neck. "I don't think I could make myself do it hard enough to leave marks, not even for you. I take it that's what you want?"

"No! Please don't actually try that! But yeah, I want to know how Verity could have made those marks herself."

"Maybe pinching? That might look like finger marks."

"Anything else?"

"Scrape at her neck with something rough? A nail file?"

"You're a genius! The marks on her neck were described as rash like. So, she could have faked it, but I don't know why she would."

"She's the murderer and wants to confuse the issue?"

"Oooh, that's a thought. She does inherit some stuff and probably thought she was getting the house too." Crystal remembered Adam had seen Verity in her garden at the time Vanessa was killed. She didn't burst Dil's bubble though.

Crystal's official shift hadn't long started when Trevor got a call from Muriel asking if they would be able to visit her, as she had more to say.

# Chapter 44

## Wednesday 2nd September

While Muriel waited for Crystal and Trevor, she thought about what she would tell them and how to say it, just as she had before telling Bert. She imagined stating baldly, 'Bert, the man you know as my brother is in fact my son.' How would they react?

They'd be surprised, she was sure. Perhaps shocked initially. Not horrified. Nobody would be. What a fool she'd been to keep quiet for so long. To be so frightened of exposure. Of rejection. If Bert could accept what she'd done and love her still, what did it matter what anyone else thought anyway?

When Crystal and Trevor arrived she showed them into the lounge and brought them tea. She sat, then got up for the biscuits they'd already declined. She was ready to talk, wanted to, but couldn't quite get started.

"You have something to tell us?" Crystal prompted.

"Yes..." Muriel looked up and saw the faded photograph which had been on the mantlepiece for decades. She fetched it and handed it to Crystal. "That's me, when I was sixteen."

Both police officers looked from the picture to Muriel.

"Even I find it hard to believe at times," she said. "Everything was so different then... No, not everything. I was young and carefree and made mistakes, just as I'm sure girls do today."

"I certainly did," Crystal said.

"I got pregnant."

They both nodded understandingly. Kindly.

"To have an illegitimate child back then would have caused a scandal. It would have been humiliating for my family and ended my hopes of gaining further education and becoming a teacher. That's what I wanted; not to be a wife and mother. The boy responsible, Albert, at the time I thought I loved him and he loved me. Maybe we did in a childish way... He went away before he knew there was a baby coming." Was Albert still alive? He was only a little older than her.

"Muriel?" Crystal spoke very gently.

"Oh, yes... I was remembering. My parents wanted another child. They devised a plan. When my condition could no longer be disguised, I went away with Mum, on the pretext we were looking after an elderly relative. Mum sent back word she was pregnant with an unexpected late baby, and that the doctor advised her not to travel until it was safely delivered. He was registered and later baptised as Mum and Dad's. I suppose that's a crime, to have lied on the documents?"

"If it was, it was committed by your parents, not you," Trevor said.

Perhaps, even now, Muriel could put it right. She'd speak to the vicar. He was interested in such records and could advise her.

"And it was all done for the best of motives," Crystal added.

"I believe so, yes. It had seemed the best thing for everyone. Bert too. It freed him from the stigma of illegitimacy. That would have disadvantaged him back then."

"Bert's your son?" Crystal asked.

"Yes."

"That's what Vanessa was blackmailing you about?"

"Yes. Nobody knew you see, or at least I hadn't thought so. Keeping the secret had once been all important, and I'd done it for so long I thought I always must. I was frightened of exposure and felt ashamed of being in a position which gave Vanessa power over me. I'd felt compelled to seem friendly towards her, which increased her social standing, her confidence. I was wretched and desperate. I knew it couldn't continue, that I needed a final solution. I could have killed her, I think. I'm not strong enough to have strangled her, but if I'd seen her on a cliff edge I'd have pushed."

"I'm not sure you would," Trevor said.

Muriel smiled. "Fortunately there are none nearby, and I realised I didn't have to. That if I once said no, and meant it, she would lose her hold over me. Yes, she might tell people, but I was coming to realise that wouldn't be as disastrous as I'd feared. Certainly not as bad as allowing things to continue as they were, to escalate. I'm still coming to terms with the fact my secret hardly matters at all. Not to me now, but for others it will be different."

"You think one of her victims killed Vanessa?" Crystal asked.

"I do, yes."

"Any idea who?"

"I'm sorry, no. If I did I would tell you. I don't like Verity, but I won't have her murder on my conscience."

"You think she's still at risk?"

"She's doing the same things, to the same people." Muriel told them again about Verity's approach to her. Without revealing the woman's name she described what she'd witnessed happen to Cherry.

"How did it all start?" Crystal asked.

"Vanessa suggested I donate to a charity for unmarried mothers. She didn't say it was payment for her silence or anything like that, but I realised immediately she knew my secret. At first I felt positive about helping those who'd ended up in the same position as I'd been in and hadn't been offered such an easy way out. Then she started asking for more than money. She persuaded me to go to her home and do her little favours which implied friendship. Those small deceits ate away at me."

"Has either woman ever approached you for other charity donations? Ones which seemed genuine?" Crystal asked.

"I was convinced all Vanessa's requests were genuine until very shortly before she died. I do still think some might have been."

"You're right. We looked into her finances, as they could reveal a possible motive, and she did donate a lot of money to charity. If it's any consolation, anything you paid her most likely did go to the good causes she said would benefit."

"Thank you. That does comfort me a little."

"And Verity? You said she didn't disguise payments to her as a charity donation?"

"No. I don't know what she intended to do with the money. She's certainly been involved in genuine fundraising activities. Mostly selling her endless raffle tickets."

"You said you're sure there are other victims. Can you tell us more about that?"

"The lady I mentioned earlier is the only person I know

for certain paid money, but I've recognised my own actions and reactions in others. The apparent friendships with Vanessa, the worry on people's faces sometimes when she talked about things which seemed unconnected to them. I think those were warnings, demonstrations of how easy it would be for her to say what they paid her to keep quiet."

There was more she could say. She drank her tea as she thought about it. "I know of at least one other person who received hints that she could tell people something about them. In this case he hasn't done anything wrong, but nasty gossip from her could make it seem that way." Muriel couldn't bring herself to repeat what the evil Vs alleged about Bert.

"Arnold?"

"No… Poor verger. He'd worry terribly about nasty lies being spread about him." Was it the same thing – that there was something wrong about Adam spending time with him? Muriel didn't believe it, but others might.

"We don't think he has any secrets. There is his relationship with Cameron."

"Nobody minds about that. We're happy for him." Possibly there were those who felt differently. If so, they'd kept their opinions to themselves. People did talk about it, and if they learned Bert was her child they'd talk about that too. For a while. Then there would be a new topic of gossip and life would move on.

"Thank you for telling us all this, Muriel. I know it must have been hard. I can assure you we won't share the information except where absolutely necessary to conduct our investigation."

"That doesn't matter now. I just hope it will help?" That wasn't quite true. Hope wasn't her only emotion, not even the main one. Telling Bert, when she'd finally done so, had been so easy it was only now sinking in that she was free. She no longer had to watch what she said, fear what others might say, or worry Bert wouldn't understand, wouldn't forgive. Even if their secret were published in the Little Mag, Little Mallow's community newspaper, it could no longer hurt them.

"Oh yes. Most definitely. Not just with the murder, but also in finding who attacked Verity."

"They're the same person, surely?" Muriel asked.

"From what you've told us that does seem most probable, but it's far from certain. We have to keep an open mind."

"Two stranglers in Little Mallow?" That was an alarming possibility.

"It does seem unlikely," Crystal agreed. "But clearly there's at least one, so you take care of yourself, until we get him locked up. Which we will, thanks to people like you sharing all they know."

# Chapter 45

## Wednesday 2$^{nd}$ September

"Poor Muriel!" Crystal said as she and Trevor drove away. "I can see now why she was so traumatised about standing up to Vanessa. She might have done it in a slightly passive way, but that's what she did."

"She's free of the worry of it now at least, and you did a great job of showing her she did the right thing."

"I hope so. I don't think it moves the investigation on. There are potentially lots more blackmail victims, which means more people with motives we're unaware of. It's possible there was someone else in Grassy Lane we don't yet know about. Nobody we've spoken to was a great witness as they were all concentrating on other things. Mrs King was gardening, Beth and Zach occupied with each other, Muriel was in a state, the plumbers were working – unless any of them were bumping Vanessa off."

"I can't help you with who did it, lass, but I wouldn't mind betting Vanessa was killed for something she said."

"That's another bet you're not going to get anyone to take, Trevs! Right, what's next then?"

"What time are you due in CID, lass?"

Crystal checked her watch. "Arthur is coming in, to explain to DI Shortfellow where he's gone wrong with his investigation, in just over an hour."

"You can't miss that! Pity I have to, but there's a cat fight in Rowner I have to break up."

"Okaaay."

"Some old dear is feeding all the neighbourhood cats and shutting them in her house, saying their owners starve and neglect them. The owners say she's stealing them."

"That sounds like fun." It very much didn't.

"Maybe one of the owners will be my age, single, and have lovely bright blue eyes?"

"Like my cousin Yvonne?"

"Get yourself off to CID, lass." He pointed dramatically in vaguely the right direction – if she'd been flying there.

"Will do. And you make sure the cat women don't get their claws into you."


As Crystal passed Ellie's house she saw her friend in the garden, so stopped to say hello.

"Got time for a cuppa?" Ellie asked.

Crystal checked her watch. "I've got twenty minutes. I really can't stay longer as our prime suspect is coming in for interview."

"Oooh. Can you tell me anything about that?"

"I shouldn't…" Crystal said as she followed Ellie inside.

"Then don't. What I most want to know is that he's locked up and can't hurt anyone else, and I guess you're not quite there yet."

"We're not." She hoped they were close, but didn't feel able to give Ellie that reassurance.

"There is something you want to tell me though?"

Ellie was right. Since the birthday party, Crystal hadn't spoken to anyone but Jason about Aunty's comments concerning dancing and weddings. She hadn't been sure there was anything to tell beyond the fact Aunty had been up to her tricks again. Crystal still thought they were right to wait a while, but after she and Jason had mentioned their concerns. she was confident they'd be announcing their engagement sometime next year. This was too big to keep to herself for long. As Ellie made tea, Crystal repeated Aunty's words as accurately as she could remember, ending with, "I think it was a hint she'd like us to get married."

Ellie grinned and shook her head. "I don't."

Really? "What else could it have been?"

"An order!"

"Ha! Yeah. Subtlety hasn't always been her strong point." Crystal drank some of her tea. She wanted to say the next bit calmly, not squeal it like a little girl picked to play the fairy princess in a school play. "It won't be for months, but I'm pretty sure Jason's going to propose."

"You don't have to accept, because he asks or it's what your family want."

"Yeah, I…"

"Like the service says, marriage shouldn't be taken on lightly."

"I know that."

"It's a big commitment for the rest of your life. You have to be really sure."

"I know, Ellie! Sheesh, I wasn't thinking of popping over to Vegas next week just because I have an urge for iced fruit cake and to see how I'd look wearing white!"

"OK. Right. Sorry. It's just you've not been together all that long and I know how much Agnes means to you. I didn't want you rushing into something for her sake and regretting it later. My parents… they were kind of pushed into getting married. They're happy now, but when I was a kid they split up for a while. It was awful – for all of us. I wouldn't wish that on anyone."

"I'm so sorry, Els." Her childhood experience, plus her strong religious faith went some way to explaining why, after years of her loving Mike and people assuming the pair of them would marry, Ellie was still single. "I'm not going to rush into anything, I promise you."

"So, what is troubling you?"

Crystal wasn't troubled, not now, but she wanted to reassure Ellie she wasn't going to rush into a huge mistake. "There's a lot to think about. Our work mostly. He's away a lot. So far I don't mind. In fact it's a good thing. I can stay with Aunty regularly without her feeling a burden, which she absolutely isn't. But long term, how will I feel when he keeps going off to interesting places and I'm stuck at home?"

"Yeah, I get that. You can't just drop a case to carry his bags, if you'll excuse the pun."

"I will – but will he get fed up with the fact I won't be able to drop a case for pretty much anything? I'll be late home a lot, miss things he wanted me to be there for. Miss things I wanted to be there for. I've not even started the job yet, so I don't know how it'll work out."

"No, but it will work out, Crystal. I'm sure of that – if you really want it to. If you really love him."

"I definitely love him, and yeah, I do think we'll find a way to make it work." She took a big breath. "And if you want my advice, you and Mike should have a talk. Explain to each other what's holding you both back. I'm sure you can work things out to."

"Want some of my advice?" Ellie asked.

"Go on."

"Get yourself over to CID or you're not going to have a job to worry about!"

As was so often the case, Ellie was right.


"Well?" Arthur was smug, there was no other word for it.

The DI slid Arthur's phone from its position between him and Neil, towards Crystal, so she could get a better look at the two photographs which allegedly provided a waterproof alibi.

One was a beautiful and atmospheric scene of mist trails on what Crystal assumed was part of the Peak District. "That's lovely," she said. It really was. The next was a shot of a castle, nicely framed by a tree at the top and wild flowers below. Presumably Peveril, as that's where he said he'd been. She also presumed the DI wasn't waiting for a critique on Arthur's technical skill.

She swiped to see if there were more. There was nothing after those two, so she went backwards. That revealed a photo of a beautiful, blonde young woman, with a big hill in the background – almost certainly another part of the Peak District. "Who is this?" she asked, turning the phone towards Arthur.

"Nobody!" Arthur snatched it back. Then, more calmly, said, "I took that a different day so it doesn't help. But if you check the last two, you'll see the first one was taken at 8.45 on the twenty-fifth of August and the second one nearly two hours later. They prove I couldn't have been in Little Mallow in time to kill my godmother."

"May I?" Neil extended his hand and was given the phone. He went back to the misty shot and showed the DI and Crystal the information on the screen was exactly as Arthur had said. He repeated that for the image of the castle.

"That's very helpful, thank you," DI Shortfellow said. "We'll return your phone as soon as possible."

"You'll return it now."

"These photographs are evidence," the DI said.

"They are. The phone isn't. Send them to your computer or whatever, if you must."

Without either his permission to keep it, or a warrant, they had no choice. Neil tapped away, then returned the phone.

"Mr Rendall, if you had visited Vanessa Meadows, how would you have got there?"

Arthur seemed thrown by the question.

"Would you have come by train?" the DI prompted.

"Oh, yes, yes I suppose so."

"And from the station to her house?"

"A bus perhaps, or a taxi."

"Is that how you got here this time?"

Arthur smirked. "I didn't come. I've just proved that."

"My apologies, I wasn't clear. I meant when you came down after learning the news, so that you could help with our enquiries." The DI did a pretty good impression of someone who knew he'd made a mistake.

"I brought my bike. I didn't know how long I'd be staying and there would be things to do, so I thought I'd need it. Do you want to see it?"

Despite being told that wasn't necessary, he showed a photo of a garish bicycle which would be hard to miss, or mistake for one belonging to someone who didn't want to stand out.

"Thank you. Is there anything more you can tell us? Perhaps you've had a chance to think about who may have had a grudge against your godmother?" The DI sounded as though he was clutching at straws and only Arthur could possibly help him crack the case.

"Everyone she met, I expect!"

"That's right from what I've found out, sir," Crystal said, hoping it was the correct thing to say.

"She taunted me. I'm going to set up a bike hire business. For years I've been doing a job I hate to raise the money. It's hard on my own. Mum left me the house but almost no cash. Vanessa kept saying she'd help. She could easily have afforded to, but kept putting it off. And with her will, she'd say I was going to inherit, then changed her mind saying I was a selfish boy. Boy! And she'd…"

Crystal wasn't totally sure if he'd stopped speaking or his voice had got so high pitched she couldn't hear it.

"Could you show me your arms, Mr Rendall," the DI asked after a pause.

Arthur pulled back both sleeves, to reveal red, sore looking skin. Eczema or psoriasis Crystal guessed. There were a lot of scratches. If any were from Vanessa or Verity it would be impossible to tell those apart from the ones Arthur had inflicted on himself. He shoved his sleeves back down. "I know what you're doing! You're trying to humiliate me to get back at me for showing up your own incompetence in not investigating this properly!"

"Will you consent to providing a DNA sample, Mr Rendall?" the DI asked.

"No! This has gone far enough. I'm leaving now."

# Chapter 46

## Wednesday 2nd September

Verity wasn't in the flower room of St Symeon's church when Muriel arrived. The hope she was still too shaken by the attack she'd suffered was dashed a few minutes later.

"I wasn't sure if I'd be up to it, but I didn't want to let you down," Verity said. She showed off the rash on her neck and received words of sympathy for her ordeal.

To Muriel's ears, it all sounded very false.

"What were you doing in the woods anyway?" Aurora asked.

"I saw two people go in... people I wouldn't have expected to see together. One of them is married..." She looked straight at Aurora.

"Yes, I was there. What are you trying to suggest? That I'm having a steamy affair, or that I stood by and watched someone strangle you?"

"No, I..."

"We've all had enough of your insinuations, Verity Houseman. You'd better be careful what you say in future."

Those words from Aurora, and the silence from Agnes and Mary, gave Muriel confidence. "Verity, I've decided that in future I shall make all my charity donations myself, not through anyone else."

If Aurora and Mary were confused by that, they didn't say so.

Agnes, who would be aware Muriel had just refused to pay blackmail, did speak. "Good idea, Muriel. It isn't fair to give Verity that extra work when she already does so much. I think we should all make everyone aware they shouldn't put her to that trouble."

The point was very clearly not lost on Verity. Aurora and Mary couldn't have fully understood, but their expressions showed they realised Verity had been put in her place.

A few minutes later Verity said, "I think I'm still suffering from what happened to me. I shall go home and rest."

"Would you like a lift?" Aurora asked the question gently.

"No thank you. The fresh air will do me good."

This was turning out to be such a good day! Muriel might still be Mure to Bert, but she was no longer mured; trapped by secrets. She was free. Even her slight doubts over Teddy's birthday party vanished and she was sure the event would be pure joy.

Muriel gave thanks for the glorious weather as she waited for the guests to arrive. The garden looked wonderful. A few balloons and pretty bunting, borrowed from Ellie Jenkins, gave it a child friendly celebration look. Nobody was likely to suspect the bunting's chief purpose was to keep the guests away from areas where they could cause damage either to the garden or themselves.

Fifteen minutes before the party was due to start, Muriel's doubts returned. It had been so long since she'd had much to do with children. They probably hadn't changed much, but what about her? She no longer had the authority of a teacher or the energy of youth, and the party wasn't really hers. She wanted to get it right for Beth. And for Teddy.

To add to her worries, a woman with a toddler and baby arrived early. "Sorry to bother you. Um, do…"

"Where party?" the toddler asked.

"Here!" Muriel told the child, then addressed the mother. "You're in the right place. Beth and Teddy won't be long."

"Oh, sorry. I didn't know."

Muriel didn't like to ask what the woman didn't know. Nor did she wish to stand in awkward silence. "Beth and I are friends." She very much hoped that's how Beth saw their incipient relationship. "As she doesn't have a garden and I do, we decided to hold the party here. I'm Muriel." She held out her hand.

"Sophie," the woman mumbled as she briefly touched Muriel's hand.

"And these two are?"

"Oh, sorry."

Thankfully before Sophie got through the ordeal of reciting her children's names, Beth and Teddy arrived. Sophie seemed no more at ease then, but her eldest child greeted Teddy enthusiastically and extracted a wrapped gift from the baby's pram.

It was clear Teddy was itching to take it, but trying to be patient until it was offered.

"Do go through into the garden," Muriel invited.

Sophie obeyed quickly, the children streaming after her.

Beth, who'd hung back a little said, "I'd say sorry for not getting here before Sophie, but she's probably apologised more than enough for both of us!"

Muriel smiled, glad of Beth's relaxed manner. "She has, yes."

"How shall we do this? Do you want to greet people as they arrive, or shall I do that and send them out to the garden?"

"It might be best if you do. Sophie was looking for you."

"OK, then. I'll just have a quick look at where I'm sending them…" They followed behind Sophie.

"Oh, wow! It looks fab, Muriel. Thank you so much for doing this." With a wave to Bert, Beth went back out the gate and disappeared from sight.

Muriel was spared agonising small talk with Sophie by her son and Teddy both insisting they watch the birthday boy unwrap his gift.

Oliver handed it over and Teddy thanked him as formally as if they were performing a business transaction. Then Teddy ripped frantically at the paper. He revealed a glove puppet in the shape of a brightly coloured giraffe. Sophie showed how a stretchy piece of fabric could be pulled all the way down Teddy's small arm to form an appropriately long neck. He set off with his arm held high, and Oliver in pursuit, showing the giraffe the garden. The two boys somehow collected Bert as they reached him and he pointed out things the giraffe was most likely to want to see.

"That was a success, what a wonderful gift," Muriel said to Sophie. On receiving no response but a blush, Muriel asked where Sophie had bought it.

"I made it," she mumbled, confirming Muriel's guess.

"How very clever!"

The other guests arrived close together.

Beth followed, informing Muriel, "That's everyone."

The everyone didn't include Zach. Muriel wondered why, but didn't risk spoiling Beth's sunny mood by asking.

# Chapter 47

## Wednesday 2nd September

After Arthur stomped out of CID, the DI recapped what they knew so far, for the benefit of the whole team. Basically they still couldn't entirely rule anyone out. Not even Arthur. "Without access to his phone, we can't be sure those photos weren't faked in some way."

"Sir, may I show them to my partner? He's a professional photographer and might have some ideas." Crystal knew CID had experts to analyse anything technical, but as the DI said, there was nothing yet to pass on to them.

"Very well."

"I wish we had more than those two. It would be interesting to compare those with the others on his phone." Crystal thought the 'evidence' photos of a higher standard than the other two she'd seen, but didn't know enough to be sure.

"Two?" Neil asked in mock surprise. "When I was given permission to copy them, I thought Mr Rendall meant all those mentioned in the interview, so I included the one of the blonde."

"I'm certain you were correct to do so. Our Mr Rendall has been very keen to co-operate, hasn't he?" the DI said.

"Sir, are we working on the assumption both attacks were carried out by the same person for the same reason?" Anne asked.

"You know better than to assume anything, DC Hetherington."

"Sorry, sir I meant…"

He waved her apology away. "Blackmail is a strong motive and there may be more victims we don't know about. That may be the reason for both attacks, but there are other possibilities. Arthur's motive is just as strong."

"He's playing games with us, sir," Neil said.

"Indeed. I don't think we have quite enough on him to hold him, or force him to give up his phone, or provide a DNA sample, but I am pushing for that."

"Arthur doesn't have a reason to kill Verity Houseman," Captain said.

"She hasn't been killed," the DI pointed out.

"She could have been trying to blackmail him," Crystal said. "I've heard that hinted, but don't see how she'd know he was guilty – if he was."

"What about the plumber, Mr Bend?" Anne asked. "He had motive and opportunity for Vanessa and we know he had the opportunity to strangle Verity."

"That's right, Aurora Evans saw him when she was walking her neighbour's dog," Captain said. "She saw Verity again after that, in good spirits. Looking suspiciously pleased with herself is how she put it. Mrs Houseman was quite vague over the timing though, so it's possible she went back for some reason and he followed her."

"Let's see what Kyle has to say, shall we?" the DI said.

"Who?" Crystal asked.

"Exactly," he said and strode away.

Crystal raised both hands in Anne's direction in an 'eh what???' gesture.

"Kyle is the real name of Hugh Bend the plumber. Do keep up!" Anne followed the DI.

It took Crystal a second or two to realise that was meant literally as well as figuratively and she hurried after them. She caught up as they reached an interview room.

"Anne, you're to lead the interview. Crystal, you're observing only."

"Yes, sir," the women said in unison.

Hugh didn't wait to be questioned before saying, "I didn't kill or attack anyone but, as you know I was close by both times. I want to clear a few things up. Did all this happen because of blackmail? That's what I've heard."

"We're considering a variety of possibilities, sir," Anne said. "If you could tell us…"

"There's nothing they could have used against me, and I wouldn't have paid if there was. I have a family to support. Vanessa tried digging, at least it felt like that. She kept saying what a close relationship I have with Kirianne. 'Almost as though she was my child' is how she put it. Vanessa said some people might be jealous of our relationship, or misunderstand. I should be careful not to be too affectionate in public. It was horrible, and now that Verity woman's started insinuating things."

"About Kirianne?" Anne asked.

That wasn't what Crystal would have asked, but then she'd probably have tried to interrupt before he got to the bit she most wanted to know about.

"No, about Vanessa. Saying I had a reason to want her dead."

"But you didn't?"

"Honestly, I don't care what the likes of her might say about me. Nobody who knows me would believe it. I didn't hurt either woman, but I was angry and warned them to shut up. I'm a big bloke, it may have seemed threatening." He ran his hands through his hair. "OK, I shook her by putting my hands on her shoulders. Maybe she thought I had ideas of strangling her. And maybe I did."

"This is Verity Houseman you're talking about?"

"No, Vanessa."

"And when was this?"

"Weeks ago. Not sure exactly. Maybe a month."

"Why did you do it?"

"She was making my daughter's life hell, tormenting her, saying she was fat and ugly. She never was, but after Vanessa started on at her she practically stopped eating... Being sick and all that. We took Kirianne to the doctor and the whole thing came out. Vanessa had said even Kirianne's own father didn't want her. She's legally my daughter now, but her mum was expecting before we met and the bloke didn't want to know, so I've been her dad since before she was born. I adopted her when Kate and I married. Vanessa wanted to push us apart, make us miserable – all of us."

"Did either woman blackmail you, or attempt to?"

Crystal was impressed with the calm way Anne was handling this, and had brought the interview under control.

"Vanessa never did. It wasn't about the money with her. She just liked to control people. Verity's different. She tried. I think she really believes I'm the murderer. She's wrong, and wrong to think I'd pay to keep her quiet. I told her that and warned her to keep away."

"Did you put your hands on her? On Verity Houseman?"

"I did not."

Anne took him through his movements when Verity was attacked. He'd left Ryan and Zach working in the house and gone to buy a replacement for a flush lever which had arrived damaged. While doing that he'd spotted Verity. "Looked like she was spying on my accountant, Aurora Evans. That short woman with all the red hair?"

"Yes, sir. We know who you mean."

"Aurora was walking a little dog. Verity was creeping about like a spy in some spoof film behind her. I followed and when Verity saw me, I warned her to leave people alone. Then I bought burgers for me and the boys and went back to work."

"What are your thoughts?" the DI asked afterwards.

"He has clear motive for the murder and by his own admission has a temper," Anne said. "However, Vanessa's death wasn't a spur of the moment thing. I can't see him drugging her and hanging around for half an hour while it worked – or her inviting him in for tea and letting him make it."

"She was expecting a visitor," Crystal pointed out. "She'd been to his house at least once and spoke to Kirianne numerous times. Maybe they knew each other better than we thought? And Hugh got his staff out the way…"

"It could be argued Zach was put in the way," Anne said.

"Hugh was setting him up?" Crystal asked. If he was ruthless enough to strangle Vanessa, he wasn't likely to worry about letting someone else take the blame. And if he'd done both of those things, and was being blackmailed about it, he wouldn't just politely ask the person to stop.

"Verity's description of her attacker fits Hugh well and he could easily have gone back after Aurora saw him. Maybe Verity looked pleased with herself because she'd rattled him and didn't realise she'd made a taunt too far?"

# Chapter 48

## Wednesday 2nd September

Nine further children arrived for Teddy's party, two of them babies. It seemed more. And they all had adults with them.

Bert organised energetic games. He had Sophie holding one end of the finishing line, stopping music, or replacing burst balloons as required. Whether he'd realised Sophie's unease and wanted to help her, or just spotted someone who looked as if they'd do as he asked, the young woman soon started enjoying herself. The children were even happier. It was wonderful to have them running around and laughing. Muriel felt incredibly nostalgic for her days as a teacher.

Just as it appeared nothing could go wrong, an unco-ordinated child in a sack veered off the course Bert had marked out. He landed sprawled in a rhododendron bush. It did look funny as he bounced back off the wiry stems. Muriel, and others, hastened to check he was OK. His laughter reassured them. The shrub had cushioned his fall and the sack protected him from scratches.

"Oh dear, I hope he hasn't caused any damage. It looks very flat." The mother, thankfully not Sophie, said.

"I'm sure it will be fine," Muriel assured her.

It was a tough plant which had got a bit big for its location, so if it did need to be cut back that might be a good thing. Bert gave it a shake, encouraging it to regain some of its previous stature.

By the end of the first hour Muriel was still happy, but very glad she wouldn't be going back to work in St Symeon's at the start of the term. Children were even more exhausting than she'd remembered, and so loud! She approached Beth and asked if it would be a good time for them to put out the food.

"In ten minutes? Zach will be here then and it looks like the kids are just beginning to calm down a little bit, so they should be ready then."

"Perfect."

When Zach arrived, Muriel signalled for Bert to come and help carry out food. Sophie came with him, so getting everything outside was a quick job. Zach brought with him a huge traybake birthday cake, and two large packets of crisps. Those, and everything else bar a few of the least interesting sandwiches, were soon eaten.

More games followed, some involving parental participation. Muriel was very pleased there were enough adults to go round and she could simply watch and cheer. She was even more pleased when Beth allowed Zach to partner Teddy, while she flopped down at Muriel's side.

"This is really amazing, Muriel. Thank you so much."

"I'm glad you agreed to it. I'm enjoying it enormously."

"Everybody is, I think. Even Sophie!"

"Did you know she made the puppet they gave Teddy?"

"No way!"

"You might want to ask her about it sometime."

"Yeah, good thinking."

Muriel had forgotten about the colouring books and packs of crayons she'd bought until Bert announced it was time for the prizes. "Who won something?" he asked.

Several hands, including Teddy's, shot up. Bert handed those children their gifts, inviting everyone to clap.

"Who was bounciest?"

"That's you love," said the mother of the child who'd fallen onto the rhododendron, pushing him forward.

Bert gave him a book and crayon set.

"You three," Bert indicated those who'd not yet won anything. "Get the judges's special prize for being really good." It wasn't clear whether he meant well behaved or talented, but everyone clapped as he awarded them exactly the same gifts as their friends had received.

Zach quietly asked Muriel how much he owed her.

"How does ten pounds sound?"

"Cheap! But it's a deal." He paid, then offered to wash up and proved he meant it by adding, "But not drying and putting away as I'd put it all in the wrong place."

Bert said that was his job and the two of them began gathering up the cutlery and crockery. Muriel would have taken the opportunity to remark on Zach's consideration and helpfulness. She didn't need to as several other young mothers did that.

Beth, Teddy and Zach were the last to leave.

"Thank you for my party, More-ree-oil," Teddy said. "Liked it lots and lots!"

"You're very welcome, young man," Muriel said, trying to contain her amusement at his pronunciation of her name.

"It's been lovely. Thank you," Beth said.

"Yeah, nice one," Zach said.

"I might go down the allotment later," Bert said, once they'd closed the gate after Beth.

"Aren't you tired after all that running round? I'm exhausted and I was only watching," Muriel said.

"A bit," he admitted. "But I've got watering to do."

"When you've done the vegetables, maybe you'd like to quench your own thirst with a beer in the pub. You've earned it."

"I might do that."

Muriel decided to have a nap, as she'd unintentionally done after Agnes's party. If anything, although very happy, she was even more tired.

First she'd check for damage in the garden. If there was a broken stem or two she'd rather trim them back now, while still feeling the glow from the party, than see them wilted in the morning.

The rhododendron was showing very little in the way of flatness. Hard to believe a person, even a small one, had landed on it with force. It looked more as though she'd carefully pushed her arm in, perhaps to put mulch over the roots.

Muriel recalled getting inside the laurel hedge at the top of Grassy Lane on the day Vanessa was killed. It had been so easy to do. She now realised that was because she'd not been the first person to do it. She'd been puzzled why she'd gone in at all.

The bicycle! She'd noticed a bicycle pushed into the hedge as she'd walked down the lane. She'd been so concerned about confronting Vanessa she'd paid little attention. It hadn't been the vicar's rickety old machine, or she'd have wondered where he was. It wasn't like Arthur Rendall's sleek and easily noticed bicycle either. Just a plain, ordinary looking thing.

When she came back it was gone and its removal had created an enticing gap. It probably didn't mean anything, and no lasting damage had been done to the hedge, but

Crystal had been very keen to know if Muriel had seen anyone else that morning. This was proof someone had been there. Muriel would call her as soon as she got in.

As Muriel walked around she was aware of someone else in the garden. Maybe one of the guests had left something behind, came to fetch it and didn't like to disturb her. She couldn't see anyone. "Hello! Anyone there?"

There was no reply, but the side gate was open. She'd made very sure it was closed when the last guest left, and Bert wouldn't have left it open. Foxes came in otherwise and caused a lot of damage digging in any soft earth, which was usually where tender new seedlings had just been planted.

Maybe she'd been right and somebody had returned for something, but instead of sensing them arriving they were in fact leaving? She'd decided that was the case when she heard a footfall on the path.

Muriel span round to see a man who had no business being there. Before she could say a word he reached out his hands and put them around her neck. Muriel was too terrified to say anything. Too shocked to attempt to reason with him or shout or scream in hopes the builders working on the house next door would hear. She couldn't move, not even attempt to step away.

He squeezed.

It hurt so much. That pain brought her back to her senses.

This then was Vanessa's killer. The person who'd attacked Verity and would murder her. Now the first shock had passed Muriel was able to move. Her strength was no match for his. She could have called for help, but had no breath to do it. Her vision blurred. Then everything went black and she knew it was all over.

# Chapter 49

## Thursday 3rd September

Although she'd miss her colleagues, Crystal wasn't going to miss the pig of a commute from the flat she now shared with Jason, into Gosport police station. She'd only done it a handful of times and it was already getting her down. She'd started to moan about it when she caught sight of Trevor's expression. "What?"

"It's Muriel. Someone strangled her yesterday afternoon."

"What? No, no. Why didn't anyone tell me?" Crystal tried to swallow her fury. It was the attacker she was angry with, not her colleagues.

"Dil Dylan called your DI. As Muriel wasn't conscious and Bert was with her, it seemed best to leave them alone."

Eighty-eight and deprived of oxygen to the point of losing consciousness couldn't be good. "And now?"

"I don't know, lass."

"What happened?"

"I don't know that either. Sorry. It's been passed to CID."

"And don't think you're swanning off there," Sergeant Freedman said. "I've got a routine enquiry for you."

"Right, skip, sure. What is it?" She was a professional. She could push down her worry and do her job.

"You're to check on the alibi of Arthur Rendall at the time Muriel Grahame was attacked. DC Hetherington will brief you."

As they walked over to the library, Crystal phoned Anne. First she asked about Muriel.

"Conscious and stable, after being on oxygen most of the night. It happened in her garden. She'd had a kiddies party and a decorator working in the house next door was promised any leftovers. Some sort of joke apparently. When she didn't answer the door he saw the side gate open, and went into the garden. He initially thought she was dead, and the DI won't mind if Arthur Rendall gets that impression, but we're not to bring up the subject."

"OK. What's the deal with him?"

"He claims he was in Gosport library at the time. He bought a coffee and has the receipt and he photographed something from the local records there and is sure his phone records will back him up even if the person he requested the book from doesn't remember him, which they probably will as he stayed late and they had to ask him to leave. Plus he was wearing that goppingly awful pink and yellow outfit. I'm sending you a picture."

"OK. Why is he a suspect? "

"He wasn't particularly until he offered a lot of information nobody asked for."

"Just like he did with Vanessa's death."

"Indeed."

"How about when Verity was attacked? Didn't he say he was on a bike ride?"

"He did, but not until asked and he can't back it up."

"Interesting."

"Indeed." She chuckled. "That seems to be my word of the week!"

Crystal wasn't amused. "What time did the attack on Muriel take place?" They'd reached the library by then, and Crystal nodded when Trevor made a few gestures she assumed meant, 'Shall I go in and ask?'

"About six, we believe."

"Anne, the library closes at five, and it'd only take him a few minutes to cycle to Little Mallow. Arthur doesn't have any kind of alibi!"

"There was a book launch last night. He says he didn't notice they'd closed to the public until he was asked to leave, shortly before seven."

That did sound fishy.

"I'll be talking to Muriel, as soon as the hospital will let me. I'll be nice, I promise. I'll update you on how she's doing."

"Thanks."

Inside the library, Trevor had found a member of staff who recognised Arthur's photo. She fetched someone else and it was confirmed Arthur had been discovered after they'd officially closed and was asked to leave. "We do a sweep round at five, to make sure nobody's shut in overnight. There wasn't any danger of that yesterday and things were a bit hectic getting ready for the event, so maybe we weren't very thorough."

"And it definitely wasn't until nearly seven you spotted him? You couldn't be confused and it was only just after five?"

"No. I checked my watch to see if we had time for a cuppa, which we didn't."

"What time did he arrive?" Trevor asked.

The lady who'd kicked him out shrugged.

"He spoke to me at about two," the other said. "I can't be exact, but it was quite a while after lunch, and quite a bit before we closed. He was annoying. I don't mind people asking for help, it's what we're here for. He seemed to think I was going to do his research for him."

"What was he researching?"

"Stuff about bicycles. Waste of time. It was very specialist stuff he wanted to know and we don't carry that kind of thing."

"OK. Thanks."

As they walked away, Crystal said, "He was lucky."

They'd nearly got back to the police station, when someone ran after them, calling, "Police, stop!"

"Isn't that our line?" Trevor asked as they turned to see what the problem was.

A third member of library staff rushed up to them. "I heard you say someone was lucky and asked Lisa what it was about. I don't know if it matters, but I asked Lisa how you knew and she said you didn't because she didn't," the woman gasped.

"Could you try that again, a bit more slowly?" Trevor asked.

"I don't know why you think he was lucky, but I thought he was because his phone was handed in."

"Oh?" Crystal prompted.

"He left without it and came back for it later."

"Do you know what times those things happened?" Crystal asked.

"I don't know when he left. The phone was handed in about four. He came back around six. Normally he'd have been out of luck, but we were setting up for the author signing, and I'd been out to collect the wine we'd ordered. I remembered him from earlier and it was me who took the phone in, so I let him in and gave it to him. I've just heard he didn't leave afterwards."

"Thank you, that's really helpful."

"So, his phone has an alibi, but he doesn't," Crystal said as they walked back into the station.

"You reckon he did it, lass?"

"Why else fake an alibi? He's been messing us about, but he'd have no reason in advance of Muriel being strangled, to think we'd care where he was yesterday afternoon and he was setting it up hours before this happened. Did you know about the party Muriel had?"

"No."

"Neither did I. Bet he didn't either and had to hang about until everyone left. He'd probably hoped to get back to the library before closing time."

"So he attacked Verity and killed Vanessa too?"

"I think so. Trouble is, we still can't prove he was in Little Mallow when Vanessa was killed. His phone records would show us, but he's refused to hand it over." Crystal had a happy thought. "Arthur has just made his phone evidence. That should give the DI his warrant!"

Crystal was further cheered by the news Muriel was well enough to answer questions, and expected to be allowed home later that day.

"By the way," Anne said. "The house next door to Muriel's isn't just being decorated."

"No, it's practically being rebuilt." Why did Anne think she'd care about End House?

"Which includes plumbing. Hugh Bend is doing it. Two people remember seeing his van parked there yesterday afternoon – but nobody saw the man himself."

# Chapter 50

## Thursday 3rd September

When Zach went to fetch a radiator bleed key from the van, he saw Kirianne getting out of her car. "Hiya. Your dad's upstairs," he said.

"Actually, it's you I've come to talk to. Got a minute?"

As it was Hugh who'd sent him out, for something Zach knew wasn't needed yet, he probably had.

"The thing is... I want to apologise for breaking up with you the way I did. I was in a bad place back then."

"I realise that – now. I'm sorry I didn't do more to help."

"It's not your fault, Zach. It's not mine either. I was ill. I've been having counselling and it's working. I feel good about the future. Making peace with the past is part of that."

"OK, well we're good, if that helps. No hard feelings."

"Thanks, but I want to explain." She sat on the low wall outside the house, and patted the space next to her.

"OK." He sat by her side. She'd looked and sounded so awkward the whole time he guessed it was something she really needed to say – maybe even practised first.

"It's tempting to blame Vanessa for everything, but I have to accept some responsibility for letting her poisonous words get to me. I don't mean it's my fault... "

"'Course it's not. She was evil. A witch Beth said, when she was nasty to her."

"She's right. Vanessa manipulated me into thinking I was fat, ugly and pathetic. That nobody would like me for myself."

She looked like she might cry – obviously she'd not forgotten how all that felt.

"Oh, Kirianne!" He put his arm round her and pulled her in for a half hug.

"When I said you'd been using me, were shallow, I really believed it. I should have realised you're not like that."

"I'm glad you think so. The truth is I asked you out mostly because you were stunning."

"I *was* stunning?"

Oooops – that was a really stupid thing to say to someone who'd got ill because she'd been made to hate how she looked. "You look great now," he said.

She grinned. "See, you're a nice bloke. You try to say the right things."

Zach relaxed. "You do look good, honest."

"I'm getting there – and I've realised that's not what's important. My worth as a person has little to do what you can see on the outside. Same for everyone."

"True." He'd been attracted to Beth because she was gorgeous. He stuck around because he loved what was on the inside too.

"I'm going to be fine, I really am. I'm stronger now. And I know who to listen to now. People like Dad."

Zach felt uneasy. Kirianne needed Hugh. What if he'd done something drastic in the hope of protecting her?

"Don't look so worried. I've been recovering for months now. Dad had no reason to kill Vanessa."

So, she had realised he'd overheard their conversation about Vanessa. Finding Vanessa's dead body had scared Zach. He'd thought some wild things. That the police would try to pin it on him because of his brother. That it was karma for what she'd said about Beth and Teddy. That Hugh sending him on that initiative test might have had a sinister motive. It was all rubbish, except maybe the karma.

"Yeah. Like I said, he's a good bloke, your dad. After what Dom did, I was in a right state. Sure I'd get the sack. Hugh said I was part of the firm now and asked how he could help."

"When Dad adopted me, he promised that no matter what happened, or what I did, he'd look out for me. Protect me. I've always known it was true. When I was at my lowest, I still knew it. That's what pulled me through."

It sounded as though she'd been even more ill than Zach had realised – in real danger. "I'm really sorry for what you went through."

"It's in the past."

And she wanted to make peace with that. "Yeah, it is."

"Friends?" Kirianne said.

"Yeah, of course."

They hugged properly, then sat side by side in a silence which started to feel awkward.

"I didn't know Hugh wasn't your real dad," Zach said.

"Don't be stupid, of course he is. Your real dad is the one who's there for you."

Would Teddy ever think of Zach as his dad? More importantly, could Beth think that way? That's what it would take for them to have the relationship he wanted.

"What are you thinking about, Zach?"

"Beth," he admitted.

"Now Beth, she really is beautiful."

"Yes she is – and you're right, that's not what's most

important about her."

She tilted her head and smiled. "What is?"

Zach thought. "Everything. She's so alive, always ready to solve problems and have fun. Nothing gets her down for long. She's strong, even fierce sometimes, because she's had to be. I love her – and her little boy. I want us to be a family, but she… She doesn't let me pay for stuff because she needs to know she can manage on her own. If I try to make plans she doesn't really listen because she's heard it all before…I get why, but I wish she'd see I'm different."

"How long have you been together?"

"I don't know about together, but I met her just after we split up."

"That's more than a year! You need to make it clear you're around long term. Her last fella did the opposite, right?"

"Yeah."

"I doubt Beth's as neurotic as me, but she's going to worry you'll be the same unless you prove different. Still being there will help, but she won't know why that is unless you tell or show her."

That made sense. He'd tried telling Beth without a lot of success. He had to find a way to show her.

# Chapter 51

## Thursday 3rd September

The DI called another briefing, which Crystal was in time to attend. When everyone had reported what they knew, he summed up Muriel's case by saying, "If she'd not been found so quickly, she'd probably have died. Party guests saw Zach, Beth and the child leave Muriel's home directly after them. The owners of the house where Beth lodges confirm she and Zach were there at the time of the attack. Our other suspects lack strong alibis. Thoughts?"

"With three women strangled, are we looking at a serial killer?" Neil asked.

"The press say so. There's no obvious motive for all three victims, so I'm afraid there will be more."

"Odd they were successful the first time, but not afterwards," Crystal said. "Verity doesn't seem like she was much stronger than Vanessa, and Muriel definitely isn't."

"The later victims weren't drugged. And the workman who found Muriel initially thought she was dead, so maybe Arthur did too?" Anne suggested.

"If it was him," Crystal said.

"Do you not think him guilty at all, or just not in the case of Muriel Grahame?" the DI asked.

"I don't know… I don't feel like it's all more of the same." DI Shortfellow had praised her instincts when Crystal was right about this sort of thing before. It'd be good if she could turn those instincts into conscious thoughts. "It feels like this is simple and it's being made unnecessarily difficult. Arthur complicates things, and I'm sure he's guilty of part of this, but not all."

"Verity's the odd one out," Captain said. "No complicated alibi from Arthur Rendall, and she wasn't badly hurt."

"If it wasn't Arthur, then who?" Neil asked. "Someone she blackmailed?"

They agreed that made sense, could apply to any of the suspects, and may well have been the motive behind Vanessa's death.

"It doesn't work for Muriel's attack. She was a victim, not a blackmailer," Anne said. "I interviewed her and I'm certain of that."

Crystal was pleased to hear it.

"It's more likely she tried to stop the other two. Vanessa was expecting her. Muriel could have slipped the sedative into her tea and waited for it to work."

Crystal wasn't pleased to hear that. "Verity described a man, and Muriel didn't strangle herself."

"Her brother, son, whatever we're calling him, might have attacked Verity, then done the same to her so she wouldn't be a suspect in Vanessa's murder."

"She nearly died!" Crystal said. "He wouldn't kill her to clear her name when she'd not even been accused."

"It was an accident. He hardly marked Verity, so tried harder and didn't take her age into account?"

Although Anne's theory sounded plausible, Crystal didn't believe it. Bert was such a gentle man, and Muriel so proper and honest. She wouldn't let Bert do such a thing to protect her, and wouldn't risk him going to prison – he'd hate being shut inside. But he did love Muriel.

Maybe Bert felt guilty for being the reason she was blackmailed and acted without her knowledge trying to put that right. Crystal could imagine that if it had been Bert who attacked her, Muriel wouldn't admit it – perhaps not even to herself. That would explain a usually sharp and observant person being unable to describe her attacker.

"Hugh mentioned seeing an old lady in Grassy Lane. He might have known it was Muriel, or has since found out, and decided to silence her," Crystal said. That idea was at least as likely as Anne's.

"OK, but that only makes sense if he killed Vanessa – which is possible," Anne said. "And despite what he said, he may have tried strangling Verity."

"It doesn't explain Arthur creating an alibi for when Muriel was attacked." Crystal was destroying her theory.

"Maybe he didn't create it? Perhaps the little twerp really did forget his phone, then heard what happened and decided to yank our chains a bit more?" Captain said.

That too was accepted by everyone as possible.

"Can we get him on obstruction?" Anne asked.

"If we can't charge him with something, I'll lose all faith in the job," the DI said. "What we... Yes?"

"Another witness for you, wanting to confess all, sir."

"Who is it this time?"

"Verity Houseman."

"OK, put her in an interview room please. Captain, will you lead and take Officer Clere with you?"

"Five minute break first, sir?" Captain suggested.

Crystal was washing her hands when her phone rang. She just caught it before Lorna Milligan gave up.

"I'm ringing about Adam," the boy's mum said. "He's back home and still really interested in the murder. He wants to make a witness statement."

Didn't everyone! "I'll be happy to come and take one from him, but I'm in CID headquarters in Portsmouth at the moment. As you can imagine, we're quite busy."

"I understand."

Lorna did, Adam might not. "Is he with you now?"

"I'll put him on."

Crystal immediately heard the boy's excited greeting.

"Adam, listen to me."

He stopped talking.

"I need you to promise to keep this conversation confidential, do you know what that means?"

"I'm not to tell anyone anything because it's top secret!"

"That's right. Nobody except your mum. So, a detective sergeant is just about to interview Verity Houseman and I'll be helping him. We don't know that she's done anything wrong. We'll use your evidence to get to the truth. Ruling people out is just as important as finding them guilty."

"I know, PC Crystal! That's why I need to tell you about Mr Grahame."

"What!" Calm down, Crystal. If Adam believed old Bert was guilty, he'd have already got his mum to pass that on.

"Officer Clere, are you ready?" Captain asked.

"Yes, I'm coming." To Adam she said, "I promise I'll come and see you as soon as I can."

As Crystal ended the call, she saw a text from Ellie. *Mike's coming down – would you and Jason like to come to dinner tonight?'*

Crystal replied with a thumbs up and raced to the interview room.

Verity took a long, whiny time to admit she'd faked the attack on her, because she believed Hugh killed Vanessa and would hurt her too. She thought that by exaggerating his threats to physical harm she'd help the police get him arrested and keep her safe. After what happened to Muriel she was now terrified. "I want witness protection!"

"That's reserved for genuine witnesses, not those who make false accusations," Captain said. It was about the first time he'd got a word in throughout her 'poor little me' act.

Crystal almost laughed when she saw Verity's reaction. Clearly she'd been expecting sympathy.

"Your best bet, Mrs Houseman, is to tell us everything you know, and nothing you don't. That's what will help us arrest the person responsible and keep you safe."

Verity nodded. "I wasn't sick the day Vanessa was killed. Vanessa told me not to go to flower arranging. She said she wasn't going and if neither of us did we'd be missed more and would therefore be appreciated more. We do most of the work and we're taken for granted. I know it looks bad lying about being ill, and that the police are already against me because I made a mistake in trusting my cousin and trying to help him, but I had no choice! Vanessa was blackmailing me. She forced me to collect gossip."

Captain put his hand on the table.

"What was Vanessa's hold on you?" Crystal asked.

Verity stared at her.

Honestly, did the woman think that accusing the police of bias, and Aunty Agnes of being lazy, and blaming everyone but herself was going to win them round? "Please answer the question, Mrs Houseman."

Verity blinked, then swallowed. "I had an affair with a married man. I won't name him because his wife doesn't know and she'd be the one to suffer."

"Noble of you. Why do you suspect Mr Bend of killing Vanessa?"

"Because of what she did to his daughter, and what she said about the two of them. She liked toying with people, getting them to act like they were her friends and punishing them if they wouldn't. She wasn't going to flower arranging because she said she was going to have some fun with him."

"She named Mr Bend?"

"It must have been... No. No she didn't." It was clear Verity really had suspected Hugh and just realised she might have been mistaken.

"You tried to gain access to Vanessa's home shortly after she died, and later tried to persuade her godson to let you take something from there."

"I'm entitled to everything in that house! He wouldn't let me look."

"What were you looking for?"

"I thought she'd have a file of information on the people she blackmailed. I wanted to protect those people. I've tried to drop hints to them that their secrets are now safe."

It took an effort for Crystal not to yell, 'Only if they pay you!' She calmed herself and asked, "You said he wouldn't let you look. Has he since done that?"

"He said you lot took her computers and paperwork and stuff. He looked so smug I'm sure it's true."

"Why did Vanessa leave you an inheritance?"

"Guilt? We used to be friends."

Afterwards, Captain said, "Well done, Crystal. I nearly

313

lost my rag with her whinging and lying. You did well not to lose it."

"I couldn't. She's wriggled out of stuff before. I'm not giving her any excuse to claim mistreatment or otherwise get any charges we might bring, dismissed."

"That's the spirit! What do you reckon? Any of it true?"

"I think she genuinely believed Hugh killed Vanessa, but it was just a guess. She did want to get this blackmail folder, so she could use it herself. I doubt it really exists. It's possible Vanessa was blackmailing her. If so, the only victim she has the slightest intention of helping is herself."

"That sounds spot on to me. Want to report to the DI?"

"Actually, could you do it? Just before we interviewed Verity another witness contacted me. Remember Adam?"

Captain grinned. "Who could forget?"

"He thinks he has something useful to tell me. It might be nothing, but I think it's worth checking out. And, um actually I was hoping to finish fairly early today. I've got a dinner date."

"Go on then."

"Don't forget to tell the DI I was brilliant!"


"Did you do arresting anyone today, PC Crystal?" Adam asked the moment his mum answered the door.

"Come and sit down, and let me get you a coffee, before you answer that," Lorna said.

"I'm good for coffee, thanks. Sitting is a good idea though. Adam, generally it's best for everyone to be comfortable when taking statements."

"OK!" He rushed off, and just about managed to wait

until Crystal's bum hit the sofa before speaking again. "The news app said there's a serial killer, but that isn't right?"

"No, Adam, it isn't."

"Because only Mrs Meadows is dead. Mrs Houseman and Miss Grahame were strangulated, but they didn't die. You need more than one person to be murdered before it's a serial killer."

Crystal smiled. Enthusiastic as he was in the pursuit of crime, he still remained more accurate than the press coverage which he must have seen. "That's true."

"But there is a murderer and people think it's Mr Grahame?"

"Some people might think that…"

"They think so because they think he hurt Mrs Meadows and the same person did all the strangulating."

"Well, yes, but he won't get in trouble for what people think or even say, just what he's done – if he has done anything and we don't yet know that."

"I do."

"Adam," his mum cautioned.

"I really do, Mum! Mrs Meadows was really horrid and Mrs Houseman is a big fat liar…"

"You mustn't say things like that, Adam."

"It's true, Mum. You know that, and PC Crystal needs to know all the facts or the wrong person could be arrested."

"Yes, I…"

"Adam's right. Verity Houseman did lie about her whereabouts at the time of Vanessa Meadow's death. She's now admitted that."

"Did she kill Mrs Meadows?" Adam asked.

"We don't yet know who that is, but have a number of suspects we're investigating and lots of leads to follow up."

"Good because even if she was horrible you should catch who killed her."

"Yes, and knowing what the victim was like can help with that." She glanced at Lorna Milligan apologetically, hoping Adam wasn't about to inadvertently reveal his mum was a blackmail victim.

"She used to say things to people in church, like she told Josh not to worry about his spots because they hardly showed. What she was doing was saying she could see them and trying to make him worry about them."

"That's very perceptive of you, Adam," his mum said.

"What's perspective? Dad does it at work, but I don't know what it is."

"I'll get him to show you, but the word I used to describe you was perceptive. It means being good at noticing things, which I'm sure is very useful for a detective."

"Definitely it is," Crystal confirmed.

"Can I do my statement now?"

"Absolutely. What did you want to tell me?"

"Mr Grahame didn't strangulate Mrs Meadows and he wouldn't have done it to Miss Grahame because she's his sister and she's nice and makes him cakes and if it was the same person who did all the strangulating then he can't have done it to Mrs Houseman either, even though she's a big fat liar and horrid."

"I follow the reasoning, and agree Mr Grahame seems an unlikely person to have hurt anyone, but we don't know for sure."

"I do! I told you!" Adam looked as close to having a

tantrum as Crystal had ever seen him.

"OK, yes, sorry. How did you work it out?" He had been very perceptive regarding Vanessa Meadows, and found evidence in previous cases, maybe she'd get lucky again.

"I was with him. It was his birthday I took him a card and said I'd do a job as a present. We collected seaweed to make his vegetables grow ginormous. We were doing it until nearly one o'clock. I knew the campanological metallurgist was coming and Reverend Grande said I could go up the tower with them and I thought I might be late. Mr Grahame said he would walk to the church with me, but when he got near the Kale and Snail his friend heard me singing happy birthday to him and so they went to have beer. I went to the church and on the way a man who was going too fast on his bicycle nearly flattened me, but I made it just in time and I went up and saw Mrs Houseman."

"Adam, this is really useful information. I think DI Shortfellow would like to know immediately – will you excuse me for a moment?"

She was soon back. "The DI is *very* interested, Adam. As soon as you and your mum are free he'll send a squad car to collect you both and take you to HQ so you can make a formal witness statement."

"On a tape and everything?"

"Yes!" In case she wasn't there in person, she wanted a chance to listen to Adam putting the DI through his paces.

"We could go now, couldn't we, Mum?"

"Not right now."

"But, Muuuum!"

"Here's the number, just call when you're ready," Crystal said, before making a hasty exit.

# Chapter 52

### Thursday 3rd September

When Muriel awoke, she knew she was in hospital, but not why. Bert was there. Had something happened to him? She tried to ask. Her throat was so sore and something covered her nose and mouth.

"It's OK, Mure. You're going to be OK."

Bert was worried, she could hear it in his voice. Worried about her? Yes, she was the one hooked up to machines.

Someone else came. Bert said she was awake and the person told her to sleep. She did.

People kept coming. They shone a light into her eyes, and did that thing for the blood pressure, asked her questions and told her to rest. Bert was always there. He told her someone had come into the garden and strangled her. Another person found her and called the ambulance. Bert had been collected from the pub by the vicar and brought to the hospital. Poor Bert, what a shock it must have been for him. How worried he must have been.

A police officer came to take her statement. A kind young woman. Muriel couldn't tell her very much. Bert answered some of the questions for her, and repeated the few words Muriel managed to croak. Somehow he knew what she was trying to say. Muriel thought she remembered a big man wearing gloves. Maybe she was thinking of what she'd heard about Verity's attack.

Arnold came to visit. He'd hardly had time to ask how she was when a doctor came to examine her.

"I know it's painful, I'll prescribe something for that, but

I'm pleased to say you're now suffering from nothing worse than bruising. You can go home, if there's someone there to look after you."

"My son," she tried to say.

"I'll look after you, Mure," Bert promised.

"And I, and most of Little Mallow, will help," Arnold promised.

Eventually Arnold drove Muriel and Bert home. She felt much better outside the hospital, and in the car which Arnold said Cameron had lent him to ensure she had a comfortable journey home.

"If there's anything either of us can do to help, please let us know," Arnold said.

She wanted to thank him. As soon as she opened her mouth, Arnold told her not to try to speak. "Not unless you want something."

She shook her head and looked out the window. They were up on Portsdown Hill, which meant she could see Portsmouth Harbour and across to the Isle of Wight. She pointed that out to Bert, who was in the back with her.

"Do you want to stop, Mure?"

She nodded and Bert told Arnold she'd like to look at the view. When Muriel could talk properly, she'd explain she'd wanted to stop because the sea looked so beautiful in the sunlight and seeing the Solent and the familiar coastline from up high was a pleasant novelty. That she'd wanted something positive, however small and fleeting, to come from the horrible experience she, and Bert, had been through.

Once home Muriel thought she should step into the garden for a minute. She'd be safe with Bert and Arnold and it might spark a memory which could help the police. She couldn't face it.

Bert suggested she go to bed. She shook her head. Only a small movement as it was painful.

"Come and sit on the sofa then."

Lots of people called to visit, or rang up on the telephone. Bert dealt with them all, bringing her any cards or gifts, passing on messages, and giving her the chance to invite the person in. She didn't. Later she'd want to see her friends, perhaps to talk and talk, but not just yet.

Bert relayed a message from Adam saying that if her throat was too sore for talking, she could write down what she wanted to say and he would do the telling people. Her laugh as she thought how good he'd be at that made her feel better everywhere except her throat.

There were a great many get well cards, and a beautiful card made by Teddy, thanking her for his birthday party.

"They hadn't heard what happened, Mure. They said they'd like to visit when you're well enough. I said you would be soon."

Muriel smiled. Bert was doing so well. He brought her frequent cups of tea, heated soup, brought little bowls of ice cream.

When Agnes arrived, Bert allowed her in.

"Don't talk," she said. "We both know I can do enough of that for two."

Muriel made a small negative movement of her head and held up three fingers.

Agnes laughed. "You're going to be OK, aren't you?"

Muriel nodded.

"Bert says you're tired. I told him you'd need to be, so you sleep tonight. He wouldn't have let me in otherwise, but I'm right aren't I?"

Muriel smiled.

"If you're up to it, I think we should sit in the garden. What's that face? Tired or scared?"

Muriel was worried she might never feel safe there again. She realised the first time would be the worst and, as she often told Bert, the longer she put it off the harder it would be. She must try soon, but not today. "Both," she croaked.

"It'll get better," Agnes said.

Bert made yet more tea, and carried it in, with cake, on a tray. Muriel hadn't made the cake. She wondered which of her many kind visitors had. Bert was sure to have thanked them, whoever it was.

After she'd chatted on and on about nothing much, Agnes said, "I asked Crystal if someone was bumping off the flower arranging group. She says it's not that and she's sure she knows who did it. That the person will be caught soon and we'll all be safe."

Muriel had been thinking only of herself. That was forgivable she thought. Agnes would certainly forgive her. Muriel took her dear friend's hand, hoping the gesture showed all she felt.

Agnes smiled. "Hurry up and get your voice back. It's not so much fun gossiping without you telling me off for it!"

# Chapter 53

### Thursday 3rd September

Crystal pulled over to answer her phone.

"This fairly early finish you wanted…" Captain said.

"Another interesting development?" Crystal hoped it wasn't too interesting. She was due at Ellie's in two hours.

"We got a call from Mrs Sheppard in Grassy Lane. They have a doorbell which records visitors. It was running while they were on holiday. As they share their pathway with house 1, she thought we'd be interested in the footage."

"Ooooh!"

"Neil's on his way. You know how he loves his tech! The DI thought you might like to meet him there."

"Right now? Yeah, I can do that."

Crystal called Jason. "You know my feminine wiles, naughty enticements, and saucy tricks?"

"I vaguely recall…"

"I'll remind you this weekend."

"We're not going out for that curry tonight, are we?"

"Nope. We're having dinner with Ellie and Mike."

"There's a catch…"

"I need you to buy dessert, find me something to wear, and bring it to Aunty's so I can shower and change there."

"For this, I get dinner with our mates and a weekend of kinky fun?"

"I said at the weekend, not all weekend! OK, OK. Deal."

Mrs Sheppard insisted Crystal and Neil came in, then went to make the tea, which both officers said they didn't need.

"Sorry we didn't think of this sooner," Mrs Sheppard said. "It was only today we realised Vanessa's killer had walked through her front door, so might be on the recording. To be honest, we've tried not to think about how close it was."

"Understandable," Crystal said. "I'm sure you'll feel better once the person is arrested. The recording might help."

"Have you watched it?" Neil asked.

"Only to check it really was running and might show something useful. Vanessa didn't like us spying on her friends as she put it, so we angled it to show people when they get to our door, not from the top of the path. It does still pick up anyone who goes next door. Not as well as here, but you'll be able to see exactly when the path was used and catch a glimpse of the person."

"That's great," Neil said.

"We didn't want to waste your time… But we didn't want to see a murderer walking down our path either. Will you need to take the thing away?"

"We should be able to just transfer the files," Neil said.

"That's good. Excuse me, I hear the kettle."

"Is it OK if we look here?" Crystal asked. She couldn't hold her curiosity in much longer and it seemed they'd have to drink tea before they could leave.

"Oh yes, of course. I won't look at it myself though."

Neil quickly found the day in question. They watched Beth leave in the morning with Teddy, and return alone. She didn't show up until almost at the house. That seemed to happen almost immediately. As the device was triggered by movement there were no long boring gaps with nothing happening – which was excellent, if slightly disorientating.

The next activity was Zach arriving, then him leaving and turning left, presumably to tell people the water was going off. There was a glimpse of him as he went to Vanessa's. Then they saw him clearly as he rejoined Beth.

"That all ties up with what we've been told so far," Crystal remarked.

"Pretty decent image quality too."

Crystal and Neil watched someone go into to Vanessa's cottage. They couldn't see the face or much of the body. Just enough to realise there wasn't very much to see.

"Thin, male," Crystal said. He was dressed in plain black clothes which didn't cling like the lycra, but…"Arthur?"

Neil replayed it. "Could be. It's not enough on its own…"

"It is to rule certain people out."

"Yeah. Let's see when he leaves."

They watched as Zach went out and turned left again. Next he went to Vanessa's, knocked, waited, and went away.

"Looking in the garden, he said didn't he?"

"He did," Crystal agreed.

They saw the thin man leave, walking casually.

"Not carrying anything, so he'd already put the tea bags and towel in the bin," Crystal said.

Then Zach came back, vanished from sight, reappeared rushing into 2. After that Hugh arrived. They saw him leave, go to Vanessa's and come back. There was no further activity until the arrival of the paramedic, then ambulance and police.

"Any good?" Mrs Sheppard asked.

"Yes, extremely useful."

"I'm so pleased. It's horrible to think that someone in Little Mallow is strangling women."

"I'm sorry, I know this is difficult, but would you mind looking at one image to see if you recognise the person?"

"The killer?" she looked terrified.

"Someone we don't recognise calling at Vanessa's house. We need to talk to anyone who was here that day in case they saw anything which might help." It wasn't a lie, just a careful phrasing so as not to influence a potential witness.

"Oh, yes. Right."

Mrs Sheppard didn't recognise the man. "He's as slim as Arthur next door. It couldn't have been him. He didn't arrive until a few days afterwards."

"Arthur was wearing very bright clothing when he came in to help with our enquiries," Crystal said. "Does he always dress like that?"

"Whenever we've seen him, yes. I suppose it might just be when he's cycling. I don't think we've seen him when he's not been going or coming back from a bike ride. More tea?"

"No, but thank you so much."

"It was delicious," Neil said.

Once outside, Neil said, "I think we can rule out most of our current suspects."

"Yeah. No way was that Muriel, Mrs King, Beth, Zach, Hugh or Bert. This isn't looking good for Arthur."

"It's almost certainly enough to get that warrant."

They high-fived each other, then Neil went back to CID HQ in Portsmouth and Crystal drove to Aunty's.

As Jason chopped strawberries, and stirred them with

meringue into fresh cream, to make Eton mess, he mentioned the photos Arthur said proved he couldn't have killed Vanessa.

"Can we see them?" Mike asked.

She'd got permission to show Jason, not anyone else. On the other hand the DI had issued no stern warning the photos weren't to go further. "Totally in confidence, OK?"

"Scout's honour," Mike said.

"Cross my heart and all that," Ellie said.

"The 'all that' is swearing on your hair straighteners."

"Crikey, that is taking it seriously!" Ellie said.

Crystal explained the oath Adam devised for his mum, which made them want to know what his vital clue had been. "I can't give details, but he ruled out both Verity Houseman and Old Bert on Vanessa's murder."

"The photos?" Mike prompted.

Crystal opened the shot of the blonde. "This isn't an alibi one. I thought it might be useful for comparison purposes." Jason had already given his opinion it was a standard holiday snap and pointed out Arthur's thumb in the corner.

"She's pretty and the scenery looks gorgeous," Ellie said. "Who is she?"

"Nobody, according to Arthur. He was on holiday on his own," Crystal said.

"He was probably going to show it to people when he got back and pretend a holiday romance," Mike said.

"That's what we thought in CID."

"If he intended showing that photo in the way we think, it's kind of a fake – could the others be faked?" Mike asked.

"I'm certain they are, but can't prove it. The details on

Arthur's phone supports what he told us," Crystal said.

"Could he have changed the settings?" Ellie asked. "My parents change their time zones as they move round."

"He made calls to Vanessa and her records match his."

"Someone else took the phone?" Mike suggested.

"He called Vanessa that morning. It was too long for 'sorry wrong number'."

"Let's see the alibi pictures," Mike said.

Crystal showed him the one of Peveril Castle.

"That's a much better one."

"That's what we thought," Crystal said.

Mike scrolled to the next photo, which he showed Ellie.

"Oh, that's lovely!"

Jason nodded. "If it's genuine he got lucky. I'd have to spend days getting up early in the hope the light and mist did what I wanted to be sure of a shot like that."

"That's why you get lots of excellent shots, not just the odd lucky one," Crystal pointed out.

"Remember you said that when we're away and I have you up before dawn to see the view in the best light!"

"Dawn?"

"You work shifts, you can handle that."

"Yes I can, but Arthur took this at 8.45."

"No, sunrise is much earlier in August."

"Are you certain it's sunrise? You can't see the sun."

"I'm totally sure – but if CID will pay for our travel and a couple of nights accommodation I'll happily prove it."

"So they're definitely fakes?" Mike asked.

"We think so. The only other one I saw, was of his bike. It

327

didn't show up well, because the background was messy. Jason keeps telling me that's a major no-no."

"Sort of thing people who get their thumb in shot do," Jason confirmed.

"The problem is proving he didn't take them when and where he and his phone say he did," Crystal said. "Our tech people will do that, and track his movements, once we make him hand his phone over, but I don't want to wait."

"Have you ever tried changing time and locations on our phone pictures?" Mike asked.

It only took Crystal a minute to snap Jason and adjust the settings to show she'd taken it the previous day, in Dover.

"Why Dover?" Jason asked.

"I put in my parents' postcode."

"Ah!" Ellie said. "I've done it now."

"And me, Mike said."

As they drove home, Jason said, "Do you think I could have been right, and Mike really is in MI5? I noticed he'd done the fake photo thing long before you said you had."

"That's why you didn't try! You were spying on the spy?"

"No, I was looking up views of the Peak District. It struck me that if he'd not taken that photo maybe it wasn't even of where he said it was."

"And?"

"Bad news. It's not just in the Peak District, it's a couple of miles away from the Mam Tor View."

"So he could have taken it, exactly when he said?"

"He could have taken a photo there. I'm still not convinced he took that one."

# Chapter 54

## Thursday 3rd September

Beth phoned Zach at work. "Is there any chance you could finish a bit early?"

She'd let him help a bit with Teddy's party and he'd taken an hour off for that yesterday. He didn't think she'd suddenly become needy and clingy, so something must have happened. "What's up, babe?"

"Can you find out first, about leaving early?"

Zach checked his watch. It wasn't quite three and they'd nearly finished the job they were on. "How early?"

"You'd need to be here about three-thirty, or four if you can borrow a car. A car would be better." Beth sounded really anxious.

Zach quickly found Hugh and explained the little he knew. "It must be serious. She never asks me for anything."

"If it's an emergency you can go. Take the van and bring it back by tomorrow morning if that helps. Ryan will give me a lift home, won't you, mate?"

"Sure thing. I'd lend you my car, but it's not insured."

"Thanks, guys. I'll tell her." Zach called Beth. "Yeah, I can make it. What's up?"

"It's Teddy, he's had an accident."

"Beth! Does he need to go the hospital?"

"No, no. He's OK, but urgently needs to see the dentist."

"OK. Good. Look, I'm coming now." He'd guessed Teddy was involved. Beth wasn't likely to get so upset on her own account. Emergency dental treatment didn't sound good, and

329

Beth hated visiting the dentist. Even taking Teddy for a routine check last week had upset her.

When Zach got there, both of them were in quite a state. Teddy was crying and Beth weirdly quiet.

"What's happened to you, then?" Zach asked Teddy.

"Broke!" he pointed at his mouth.

"Let's see. Open wide!"

Zach immediately spotted a small chip was missing from a front tooth. He said, "Wider than that! Pretend you're a hungry hippopotamus." He demonstrated tipping his head back and opening his mouth as wide as he could, then pretended to take a big bite out of Teddy's arm.

Teddy laughed and bit Zach. Not hard at all, but it left a wet mark on his forearm.

Zach pretended to count teeth marks. "All there, but what's this? You broke one? How did that happen?"

"Felled over."

"He was playing with that giraffe and tripped."

"Oh! I get it now. Giraffe hurt his tooth. So, we're going to go and see the nice dentist man and get him to check if it's OK?"

"Denist not nice."

"It's a lady," Beth said.

Ooops. He shouldn't make stupid assumptions. "Same one he saw the other day?"

"Yes. Zach, what if he needs a filling, or to have the tooth out?"

"Teddy, mate, can you get your giraffe ready?"

The little boy looked doubtful, but nodded.

"If Teddy needs treatment, then the nice dentist lady will

do what has to be done, and he'll be fine. And when he's older he'll get a nice new tooth."

"Yeah... I don't know if I can do this."

"You don't have to. I'll take him." Teddy seemed fine and Zach thought he'd only been crying because he'd picked up on his mother's fear. "Let me do it, Beth."

"It's why I called you," she admitted.

"I'm in the van. He'll like that. You go and put the car seat in, and I'll bring him down. Then call the dentist and explain. Tell them Teddy's nervous, OK?"

"OK."

As predicted, Teddy was delighted to be driven in the work van. As the seat Beth had, to make sure he was protected in any vehicle they might travel in, was rear facing he couldn't see where they were going. Luckily his giraffe glove puppet could and, via Zach, provided a running commentary.

"Well, what do we have here then?" asked the dentist, who really did seem nice to Zach.

"Major disaster! Giraffe, and Teddy the hungry hippopotamus, had a catastrophe and both have done colossal damage to a tooth."

"I'd better have a look then. Teddy, will you hold Giraffe nice and still, so I can take a look?"

Zach lifted Teddy into the chair and said, "Open wide. No, wider than that!"

Teddy opened the glove puppet's mouth.

The dentist looked inside, and waved her tools close to the toy's mouth. "Hmm, not too bad. There's nothing I need to do about that chip in the front, but you need to tell him about cleaning his teeth properly. If he doesn't, he might have trouble later."

"We'll tell him, won't we, Teddy?"

Teddy nodded. "Open wide?"

"Yes, your turn."

Teddy tipped his head back and opened his mouth wide.

"Oh, this looks much better! I'm just going to use my little mirror to check." She gently examined Teddy's mouth. "You've been cleaning your teeth really well, young man. Great job! Keep that up and you'll always have good teeth, even if you do have a little chip in one for a while."

To Zach she said, "It's fine. No treatment needed for either patient. You were right to bring him in though."

As they were leaving, the dentist said she hoped to see all three of them for Teddy's next check up.

Zach mentioned that to an extremely relieved Beth. "I could change dentists to there and let him see me being examined and fine. I think it should be all of us though."

"That's six month's in the future. Anything could happen," Beth said.

"Not anything. I'm not going anywhere. But yeah, six months is quite a long time. Maybe long enough to get you in that chair too. I'd hold your hand and I'm sure Teddy would lend you Giraffe."

"I don't know… But thanks for today, Zach. You were brilliant."

He put his arms around her. "I'm here for you, Beth. You and Teddy, whenever you need or want me."

"You're like family should be," she said through tears, as she held him tight.

At home, after Zach had explained to his mum what happened, he said, "Beth's offered to do your wedding flowers if you'd like."

"I would like that very much. I was thinking of asking, but didn't want to put her in a difficult position."

"What would be difficult about it?"

"It's not happening until February."

"Not many flowers around then?"

"No, you numpty! Well, there might not be, but I'm sure a florist can cope with that. February is six months away."

"Beth said that. I still don't get it."

"She might not expect you to still be around then."

"I told her I would be."

"Sometimes telling someone isn't enough, Zach. Sometimes you have to show it."

Mum wasn't the only person to give him that advice. Kirianne had too. 'Like family should be,' Beth had said.

Zach was going to stop listening – and start doing.

# Chapter 55

## Friday 4<sup>th</sup> September

As everyone in CID had hoped and expected, a warrant was obtained to arrest Arthur Rendall, examine his phone, and take a DNA sample. Neil and Captain made the arrest and reported he'd made no fuss at all.

"Biggest problem was stopping him confessing everything before we could get it all on tape," Captain said.

"You've already interviewed him?" Crystal was disappointed. Realistically she was never going to have been allowed to question him, but she'd have loved to sit in.

"I wouldn't say 'interview'. He talked, we listened."

"You got everything you need?" The right person being arrested and a strong case built, was what mattered, not who was there at the end.

"More than enough." Captain grinned. "We don't think he's finished telling us how clever he was, and why it had to be done though. I'm sure he'd be happy to inform you."

"Really?"

"I'll go ask him, shall I?"

"Please… and maybe the DI?"

When Captain left, Anne said, "The DI already agreed. I said it might help your interview skills to listen to a confession, without the pressure of knowing any mistake on your part might result in them getting away with it."

"That was a great idea. Thank you."

"I was thinking… If I was to be your mentor, I'd need Neil's help with that to start with, so you'd be getting two for the price of one. I'm not sure if that might be too much of a good thing?"

"Not at all – I've always liked a bargain!" She really hoped things worked out just the way Anne had said.


As predicted, Crystal, and Anne who said she'd observe only, were fully informed of Arthur Rendall's clever plan to perform the necessary duty of ridding the world of Vanessa Meadows. He said he'd been thinking about it for a long time. When Vanessa insisted he visit on the anniversary of his mum's death, he knew it was a sign to act. His holiday had been booked, but he'd taken similar trips before and knew it would be easy to ask for breakfast to be left for him and to slip out very early in the morning.

He'd cycled to the train station, taking a travel brochure with him, so he could photograph it on the way to give him an alibi. He'd also called Vanessa with a grovelling apology that he'd be late.

"She hung up on me! Something she lived to regret, although not for long."

He said he'd acted cowed when he arrived and offered to make the tea. Once she'd drunk it, all he had to do was wait until the sedative took affect, kill her, and tidy up, before cycling away to resume his holiday.

"You took your bike on the train?" Crystal asked when he paused for breath.

"Of course not! That would have been far too distinctive. I left that the other end, after disguising it a little by removing some of the coloured tape and reflectors. I took one from Fareham station. Combination locks are no problem for anyone with half a brain."

"Right." Crystal should have thought of him stealing one. It wasn't long ago she'd learned how easy that was. And, as the other thief had told her, if it was returned before the owner needed it again, they'd never know it was missing.

"You hid it at the top of the lane, didn't you?" That would account for the gap spotted, and used, by Muriel.

"I had to. I saw a plumber's van. They might have noticed me and remembered."

They'd noticed, but mistaken him for the postman. Crystal guessed Arthur was the man who almost knocked Adam down, in his haste to get away from the scene.

"Where did you get the sedative?"

"Surplus medication is often returned to chemist shops for disposal. Someone brought in a lot of stuff which was left over after a relative died. I recognised the pills Mother took to end her life, so kept them myself. I planned to get Vanessa drowsy and tell her how she'd destroyed the life of the one person she considered to be a friend, and had made my life hell. She claimed to be a Christian and had pledged, when I was a baby, to support me. She always did the opposite, running me down at every opportunity. I wanted her to see what she'd done, to be sorry, to stop, that's all."

"So, what happened?"

"She laughed. When I told her about Mum she laughed and said, 'So Ivy listened to me in the end did she? Never did when we were kids, always had to have the upper hand.' I had to stop her laughing."

"How did you do that?" She knew of course, but had to try to avoid leading questions.

"I strangled her."

"Can you describe how you did it?"

336

"I walked over to her in the chair. She didn't try to get up, just taunted me, saying I was wet and didn't have the nerve to touch her. I put a hand on her mouth, to make her be quiet. Then I put them round her throat and squeezed. I stopped when I saw fear in her eyes. She smiled, thinking she'd won, that she'd have a hold over me forever. She would have, or maybe gone to the police, so I finished the job. It took a long time."

Crystal might have felt some sympathy for Arthur, if he didn't seem so self satisfied. No way was he going to get away with claiming he was goaded into manslaughter. Not when he'd planned it months in advance. Maybe he could plead insanity. He seemed to consider his behaviour totally reasonable.

"And the others? Why attack Verity Houseman?"

"I never touched her!"

Crystal would have believed him, even without Verity admitting she'd faked that. "And Muriel?"

"I didn't kill her, just did enough to confuse your feeble attempts at an investigation."

"You hurt her very badly. She's 88, the shock alone could have killed her."

He looked serious for the first time. "Is she OK?"

"We hope she will be." Crystal asked about the photos and he confirmed what she already knew. Then she took him through the events of Vanessa's death again.

Arthur seemed pleased to tell her but finished with, "She did win in the end, didn't she? I'm still not free of her. I'll never be free of what I did to her."

Crystal didn't think he would.

Afterwards she said, "Thank you for that, Anne. It was

337

awful, but I'm glad I did it."

It wasn't just the end of the case, but the end of Crystal's time as a uniformed officer. She returned to Gosport police station, to collect her few personal items and say a formal goodbye ahead of her leaving party.

To her surprise DI Shortfellow turned up. He'd come to inform everyone of the result and thank them for their efforts, with routine enquiries and making it possible for Crystal to take an active part in the investigation. "Your loss is very much CID's gain."

"It's been emotional," Crystal said, before it got too much that way. "I'm out of here. I'll see you all later. Seven in Nelson's, right?

"I told you she'd do it," Trevor said.

"Not exactly difficult. Having my leaving do the evening I leave in the nearest pub?"

"Come on, how did you work it out?" Sergeant Dylan asked.

"I'll give you twenty questions, yes or no answers only," Crystal said, trying not to smirk.

Sergeant Freeman explained to the DI those had been the terms given to Crystal.

"How many did she use?" DI Shortfellow asked.

"She asked me one," Trevor said.

Everyone else kept quiet for a minute, then started asking questions.

"Sorry, just remembered I'm off duty," Crystal said. "We'll have to do this later!"

# Chapter 56

### Friday 4th September

When Muriel awoke on Friday morning, although still painful, her neck and throat were considerably improved. A cup of tea and painkiller helped. A look in the mirror did not.

"Would you like breakfast, Mure?" Bert asked.

She found that not only was she hungry, she was able to say so.

Bert decided he'd spend the day working in the garden rather than go to the allotment. Muriel wouldn't have asked him to do that. Neither did she tell him it wasn't necessary. She was glad of his company, and glad he turned most visitors away. It was kind of them to come, but she didn't want to have the same painful conversation over and over.

The vicar, Jerry Grande, was admitted. He prayed with Muriel, which brought some comfort.

Dr Crosby, her own GP, came. "Technically this is a social call," he said. That didn't stop him examining Muriel, and agreeing with the hospital's assessment she should make a full recovery. "Rest is important. I also prescribe gentle walks and a little light gardening as soon as you're ready."

Muriel could only hope that time would come.

Crystal was another person to be admitted, although Bert did attempt to put her off.

"I won't stay long and I won't make your… I won't make Muriel talk," she promised him.

"This will probably be the last time you see me in uniform," she told Muriel. "It's my leaving party tonight and I join CID on Monday. I wanted to see how you are, and there's something I think you'll want to know."

"I'm told there will be no lasting effects," Muriel managed to say. After a day of reading, drinking tea and generally being cosseted by Bert, she believed that physically she would recover. She was far less certain she would do so mentally. She'd been attacked in her own garden, her place of sanctuary and, perhaps worse, she didn't know who she could trust.

"That's great and I have news which might speed things up. We've arrested the person responsible both for killing Vanessa and attacking you. There's lots of paperwork and procedures to be got through, but we have the right person. He's confessed, been charged, and will remain in custody until his trial."

The young police officer's words left no room for doubt. Oh, the relief! "Who?" Muriel asked.

"Arthur Rendall, Vanessa's godson."

"He seemed nice."

"He says Vanessa goaded him beyond endurance and that he didn't intend to hurt you, just confuse the investigation."

"I imagine he wasn't thinking straight. Desperate people do desperate things."

"That will probably be his defence – the not thinking straight and maybe it's true. He said he'll never be free from Vanessa."

"No, I don't suppose he will be. Many others are because of him, aren't they?"

Crystal nodded. "Whatever Vanessa knew died with her.

Verity had a good idea who the victims were, and tried to continue where she left off, but didn't know any of the secrets. We're not even sure Vanessa really did – she just probed until she found weak spots, promised discretion and started asking for little favours."

Muriel thought that over. She could no longer recall exactly how Vanessa had initially raised the subject of Muriel having a secret to keep. Verity had definitely not made any specific allegations.

"Will you be able to speak to Mr Rendall again?"

"Probably," Crystal said.

"Then please tell him that he's freed others – and that I forgive him for what he did to me." She did. Nobody but God could forgive him for taking Vanessa's life.


Muriel felt so much better after Crystal's visit that she asked Bert to bring her a cup of tea into the garden. "And all the cards people have brought."

Bert walked out with her, carrying a cushion. Once satisfied she was comfortable he went in for the cards, and to switch on the kettle.

Although glad to be in her garden, Muriel didn't look at it. She didn't want to spot jobs which needed doing before she felt strong enough to attend to them. Instead, she concentrated on the cards. Most were in nice neat envelopes. One was far too large and exuberant for such conventionality – another created by Teddy. Inside was a short note from Beth.

*'We're so very sorry to hear what happened to you. Sending love and prayers for a speedy recovery. I wouldn't normally make a get well message all about me, but I feel*

*sure my good news will please you. Zach has asked me to marry him, and I've accepted. We'll all come and see you when you're a little stronger. Much love, Beth.'*

Muriel got out of her garden seat and went into the kitchen. "Don't bother with the tea, Bert. I'll have it at Agnes's, if you'll lend me your arm to walk there?"

"OK, Mure, if you're sure."

"I'm sure." She had a lot to tell her friend.

They'd not gone far when Cameron's nice comfortable car pulled up. "My dear lady, we were just coming to see if we could render you any assistance," he said.

Muriel smiled at him and Arnold. "I'd like a lift please."

"Of course. Where to?"

"First stop the post office." She'd tell Mary, and anyone else who happened to be there, that the murderer had been arrested and they were now safe from the fear of further attacks. She'd also say Vanessa had been a blackmailer, but had left no evidence of anyone's secrets. She'd repeat her own decision not to make further charity donations via Verity. It shouldn't take long for that to reach the ears of Cherry Baines and all the other victims of the evil Vs.

"And then to visit Agnes Patterson." She too would be relieved the murderer had been caught, if Crystal hadn't already told her. She'd be pleased to know Verity's career as a blackmailer, and perhaps her liberty, were at an end.

However, it was the news of a forthcoming wedding which Muriel was most looking forward to discussing. That would bring Agnes joy. So would being able to tease Muriel for spreading gossip. She'd be right, as Muriel intended to do that from now on – whenever it was true, and the results would be positive.

Thank you for reading this book – the third in my Little Mallow cosy mystery series. I hope you enjoyed it. If you did, I'd really appreciate a short review on Amazon, Goodreads – or anywhere else.


I can be found at www.patsycollins.co.uk You may like to sign up for my newsletter and get an exclusive mini ebook set in Little Mallow, plus news of the latest releases, special offers, competitions and behind the scenes insights. A link can be found on the website, or you can use subscribepage.io/ItLSNa

# More Books by Patsy Collins

Novels –

Firestarter
Escape To The Country
A Year And A Day
Paint Me A Picture
Leave Nothing But Footprints
Acting Like A Killer
Disguised Murder and Community Spirit in Little Mallow
Dependable Friends and Deceitful Neighbours in Little Mallow

Short story collections –

Over The Garden Fence
Up The Garden Path
Through The Garden Gate
In The Garden Air
Beyond The Garden Wall

No Family Secrets
Can't Choose Your Family
Keep It In The Family
Family Feeling
Happy Families

All That Love Stuff
With Love And Kisses
Lots Of Love
Love Is The Answer

Slightly Spooky Stories I
Slightly Spooky Stories II
Slightly Spooky Stories III
Slightly Spooky Stories IV
Slightly Spooky Stories V

Just A Job
Perfect Timing
A Way With Words
Dressed To Impress
Coffee & Cake
Not A Drop To Drink
Criminal Intent
Crime In Mind
Making A Move
Days To Remember
A Clean Bill Of Health

Printed in Dunstable, United Kingdom